10

26/2/18

D1341221

BoR

energy and scope' *Sunday Telegraph*

'A thoroughly readable romp of a novel, filled with excel-
lent set pieces, comic digressions, love interest, subterfuge
and betrayal. We are left thirsty for more' *New Statesman*

467 297 20 7

The Shadow Lines

Amitav Ghosh

JOHN MURRAY

First published in Great Britain in 1988 by Bloomsbury Publishing Ltd

This edition published in 2011 by John Murray (Publishers)
An Hachette UK company

5

A CIP catalogue record for this title is available from the British Library

ISBN 978-1-84854-417-8

Typeset in Adobe Caslon by
Palimpsest Book Production Limited, Falkirk, Stirlingshire

Printed and bound by
Clays Ltd, St Ives plc

John Murray policy is to use papers that are natural, renewable and recyclable
products and made from wood grown in sustainable forests. The logging and
manufacturing processes are expected to conform to the environmental
regulations of the country of origin.

John Murray
338 Euston Road
London NW1 3BH

www.johnmurray.co.uk

For
Radhika and Harisen

Going Away

In 1939, thirteen years before I was born, my father's aunt, Mayadebi, went to England with her husband and her son, Tridib.

It startles me now to discover how readily the name comes off my pen as 'Mayadebi' for I have never spoken of her thus; not aloud, at any rate: as my grandmother's only sister, she was always Mayathakuma to me. But still, from as far back as I can remember, I have known her, in the secrecy of my mind, as 'Mayadebi' – as though she were a well-known stranger, like a film star or a politician whose picture I had seen in a newspaper. Perhaps it was merely because I knew her very little, for she was not often in Calcutta. That explanation seems likely enough, but I know it to be untrue. The truth is that I did not *want* to think of her as a relative: to have done that would have diminished her and her family – I could not bring myself to believe that their worth in my eyes could be reduced to something so arbitrary and unimportant as a blood relationship.

Mayadebi was twenty-nine when they left, and Tridib was eight.

Over the years, although I cannot remember when it happened any more than I can remember when I first learnt to tell the time or tie my shoelaces, I have come to believe that I was eight too when Tridib first talked to me about that journey. I remember trying very hard to imagine him back to my age, to reduce his height to mine, and to think away the spectacles that were so much a part of him that I really believed he had been born with them. It wasn't easy, for to me he looked old, impossibly old, and I could not remember him looking anything other than old – though, in fact, at that time he could not have been much older than twenty-nine. In the end, since I had nothing to go on, I had decided that he had looked like me.

But my grandmother, when I asked her, was very quick to contradict me. She shook her head firmly, looking up from her schoolbooks, and said: No, he looked *completely* different – not at all like you.

My grandmother didn't approve of Tridib. He's a loafer and a wastrel, I would sometimes hear her saying to my parents; he doesn't do any proper work, lives off his father's money.

To me, she would only allow herself to say with a sardonic little twist of her mouth: I don't want to see you loafing about with Tridib; Tridib wastes his time.

It didn't sound terrible, but in fact, in my grandmother's usage, there was nothing very much worse that could be said of anyone. For her, time was like a toothbrush: it went mouldy if it wasn't used. I asked her once what happened to wasted time. She tossed her small silvery head, screwed up her long nose and said: It begins to stink.

As for herself, she had been careful to rid our little flat of everything that might encourage us to let our time stink. No chessboard nor any pack of cards ever came through our door; there was a battered Ludo set somewhere but I was allowed to play with it only when I was ill. She didn't even approve of my mother listening to the afternoon radio play more than once a week. In our flat we all worked hard at whatever we did: my grandmother at her schoolmistressing; I at my homework; my mother at

4

her housekeeping; my father at his job as a junior executive in a company which dealt in vulcanised rubber.

Our time wasn't given the slightest opportunity to grow mouldy.

That was why I loved to listen to Tridib: he never seemed to use his time, but his time didn't stink.

Sometimes Tridib would drop in to see us without warning. My grandmother, for all her disapproval of him, would be delighted whenever he came – partly because she was fond of him in her own way, but mainly because Tridib and his family were our only rich relatives, and it flattered her to think that he had gone out of his way to come and see her.

But of course, she knew, though she wouldn't admit it, that he had really come to nurse his stomach. The truth was that his digestion was a mess; ruined by the rivers of hard-boiled tea he had drunk at roadside stalls all over south Calcutta. Every once in a while a rumble in his bowels would catch him unawares on the streets and he would have to sprint for the nearest clean lavatory.

This condition was known to us as Tridib's Gastric.

Once every few months or so we would answer the doorbell and find him leaning against the wall, his legs tightly crossed, the sweat starting from his forehead. But he wouldn't come in right away: there was a careful etiquette attached to these occasions. My parents and grandmother would collect at the doorway and, ignoring his writhings, would proceed to ask him about his family's doings and whereabouts, and he in turn, smiling fixedly, would ask them how they were, and how I was, and finally, when it had been established to everyone's satisfaction that he had come on a Family Visit, he would shoot through the door straight into the lavatory. When he emerged again he would be his usual nonchalant, collected self; he would sink into our 'good' sofa and the ritual of the Family Visit would

5

begin. My grandmother would hurry into the kitchen to make him an omelette – a leathery little squiggle studded with green chillies, which would lie balefully on its plate, silently challenging Gastric to battle. This was the greatest sign of favour she could show to a visitor – an omelette made with her own hands (it fell to the less favoured to feast on my mother's masterly tidbits – hot shingaras stuffed with mincemeat and raisins, or crisp little dalpuris).

Sometimes, watching him as he chewed upon her omelette, she would ask: And how is Gastric? or: Is Gastric better now? Tridib would merely nod casually and change the subject; he didn't like to talk about his digestion – it was the only evidence of prudery I ever saw in him. But since I always heard my grandmother using that word as a proper noun, I grew up believing that 'Gastric' was the name of an organ peculiar to Tridib – a kind of aching tooth that grew out of his belly button. Of course, I never dared ask to see it.

Despite the special omelette, however, my grandmother would not let him stay long. She believed him to be capable of exerting his influence at a distance, like a baneful planet – and since she also believed the male, as a species, to be naturally frail and wayward, she would not allow herself to take the risk of having him for long in our flat where I, or my father, might be tempted to move into his orbit.

I didn't mind particularly, for Tridib was never at his best in our flat. I far preferred to run into him at the street corners in our neighbourhood. It didn't happen very often – no more than once a month perhaps – but still, I took his presence on these streets so much for granted that it never occurred to me that I was lucky to have him in Calcutta at all.

Tridib's father was a diplomat, an officer in the Foreign Service. He and Mayadebi were always away, abroad or in Delhi; after intervals of two or three years they would sometimes spend a couple of months in Calcutta, but that was all. Of Tridib's two brothers, Jatin-kaku, the elder, who was two years older than Tridib, was an economist with the UN. He was always away too, somewhere in Africa or South East Asia, with his wife and his daughter Ila, who was my age. The third brother, Robi, who was much younger than the other two, having been born after his mother had had several miscarriages, lived with his parents wherever they happened to be posted until he was sent away to boarding school at the age of twelve.

So Tridib was the only person in his family who had spent most of his life in Calcutta. For years he had lived in their vast old family house in Ballygunge Place with his ageing grandmother.

My grandmother claimed that he had stayed on in Calcutta only because he didn't get along with his father. This was one of her complaints against him: not that he didn't get along with his father, for she didn't much care for his father either – but that he had allowed something like that to interfere with his prospects and career. For her, likes and dislikes were unimportant compared to the business of fending for oneself in the world: as far as she was concerned it was not so much odd as irresponsible of Tridib to shut himself away in that old house with his grandmother; it showed him up as an essentially lightweight and frivolous character. She might have changed her opinion if he had been willing to marry and settle down (and she hadn't any doubt at all that she could have found him a rich wife), but every time she suggested it he merely laughed. This was further proof that he lacked that core of gravity and determination which distinguishes all responsible and grown-up men; a sure sign that he was determined to waste his life in idle self-indulgence. And yet, although she would pretend to dismiss him with a toss of her head, she never ceased to be wary of him, to warn me against

7

his influence: at heart she believed that all men would be like him if it were not for their mothers and wives.

She would often try to persuade me that she pitied him. Poor Tridib, she would say. There's nothing in the world he couldn't have done with his connections – he could have lived like a lord and run the country. And look at him – oh, poor Tridib – living in that crumbling house, doing nothing.

But even as a child I could tell she didn't pity him at all – she feared him.

Of course, even she would acknowledge sometimes that Tridib did not really do 'nothing'. In fact, he was working on a PhD in archaeology – something to do with sites associated with the Sena dynasty of Bengal. But this earned him very little credit in my grandmother's eyes. Being a schoolteacher herself, she had an inordinate respect for academic work of any kind: she saw research as a life-long pilgrimage which ended with a named professorship and a marble bust in the corridors of Calcutta University or the National Library. It would have been a travesty to think of an irresponsible head like Tridib's mounted in those august corridors.

Part of the reason why my grandmother was so wary of him was that she had seen him a couple of times at the street corners around Gole Park where we lived. She had a deep horror of the young men who spent their time at the street-corner addas and tea-stalls around there. All fail-cases, she would sniff; think of their poor mothers, flung out on dung-heaps, starving . . .

Seeing Tridib there a few times was enough to persuade her that he spent all his time at those addas, gossiping: it seemed to fit with the rest of him.

But the truth was that Tridib came there rarely, not more than once or twice a month. I would usually hear when he came: Nathu Chaubey, the paanwala who sat in the stall at the corner of our lane, or my friend Montu, who could see the far side of the lane from his bathroom window, or someone at the second-hand bookstalls, would tell me. They all knew I was related to Tridib.

When I go past Gole Park now I often wonder whether that would happen today. I don't know, I can't tell: that world is closed to me, shut off by too many years spent away. Montu went away to America years ago and Nathu Chaubey, I heard, went back to Benares and started a hotel. When I walk past his paan-shop now and look at the crowds thronging through those neon-lit streets, the air-conditioned shops packed in with rickety stalls and the tarpaulin counters of pavement vendors, at the traffic packed as tight as a mail train all the way to the Dhakuria overbridge, somehow, though the paan-shop hasn't changed, I find myself doubting it. At that time, in the early sixties, there were so few cars around there that we thought nothing of playing football on the streets around the roundabout – making way occasionally for the number 9, or any other bus that happened to come snorting along. There were only a few scattered shacks on Gariahat Road then, put up by the earliest refugees from the east. Gole Park was considered to be more or less outside Calcutta: in school when I said I lived there the boys from central Calcutta would often ask me if I caught a train every morning, as though I lived in some far-flung refugee camp on the border.

I would usually hear that Tridib was around on my way back from our evening cricket game in the park. My cricket game was the one thing for which my grandmother never grudged me time away from my homework: on the contrary, she insisted that I run down to the park by the lake whether I wanted to or not. You can't build a strong country, she would say, pushing me out of the house, without building a strong body.

She would watch from her window to make sure I ran all the way to the park.

But if I happened to hear that Tridib was around I would double back through the park and the back lanes. Someone would always be able to tell me where he was: he was a familiar figure within the floating, talkative population of students and would-be footballers and bank clerks and small-time politicos and all the rest who gravitated towards that conversation-loving stretch of road between Gariahat and Gole Park. It did not occur to me then to wonder why he was well known, or known at all – I simply took the fact for granted, and was grateful for the small privileges his presence secured for me on those streets: for the odd sweet given to me by a shopkeeper of his acquaintance; for being rescued from a fight in the park by some young fellow who knew him. But in fact it seems something of a mystery to me now, why they put up with him: he was never one of them, he didn't even live there, and he often didn't have much to say. He was usually content to listen to their loud quicksilver conversations in silence: often when he came he would have about him the tired, withdrawn air of a man who has risen from some exhausting labour and ventured out to distract himself.

But occasionally, when he was in the mood and some-body happened to say something that made a breach in his vast reservoirs of abstruse information, he would begin to hold forth on all kinds of subjects – Mesopotamian stelae, East European jazz, the habits of arboreal apes, the plays of Garcia Lorca, there seemed to be no end to the things he could talk about. On those evenings, looking at the intent faces of his listeners, watching his thin, waspish face, his tousled hair and his bright black eyes glinting behind his gold-rimmed glasses, I would be close to bursting with pride.

But even at those times, when he was the centre of

everybody's attention, there was always something a little detached about his manner. He did not seem to want to make friends with the people he was talking to, and that perhaps was why he was happiest in neutral, impersonal places – coffee houses, bars, street-corner addas – the sort of places where people come, talk and go away without expecting to know each other any further. That was also why he chose to come all the way from Ballygunge to Gole Park for his addas – simply because it was far enough for him to be sure that he wouldn't meet any of his neighbours there.

Perhaps they put up with him simply because he *wasn't* like them, because he was different – partly also because they were a little frightened of him: of the occasional, devastating sharpness of his tongue, and of the oddly disconcerting streams of talk that would suddenly come gushing out of him. But of course, he also had his uses: there was a streak of intensely worldly shrewdness in him which would stand them in good stead every once in a while. For example, he would give a student precise and detailed instructions on how to write an examination paper, because he happened to know that Professor So-and-so was going to correct it, and he liked answers that were slanted just so, and the student would do as he had said, and get a first class. Or else when someone was going to appear for a job interview he would tell him what he was likely to be asked, and when the interview was over it would turn out that Tridib's predictions had been dead right. But equally his advice would sometimes seem deliberately misleading, perverse. Once, for instance, he told a young man who was going to be interviewed by a multinational company that the firm, once famous for its stuffiness, had recently been bought by a Marwari businessman and become very nationalist, and that he would not stand any chance at all of getting in unless he went to the interview dressed in a dhoti. The young man went off to the interview duly clad in dhoti, and found that the doorman wouldn't let him in.

Nobody was ever quite sure where they stood with Tridib: there was a casual self-mockery about many of the things he said which left his listeners uncertain about whether they ought to take what he said at face value or believe its opposite. As a result, inevitably, there were all kinds of conflicting rumours about him – especially because he was secretive about his family and his circumstances to an extraordinary degree – even more than was wholly warranted by the fact that everybody young was turning Maoist at that time. Someone would remark knowingly that he had heard that Tridib's family was rich and powerful, that his father was a diplomat, the son of a wealthy judge, and his brother was a brilliant economist who had a job with the UN and lived abroad. But no sooner would he say it than a sceptical voice would cut him short and say: Where do you live, mairi? D'you think we've all dropped out of the sky that we'll believe all that – don't you know he's married and has three children and lives with his widowed mother in a slum near Santoshpur?

And since there was something just a little improbable about the son of a diplomat, scion of a rich and powerful family, turning up at those street corners for years on end, it was the latter kind of story that people tended to believe. Sometimes I would try to tell them the truth. But I was just a boy and I happened to have a reputation for being wide-eyed and gullible. Besides, they all knew we lived in a small flat down the lane; if I had tried too hard to persuade them that we had rich and powerful relatives they would only have thought that I was giving myself airs.

When I was about nine Tridib once stayed away from his haunts in Gole Park for so long that the regulars began to wonder what had happened to him. I was the only one who knew, because I had stopped by at his house once (as I often did in those days) on my way to my maths tutor's house, in the afternoon. This was during the time he was telling me the story of his journey to England in instalments.

I had found him, as always, lying on a mat in his room at the top of the house, reading, with a cigarette smouldering in an ashtray beside him. When I told him that people were asking about him at Gole Park, he put a finger to his lips.

Shh, he said. Don't tell them a thing. Do you know what? I think I may have discovered the mound where the kings of the Sena dynasty used to bury their treasure. If the government finds out, they'll take everything. Don't say a word to anyone and don't come here again for a while – you may be followed by secret agents.

I was thrilled: I hugged the secret to my chest every time I was asked about him. He'd gone, I would say. He's vanished.

Then, one evening, on my way to the park, I heard he'd surfaced at Gole Park again. I doubled back and found him at his favourite adda, on the steps of an old house, surrounded by his acquaintances. I waved to him, from between someone's legs, but he was busy answering their questions and didn't see me.

Where have you been all this while, Tridib-da? somebody said. It must be three or four months . . .

I've been away, I heard him say, and nodded secretly to myself.

Away? Where?

I've been to London, he said. To visit my relatives.

His face was grave, his voice steady.

What relatives?

I have English relatives through marriage, he said. A family called Price. I thought I'd go and visit them.

13

Ignoring their sceptical grunts, he told them that he had been to stay with old Mrs Price, who was a widow. Her husband had died recently. She lived in north London, he said, on a street called Lymington Road; the number of their house was 44 and the tube station was West Hampstead. Mrs Price had a daughter, who was called May.

And what's she like? a voice asked. Sexy?

He reflected on that for a moment, and said, no, she wasn't sexy, not in the ordinary way – she was thick-set, with broad shoulders, and not very tall. She wasn't beautiful or even pretty in the usual sense, for she had a strong face and a square jaw, but she had thick straight hair which came down to her shoulders in a glossy black screen, like a head-dress in an Egyptian frieze, and she had a wonderful, warm smile which lit up her blue eyes and gave her a quality all her own, set her apart.

And what does she do? someone sneered. Is she a wrestler or a hairdresser?

She's a student, said Tridib. At least, a kind of student – she's studying at the Royal College of Music. She plays the oboe, and one day she's going to join an orchestra.

It was then, I think, that I could restrain myself no longer. I thrust myself forward through the thicket of trousered legs and cried: Tridib-da, you've made a mistake! I met you last month, don't you remember? You were in your room, lying on your mat, smoking a cigarette. You were looking for . . .

There was a howl of laughter and a chorus of exclamations: You fraud, you liar, you were just making it all up, you haven't been anywhere . . .

Tridib did not seem to be at all put out, either by what I had said or by their laughter. He laughed too, shrugging good-naturedly, and said: If you believe anything people tell you, you deserve to be told anything at all . . .

Leaning towards me, he pinched my cheek and grinned. Isn't that so? he said, with an interrogatory nod, his spectacles glinting in the lamplight.

His aplomb gave an uneasy edge to the laughter and the comments around him: it seemed now that he had made them the victims of a complicated private joke. There was an edgy hostility in their voices when he left. You can't believe a word he says, somebody exclaimed, he just likes to bamboozle people and play jokes on them. But another, sharper voice broke in and said: Joke? He wasn't joking, he believed everything he said: it was no joke, the fact is that he's a nut – he's never been anywhere outside Calcutta.

I was furious with myself now for having exposed Tridib to their ridicule. You don't know what you're talking about, I cried. I was shouting at the top of my voice, so they listened.

Still shouting, I told them the truth as I knew it: that Tridib *had* been to London, with his parents, many years ago, when he was a boy. They had taken his father there for an operation, which couldn't be done in India. They had had to go, even though it was 1939 and they knew there might be a war. His brother Jatin had been left behind in Calcutta with his grandparents because he was older and couldn't be away from school for so long. And yes, there *was* a family called Price, who lived in West Hampstead, but they weren't relatives – they were very, very old friends of Tridib's family, because Mrs Price's father, Lionel Tresawsen, had lived in India when the British were here, and he and Tridib's grandfather, who was a very important man, a judge in the Calcutta High Court, had been friends. Long after Lionel Tresawsen went back to England his daughter had married a man who had taught her in college, whom everyone called Snipe because his name was S. N. I. Price. When she'd heard that Tridib's father was ill she had written to them and sent telegrams to say that they must stay with her in London, because she'd bought a big house, and she'd been wanting to take in lodgers anyway. And it *was* true that she had a daughter called May, but she was a little baby when Tridib was in London, and as far as I knew he hadn't seen her since. And Mrs Price had had a brother too, called Alan, who had been in Germany before the war . . .

I gave up, exhausted.

That's an even better version than Tridib's, somebody said, with a snort of laughter.

It's true, I shouted back at him. If you don't believe me, ask . . .

Tridib? A voice prompted, and they doubled up with laughter.

I pushed my way out and ran all the way down the lane and up the two flights of stairs to our flat. I was an hour late, and my grandmother was very angry. In her controlled, headmistress's voice she asked me where I had been, and when I didn't answer she raised her hand, drew it back and slapped me. Where have you been? she asked again, and this time I blurted out that I'd been down at the corner. She slapped me again, really hard. Haven't I told you, she said, you're not to go there and waste your time? Time is not for wasting, time is for work.

I met May Price for the first time two years after that incident, when she came to Calcutta on a visit. The next time I met her was seventeen years later, when I went to London myself.

I went to England on a year's research grant, to collect material from the India Office Library, where all the old colonial records were kept, for a PhD thesis on the textile trade between India and England in the nineteenth century. More than a month passed after I arrived in London, before I could meet May again.

I had to go to a great deal of trouble to find her. She was playing in an orchestra and living on her own in a bedsit in Islington. Mrs Price gave me her phone number and I called her several times, but she was never in. And then, one morning, while looking through the entertainment page of the *Guardian*, I saw a notice which said that her orchestra would be playing the Dvorák Cello Concerto that evening at the Royal Festival Hall.

I went there early that evening: I could only afford a ticket for a place on one of the benches behind the orchestra, and I had heard they sometimes sold out very early. But as it turned out I managed to get a seat quite easily: the soloist was a Swedish cellist who clearly did not have much drawing power.

When I went in, I discovered that my seat was directly behind the woodwind section. Soon I saw her; she was fussing with her music-stand, dressed, like all the other women in the orchestra, in a black skirt and white blouse. I watched her as she arranged her music and chatted with an elderly horn player who was sitting in front of her. Her hair was still cut exactly as I remembered it from the time she had stayed with us in Calcutta: falling thick and straight to her shoulders, mantling her neck and the sides of her face; but where I remembered it as dark and shiny, it was streaked now with bands of grey which shimmered when they caught the light. Her shoulders, always broad for her height, had thickened; she seemed almost top-heavy now, for she hadn't added an inch to her waist. I caught a glimpse of her face when she turned to say something to a woman who was sitting in the row behind. She had deep lines running from the corner of her mouth to her nose, and her eyes, which had once been a clear, bright blue, had grown pale and prominent.

Watching her through that concert, I thought of her as she was when she came to stay with us in Calcutta, all

17

those years ago. We had moved to a much larger house then, and she had been given the guest room, downstairs. In the evenings, whenever I managed to elude my mother and grandmother (who didn't want me to bother her), I would slip into her room, sit on the floor and listen to her playing scales on the recorder she had brought to practice on. Often she would blush with embarrassment, put her recorder down and say: Look, this must be so boring for you, all these horrible scales.

But I wouldn't let her stop. I would insist that she go on playing, and I would sit there entranced, and watch her blowing into her recorder, frowning, the muscles in her cheeks knotting in concentration.

She was not frowning when she played in that concert in the Festival Hall: it was evident that her mastery of her instrument was so complete now that she had to give little thought to the music. All through that concert she, and most of the other musicians around her, performed with a bored mechanical precision, very much like veteran soldiers going through a familiar exercise at their sergeant-major's command.

When the concert was over I waited in my seat until the audience had left and the members of the orchestra were busy packing their instruments. Then I leant over the railing and called out her name. She looked up, narrowing her eyes. She saw me and gave me a politely puzzled smile. Then, to my surprise, she recognised me, and her face lit up and she waved. Pointing at the exit she mouthed the words: I'll see you outside.

I went out into the plush, chandeliered foyer and waited. Five minutes later, I saw her, picking her way through the last stragglers, her shoulders rolling, like a boxer's, as she walked towards me. We met half-way down the foyer and froze in mutual embarrassment. She put out a tentative hand, and then suddenly she smiled, rose on tiptoe, pulled my head down and kissed me on the cheeks, her oboe clattering against my neck in its leather case.

As we made our way out, I asked her how she had recognised me, after all those years. She gave it a moment's thought and said: I put two and two together I suppose – I knew you were in London; Mother told me.

She stopped to give me a quick, appraising look. And besides, she said, it's not as though you don't bear a family resemblance to the boy I met in Calcutta – and I remember him very well.

Her voice had a deep, gravelly, almost masculine texture; I couldn't decide whether it had always been like that or whether it had changed.

While she was leading me towards Waterloo tube station through a maze of concrete walkways, she stopped to ask: Have you got anything planned for the rest of the evening?

I shook my head, trying not to look too eager.

Well, she said, pausing to think; you could always come back with me to my bedsit, for dinner. I can't offer you very much – just a beansprout salad and some grilled fish. I don't know whether you care for that kind of thing?

Yes, I said, nodding. That would be very nice.

She gave me a quick smile. If it's any consolation, she said, remember I sprouted the beans myself.

In the tube, on our way to Islington, I told her how bored she had looked through the concert. She nodded sheepishly. Yes, she said; you've guessed my guilty secret. I only stay on with the orchestra because I've got to make a living somehow . . .

She cleared her throat, hesitated, and went on to add: You know – I spend most of my time working for Amnesty and Oxfam and a couple of other relief agencies, small ones, you won't have heard of them.

I asked her a few questions and she described the project

she was working on just then with a businesslike brisk-ness: it was something to do with providing housing for the survivors of an earthquake in Central America. It was evident that she found a great deal of satisfaction in her work.

Her room was on the first floor of a house that looked out on Islington Green. As she stepped in and switched on the lights, a television set near her bed lit up too, auto-matically. She hurried across the room and switched it off.

Turning to face me she said, guiltily, as though she were making a confession: I leave it on all the time. It's my only real indulgence. It fills up the room – it feels a bit empty otherwise.

It was a large, pleasant room, full of plants; its windows looked out over the trees on the Green. There was very little furniture in it – an armchair, a desk, and a large bed, pushed up against the wall at the far end of the room. There were also a few cushions, with bright Gujarati mirror-work covers, scattered on the floor, but they looked as though they had been thrown there more to fill up empty space than to be sat on: it did not look like a room where visitors were often expected.

With a formal, faintly ironic little bow May invited me to amuse myself by looking through her bookshelf while she made our dinner. Glancing through her collection of Russian novels in paperback, miniature music scores and illustrated health books, I came upon an old photograph. It was pinned, along with a dozen other scraps of paper, on to one of those large boards that I had seen hanging over many student desks in London. It was a picture of her, taken a long time ago.

While I was looking at it she darted out of her cupboard-like kitchenette to fetch something from the refrigerator. She noticed me standing in front of her board and came and stood beside me. When she saw what I was looking at she gave me a quick glance and opened her mouth to say something. But then, changing her mind, she whipped around again and went back to the kitchenette. Curious now, I followed her there and stood leaning against the wall, watching her as she bent down to look under the grill. I remarked casually that the picture must have been taken a long time ago: that was exactly how she had looked, if my memory served me right, when she had stayed with us in Calcutta.

Not quite exactly, she said, watching the grill, her voice ironically precise; it was taken at least a couple of years before that.

She looked at me, dusting her hands, raising her eyebrows as though in surprise. That was the picture, she said, a copy of which I was once privileged to send to Tridib.

Later, when we were eating our dinner, I discovered that in 1959, when he was twenty-seven and she nine-teen, they had begun a long correspondence. Tridib had written first, she told me. He had always sent Mrs Price cards at Christmas, ever since they left London in 1940. But that year he had sent two, one to Mrs Price and one to her. He had inscribed a little note in her card saying that he remembered her very well, though she could not possibly remember him, that it would be a great pity if they lost touch altogether, and he hoped that some day she would find time to write to him. She was both touched and intrigued: she had already heard a great deal about him.

Smiling at the memory, she told me how his card had reached her just when she was trying to get over an adoles-cent crush on a schoolboy trombonist, who had had no time for her at all and had not been overly delicate about making that clear. It was nice to feel that *someone* wanted to befriend her. She had written back, and after that they had written to each other regularly – short, chatty letters, usually. Soon, penfriend-like, they had exchanged photographs.

I like to think that Tridib received May's photograph the day he came to Gole Park and told us that made-up story.

Actually my grandmother was wrong about Tridib: he was nothing at all like the hardened gossip-lovers who spent most of their time hanging around the street corners at Gole Park. He was often maliciously dismissive of those people; marine mammals, he would say of them, creatures who sink to the bottom of the sea of heartbreak when they lose sight of the herd.

The truth was that, in his own way, Tridib was something of a recluse: even as a child I could tell that he was happiest in that book-lined room of his, right at the top of their old family house. It was that Tridib whom I liked best; I was a bit unsure of the Tridib of the street corners.

His niece Ila and I used to disagree about this. We talked about it once, when we were about sixteen. I was soon to leave to go to college in Delhi, I remember, and Ila and her parents had just flown in from Indonesia for a short holiday.

Soon after they arrived in Calcutta, they came to visit us. I still remember how my grandmother gasped when Ila climbed out of the car, the tasselled end of her long thick braid swinging freely in front of her. Even my grandmother, who was very critical in all matters to do with appearance, especially where Ila and her family were concerned, pinched her chin and said: Our Ila is growing into a real beauty – she's taken after Maya.

But as for me, I was disappointed: ever since I could remember, Ila had worn clothes the like of which neither I nor anyone else I knew in Calcutta had ever seen, and here she was now, dressed in a simple white sari with a red border, like any Bethune College girl on her way to a lecture.

Soon, growing tired of our parents' conversation, we went out, the two of us, for a walk. Involuntarily we found ourselves walking towards the lake. But when we reached it and spotted an empty bench, we both remembered how we used to sit on those benches when we were children, with our arms around each other's waists, pretending to count the birds on the little island in the middle of the lake, and, suddenly embarrassed, we turned and hurried off towards the Lily Pool Bridge, in the distance, the awkwardness of our silence making me trip where there was nothing to trip on.

At last, because I could think of nothing else to say, I asked her whether she remembered those days when we were children and she and Robi used to come to Calcutta in the summers, and three of us used to go up to Tridib's room whenever we were bored and listen to him, in the still, sultry heat of the afternoons, while he lay on a mat, propped up with pillows, cigarette smoke spiralling out of his fingers, and spoke to us in that soft, deep voice of his, about the behavioural differences between the Elapidae and Viperidae families of snakes, or the design of the temples at Karnak, or the origins of the catamaran. Or, for example, the time when Robi and I decided to become explorers in the Empty Quarter, and went running up to his room to ask for a few tips before setting off. He had smiled and gone on to tell us in ghastly detail about the circumcision rites of one of the desert tribes. And then, spectacles glinting, he had said: So before you leave you'd better decide whether you would care to have all that done to your little wee-wees, just in case you're captured. I asked her if she remembered how Robi and I had spread our hands instinctively over our groins, and how angry we had been when she had laughed.

Mere vagina-envy, she said, laughing, and I tried to keep my face impassive as though I was accustomed to girls who used words like that. But I could tell she didn't remember.

I asked her, then, if she had any memory of the stratagems we used to employ to get Tridib to tell us about the year he had spent in London, during the war; of how we used to pore over his photographs when we could persuade him to bring them out; of how he used to tell us about the people in them, pointing out Mrs Price with May in her arms, or Alan Tresawsen, her brother, with his bad arm hanging limply at his side, and her husband Snipe, who used to treat himself with Yeast-Vite tonic for his neuralgia and bile beans for his blood, Doan's kidney pills for his backaches and Andrews Salt for his liver, Iglodine for his cuts and Mentholatum for his catarrh; Snipe, who had once sent Tridib to the chemist's shop on West End Lane to buy him a glue called Dentesive so that his dentures would not be shaken out by the bombs.

Yes, she said nodding, mildly puzzled by my insistence, she did have a faint recollection, but she could not exactly say she remembered.

But how could you forget? I cried. She shrugged and arched her eyebrows in surprise, and said: It was a long time ago – the real question is, how do *you* remember?

But of course, to me it wasn't a question at all.

I tried to tell her, but neither then nor later, though we talked about it often, did I ever succeed in explaining to her that I could not forget because Tridib had given me worlds to travel in and he had given me eyes to see them with; she, who had been travelling around the world since she was a child, could never understand what those hours in Tridib's room had meant to me, a boy who had never been more than a few hundred miles from Calcutta. I used to listen to her talking sometimes with her father and grandfather about the cafés in the Plaza Mayor in Madrid, or the crispness of the air in Cuzco, and I could see that those names, which were to me a set of magical talismans because Tridib had pointed them out to me on his tattered old Bartholomew's Atlas, had for her a familiarity no less dull than the lake had for me and my friends; the same tired intimacy that made us stop on our way back from the park in the evening and unbutton our shorts and aim our piss through the rusty wrought-iron railings.

I began to tell her how I longed to visit Cairo, to see the world's first pointed arch in the mosque of Ibn Tulun, and touch the stones of the Great Pyramid of Cheops. I had been talking for a while when I noticed that she wasn't listening to me; she was following a train of thought in her mind, frowning with concentration. I watched her, waiting eagerly to hear what she would have to say. Suddenly she clicked her fingers, gave herself a satisfied nod, and said aloud, inadvertently: Oh yes, Cairo, the Ladies is way on the other side of the departure lounge.

I had a glimpse, at that moment of those names on the map as they appeared to her: a worldwide string of departure lounges, but not for that reason at all similar, but on the contrary, each of them strikingly different, distinctively individual, each with its Ladies hidden away in some yet more unexpected corner of the hall, each with its own peculiarity, like the flushes in Stockholm's Arlanda, so sleekly discreet that she had once missed two flight calls because it had taken her so long to understand how the handle worked. I imagined her alighting on these daydream names – Addis Ababa, Algiers, Brisbane – and running around the airport to look for the Ladies, not because she wanted to go, but because those were the only fixed points in the shifting landscapes of her childhood.

When I went to London, a decade later, often when Ila suggested going out somewhere, to a film in Brixton perhaps, or to a new Vietnamese restaurant in Maida Vale,

I would jump to my feet and, before I knew it, I would cry: Yes, let's go, let's go on the *Underground*. She would burst out laughing and mimic me, saying: You'd think we were going on the bloody *Concorde*.

To her the Underground was merely a means of shifting venue: it would irritate her to see how excited I got when we stepped on to the escalators; she would watch me as I turned to look at the advertisements flashing past us on the walls, gulped in the netherworld smell of electricity and dampness and stale deodorant, stopped to listen to the music of the buskers booming eerily through the permanent night of the passageways, and in annoyance she would tug at my elbows and hiss: Hurry, hurry, you can't stop here, you'll hold people up. And if I still lingered she would snap at me impatiently: For God's sake stop carrying on like a third-world tapioca farmer – it's just the bloody Underground.

And I would say to her: You wouldn't understand: to you Cairo was a place to piss in.

I could not persuade her that a place does not merely exist, that it has to be invented in one's imagination; that her practical, bustling London was no less invented than mine, neither more nor less true, only very far apart. It was not her fault that she could not understand, for as Tridib often said of her, the inventions she lived in moved with her, so that although she had lived in many places, she had never travelled at all.

All through her childhood, every time her family came back to Calcutta for a holiday, they brought back souvenirs from wherever they happened to be living at that time. Her parents would bring back all kinds of things – Indonesian leather puppets or improbable North African stools with camel-like humps. But there was only one kind of souvenir that Ila ever thought of bringing back and I was the only person to whom she would show them. We would slip away to the shade of the rusty water tanks on the roof of their house, and there, with a tight little smile, she would produce a large manila folder.

They were always the same, and in time they came to mean as much to me as they did to her: they were the Yearbooks of the International Schools of whatever city she happened to be living in at that time.

They were always full of photographs. There would be one of each student and then pages of others – of groups of friends, of parties and tennis matches, of whole classes together. For a long time I could not believe that they were really pictures of a school, because in the pictures the boys and girls were standing around all mixed up together, and besides, not one of them was in uniform. To me, the clothes they were wearing in those pictures seemed to have as little to do with school as the costumes at a circus.

Then Ila would point herself out, and there she would be, dressed in jeans or a skirt, and even, once, a Persian lambskin waistcoat. She would show me her friends, standing beside her, and I would roll their names around my tongue – Teresa Cassano, Mercedes Aguilar, Merfeth ash-Sharqawi – names of girls mainly at first, and then, as we grew older, boys too – Calouste Malekian, Cetshwayo James, Juin Nagajima – names which imprinted themselves on my memory so that years later I recognised Mercedes Aguilar at once when she turned up in a photograph two continents away from where she'd been when I had first seen her in those photographs.

Ila's closest friends were always the most beautiful, the most talented, the most intelligent girls in the school. She would point them out to me in the pictures of picnics and fancy-dress dances. The three of us went to that together, she would say, Teresa and Merfeth and I; and we spent the whole evening talking to each other – you should have seen the boys buzzing around us – but Teresa decided that we weren't going to dance that evening, just like that, so . . . And she would point Teresa and Merfeth out to me, laughing, slender girls, making faces at the camera. But somehow, though Ila could tell me everything about those parties and dances, what she said and what she did and what she wore, she herself was always unaccountably absent in the pictures.

When we were fourteen she once pointed to the picture of a boy who, to me, already looked like a grown man, with a face like an American film star, square-jawed and cleft-chinned, with long black hair that curled down to his shoulders. His name is Jamshed Tabrizi, she said, he's a fencing champion and this year his father gave him a BMW sports car for his birthday; he can't drive it yet because he's not old enough, but their chauffeur brought it around to the school one day. It's red, like lipstick, and as soon as he gets his licence, we're going to drive down to the beach at Pattaya on Sundays; it's just a few miles from Bangkok.

And then, in a rush, looking at me sideways, she added: He's my boyfriend.

But a few pages later, in their class photograph, there he was, right in the foreground, in the centre of the front row, grinning, broad-shouldered, a head taller than anyone else, with his arms thrown around the shoulders of two laughing blonde girls. And before she flipped the page I caught a glimpse of Ila herself, on the edge of the back row, standing a little apart, unsmiling, in a plain grey skirt, with a book under her right arm. She saw that I had noticed, and when I came upon that Yearbook again a week later I discovered that that page had been torn out. I felt a constriction in my throat, for suddenly it seemed to me that perhaps she was not so alien, after all, to my own small, puritanical world, in which children were sent to school to learn how to cling to their gentility by proving themselves in the examination hall.

Those schools were all that mattered to Ila; the places themselves went past her in an illusory whirl of movement, like those studio screens in old films which flash past the windows of speeding cars.

I confronted her with this once, in London, when the three of us, she, Robi and I, happened to be together in a pub, the Kembles Head, on Long Acre, a short walk from Covent Garden. Robi was stopping by in London on his way to Harvard. He was on leave from his job in the Indian Administrative Service, so that he could take up a fellowship in administration and public affairs for six months. We had decided to spend the evening together.

Ila laughed when I reminded her about those Yearbooks and, picking up her glass of whisky, she said: Of course those schools mattered to me, schools are all that matter to any child, it's only natural. It's you who were peculiar, sitting in that poky little flat in Calcutta, dreaming about faraway places. I probably did you no end of good; at least you learnt that those cities you saw on maps were real places, not like those fairylands Tridib made up for you.

But of course, among other things, Tridib was an archae-ologist; he was not interested in fairylands: the one thing he wanted to teach me, he used to say, was to use my im-agination with precision.

For instance, when Ila and I were ten, her family came to Calcutta from Colombo for a holiday. Ila came with Tridib and her mother to visit us, and her mother, in her kindly way, knowing how fascinated I was by the coun-tries they lived in, asked Ila to tell me a story about their house that she thought would interest her.

Their house was in a quiet part of Colombo where diplo-mats and senior civil servants and people like that lived.

29

It was an area where sprawling bungalows with huge lawns were threaded through by lanes that were often flooded with puddles of scarlet gulmohur and yellow jacaranda. Their house was at one end of a very quiet lane. It was a big house with large verandas and a steeply sloping roof covered with mossy tiles. The garden was at the back. It seemed to stretch out from inside the house; when the French windows were open the tiled floor of the drawing room merged without a break into the lawn. It was a quiet secluded garden, with a bronze vat, taller than a child, standing like a brooding tumulus in a corner. And it had a blue-tiled lily pond in the centre, in which plump, fantailed goldfish flashed their white bellies at the sun.

There was only one problem: adjoining the garden at the back was a poultry farm. This caused Ila's mother a good deal of worry, apart from the bother of the smell and the noise, for she had heard that snakes were certain to appear wherever there were chickens. Still, the house was surrounded by a very high wall, and when the breeze was blowing in the right direction the garden was as tranquil as a Japanese cloister.

One morning, soon after they moved in, their cook Ram Dayal came running upstairs and burst in upon Ila's mother who was taking her mid-morning nap in an easy chair on a veranda.

Mugger-muchh, shrieked Ram Dayal. Save me, burra-mem bachao me from his crocodile.

He was a tall, willowy, usually drowsy man, but now his eyes were starting from his gaunt face and his lips were flecked with spittle.

Never heard of such a thing, Ila's mother said to us. Crocodile in my garden; almost fell out of my easy chair.

My grandmother and I looked carefully away from each other, but ever afterwards the thought of Ila's mother, with her rounded figure, as soft and plump as two buns squashed

30

together in a schoolbag, falling out of her easy chair at the thought of a crocodile in her garden, was enough to reduce us to helpless laughter.

Man was in a state, she snorted. Never seen anything like it.

But now, being the woman she was, she folded her tiny hands in her lap, pushed her knot of hair back to the top of her head and sat up in her chair in the way the family had come to know so well, that characteristic pose that had earned her the nickname of Queen Victoria.

Shatup Ram Dayal, Queen Victoria snapped. Stop buk-bukking like a chhokra-boy.

Dekho burra-mem, he said again, his thin voice vanishing into a screech. There it is, in the garden.

And right he was, Queen Victoria said, her voice shrill with amazement. Damn and blast, there it was – a heck of a huge great big lizard, all grey and black, nasty great-big creature, with a little pointed head and a tongue like a bootlace, wandering about in my garden like a governor at a gymkhana.

But being, as she was, the daughter of a man who had left his village in Barisal in rags and gone on to earn a knighthood in the old Indian Civil Service, she retained her composure.

Muro-it, Ram Dayal, she cried. Catch hold of it before Ila-mem sees it, and cut its head off.

(As though it were a *penis* or something, Ila said to me years later.)

But Ram Dayal was knocking his head against the wall now, the whites of his eyes showing, tears zig-zagging down his cheeks. Why did I come to Lanka? he wailed. I knew Ravana would come to get me.

Shatup Ram Dayal, Queen Victoria snapped. She rang the little bronze bell she always carried to summon Lizzie, Ila's recently arrived Sinhalese ayah.

Yes madam? Lizzie said from the doorway. She was a thin, middle-aged woman with a stern mouth and a small, wasted face, always very neatly dressed in the blouse and sari of her native Kandyan foothills.

Waving a hand with careful nonchalance, Queen Victoria said: Lizzie, at it-garden looking-looking.

The animal was sunning itself now, its grey chest raised high on stiff forelegs.

Lizzie, what it-thing being-being? Queen Victoria said.

She always spoke like that to Lizzie, though Lizzie spoke very good English and even knew a little Hindi. It was a language she had invented on the spot when Lizzie first came to them on the recommendation of a senior Sinhalese civil servant.

Lizzie looked at it and laughed.

That's a thala-goya madam, she said. Very common here, very gentle animal.

Queen Victoria glared at the reptile.

Gentle, by Jove! she said to us. Wretched beast could have passed for a bloody tyrannosaurus.

She turned to look at Lizzie. No possible, she said, it-thing killing-killing?

Kill it? Lizzie cried, once she had decoded this. But why to kill it? They keep snakes away.

She ran downstairs, and a few minutes later they saw her go into the garden with an armful of cabbage stalks and vegetable peel. She scattered them on the grass and the animal darted forward and began to feed.

Hai, hai, hai, gasped Ram Dayal. Hai, hai, *hai*!

Determined not to be outdone by Lizzie, Queen Victoria stiffened her back and went out into the garden herself, taking a few vegetables with her. The animal fixed its eyes balefully upon her as soon as she stepped into the lawn. She froze. Then, drawing on her last reserves of courage, she managed to mutter to it: Eating-eating nice veggie-veggies? which was only her Lizzie-language turned inside out, but the animal's tail seemed to flicker in answer and from that moment onwards she considered it a part of her household: she was always at ease with anything and anybody who would respond to one of her private dialects.

After that, even though many of her Sinhalese acquaintances were alarmed to find a monitor lizard on her lawn and told her stories about how they had been known to break children's shinbones with a swipe of their tails, she allowed it the run of her garden, except, of course, when she had parties, when Lizzie was made to tie it to a tree with a length of rope.

One day, early in the morning after one of her parents' parties, when the lawn was still dotted with cigarette stubs and half-eaten snacks, Ila went out into the garden to read. She had a book with her that she had had to put away the night before when she was only twenty pages from the end, because Lizzie had switched off the lights in her bedroom. She flopped into a deckchair beside the lily pond and in a moment she was absorbed in her book. Ten pages later, still engrossed, she heard a soft splash in the lily pond. It was a very gentle splash, no louder than the sound of a goldfish's tail flicking the surface. But she stirred, and, not quite taking her eyes off the page, she caught a glimpse of a shadow, as slim and sinuous as a branch of oleander, stretching from the edge of the lawn, under her chair and into the pool.

Then the shadow rippled, and this time she looked up properly and saw scales glinting on a long muscular body.

She screamed, and the book dropped out of her hands. It hit the edge of her chair and tumbled off, and she heard a dull, fleshy thud as it struck scales and muscle.

The whole length of the snake's body flashed past under

the chair with an angry rustle, and then, somewhere behind her, she heard a slow prolonged hiss. She turned, slowly, stiffly, in the way one has to when one knows that one's lungs are suddenly empty and one's muscles have gone rigid with fear.

The snake's head was about a foot from her back. Its body lay curled, in tight regular coils, flat on the earth, while its head had reared up, higher than the back of the chair. She was whimpering now, trying to call out, but at the same time, looking at the snake's head, she saw it more clearly than she'd ever seen anything before, with the telescopic clarity of absolute concentration. She could see its tiny eyes, the flaring nostrils at the end of the sharply pointed head, the tongue, no longer flickering, drawn into the soft pink mouth in readiness, the fangs, erect now, and dripping.

Then she heard another sound at the far end of the garden and dimly, without turning her head, she saw the thala-goya thrashing at the end of its rope, battering the tree it was tied to with its tail. The snake heard it too, and it hesitated for a moment with its body arched. Its eyes settled upon Ila again and its neck bent still further back till it was like a drawn bow. Then its head flashed forward.

At that moment, reflexively, Ila turned her body, a very small movement, but enough to overbalance the chair. She fell, the chair tumbled over with her, and the snake's fangs glanced off its steel legs.

It reared back again like a snapping whiplash. Ila tried to push herself up, but her hands slipped and she fell back. And then, with all the suddenness of a knot springing undone, the coiled snake dropped its head on the grass and shot away towards the wall. She looked up to see the thala-goya lumbering after it. It had bitten through the rope. But the snake was quicker and it had slithered over the wall long before the thala-goya could cross the lawn.

So, young chap, Queen Victoria said, patting my head, her eyes twinkling. What do you make of that?

I glanced instinctively towards Tridib. He was looking at me, eyes narrowed, head cocked. I was nervous now: I could see that he was waiting to hear what I'd have to say, and I didn't want to disappoint him. My mother and grandmother were exclaiming with horror about the snake, asking Queen Victoria how big it was, whether it was poisonous or not. Taking my cue from them, I chose a safe course: hoping to earn Tridib's approval by showing him how well I remembered everything he told us, I asked Queen Victoria whether the snake was of the species Boidae or Elapidae.

Queen Victoria goggled at me and mumbled something to the effect of: Well that's a bit of an uppercut, young chap; I don't think I could tell you in a month of Sundays.

While she was mumbling I stole a glance at Tridib. He had pursed his lips and was shaking his head in disappointment. I sat out the rest of their visit in crestfallen silence.

On the stairs, when I was going down to see them off, while Ila and her mother lingered over their goodbyes, Tridib said to me casually that, if one thought about it, there was nothing really very interesting about snakes – after all, if I saw one in the lake, for example, what would I do? I'd come back home and tell everyone, but in a few minutes I'd forget about it and get back to my homework: the snake would have nothing whatever to do with my real life.

I did not particularly care for the suggestion that my homework was my real life, but I kept quiet anyway: I could see he was leading up to something else.

When we had almost reached the ground floor, he said: Did you notice that Ila's house had a sloping roof?

I shook my head: the detail had escaped me. I could not see that it had any relevance at all to the story. He must have seen the puzzlement on my face, for he put his hands on my shoulders, turned me around and asked me whether I could imagine what it would be like to live under a sloping roof – no place to fly kites, nowhere to hide when one wanted to sulk, nowhere to shout across to one's friends.

He got into the car, stuck his hand out through the window and gave me a punch on my chest, leaving me more puzzled than ever.

But later that evening, and for many evenings afterwards, while I sat under my grandmother's watchful eyes, pretending to do my homework, I puzzled over what Tridib had said, and in a while I began to imagine the sloping roofs of Colombo for myself: the pattern they made if one wheeled in the sky above them, how sharply they rose if one looked at them from below, the mossiness of their tiles when one saw them close up, from a first-floor window, and soon I felt that I too could see how much more interesting they were than the snake and the lizard, in the very ordinariness of their difference.

And still, I knew that the sights Tridib saw in his imagination were infinitely more detailed, more precise than anything I would ever see. He said to me once that one could never know anything except through desire, real desire, which was not the same thing as greed or lust; a pure, painful and primitive desire, a longing for everything that was not in oneself, a torment of the flesh, that carried one beyond the limits of one's mind to other times and other places, and even, if one was lucky, to a place where there was no border between oneself and one's image in the mirror.

I listened to him bewildered, wondering whether I would ever know anything at all, for I was not sure whether I would ever experience desire of that kind.

What could I say of this to Ila as she sipped her whisky

in the Kembles Head? Ila lived so intensely in the present that she would not have believed that there really were people like Tridib, who could experience the world as concretely in their imaginations as she did through her senses, more so if anything, since to them those experiences were permanently available in their memories, whereas with her, when she spoke of her last lover's legs, the words had nothing to do with an excitement stored in her senses, but were just a string of words that she would remember while they sounded funny and then forget as completely as she had the lover and his legs.

For Ila the current was the real: it was as though she lived in a present which was like an airlock in a canal, shut away from the tidewaters of the past and the future by steel floodgates.

Once, a couple of days after I arrived in London, she took me to Covent Garden to see the sights. We met at the tube station and she led me eagerly into the vast, steel-roofed piazza and took me around the used-clothes stalls and the vegetable market. But she must have seen that I was bored, for she soon decided that she had had enough of showing me around, and stalked off across the paved square, and disappeared into one of the roads that leads to Charing Cross.

Hurrying after her to make amends, I happened to look up and spotted a window with a sign painted on it. I sprinted down the road, caught up with her, brought her back and showed her the sign.

It says Victor Gollancz, she said. So what?

In answer I took her arm and led her through the door. There was an office inside with a wooden counter at one end and a few cabinets full of books along the walls. An elderly woman was sitting behind the counter, looking at me nervously over the top of her spectacles.

Can I help you at all? she said.

Could you tell me, please, I said, whether this is where the Left Book Club used to be, before the war?

Oh dear, she said, don't know about that, I wasn't here then. Would you like me to ring the director?

I shook my head, thanked her and led Ila out again. She was indignant now, as well as surprised. What's the matter with you? she said.

So, as we stood outside on the pavement, I tried to recall for her how Tridib had told us that Alan Tresawsen, Mrs Price's brother, had worked there before the war, in the Left Book Club; that it must have been right there, perhaps even in that office which we had just entered, for the Club had been a part of Victor Gollancz's publishing house . . .

Ila looked at the window again, with mild interest, shrugged, and said: Looks like any musty old office now, doesn't it?

To me it didn't, for having seen it first through Tridib's eyes, its past seemed concurrent with its present. But I did not say so: instead I looked at Ila, at her finely planed, high-cheekboned face, her long, brown eyes, and her shining black hair, curling down to her shoulders, and she felt my gaze on her and, smiling, thrust her arm through mine and led me off to a Chinese café she knew in Neal Street.

And so, as always, it was Ila – Ila of whom it was said, when we were children, that she and I were so alike that I could have been her twin – it was that very Ila who baffled me yet again with the mystery of difference.

While the pub filled up with young bankers wearing pin-striped suits and diamond earrings, and publishers' secretaries with purple-streaked hair, I tried to tell Ila and Robi about the archaeological Tridib, the Tridib who was much more contemptuous of fairylands than she would ever be; the Tridib who had pushed me to imagine

38

the roofs of Colombo for myself, the Tridib who had said that we could not see without inventing what we saw, so at least we could try to do it properly. And then, because she shrugged dismissively and said: Why? Why should we try, why not just take the world as it is? I told her how he had said that we had to try because the alternative wasn't blankness – it only meant that if we didn't try ourselves, we would never be free of other people's inventions.

But I *am* free, she said laughing.

You're lucky, I answered. I'm not: at least in London.

Why? she asked, draining her whisky. Because of the Raj?

I began to laugh. And then, because I knew she had forgotten, I tried to recall for her how, when we were eight-year-old children, she herself had once invented London for me.

Ila's family came to Calcutta for Durga Puja that year, because after many years her grandparents were going to be there too, just in time for the festival. Ila's father was on sabbatical leave from his job with the UN at the time. He was spending the year teaching in a university in the north of England. He had been glad to accept when the university invited him to be visiting professor in their newly founded institute of development studies. Ila and her mother had looked forward to it too, but once they arrived they ran into a problem they hadn't allowed for: the rooms Ila's father had been given weren't big enough for a whole family. In any case, Queen Victoria was not at all enthusiastic about living in that cold northern town. What would she do all day long, she said, in that grey place, surrounded by terrifying teddy boys and belching factories? She would much rather be in London. But then, where would they live in London and where would Ila go to school?

39

They were in a quandary when Mrs Price stepped in, in a way to which their family had by then become accustomed. They could be her lodgers in London, she had suggested, and go up to visit on weekends. She would be glad to have people in the house: it was two years since Snipe had died but the house still felt empty, and it would be emptier still now that May had decided to move out. And as for school, they would be able to work something out – there were many schools near by.

So that was where Queen Victoria and Ila were living when they came to Calcutta for that holiday – in Mrs Price's house in West Hampstead. Mrs Price had even arranged for Ila to go to school with her son.

They flew into Calcutta a few days before the festival began. Soon after they arrived Queen Victoria rang my mother and invited all of us, my parents, my grandmother and I, to drive out with them to visit their old family house in Raibajar.

My mother was delighted. She loved to go on long drives, and at that time, when the minor success my father was to achieve as an executive in the rubber industry was still a little while away, he was working too hard to go anywhere on weekends. In fact, since we did not have a car, and money was too tight to pay for holidays, we never went anywhere.

When my mother went to ask my grandmother whether we could go, her eyes were sparkling, and as she went up to the desk at which my grandmother was correcting her schoolbooks, she pinched my nose and whispered in my ear, very softly, so that my grandmother would not hear her: Picnic, picnic.

But my grandmother, when she was asked, frowned over the top of her spectacles and told my mother sharply that she ought to have known that Queen Victoria only wanted us along so that Ila would have someone to play with; that we weren't beggars yet to grab at everything she held out to us.

I could gauge my mother's disappointment from the way her fingers dug into my shoulder. There's nothing wrong with going on a drive with them, she blurted out, and then, confronted with my grandmother's glare, fell into a resentful silence.

Then I went up to my grandmother's desk and spoke to her, and instead of pleading I reminded her how my father had taken Ila to the zoo with me the year before and of how many times she herself had fed Queen Victoria with the very best ilish from the Gariahat fish market. At that she relented, as I had known she would, because she talked to me more than she did to anyone else and so I knew something of the fears she had accumulated in the long years after my grandfather's premature death, when she had had to take her schoolteaching job in order to educate my father: I could guess at a little of what it had cost her then to refuse her rich sister's help and of the wealth of pride it had earned her, and I knew intuitively that all that had kept her from agreeing at once was her fear of accepting anything from anyone that she could not return in exact measure.

Early in the morning, two days later, the four of us, my parents, my grandmother and I, walked down to Gole Park where they had arranged to meet us. It was the day before Shoshti, a perfect Puja day, with the clear October sunlight lying golden in the galis; the air cool, free at last of the damp summer heat. We looked into the back lanes as we walked, exclaiming over the bright pandals and awnings – some not yet finished and others with the images installed and their loudspeakers already humming.

We waited outside the Ramakrishna Mission building and watched the pavements near the sweet-shops being washed and then dirtied again by the crowds hurrying to get to Gariahat while the fish and the vegetables were still fresh. Then I spotted their old Studebaker making its stately way down Gariahat Road towards us. As the prospect of seeing Ila again became suddenly imminent, I could not keep still any more. There they are, I cried, jumping up and down, pointing. There, look, look.

I can see Maya, my grandmother said, following my finger. But where's the Shaheb?

My grandmother had called her brother-in-law, Mayadebi's husband, the Shaheb, ever since she heard his mother saying of him once, very proudly, that her son was so Europeanised that his hat wouldn't come off his head. She even called him that when she was speaking to him directly. This never ceased to upset my father, who was always careful to speak of him to his colleagues as: My meshomoshai, His Excellency, the Indian Consul-General in Sofia (or wherever he happened to be), Shri Himangshushekhar Datta-Chaudhuri.

There he is, my grandmother said drily. In the back seat, all by himself, leaning back with his pipe, as though he were setting out on a state visit. I wonder which of his uniforms he's wearing today.

It was my grandmother's theory that the Shaheb's wardrobe was divided into sets of hangers, each with its own label: Calcutta zamindar, Indian diplomat, English gentleman, would-be Nehru, South Club tennis player, Non-Aligned Statesman, and so on. It was certainly true that there was always a rigorous completeness about the Shaheb's appearance: in Calcutta the fall of his dhoti was always perfect – straight and starched – the top button of his kurta open in an exact equilateral triangle; in Lagos the pockets of his safari suits were never too obtrusive; his suits, when he wore them, looked as though they had been moulded on to him by the lost-wax process – whatever he wore, there was always a drilled precision about his clothes which seemed to suggest that he was not so much wearing them as putting them on parade. He looks like a dressed-up doll in a shop window, my grandmother used to say. No wonder everyone stares at him.

But that was not fair, for people would have stared at him anyway because of the extraordinary, indeed startling, distinction of his appearance. He was tall and slim, with a long, regular face, a sweeping nose, lustrous, melancholy eyes, and a lot of straight hair that was greying discreetly at the sides, like gunmetal in a frost. Wherever he went, heads turned towards him like spotlights following a model.

Look, look, my grandmother whispered in my ear as the car drew up to the pavement. He's got a new one today.

When the car drew up, we saw that he was wearing a pale green corduroy jacket with a silk cravat.

Then Mayadebi jumped out and she and my grandmother hurried towards each other and embraced, laughing, and talking quickly in that language that none of us could understand properly, their old Dhaka dialect. After I had touched Mayadebi's feet I looked up and saw they were holding hands over my head, like schoolgirls, smiling with their lips pressed together, full of merriment, in exactly the same way, as though there was a mirror between them.

But of course, Robi remarked, drawing patterns on the table with his beer, the fact was they hadn't looked at all like each other; they were completely different. He cocked his head, looked me over and shook his head: he couldn't see any sign of her in me either, he said, wrinkling his nose. Then he laughed and flicked a bit of foam at me off the top of his glass.

Why, he said, I looked much more like her than you ever did.

I could not argue with that: even my grandmother had always said so. She would put a finger on Robi's strong rounded chin and say: You get that from me; that's mine. It was because of that resemblance perhaps that she had always loved him best of Mayadebi's three sons. She would look at him and marvel at how he was always half a head taller than anyone else of his age, at the strength in his long, sinewy legs. She would press her thumb against the muscles in his forearms, already hardened at the age of nine by all the games he played, and she would say: You're strong, don't ever forget that, you're *strong*. Then she would turn to me and say: Watch Robi, he's *strong*, he's not like the rest of you in this country.

Once, when Robi could not have been very much older than twelve, my grandmother received a letter from Mayadebi which said, or rather hinted, that Robi had got into trouble in the boarding school in north India to which he had recently been sent, and that she, Mayadebi, was thinking of flying back to take him out of the school. My grandmother was worried enough to send a message to Tridib, asking him to come to our flat; she thought he would be able to tell her what had happened.

When Tridib turned up at our flat a week later, he merely shrugged when she asked him what had happened, and said that it was nothing at all: Robi had got himself into a bit of trouble because he'd beaten up an older boy who was a notorious bully and who'd chosen to pick on one of Robi's friends – a boy who couldn't defend himself because he had a club foot. He'd beaten up the bully so badly that he had had to spend two days in hospital.

So were the teachers upset? my grandmother asked. Had they written to Mayadebi?

Tridib laughed and said, no, it wasn't anything like that. The teachers were probably not wholly displeased, and they certainly hadn't written to Mayadebi. And as for the boys, Robi had become a hero amongst them over night. But

Mayadebi had got to hear of the incident somehow and she had worked herself into a terrible panic.

Why? my grandmother asked in astonishment. What was she worried about?

She was worried because Robi had chosen to fight him at all, Tridib said. She thought that he'd change; that he'd become like the boy he'd beaten. She didn't think he was strong enough or old enough to resist taking his place.

My grandmother's mouth tightened into a thin line. Of course Robi had to fight him, she said with a dismissive flick of her fingers. What else could he have done? Maya ought to be proud of him. *I'm* proud of him; but then, he's like me, not like Maya.

She was silent for a while, leaning back in her chair, with her hands folded in her lap. Then, gazing absently at the wall, she said: It doesn't surprise me. Maya was always a fool in some ways. Even when *we* were students.

And then, her voice slow and dreamy with the effort of recollection, she told us about a boy who had been in college with her in Dhaka, decades ago, in the early twenties.

He was a shy, quiet boy, with a wispy little beard, who lived in the lane next to theirs in Dhaka's Potua-tuli. He always sat as far back as possible in the lecture room and since he never said anything nobody took much notice of him.

Then one morning, when they were half-way through a lecture, a party of policemen arrived, led by an English officer, and surrounded the lecture room. Their lecturer tried to protest, but he was silenced by the policeman. As for the rest of them, they sat there whispering, excited, but subdued too, for they didn't want to draw attention to themselves.

Weren't you frightened? I asked.

A little, she said, fingering the thin gold chain she always wore around her neck. But not very much; we were quite used to police raids in those days. There were raids all the time in the colleges and the university. We'd grown up with it.

For a brief moment I thought she was joking.

Why? I said. What had you done?

So then, because she was rolling her eyes and evidently didn't know where to begin, Tridib, who had been listening intently, told me a little about the terrorist movement amongst nationalists in Bengal in the first few decades of this century: about secret terrorist societies like Anushilan and Jugantar and all their offshoots, their clandestine networks, and the home-made bombs with which they tried to assassinate British officials and policemen; and a little about the arrests, deportations and executions with which the British had retaliated. My grandmother sat perched on the edge of her chair while he was talking, as fragile as a porcelain bird, smiling at the growing astonishment on my face as I tried to fit her into that extraordinary history.

When he had finished she went on with her story.

After their lecturer had been sent away, the English officer drew his pistol and looked over the room, carefully comparing the faces in front of him with that on a piece of paper that he was holding in his hand. He went about it slowly, painstakingly, while they sat there, sweating under his gaze. After he had been at it for what seemed like hours, he gave a thin little smile, and his eyes came to rest on someone at the back of the room. They all turned to look, and at once a sigh of collective astonishment whistled through the room.

It was the shy, bearded boy: he was standing now, his face impassive, his back erect, his gaze fixed on the policeman, clear, direct and challenging. He seemed

46

absolutely unmoved, but watching him carefully she saw him drumming on his thigh for a brief moment with one of his fingers, and she knew then that he was frightened, more frightened perhaps than she would ever be. But neither then nor later, when they handcuffed him and led him out of the room, did he betray his fear again or allow his gaze to drop from the officer's face.

She scratched my head gently, and looking up, I saw her drawing her knuckles across moist eyes.

When I look at Robi, she said, I always think that if he'd been there he'd have stood there like that too, with his head erect, unflinching.

She laughed throatily, patting my head. But I'm not so sure about you, she said.

But the boy, Tridib wanted to know; what had happened to him?

They had heard afterwards that he had been a member of one of the secret terrorist societies since he was four-teen. He'd been exercising with them in their gymnasium, learning to use pistols and make bombs, smuggling messages and running errands. A few months before he was arrested he had finally been initiated into the society. The first mission they had given him was to assassinate an English magistrate in Khulna district. All his prepar-ations were ready; he was to leave for Khulna at the end of that week. But the police found out – their network of informers was legendary. The boy was tried and later deported to the infamous Cellular Gaol in the Andaman Islands.

After that, whenever she and Mayadebi were walking past the gali in which the boy had lived, she would point it out and tell her the story.

And do you know? she said, laughing. Maya would be frightened every time, and she would hold on to my hand and hurry me past the gali.

What about you? said Tridib. What did you think?

I used to dream of him, she said softly. For years afterwards I would lie in bed and conjure up his face, complete with that absurd, stringy little beard of his.

She was fascinated, long before that incident, by the stories she had heard about the terrorists: about the heroism of Khudiram Bose and the sad death of Bagha Jatin, hunted down on the banks of the Buribalam river, betrayed by treacherous villagers who had been bought with English money. Ever since she heard those stories she had wanted to do something for the terrorists, work for them in a small way, steal a little bit of their glory for herself. She would have been content to run errands for them, to cook their food, wash their clothes, anything. But, of course, they worked secretly; she didn't know how to get in touch with them, and even if she had it would have been twice as hard for her to get in, because she was a girl, a woman. She often speculated about some of the people she knew: maybe he's one of them, should I ask, or hint, or will he turn out to be an informer for the police? And of course, when he finally turned up, she hadn't recognised him. She'd been expecting a huge man with burning eyes and a lion's mane of a beard, and there he was, all the while, at the back of her class, sitting shyly by himself. She could so easily have talked to him. He would have been handsome too, she had decided later, if only he would shave that beard of his. Lying in her bed, she would think to herself – if only she had known, if only she had been working with him, she would have warned him somehow, she would have saved him, she would have gone to Khulna with him too, and stood at his side, with a pistol in her hands, waiting for that English magistrate . . .

I gazed in awed disbelief at the delicate outline of her face, at the polished silver of her hair, and the filigreed tracery of veins on her cheek.

Do you really mean, Tha'mma, I said, that you would have killed him?

She put her hands on my shoulders and, holding me in front of her, looked directly at me, her eyes steady, forthright, unwavering.

I would have been frightened, she said. But I would have prayed for strength, and God willing, yes, I would have killed him. It was for our freedom: I would have done anything to be free.

Robi and I sized each other up, he lounging languidly against the Studebaker, dressed in long trousers, and I, all too acutely aware of the shortness of my be-shorted legs. The Shaheb climbed out of the great blue car and greeted my grandmother with a smile, bending forward from the waist in a kind of abbreviated bow. My grandmother gave him a quick nod, pausing in her conversation with Mayadebi only to raise herself on tiptoe and sniff absentmindedly at his face. He pretended not to notice, but later my father scolded my grandmother and said she shouldn't have sniffed at him like that, in front of everybody; did she think he hadn't understood that she'd been trying to find out whether he'd been drinking? He had: he'd frowned when she did that bit of sniffing and tiptoeing.

And no wonder, my grandmother told him tartly, because he *had* been drinking: his breath was steaming like turpentine – at nine in the morning!

But *I* couldn't smell anything, my mother said.

The Shaheb had won my mother's heart that day: having recently seen a picture of him in a newspaper in which he was standing behind the Foreign Minister's chair at a negotiating table, she had come to believe that the kindly and avuncular man she remembered was now in a position of such power and importance that his mind could not but be permanently preoccupied with matters of state. Thinking herself to be ignorant of such weighty things, she had long been in secret dread at the thought of speaking to him. And sure enough, after she had touched his feet, he had peered at her and cleared his throat in a statesmanlike way, exactly as she had feared, but just when she was all but trembling with fright at the thought of having to offer an opinion on some tangled issue in international politics, he had patted her on the back, and in his beautiful Calcutta voice, rich with pipe smoke and whisky, he had said: I hope you aren't having any trouble getting eggs in the market?

When she had answered as best she could, he had gone on to ask whether the price of vegetables had gone up since he was last in Calcutta and whether kerosene was still as difficult to get as it used to be.

My mother was touched that so important and distinguished a man should take so keen an interest in such trivial and unlikely matters, but she was a little puzzled too, for though the questions had been asked with every semblance of interest, they had followed so quickly upon each other that they had seemed almost practised – and yet she could not imagine any circumstance in which a man like him could have practised them, since she could not bring herself to think that the ministers with whom she believed him to spend his time were much interested in small-talk about the price of eggs and the availability of kerosene. As for my father, he was mystified by the Shaheb's conversation with my mother. He had long admired the Shaheb to the point of adulation – partly because he was our only important relative, but mainly because the kind of elegance and dignity to which the bosses of the rubber industry fruitlessly aspired came to him so effortlessly. And in that image of well-groomed distinction there was no place for this sudden interest in eggs and vegetables and other matters domestic.

The mystery was not solved till some years later, when

my father in the course of a business trip to Africa happened to spend a few days with Mayadebi and the Shaheb in Conakry. There at an embassy dinner he overheard the Shaheb conducting precisely the same conversation, merely substituting mutton for eggs, with the wives of two third secretaries successively.

Those are the right things to say to a Mrs Third Secretary, he explained to my father on the way home. They're new to the business, you see, and it keeps their morale up: they like to know that H.E. himself takes an interest in their little difficulties.

So you see, my father explained to my mother when he came back from his trip to Africa; that day when we went to their house in Raibajar he had given me parity with a third secretary.

In fact, during my father's visit to Conakry, his rather sudden professional success had proved to be something of a problem for the Shaheb: he had his own promotion scheme for the world, and my father had not risen very far within it. So, in the beginning, his conversations with my father were oddly disjointed, until one evening, upon being asked a series of long and very detailed questions about the government's export policy, my father had realised that the Shaheb had finally resolved the question of precedence by raising him to the rank of First Secretary (Commercial).

By the time my mother had finished talking to the Shaheb I was beside myself with worry. I tugged at her sari and shouted, demanding to know where Ila was, hadn't she promised me that she'd be coming too? She shook her head helplessly, so I ran over to Ila's father and asked him why Ila hadn't come yet, wasn't she coming? He gripped my shoulder, shook his head and said, no, he was sorry, but he'd left her behind in London, she wasn't coming.

I had seen the wink he had shot my father, but I was struck dumb with disappointment all the same: with people of his age, the worst was the natural thing to believe. But Mayadebi heard him too, and she must have noticed that I was near tears for she led me away and told me not to worry, I'd be seeing Ila in a minute, she was following in the other car, with her mother and Tridib, and of course, Lizzie-missy, and Nityananda, their family cook . . .

And then there it was, the new grey Ambassador the Shaheb had bought for his sons' use, on the far side of the roundabout, with Ila leaning out of the window, her long hair streaming out in the wind. I burrowed into my grandmother's sari, suddenly terrified at the thought of meeting her again.

Why, you silly boy, my grandmother said. There she is, there's Ila; weren't you waiting for her?

Tridib brought the car to a dramatic halt and they climbed out slowly: Queen Victoria, so portly now that we gasped; Tridib himself, who flashed me our secret Inca salute before disappearing around the corner for a cigarette; Lizzie-missy, who had been living in their house in Calcutta while they were away in London; Nityananda, the cook, who had been with the Shaheb and Mayadebi for fifteen years, who came to attention now, staring into the middle distance, mindful of what he'd been taught when he was in the army.

But Ila stayed in the car, looking out of the window at the bird-shitted statue in the centre of Gole Park.

Suddenly, all together, everyone remembered her.

I can't see Ila, Mayadebi said.

Probably asleep somewhere, said my grandmother.

Probably sulking, said Robi.

God, she must be big now, said my mother.

Not big enough, said Queen Victoria. Doesn't eat a thing, my poor baby.

Big enough for an automatic watch, said her father. Gave her a gold Omega for her eighth birthday.

But where is she? asked Mayadebi.

Oh my goodness, Lizzie, Lizzie, Queen Victoria roared. Ila-mem at once here fetching-fetching. Where she being-being?

Lizzie-missy went to the car and we heard her thin voice scolding. After a while Ila climbed out, very slowly, and stood leaning against the door of the car, rubbing her eyes with her fists. When she looked up, her eyes met mine and we stared at each other across the breadth of our assembled family.

She was wearing clothes the like of which I had never seen before, English clothes, a white smock with an appliqué giraffe that had its hooves resting on the hem while its neck stretched almost as far up as her chin.

It couldn't have been that one, Ila said loudly, her voice echoing on the dark shop windows of Long Acre as we walked towards the lights of Soho. She laughed and, thinking tipsily hard, said no, it couldn't have been, she hadn't got that one till much later. And Robi, tapping her on the back, reminded me that she had had trunks full of dresses, it could have been any of a thousand.

But I do remember. I can see her in it. I can still hear the starch that Lizzie-missy had washed into it, I can see the creases left by her iron, I can feel the gauzy texture of the cloth, I can smell the faint milky smell of the baby's talcum powder that Lizzie-missy has poured over her, I can even see the patch of white it has left on her neck and the two rivulets of sweat that have wound their way through it.

Why are you staring at her like that? my mother said. Go and talk to her.

At that I shrank even further back.

I don't know what the matter with him is, my mother

said, complaining loudly, to everyone. He's been waiting for her for days. He asks about her every night: where's Ila? when is she coming? He won't go to sleep at night until I tell him, she's coming soon, don't worry . . .

Now listen to that, said Queen Victoria, looking at me fondly. What a sweet little man. Do you hear that, Ila? He asks about you every day.

Ila smiled and turned her head away with a tiny shrug.

I knew then, for certain, that she had not asked about me as I had about her.

At that moment I hated my mother. For the first time in my life she had betrayed me. She had given me away, she had made public, then and for ever, the inequality of our needs; she had given Ila the knowledge of her power and she had left me defenceless, naked in the face of that unthinkable, adult truth: that need is not transitive, that one may need without oneself being needed.

To stop them saying any more I ran over to the car and jumped in.

You can sit in front, Ila said; with Tridib-kaku and Nityananda. I'm going to sleep.

We drove away soon. I sat between Nityananda and Tridib in the front seat, while Ila, her mother and Lizzie-missy dozed at the back. It took us much longer than usual to drive through the city: cars have no privilege on the roads at that time of the year; the streets are overwhelmed by the festivities. We had to inch forward near Gariahat, with Nityananda and Tridib hanging out of the windows, begging shoppers to make way. Near Sealdah it took us almost half an hour to skirt around a *pandal* that was jutting out from the pavement, right into the middle of the street. The car got hotter and hotter and Tridib began to shout curses at everything that crossed our path, his wire-rimmed glasses glinting in the sunlight, dwarfing his waspish, angular face. The traffic came to a virtual standstill again near Dakshineshwar. We crawled along till we reached the bridge, and then looked down in awe, from our height, at the vast crowds circulating in the courtyard of the temple below, like floodwaters sweeping through a garden. But once we had crossed the bridge the traffic grew thinner, and soon we were speeding along the Grand Trunk Road. Then Tridib relaxed a little and leant back, smelling as he always did of fresh cigarette smoke and soap. I asked him a few questions but he seemed abstracted and wouldn't say much, so soon I dozed off too.

When I woke up, Nityananda was shaking my arm excitedly, crying: Wake up, wake up, there it is, there's the house, look, look.

It appeared suddenly on the edge of the windscreen: a bright yellow patch on a gentle knoll, rising like a cake out of that table-like plain. In a few minutes we reached an arched gateway that had outhouses on either side of it. The cars slowed down a little, and as we were overtaken by the cloud of dust that had been following us, children swarmed out of the outhouses and ran along with the car, waving and shouting. The house had vanished behind a forest that stretched all the way up the knoll, the trees growing so thick and close together that they hid the house like a curtain. Tridib, grinning, told me to take a good look, for I wouldn't see trees like those again for a long time: his grandfather had wanted to live in a tropical rain-forest so he'd imported those trees from Brazil and the Congo.

Then Nityananda nudged me, pointing to the left, and turning I saw a troop of monkeys hanging on the vines, staring down at us, somersaulting in alarm. The car turned a corner, still climbing steeply, and suddenly the house was in front of us: newly whitewashed and plastered, shining golden in the mid-morning sunlight, a festoon of flapping saris hanging wetly from the roof, a row of columns stretching across the portico in a broad, gap-toothed smile.

The paved terrace in front of the house was already buzzing when the cars drew up. The durwans who looked after the house had lit two fires from which thin feathers of smoke were now rising into the sky. Their wives had settled down in the shade of the portico, surrounded by mounds of vegetables. In readiness for Nityananda, huge brass pots had been set out on the terrace.

We were surrounded as soon as we got out of the car. Ila vanished into a knot of people, all eager to examine and exclaim over the only grandchild of the house. She let them fuss over her for a while, then suddenly she broke free of them, snatched at my hand and dragged me across the paved terrace. Come on, she whispered urgently, let's hide.

I shot a glance back, over my shoulder. They're running after us, I shouted. What'll we do now?

Just follow me, she panted, vaulting up the plinth of the portico. We dodged through the columns into a vast, musty hall. Stumbling into it, blinded by the gloom, we bumped into each other, and then tripped and fell on a flight of cold marble stairs. Narrowing my eyes, I tried to see where they led. But I could only see a few feet ahead, and beyond that the stairs vanished into darkness. I could hear the durwans and the children racing across the courtyard now, shouting to each other.

It's too dark up there, I whispered to Ila. Where shall we hide? They're almost here.

She gestured at me impatiently to be quiet. She was looking around the hall, hesitating as though she had forgotten her way around the house. I pushed her, urging her on, my belly churning with a breathless hide-and-seek excitement.

Shut up, she snapped, pushing me back. And just when

I was about to make a dash for a dim, high door on the far side of the hall, she cried: Come on, I remember now! and began to feel her way around the staircase. I followed her until we came to a low wooden door, hidden away behind the stairs. She found a knob and gave it a tug. The door creaked but showed no sign of coming open.

Come on, pull, she said to me breathlessly. Aren't you good for *anything*?

I could hear feet thudding on the portico now. I caught hold of the knob and we pulled together, as hard as we could. The door creaked and a gust of musty air blew into our faces. We pulled harder still and the door opened, no more than a few inches wide, but enough for us to squeeze through. We slipped in and managed to push the door shut. A moment later we heard them pouring into the hall.

We tumbled down a couple of steps to a stone floor and lay there panting. We could hear them scattering in the hall now, some running up the staircase, some looking in the corners, shouting excitedly to each other. Ila smiled gleefully and squeezed my hand.

You watch, she said, none of them will think of looking in here.

For a while all I could see was a pale green glow filtering in through a window, set so high up in the wall that it seemed like a skylight. Its small rectangle of glass was mildewed over on the outside by grass and moss.

Look! I said to Ila. There's grass growing on that window.

Yes, she said. The window's on the ground. If you want to look in here you have to lie flat on your stomach.

But then, I said in amazement, this room must be under the ground.

Yes, of course, she said. You fool: couldn't you tell?

I shivered. I had never been underground before: as far as I knew only the underworld lay below the ground. I looked around and the cavernous room seemed suddenly full of indistinct shapes, murky green in that strangely aquatic light, like the looming heads of rock in a picture that Tridib had once shown me, of the cave of a moray eel.

What are these things in here? I said. Why does this place smell like this?

We could hear Lizzie-missy shouting for Ila in the hall.

Let's go back, I said. We've been here long enough.

Ila clapped a hand over my mouth. Shut up, she whispered angrily; you can't go, now that I've brought you here.

Queen Victoria was shouting too, scolding Lizzie-missy: Why you let her running-running? Tridib was arguing with her: Let them be, they're just playing somewhere . . . Their voices drew away slowly and we knew that they had gone outside, back to the terrace.

I don't like this place, I whispered to Ila. I don't want to stay here.

Coward, she said. Aren't you meant to be a boy? Look at me: I'm not scared. It's just some old furniture covered up with sheets. That's all.

But what are we going to do in here? I said. It's so dark . . .

I know what we can do, she said, clapping her hands together. We can play a game.

A game! I cried, peering at the grey-green shapes rising out of the darkness. What kind of game can we play in a place like this?

I'll show you, she said. It's a nice game, many boys like it.

But there's no room in here, I protested. And I can't see very far.

She sprang up. I know where we can play, she said. I just hope it's still there.

I followed her as she picked her way through the looming shrouded shapes, stumbling in the darkness, raising little storms of dust. She led me to the far end of the room where it was so dark I could hardly tell where she was.

Yes, she cried in triumph, pointing at a vast, sheet-covered mound. It *is* still here. Help me pull off the sheet, come on.

I caught hold of one end of the sheet and she of another. We tugged, but instead of coming off, the sheet seemed to atomise in our hands, and for a moment everything vanished into a cyclone of dust.

I can still see it, taking shape slowly within that cloud of dust.

Like a magician's rabbit, laughed Ila.

Nothing as simple as that, said Robi wryly. No, at least a castle on a misty mountain top.

But in my memory I see it emerging out of that storm of dust like a plateau in a desert.

It was a table, the largest I had ever seen; it seemed to stretch on and on. I used to wonder later whether this was merely a legacy of a child's foreshortened vision: an effect of that difference in perspective which causes all objects recalled from childhood to undergo an illusory enlargement of scale. But three years later, when I took May, a fully grown 24-year-old adult, into that room and showed her the table, even she gasped.

Heavens! she said. It's huge: what could it possibly have been used for?

Tridib once told me all about it. My grandfather bought it on his first visit to London, he said, some time in the 1890s. He saw it at an exhibition in the Crystal Palace and couldn't resist it. He had it shipped to Calcutta in sections, but when it arrived he didn't know what to do with it so he had it put away here. And so it was forgotten until you rediscovered it.

May walked around it, frowning. I wonder how much

59

he paid for it, she said, running her thumb along the grain of the dark, heavy wood.

I wonder how much it cost to have it shipped here, she said loudly, her voice echoing in the shadows of the room. I wonder how many proper roofs that money would have bought for those huts we saw on our way here.

The indignation in her voice stabbed accusingly at me. I don't know, I said, lowering my head.

She tapped on the wood with her knuckles. Why did he bring *this* back, for God's sake? she cried. Why this worthless bit of England; why something so utterly useless?

She was biting her lip in bewilderment now, shaking her head.

I could think of no answer to give her: it seemed impossible to me to think of that table as an object like any other, with a price and a provenance, for I had seen it taking shape with my own eyes, within a cloud of dust, in that very room.

All right, said Ila, let's go under it.

Under it? Aghast, I tugged at the back of her smock and asked her what kind of game we could possibly play under it.

Come, she said; she was already on her knees crawling through the dust. Come on, I'll show you. It's the game I play with Nick.

Nick? I said, suddenly alert. Who's Nick?

Don't you know Nick? she said, and turning to look back at me, over her shoulder, she said: Nick's Mrs Price's son, May's brother. We live in their house in London. He and I walk to school together in the morning and come back together in the afternoon, and then afterwards, every evening, we go down together to play in the cellar.

She reached for my hand and tried to pull me down. Come on, she said. I'll show you: it's a game called Houses.

No, I said, shaking my head, confused by the questions that were now stirring in my head.

This Nick, I found myself asking her. How big is he?

Oh he's big, she said, perching on the footrest. He's very big. Much bigger than you: much stronger, too. He's twelve, three years older than us.

I squatted beside her on the dusty floor, thinking.

What does he look like? I asked presently.

She screwed up her face and thought hard. He has yellow hair, she said after a while. It always falls over his eyes.

Why? I said. Doesn't he comb it?

He does comb it, she said. But it still falls over his eyes.

It must be long like a girl's.

No, it's not a bit like a girl's.

Then why is it so long?

It is not so long, she said. It's just very straight, and when he runs or something it falls over his eyes. He can even touch it with his tongue sometimes.

I spat on the floor in disgust. We watched the spit turning into a tiny pool of foaming mud.

He must be filthy, I said. Eating his own hair.

You're just jealous, Ila said grinning, because your own hair is so short. Nick looks sweet when his hair falls over his eyes: everyone says so.

After that day Nick Price, whom I had never seen, and would, as far as I knew, never see, became a spectral presence beside me in my looking glass; growing with me, but always bigger and better, and in some ways more desirable – I did not know what, except that it was so in Ila's eyes and therefore true. I would look into the glass and there he would be, growing, always faster, always a head taller than me, with hair on his arms and chest and crotch while mine were still pitifully bare. And yet if I tried to look into the face of that ghostly presence, to see its nose, its teeth, its ears, there was never anything there, it had no features, no form; I would shut my eyes and try to see its face, but all I would see was a shock of yellow hair tumbling over a pair of bright blue eyes. And as for what he did, what he said, what he thought about, in the three years between the moment when Ila first told me about him and that day when I took May down to that underground room, I knew nothing at all about him except one little snippet of a story that my father told me about him once, soon after returning from a trip to England.

My father had telephoned Mrs Price soon after he arrived in London, just in case Ila and Queen Victoria were still there. It turned out that they had left long ago, but Mrs Price insisted that he come to tea with her anyway. He went, and when Mrs Price led him into her drawing room, he found Nick there too, dressed in his school uniform but with his tie hanging loose around his neck. He shook hands with my father and sat down quietly in an armchair in a corner. My father could not help being impressed: he had never seen such a definite air of self-possession in a child of thirteen.

For a while my father and Mrs Price chatted about Mayadebi and the Shaheb (who were in Romania and had invited her to visit them there), about May, who was away at the festival in Bayreuth, and Tridib. Mrs Price remembered, laughing, that Tridib had once decided that he wanted to be an air-raid warden when he grew up. So then my father turned to Nick, for he hadn't said a word yet, and asked him whether *he* knew what he wanted to be when he grew up.

Nick tipped back his head, with a little smile, as though he were surprised that anyone should ask, and said, yes, of course he knew, he'd known for years; he wanted to be like his grandfather, grandfather Tresawsen, whose picture was hanging over there, above the mantelpiece.

To my intense disappointment, my father could tell

me nothing about Nick's grandfather, except that in the picture he had had a square face, white hair and a walrus moustache.

So, as always, it fell to Tridib to tell me, sitting on the grass in the Gole Park roundabout one evening, how Mrs Price's father, Lionel Tresawsen, had left the farm where he'd been born – in a village called Mabe, in southern Cornwall – and gone off to a nearby town to work in a tin mine; how he'd gone on from there – for no matter that he had very little education, he had deft hands, a quick mind and a great deal of ambition – to become the overseer of a tin mine in Malaysia; and then further and further on, all around the world – Fiji, Bolivia, the Guinea Coast, Ceylon – working in mines or warehouses or plantations or whatever came his way; how finally he had surfaced in Calcutta, making his living by working as an agent in a company which dealt in steel tubes, and then, later, gone on to make, if not exactly a fortune, certainly a respectable sum of money, by starting a small factory of his own, in Barrackpore. It was then, prosperous at last, in his middle age, that he married. His wife was the widow of a Welsh missionary doctor, and she bore him two children, Elisabeth and Alan. When Elisabeth was twelve and Alan ten, she made her husband sell his factory and move back to England: she was determined that her children would have all the advantages of a proper education, university and all. And so they went back and settled in the bucolic tranquillity of a small Buckinghamshire village.

But in fact there was much more to Lionel Tresawsen than money, steel tubes and children. In his youth, for example, he had been a prolific inventor. After he died, his wife discovered that in the period of five years when he was living in Malaysia he had taken out no less than twenty-five patents – for gadgets ranging from mechanical shoe-horns to stirrup-pumps for draining water out of flooded mines.

He had given up inventing in disgust when manufacturers had proved strangely indifferent to his inventions. And then there was the Lionel Tresawsen of middle-age, who had tried to set up a homeopathic hospital in a village near Calcutta; and the almost-old Lionel, who had developed an interest in spiritualism and begun to attend the meetings of the Theosophical Society in Calcutta, where he met and earned the trust and friendship of a number of leading nationalists. This had, of course, estranged him and his wife from most circles of British society in the city and led to innumerable colourful slights and insults at clubs and tea parties, but that had made very little difference to Lionel Tresawsen, since those people had never been particularly pleasant to him anyway. He had also begun to attend seances conducted by a Russian medium, a large lady who had married an Italian who ran a restaurant in Chowringhee. It was at those offices that he met Tridib's grandfather, Mr Justice Chandrashekhar Datta-Chaudhuri, who liked indulging in matters spiritual when the High Court was not in session: their friendship was sealed across innumerable planchette tables while waiting for the large lady to summon her favourite spirit, the all-seeing astral body of Ivan the Terrible.

Listening to Tridib that evening, I thought I understood what Nick had meant when he had said to my father, with such untroubled certainty, that yes, of course he knew what he wanted to do, he wanted to travel around the world like Lionel Tresawsen, to live in faraway places half-way around the globe, to walk through the streets of La Paz and Cairo. At that moment, looking up at the smoggy night sky above Gole Park, wondering how the stars looked in London, I thought I had found at last the kindred spirit whom I had never been able to discover among my friends.

I couldn't hold my questions back any more after I had shown

May the footrest under the immense table, where Ila had been sitting when she first introduced me to Nick Price. Is his hair really yellow? I cried. And does it really fall over his eyes?

May gave this a bit of thought and said, no, yellow was not quite the word she would use, it was sort of straw-coloured hair, but yes, it did fall over his eyes.

And what was he like? I found myself asking her. Did he like school, and what was he going to do afterwards?

I was being clever. I didn't want her to know that I already knew.

She found an upturned chair, righted it, and sat down. Oh, he's a very grown-up little boy, she said. He knows exactly what he's going to do after school.

What?

He's going to join a firm of chartered accountants, and once they've trained him he's going to get a nice job with a huge salary preferably abroad, not in England. England's gone down the drain, he says. It can't afford to pay anyone properly except old-age pensioners.

What's a chartered accountant? I said.

She smiled and wiped the back of her hand across his face, leaving a dark smudge on her cheek.

I don't know, she said, with a snort of laughter. I think they have big books full of numbers on which they make little marks with red pencils.

I steadied myself against her chair. But May, I said, doesn't he want to travel – like your grandfather . . . ?

Oh, travel doesn't mean the same thing to everyone, she said. She gave me a long speculative look, narrowing her eyes, and said: I wonder whether you'd like him.

65

Of course I'd like him, I cried. I like him already.

You don't know him, she said. He's not at all like us, you know.

What do you mean 'us'? I said.

Not much like me, she said. Nor like our parents, or Tridib, or you, or anyone . . .

She stood up, dusted her shirt and said, under her breath, to herself, as though in reproof: But all the same he's a dear old chap.

I hope I'll meet him some day, I said.

I'm sure you will, she said, smiling. I wonder what you'll have to say to him when you do?

I met him seventeen years later, in London.

The day before Robi was to leave for Boston, Ila arranged to take the two of us to meet Mrs Price. I was delighted: I had been planning to visit her ever since I arrived in London, four weeks before, but somehow I had not quite picked up the courage to go on my own.

Ila and Robi met me at the Indian Students' Hostel in Bloomsbury where I was staying temporarily. They arrived late in the afternoon when I was in the dining hall, drinking tea and eating dum aloo and puris, while listening to a bearded student leader from Allahabad who was campaigning to be elected president of the hostel union.

The moment I saw Ila coming through the door, I could tell from her pursed lips and shining eyes that she was nursing a secret. But when I asked her what it was, on the way to the Goodge Street tube station, she shook her head and hurried on ahead of us.

It was not till the red sign of the Mornington Crescent tube station had flashed past my window like a palmed card that Ila sprang her surprise.

Do you know who's going to be waiting for us at the station when we get there? she said.

May? said Robi.

66

No, not May, said Ila. May's away touring with her orchestra.

Then who? Go on, tell us.

Nick, she said, her eyes shining. Nick Price. I haven't seen him in, it must be all of ten years. He was a pimply youth of nineteen then, and I was a buck-toothed belle with braces.

But I thought he was away in Kuwait, said Robi. Getting rich, doing chartered accountancy or whatever.

He was, said Ila. He's been away for a very long time. But he came back unexpectedly a couple of weeks ago – I don't know why. Mrs Price didn't talk about it much.

She looked out at the black walls of the tunnel, smiling to herself.

I'll tell you what, she said presently. After we've been to see Mrs Price, I'll treat you two to dinner at my favourite Indian restaurant – it's a small Bangladeshi place in Clapham. You'll like it. We can ask Nick too – maybe he'd like to come.

I knew him the moment I saw him. He was at the far end of the platform, standing under a 'Way Out' sign. He was wearing a blue suit, a striped institutional tie and a dark overcoat. He looked very tall and broad to me at first, just as I had imagined him. But when he and Robi met half-way and shook hands, I saw that I was wrong, that my eyes had been deceived by the distorted perspectives of the long, straight lines of the platform: I saw that most of his breadth lay in the thickness of his overcoat and that his head reached no higher up Robi's shoulder than did mine.

When he turned to Ila, and stuck out his hand, I wondered whether he looked older than he ought because his face had been burnt and coarsened by the desert sun. But it wasn't that: it was because of a premature, slightly suspicious gravity that made him wrinkle up his eyes appraisingly when he talked, like a banker who has seen too many good debts turn bad.

Ila laughed, looking at his outstretched hand, and raising herself on tiptoe she flung her arms around his neck and kissed him, full on the mouth. The blood rushed to his face and he laughed too, awkwardly, and his face suddenly unwrinkled, and throwing his arms around her he hugged her to his chest, and then, when he was kissing her, I saw that his hair had fallen over his eyes in exactly the way Ila had described on that long-ago October morning.

So, when he walked up to me, flicking his straw-coloured hair back, and said: How nice to meet you, I've heard so much about you from my mother and May and everyone ... what could I say? I said: I'm not meeting you for the first time; I've grown up with you.

He was taken aback.

That must have taken some doing, he said drily, since I grew up right here, in boring suburban old West Hampstead.

I've known the streets around here for a long time too, I said.

And then I began to show off.

When we came out of the tube station I stopped them and pointed down the road. Since this is West End Lane, I said, that must be Sumatra Road over there. So that corner must be where the air-raid shelter was, the same one that Robi's mother and your mother and your uncle Alan ducked into on their way back from Mill Lane, when one of those huge, high-calibre bombs exploded on Solent Road, around the corner, blowing up most of the houses there. And that house, that one, just down the road, over there, on the corner of Lymington Road, I know what it's called: it's called Lymington Mansions, and an incendiary bomb fell on it, and burned down two floors. That was on the first of October 1940, two days before your uncle died.

Nick Price inclined his head at me, in polite incredulity. He turned to Ila and they walked on ahead, cutting me short. Robi fell into step beside me and, jabbing me in the ribs, told me not to bullshit; didn't I know that the Germans hadn't developed high-calibre bombs till much later in the war? In 1940 they simply hadn't possessed a bomb that was powerful enough to knock down a whole street.

But that's what happened, I said.

How do you know? Robi said.

Because Tridib told me.

How was *he* to know? He was just a kid, nine years old. Every little bomb probably seemed like an earthquake to him.

Look, I said, that's what happened.

OK, Robi said. Since you're so sure, let's go and take a look at that road of yours and see what it's like now.

All right, I said. I called out to Nick and Ila: We're going over there to take a look at Solent Road, where the bomb fell.

Ila made an impatient face. You and your silly bombs, she said. We're late already; hurry up. We'll wait for you at the corner.

Solent Road's over there, said Nick, laughing. Do tell us if you find it all bombed out.

He did not have to tell me where it was. I knew already, for the map was in my head: down Sumatra Road, fourth turning to the right.

Here we are, said Robi, when we got there. That's your bombed-out road.

It was a short road, lined with trees and hedges on either side. The trees were a pale honey-green – the colour of English greenery – but gentler still now, gilded by the steep afternoon sunlight. The red brick houses were all exactly the same, on both sides of the road: with sharply pointed tiled roofs and white window frames and doorways, each with its own patch of garden hidden behind a hedge. There were rows of small cars parked on either side of the road. Right beside us was a small blue Citroën with a sticker on the windshield which said: Save the Whales. On the back seat there was a pile of oddly shaped green bottles and next to them a kind of plastic bucket strapped to the seat.

I found myself suddenly absorbed in the trappings of the lives that went with that car.

Are those wine bottles? I asked Robi.

No, you fool, he laughed. Those are mineral water bottles.

And that; what's that? I asked, pointing to the plastic bucket.

That's a seat for a baby, he said impatiently. Haven't you seen one before? It's to keep a baby safe inside a car.

I could not take my eyes off the Citroën.

Enough of that bloody car, said Robi. Take a look at your bombed-out Solent Road now.

I looked up at the quiet, pretty houses on that tranquil road. I caught his eye and we both burst into laughter.

Not exactly what you had expected, Robi said.

I did not tell him then, but he was wrong.

I had not expected to see what Tridib had seen. Of course not. I had not expected to see rubble sloping down from burnt-out houses like scree in a mountain quarry, with a miraculously undamaged bathtub balanced precariously at the top; nor had I expected to find the road barricaded by policemen while the men from the Heavy Rescue Service tried to dig beneath the rubble for the lost pensioner. I had known that I would not see uprooted trees or splintered windows or buckled flagstones: I had expected nothing of all that, knowing it to be lost in a forty-year-old past.

But despite that, I still could not believe in the truth of what I did see: the gold-green trees, the old lady walking her Pekinese, the children who darted out of a house and ran to the postbox at the corner, their cries hanging like thistles in the autumn air. I could see all of that, and yet, despite the clear testimony of my eyes, it seemed to me still that Tridib had shown me something truer about Solent Road a long time ago in Calcutta, something I could not have seen had I waited at that corner for years – just as one may watch a tree for months and yet know nothing at all about it if one happens to miss that one week when it bursts into bloom.

I wanted to know England not as *I* saw her, but in her finest hour – every place chooses its own, and to me it did not seem an accident that England had chosen hers in a war.

Nick and Ila were waiting for us where we had left them, at the corner where Sumatra Road joined West End Lane. Nick was talking and he did not notice us.

One can't really *like* Kuwait, we heard him say. There's nothing to do there except drink and watch video films. I'm quite relieved to be back.

So have you got yourself a new job? Ila asked.

Oh, I'll start looking around soon, he said. It shouldn't be a problem; I have a lot of experience.

He stopped to run his fingers through his hair.

You may say what you like about Kuwait, he said. But there's serious money to be made out there. Really serious money. Nothing like the chickenfeed I'd get working for some tuppenny company in the Midlands.

Then he saw us and exclaimed: Ah, there you are. So did you find your bombed-out road?

He found it all right, said Robi. But instead of the remains of some dreadful battlefield, all he got to see was a little old lady with a blue rinse, out walking her Pekinese.

But still, said Nick, you did find your way there. Now would you like to have a go at finding your way to 44 Lymington Road?

I could try, I said.

Go ahead then.

It was easy enough on the A to Z street atlas of London that my father had brought me. I knew page 43, square 2, by heart: Lymington Road ought to have been right across the road from where we were. But now that we had reached the place I knew best, I was suddenly uncertain. The road opposite us was lined with terraces of cheerfully grimy red-brick houses, stretching all the way down the length of the road. The houses were not as high or as angular as I had expected.

But still, as far as I could tell that was where Lymington Road should have been, so I pointed to it and asked whether that was it.

Yes! said Nick. Good boy: got it first time.

We crossed West End Lane at a zebra crossing and I went ahead of the others, absorbed in taking in the details of the woodwork over the doorways, the angles of the bow windows that jutted out into the little patches of garden, the patterns of the wrought-iron gates. Then I caught a glimpse of a cricket field in the distance and at once I knew where number 44 was. I shouted to the others, pointing at the house. They smiled to see me so excited and when they caught up with me Nick burst into laughter.

Well, he said, following my pointing finger, you're positively a mystic from the east. You've done it again.

When we reached the house, I leaned over the hedge to look into the garden before Nick could unlatch the little gate. The cherry tree in the garden was much taller than I had expected.

The front door opened when we were half-way down the path that led through the little patch of garden. Mrs Price had seen us coming; she stood framed in the doorway. She was a small woman, very thin and stooped with age. Her face was small too, but she had large, prominent eyes, like May's. She had a tight wreath of silver curls, and a short-sighted, slightly worried frown was etched into the lines of her forehead. She was wearing a severe military-green skirt, a white blouse and a grey cardigan. I had seen many pictures of her, but they had not prepared me for the transparent, almost translucent quality of her complexion: even at a distance, I could see an intricate circuitry of veins filigreed on her skin.

She met us half-way up the path and kissed Ila, and shook hands with Robi and me. She was glad, she said to me, that we had met at last, it was such a pity May was away, she would very much have liked to meet me, she spoke so often of the kindness my family had shown her in Calcutta . . .

Nick, hugely amused, told her how I had shown them the way to the house, and how I had known that they had a cherry tree.

I've heard so much about it, you see, I said awkwardly. I was embarrassed now.

Well, said Mrs Price, smiling, we must give you a guided tour, but come and have a glass of sherry first.

She led us into the hall, showed me where to hang my coat, and ushered us into a large, sunny room.

Well, here we are, she said, turning to a tray that had a decanter and several glasses on it. And what will you have to drink?

She had to repeat herself twice before I heard her; I was absorbed in looking around the room.

Tridib had once shown me pictures of that room.

Soon after he and his parents went to stay at 44 Lymington Road in 1939, Mrs Price invited her brother Alan and the three friends with whom he shared a house in Brick Lane to come to tea with her. The Shaheb was still on his feet at the time; he was to have his operation a month later. He had recently bought a camera, and that afternoon he took a number of pictures.

There is something strikingly different about the quality of the photographs of that time. It has nothing to do with age or colour, or the feel of the paper. May remarked on it at once when Tridib took the two of us up to his room and opened his old scrapbook.

It's nothing to do with fading or anything, she said, pointing at a picture of, her parents. It has to do with the way the camera looked at people then.

In modern family photographs the camera pretends to circulate like a friend, clicking its shutters at those moments when its subjects have disarranged themselves to present to it those postures which they like to think of as informal. But in the pictures of that time the camera is still a public and alien eye faced with which people feel bound either to challenge the intrusion by striking postures of defiant hilarity, or else to compose their faces and straighten their shoulders, not always formally, but usually with just that hint of stiffness which is enough to suggest a public face.

For example, in the foreground of one of those pictures, there is a large, shallow pit. Snipe has been digging that pit for the last two weeks in the back garden. This pit is intended to be the foundation of an Anderson air-raid shelter, his second line of defence against the expected German bombs. It is a serious pit therefore. But in the picture it looks anything but that; it looks like a dishevelled flowerbed. It was probably as some kind of joke that they decided to stand beside it; one of Tresawsen's friends must have thought of it. Perhaps moments before the picture was taken they were doubled up with laughter, looking down at this pathetic would-be shelter. But now that the camera is upon them only one of them is laughing, defying the lens. The rest have composed their faces.

74

Snipe is at the far left of the group. He is dressed in a crumpled corduroy jacket and a woollen tie that is somewhat askew. He is not a big man, but he has broad shoulders which he does not carry well. He is stooping slightly, his head inclined towards the camera, so that the light has fallen on the bald patch on his crown. He looks a great deal older than everyone else in the photograph, which of course he is, but not so much as he looks. He is holding a spade in his hands, perhaps in an attempt to enter into the spirit of the joke. But the spade looks comic in his hands in a way he has not intended. It is evident from the gingerly way in which he is holding it that it is an unfamiliar instrument in his hands: he is cradling it like a baby. He is unmistakably an academic. For the moment, however, he has temporarily left his job as a lecturer in Middle English at a Hampstead college, and has been assigned to the Ministry of Food 'for the duration'.

On Snipe's right a tall, pale young man with a very thin face is squinting at the camera through very thick spectacles. This is Dan. He is wearing a cloth cap and a faded Fair Isle sweater, and he has a long scarf draped around his neck. A rolled-up newspaper is sticking out of the pocket of his jacket.

That newspaper was the first thing Tridib noticed when Mrs Price introduced him to Dan. He could not resist standing on tiptoe when Dan was being introduced to Mayadebi, and picking it out of his pocket. Mayadebi noticed and spoke to him sharply, under her breath. Dan heard her. His pale face turned flaming red, and, stammering with embarrassment, he said something like: Oh, it's just a paper, he's welcome to it. He fished it out of his pocket and held it out to Tridib.

Tridib gave it a long look and asked whether it was the *News Chronicle*. Dan shook his head apologetically, turning redder still. So then, Tridib asked, if it wasn't the *News Chronicle*, which one was it?

Tridib often ran down to West End Lane to buy papers for his father, so he was already familiar with those he had seen on the newsagents' racks. His favourites were the *Sphere* and *Picture Post*, but he liked the *News Chronicle* too, especially the pictures.

It's the *Daily Worker*, Dan told him, and Tridib lost interest and handed the paper back to him. He had neither heard of nor seen any paper called that. Why didn't he read the *Sphere* instead? he asked Dan.

He did, Dan told him, he read it sometimes, though not often. And as for the *Daily Worker*, he didn't read it at all; he just happened to work for it.

Tridib could not help being impressed, for even though he had never heard of it, it was evidently a paper, printed, like every other paper, and with a few pictures too. He stepped back, looked Dan up and down, and asked whether he really, seriously meant that he wrote for that paper. He hadn't met anyone before who wrote in a paper.

Yes, Dan told him, scratching his head, he did. So then, naturally, Tridib asked him what he wrote about, and Dan scratched his head again and made a long face and told him that he wrote about trade unions and strikes and things like that.

It embarrassed Tridib to admit that he hadn't heard of so many things, all on the same evening, but he was curious, so in the end he abandoned his pride and said: What is a trade union?

At that Dan squatted beside him, his head level with Tridib's, and thought very hard, for quite a long time. But before Dan could answer, Mrs Price took Tridib away and handed him a plate with a piece of cake on it. Afterwards he heard her saying to Dan, with a conspiratorial smile: He's always asking these horribly difficult questions – and he was proud of himself for the rest of the evening, for having asked a question clever enough to have posed a problem for a man who wrote in a paper.

Long afterwards Tridib discovered that Dan had once been a figure of some prominence on the Trotskyist Left. He was the son of an eminent Cambridge physicist who had done a degree in chemistry, and then gone on to study at the London School of Economics. After that he had worked as a journalist for a while, on a number of left-wing papers, but soon he had gone off to fight in the Spanish Civil War. He had earned an honourable wound, gone back to England and helped in the writing of a couple of widely read pamphlets, mainly on Nazism. There was never any doubt in Tridib's mind that Dan was Tresawsen's political mentor.

In the photograph, a young man is lying stretched out at their feet, with his head propped up on his hand, laughing defiantly at the camera. He has a pudgy face with prominent cheeks and curly hair, the kind of face that goes with a stocky, rounded body. His bent elbow is resting heavily on one of Tresawsen's shoes, but Tresawsen is ignoring it. This is Mike.

When they arrived, Mike was drunk in a good-naturedly boisterous kind of way. His eyes were bleary and his cheeks pink; to Tridib he smelt of stale beer, like the draughts that blew out of the doors of pubs on the Finchley Road. He was bundled up in a dishevelled trenchcoat and a grimy cloth cap. Tridib had found it hard to understand him when he talked; Mrs Price had explained to him later that that was because Mike had a strong Irish accent.

Mike had taken an immediate dislike to the Shaheb. He had leered at the Shaheb's tweed jacket and striped tie while they were being introduced, and then, swaying exaggeratedly on his feet, he had said: So where's *you* from then?

The Shaheb, flustered, straightened his tie and said: I'm Indian.

Mike shut one bleary eye and looked him up and down. You don't look much of an Indian to me, he said. Killed any Englishmen yet?

The Shaheb retreated a step in horror, shaking his head. Tridib began to giggle.

So what makes you Indian then? said Mike, advancing a step.

Then Tresawsen stepped between them and led him away.

Tresawsen himself is in the centre of the photograph. He is standing very straight, and since he is tall anyway, he towers over everybody else. He has a long face, with direct, deep-set eyes. There are sharp lines fanning out from the corners of his eyes and lips. He is only twenty-eight, but here he looks as though he has already reached that indeterminate age which could lie anywhere between the beginning and the end of middle age. The right sleeve of his jacket is hanging at his side in a way that makes it very hard to tell that there is anything wrong with his arm. But in fact the bones of that arm are made mainly of metal and he cannot use it except in a very rudimentary way. He has always claimed that he injured himself in a motorcycle accident. But Mrs Price doesn't quite believe him, or rather, she thinks there was more to it.

The first she ever heard of it was when she received a letter from France, telling her that he had had an accident and was in hospital in Verdun, that he had hurt his arm very badly, but that she was not to worry, because the doctors had said he would be all right. The letter was signed Francesca Halévy, and a figure seven in the date had been crossed in the waist. She didn't know what to think. She had thought him to be in Stuttgart, teaching English, but she'd read that they had had trouble there, and now here he was on the other side of the border, and what's more, in a town whose name had the most dreadful associations for everybody of her generation, lying in a hospital, being looked after, presumably, by a woman who sounded both Jewish and German. But when she wrote offering to go herself, her correspondent replied by return of post to say that it wasn't necessary, she was looking after Alan herself, and he would soon be well.

But when he came back to England, a month later, he looked anything but well. She had wanted him to stay with her in Hampstead for a while so that she would be able to nurse him herself, but he'd only stayed a week before moving out to Brick Lane. She had asked him once what had happened, and he'd given her an oddly evasive, self-deprecating kind of answer, muttering something about running his motorcycle off the road at night. Mrs Price, now stricken with guilt for not having gone to visit him in France, had felt that she had lost the right to press him for a proper answer.

But still, to her relief, he seemed cheerful when she met him again. His friends had introduced him to somebody called Victor Gollancz, he told her, a publisher who ran a club called the Left Book Club. He'd been offered a job helping to edit the Club's newsletter, he said.

He was still working with the Left Book Club when that picture was taken, at their office in Henrietta Street, off Covent Garden. But when the war began and the Club's offices moved to Berkshire, he resigned and stayed on in London, earning a little money occasionally by writing for the *Tribune* and the *Observer*, and helping out sometimes at the Socialist Bookshop on St Bride's Street, near Holborn.

Francesca Halévy is standing between Dan and Tresawsen. She is slim and tall, with dark hair and a wonderfully sad, aquiline face. One of her arms is lying on

Dan's shoulders, while she has arched the other, dancer-like, over her head. She is dressed in a long, black skirt and a narrow-waisted jacket. Mayadebi and Mrs Price, standing on the edges of the group, are both looking at her intently, awestruck by her elegance.

Mrs Price has often speculated about Francesca to Mayadebi: she knows that Francesca shares that house in Brick Lane with the three men. But the trouble, as she puts it, is that she doesn't know which of them exactly Francesca shares it *with*. It ought, by rights, to be Alan, she thinks, because she is convinced now that Alan injured himself in trying to smuggle her out of Germany. But at the same time Francesca seems to be *very* familiar with Mike: Mrs Price has actually seen her once, tucking in his shirt, in public. Mrs Price doesn't really like Francesca, though she tries hard – she is altogether too elegant, too brilliant, too worldly . . . She can't help hoping that her brother won't, isn't . . .

There is another picture of them, taken in the drawing room. This is Tridib's favourite. It is a shadowy, indistinct picture, taken in the failing evening light, on a very long exposure. They are bunched around a large armchair. A part of the drawing room is visible behind them. It seems a very large, bare room; there is little furniture in it and nothing at all on the walls. The door at the other end, which opens out into the back garden, is visible, but it is no more than a dark smudge, blacked out with a heavy curtain.

Francesca is sitting in the chair and Mike and Dan are perched on its arms. All three of them have moved, and their faces are a blur on the photograph. They are laughing – perhaps at the Shaheb's insistence on taking pictures of them. Mrs Price and Mayadebi are standing behind the armchair, with Alan Tresawsen in between, towering above them. Mrs Price has May in her arms, a tiny white bundle, and she is looking down at her, smiling proudly, her hair tied up on top of her head in a swirl of blonde pigtails.

Tresawsen is looking down from his great height at Mayadebi; he looks gentle and perplexed.

A few minutes before this picture was taken Tresawsen and Mayadebi spoke to each other for the first time. They hadn't exchanged a word all evening, so they were both a little awkward when they found themselves standing next to each other, for the picture. At length, clearing his throat, Tresawsen had remarked: You've chosen an unfortunate time to come to England, haven't you? It must be worrying to be stranded so far away from home with a war looming ahead.

Yes, Mayadebi had replied, I am worried, but for my son and husband. It wasn't a matter of choice, but if it were I couldn't have chosen any better time to come to England myself.

He was taken aback: Why?

Well, she said, laughing, the couple of months she had spent in London had been so exciting – the atmosphere had changed so dramatically, even within the last few weeks. People were becoming friendlier; in the shops, on the streets, she couldn't help noticing. Everyone was so much nicer now; often when she and Tridib were out walking people would pat him on the head and stop to have a little chat with her; the shopkeepers would ask her how her husband was, and when he was to have his operation. But it wasn't just her – everyone was being friendly with everyone else; why, just that morning his sister, Elisabeth, had said that old Mrs Dunbar who lived down the road had actually been civil for the first time in living memory . . .

Yes, he said, that's true – there's a kind of exhilaration in the air.

Yes, that's the right word, said Mayadebi: exhilaration.

I've been lucky, I've been able to watch England coming alive. I wouldn't have seen that if I hadn't been here now.

Tresawsen laughed. People don't believe me, he said, but it's the same over there – in Germany – though of course in a much more grotesque way. It was odd coming back here – like stepping through a looking glass.

It was then that the Shaheb clicked his shutter. Mayadebi is looking up at Tresawsen, smiling shyly; her sari has slipped off her head. Although she is as old as Tresawsen and the mother of two children besides, she looks half his age: clear-eyed, innocent and luminously beautiful.

This is Tridib's favourite picture: he loves the quizzical, faintly perplexed look on Tresawsen's face; he loves the way Mayadebi smiles as she looks up at him. When he makes up stories about his hero, Tresawsen, they always end with him looking like that and Mayadebi smiling up at him.

I have one final image of Tridib on that evening: he is standing by the window, watching through parted curtains as Tresawsen and his friends walk down Lymington Road on their way back to Brick Lane. It is late now, and the gentle late-summer twilight is darkening into night. The lamps on the street light up as they step out of the house. Caught in that sudden glow of light, Mike rocks back on his heels with the balanced agility of a practised boxer, and throws a flurry of quick short punches at Tresawsen. But Tresawsen is quick too, and he sways easily away from Mike's fists, drawing him off balance, and then his left arm shoots out and catches Mike square in the middle of his chest. Mike is brought up short, winded, his arms sag and drop, and he makes a face and lets his tongue loll out. Then they all throw their arms around each other's shoulders, and Francesca tucks her hand into Dan's and they walk off down the street in a tight little phalanx singing so loudly that Mrs Price's neighbours part their curtains.

Tridib could see them quite clearly, years later, walking

down that road in the creeping darkness, holding tightly on to each other. But he knew that the clarity of that image in his mind was merely the seductive clarity of ignorance; an illusion of knowledge created by a deceptive weight of remembered detail. He knew, for example, that they were on their way to their house in Brick Lane, that they would turn left at the end of Lymington Road, towards the West Hampstead station. But of the world they were going to, that house in Brick Lane, he knew nothing; nothing at all of the web of trust and affections and small jealousies that must have held it together. In one part of his mind that house figured as a bright, pure world, a world built on belief, but in another he knew that to be real it must have had room in it somewhere for petty, tawdry little jealousies. It would drive him to despair that he could not guess where that tawdriness lay: did it lie, for example, in unwashed bathtubs, in arguments over who was to pay for the sugar that week, or in quarrels over who was to share whose bedroom? Whatever it was, at that moment, walking down Lymington Road, with their arms clasped around each other, they were exactly one week away from the announcement of the Nazi-Soviet pact, after which nothing in their house would ever be the same again. Which was the more real, their dirty bathtubs and shared bedrooms or that other reality, waiting one week away? Most of all he would despair because he could not imagine what it would be like to confront the most real of their realities: that within two years three of the four of them would be dead. The realities of the bombs and torpedoes and the dying was easy enough to imagine – mere events, after all, recorded in thousands of films and photographs and comic books. But not that other infinitely more important reality: the fact that they *knew*, that even walking down that street, that evening, they knew what was coming – not the details, nor the timing perhaps, but they knew, all four of them, that their world, and in all probability they themselves, would not survive the war. What is the colour of that knowledge? Nobody knows, nobody can ever know, not even in memory, because there are moments in time that are not *knowable:* nobody can ever know what it was like to be young and intelligent in the summer of 1939 in London or Berlin.

And in the meanwhile, there they are, in that gilded summer, laughing and singing on their way back to Brick Lane.

The room Mrs Price led me into was large and airy, and it teemed with furniture – sofas, delicate spindly chairs and armchairs with tall curved backs, a chaise-longue, little tables with spidery legs. Every available surface was crowded with things: tall blue Chinese vases, little porcelain plates with gold rims and floral designs, bowls filled to the brim with rose petals, ormolu clocks and silver-framed photographs. The walls were quilted over with arrays of water-colours, woodcuts and botanical drawings. Mrs Price saw me looking around in astonishment, and said, guiltily, as though explaining away a vice, that she was a church-sale addict, that the things in that room were only a small fraction of a lifetime's collection.

Ila said: Well, at least the room's a surprise, isn't it?

Yes it was, I told her, a real surprise, and then Nick, smiling, asked me if I thought I could find my way around the house as I had through the streets.

I had to think a bit to orient myself. I turned to face the door and said: Correct me if I'm wrong, but if I go out of this door and turn right and keep walking straight for a few paces, that would take me to the kitchen, wouldn't it? And if I were to turn right before I reached the kitchen, wouldn't I come upon a flight of stairs that would lead me down to the cellar if I were to go down them?

It was my turn to laugh now, at their astonished faces.

It's incredible, Ila sighed, shaking her head. How does he do it?

And all the while, of course, it was she herself who had shown me.

She had taken my hand and pulled me under the table, and when I was sitting beside her, she had drawn a line in the dust and said: Now remember, that's the road outside, and that, over there, is where they play cricket.

Then, boxing off a small dusty square, she said: That's the garden, and that's the cherry tree, and there's the front door, and after you've rung the bell and wiped your feet on the door mat you can come in.

She drew a long narrow rectangle, pointing inwards from the door.

That, she said, is the hall.

She added another large square to the left.

That's the drawing room, she said. It looks out into the garden, through the big windows, like this, and you can go through this door, into the dining room, and through that again into the kitchen, right back over there. And then there's the kitchen garden out at the back.

While I was staring at this dusty chequerboard of lines, she crawled around me, to my right, and drew another room, a smaller one this time.

That's the bedroom where Ma and I live, she said. It's right next to the hall.

She added a couple of lines to it and said: That's the cellar, and that's the staircase. That's where Nick and I play Houses sometimes.

Why do you play down there? I said. Why don't you play under a table, like this?

It's the same thing, she said. This table is like a cellar anyway.

Doesn't anybody know you go down there? I said. Don't they stop you?

85

Of course they know, she said. Why should they tell us not to? They know we're just playing.

Why don't you play here in the drawing room, or there in the garden, or out there where they play cricket?

You can't play Houses out in the garden, she said. It has to be somewhere dark and secret . . .

She crawled around me again, through the hall and into the drawing room. Then she squatted and drew a thin rectangle next to the drawing room wall.

That's the staircase, she said. You have to climb up it and then you come to the bedrooms.

She drew another set of lines, right next to the staircase. That's Aunty Elisabeth's bedroom, she said. It's right above the drawing room. If you look out of these windows you can see the cricket field.

I shook my head violently; something about those lines had begun to disturb me.

You're lying, I shouted at her. That can't be a staircase because it's flat, and staircases go up, they aren't flat. And that can't be upstairs because upstairs has to be above and that isn't above; that's right beside the drawing room.

I dropped to my knees and began to scrabble around in the dust, rubbing out the lines, shouting: You're lying, you're mad, this can't be a house . . .

She put her hands against my chest and pushed. She wasn't very strong, but she managed to push me back on my heels.

You're stupid, she said. Don't you understand? I've just rearranged things a little. If we pretend it's a house, it'll be a house. We can choose to build a house wherever we like.

No! I cried. It won't be a real house. It can't be.

Why? she asked, smiling.

Frowning, I puzzled over the pattern in the dust.

86

It can't be a real house, I said at last, because it doesn't have a veranda.

Veranda? she said in amazement, rolling the word slowly around her mouth as though she had forgotten its taste. What shall we do with a veranda?

She was uncertain now, biting her nails, unable to find a place for verandas in the world of her invention. And, I, sensing her confusion, felt a sudden, predatory thrill of triumph.

I gave her a shove. Of course we must have a veranda, I said. Otherwise how will we know what's going on outside?

There was much more to say, I knew, but I could not think of how to say it: a nice house had to have a veranda; why, even our small flat had a veranda. To me the necessity of verandas was no more accountable than the need for doors and walls.

I fell on my knees and, leaning over her house, I rubbed away a line and drew another in its place.

Look, I said. There's our veranda.

She stared at me aghast, rubbing her knuckles against her teeth. I could tell from the brightness of her eyes that she was close to tears.

You can't do that, she said. You can't put it there.

I rocked back on my haunches, hugging my knees: Why not?

Because, she said, that's going to be Magda's room.

Magda? I said. But Magda isn't here.

Magda was Ila's doll. I had seen it once. It was a huge doll, almost as big as Ila, with pink cheeks and snow-white arms, bright gold hair, and blue eyes that opened on their own every time it was picked up. The eyes had intrigued me; I'd wanted to see whether they were real. But when I had put out my hand to touch them, Ila had slapped my fingers away and shouted: You can't touch Magda.

And anyway, I said warily to Ila, why should a doll need a room?

Not Magda the doll, Ila cried. This is the real Magda – our baby. A house has to have a baby.

What does Magda look like?

She has nice golden hair, said Ila frowning, trying to remember.

She has blue eyes and she goes to school every day.

Kindergarten? I said.

No, of course not. She goes to a proper school.

But then, I interrupted triumphantly, she can't be a baby. She has to be as old as us.

Stupid, Ila said. We're grown-ups now; it doesn't matter how old she is.

She yawned, stretched, and rubbed her eyes.

First, she said, we have to wake up, get out of bed and change. And then you have to go to work. I'll take Magda to school after you've gone.

She reached for the hem of her dress, slipped it over her head and draped it over her shoulder.

There, she said, grinning, hugging her chest. Look, I'm changing.

She was bare-chested now, naked, but for her blue, frilled underwear. She looked very thin and fragile, her dark body a wispy shadow in the gloom. Her shoulders were pointed, the bones forming sharp-edged ridges under the skin. I was puzzled by her stick-like bones. I stretched out my hand and ran my fingers over the china-thin ribs, up to the ridges of her shoulder and along the curve of her arm, down the sharp angle of her elbow, and up again, to the nutlike wrist she had dug into her chest. There was a spot above her nipple, a tiny, black bump.

What's that? I said, rubbing it with my thumb.

Stop that, she said giggling.

I thought I could feel the bump rolling under her skin,

88

like a tiny pea or a mustard seed, embedded inside. I pinched it, wondering whether it would burst. She shivered, and I shivered too, taking myself by surprise.

Stop that, she said sharply. But I couldn't stop – I was curious about her bump, intrigued by its velvety hardness; I wondered whether it had a taste, I wanted to feel it with my tongue.

But she slapped my head away and pushed me back.

Stop it, she said. You have to go to work now. We'll pretend you've already changed.

I peered apprehensively around the murky room. Where do I have to go to work? I asked.

There, she said, pointing at a crazily tilted chest of drawers. That's your office. Go on now. You can't come back until I tell you and you can't look back at the house to see what I'm doing.

I darted out, ran to the chest of drawers, and stood there with my eyes shut, counting loudly, as we did when we played hide-and-seek. An age seemed to pass, though it was probably no more than five minutes, for I'd only counted twice to one hundred. Then Ila called out: All right, you can come back now. Magda's back home from school.

She was waiting for me in the garden. Leaning against the cherry tree. Before I reached the wicket gate that opened out into Lymington Road, she shouted out: Do you know what happened to Magda today?

What? I said, following her into the house. What happened to Magda?

Before she would tell me, she took me into the drawing room and made me sit down.

The children in Magda's new school had never seen anyone like her. It was terrible for her on her first day at school. They stared and stared until Mrs Tolland had to tell them not to. But even then, though they were scared of Mrs Tolland, they'd still pretend to drop their books and pencils just so they could turn around to look at Magda. They were still staring at her now, after she'd been there two whole weeks.

The reason they stared like that, all of them, girls, boys, even the teachers, was that they'd never seen anyone as beautiful as Magda. They had never seen hair that shone like hers – like a bright, golden light. They had never seen such deep blue eyes, nor cheeks as pink and healthy and smiling as hers. And they hadn't seen clothes like hers either: so clean and so beautifully ironed that they looked more like the dresses you see in shop windows in Oxford Street than a school uniform. Even the bag she took to school was so much nicer than theirs: a beautiful leather bag her father had bought for her in Florence, not a bit like the ugly satchels *they* brought with them.

You couldn't blame them for staring: they'd never seen anyone as beautiful as Magda. And they liked her too: they all wanted to be friends with her – girls, boys, teachers, all of them. On the playground they would sometimes come up to her and whisper in her ear: I want to be your best friend.

But there was one girl who hated Magda from the very first day. Her name was Denise.

Now Denise was ugly. She had dirty red hair which hung down from her head like greasy quills. She didn't have a mother to wash her hair for her; her mother had left her and run away to Australia. And her skin, her skin was like dirty ice-cream – pale and grainy and peppered with blackheads. Even the teacher shuddered every time she looked at Denise.

But Denise was very big, bigger than the biggest boy in the class. And she was very strong too: she had once knocked out a boy's teeth with a punch.

So everyone was nice to Denise because everyone was

afraid of her. It was Denise who decided who could be friends with whom and if Denise didn't like someone, well, that was it, she made sure no one spoke to her.

But once Magda arrived Denise could see that she wasn't going to have it all her own way any more. She saw how the other children looked at Magda; she could see they wanted to be her friends. And even though she tried to stop them she knew they talked to Magda whenever she, Denise, was out of their sight.

As the days went by the more Denise hated Magda.

Then today it happened.

Mrs Tolland asked Denise to write a sentence on the blackboard. Denise went to the blackboard, and when she'd finished the class saw that what she'd written was: John cot the ball.

The whole class burst into laughter.

Then Mrs Tolland asked Magda to write the sentence. And of course Magda knew, so she wrote: John caught the ball, in her beautiful round handwriting.

Good girl, Mrs Tolland said to her, and then she turned to Denise and said: Well, Denise, perhaps you ought to take English lessons from *her*, even though it's your own language, not hers.

Everyone turned to look at Denise and laughed and laughed. Denise had to sit there and listen.

When Magda was going back to her desk, she heard Denise say: See you outside, little wog. She saw how Denise had gone red in the face and she was scared.

So today, after school, she decided not to come back the way she usually does. Most days she walks through the park near Hillfield Road, but today she didn't. She thought she would hurry past the park and take the other road instead.

After school, that was what she meant to do. But when she turned the corner near the park, keeping her head down so that nobody would notice her, she heard someone shout: Little wog, nig-nog!

She didn't turn to look, but she knew it was Denise; she could tell from the voice. She began to walk faster.

But the voice followed her, shouting: Don't run, little wog, nig-nog.

Now Magda began to run. She ran across the road without stopping to look right or left, as she'd been told to. She was very scared now. She dropped her bag, and though she knew Baba would be furious with her if she lost it, she didn't dare stop. She was running as fast as she could, in a straight line. She could hear them running too, three or four of them, right behind her, catching up. But she was running fast now, faster than she ever had before, and she could tell that some of them were giving up. Now there was only one pair of feet running after her. She could hear them clearly, thudding on the pavement behind her.

Something hit her between her shoulders, and she fell sprawling on the pavement. When she looked up, Denise was scowling down at her, panting: Bloody wog, nig-nog.

An open hand came slashing down and struck Magda on the face. Magda's cheek hit the pavement. She could see her blood spattering in the dust.

Denise was crouching over her. Her face was so close that Magda could smell the Mars bars on her breath.

Nig-nog, she said, filthy little nig-nog, and she stuck her fist into Magda's mouth. Then she swung her hand back again. Magda shut her eyes, covered her face and waited. There was nothing else she could do; Denise was too strong for her.

And then there was a little yelp of pain and she heard Denise being pulled off her. She didn't dare look at first.

When she opened her eyes, there he was, with his hands on his hips, standing over her.

Go on, Nick Price said to Denise. Go on, get out of here.

Denise made a face and scrabbled to her feet.

When she was gone, Nick Price knelt down beside Magda and wiped her face with the sleeve of his shirt. He helped her to her feet and put a sweet in her mouth and, taking her hand in his, he said: Come on, I'll take you home now.

That was how Nick Price had looked to me, under that table: a boy in shorts, like me, but much bigger, his head a blaze of yellow, rescuing a little girl from her tormentor.

But then, unaccountably, Ila had burst into tears.

When I had finished telling May this story, in that very room, three years later, she'd put a hand on my shoulder and said: Come on, let's go out, it's terribly dark in here.

I led her out into the brilliant sunlight of the portico, and she flopped down on one of the stairs that led down into the paved courtyard. Reaching for my hand, she pulled me down beside her.

That wasn't quite what happened, she said gently. You do know that, don't you?

I shook my head.

I happened to be at home that day, she said. And I know that Nick didn't stop to help Ila. He ran all the way back. He used to run back home from school early those days. Why?

May plucked out a peepul leaf that was growing out of the brick staircase and fanned herself with it.

I'm not sure, she said. But I think Nick didn't want to be seen with Ila. Ila didn't have any friends in school, you see. Perhaps it was just that she was shy. But after she began going to school Nick used to come home much earlier than he used to. Then that day something happened in Ila's class, and I think Nick got to hear of it. He ran back even earlier than usual and went straight up to his room. Mummy asked him what the matter was but he wouldn't tell her. An hour or so later, just when we were beginning to worry about Ila, a policeman brought her back. She was a bit bruised, but otherwise all right. She never told us what happened but she didn't go back to school after that. And then, soon after, they left.

I tried then to think of Ila walking back from school alone through the lanes of West Hampstead. I could see her swinging her schoolbag in time with her footsteps, faster and faster, until she was almost running, laughing out loud, so that people turned to smile after her; Ila walking, smiling to herself as I had sometimes seen her, her dimple rippling on her cheek. Ila walking alone in a drizzle under that cold grey sky: Ila who in Calcutta was surrounded by so many relatives and cars and servants that she would never have had to walk so much as the length of the street – and as for alone, why there we were, all of us, I, her relatives, her friends, all waiting to walk with Ila, Ila the sophisticate, who could tell us stories about smart girls and rich boys in far-away countries whose names we had learnt from maps. Ila walking alone because Nick Price was ashamed to be seen by his friends, walking home with an Indian.

You shouldn't think too badly of him, May said. She was pleading with me now. He was very young, and at that age children want everyone to be alike.

Many years later, when my grandmother had been lying in bed for months with what was to prove to be her final illness, one evening, while I was sitting by her bedside, I found myself telling her the story Ila had told me and about the odd little ending that May had added.

That evening, although she was surrounded by oxygen cylinders, bottles of glucose, disposable syringes and all the other paraphernalia of her sickness, she seemed more cheerful than she had been in a long time. When she had heard me out she said: I don't blame the boy. It was Ila's fault. It was her own fault, and Maya's fault and the fault of that half-witted mother of hers. It was bound to happen: anyone can see that. She has no right to be there. She doesn't belong there.

She buried her head in a towel and began to cough. In the two weeks that had passed since I came back from Delhi for my college's summer holidays I had been kept up every night by that hollow, echoing cough. After a quarter of an hour the fit left her and she fell back panting, on her pillows. She turned to look at me, with a hand-kerchief clamped over her mouth. I knew then, from the brightness of her eyes, that she was about to go into one of her sudden rages. I rose guiltily from my chair, angry with myself for having told her the story, and tried to calm her.

It doesn't matter, Tha'mma, I said, pulling her shawl over her thin, trembling shoulders. It doesn't matter. Lie down now and rest.

Ila shouldn't *be* there, she said, stammering hoarsely. She doesn't belong there. What's she doing in that country?

She's just studying there for a while, Tha'mma, I said gently. At that time Ila was at University College in London, doing a BA in history.

But she shouldn't *be* there, my grandmother cried, pushing my hands feebly away.

I leant back in my chair looking helplessly at her. Over the last few months the flesh had wasted slowly away from her face so that the skin on her cheeks hung down now, like dry, brittle leather.

Ila has no right to live there, she said hoarsely. She doesn't belong there. It took those people a long time to build that country; hundreds of years, years and years of war and bloodshed. Everyone who lives there has earned his right to be there with blood: with their brother's blood and their father's blood and their son's blood. They know they're a nation because they've drawn their borders with blood. Hasn't Maya told you how regimental flags hang in all their cathedrals and how all their churches are lined with memorials to men who died in wars, all around the world? War is their religion. That's what it takes to make a country. Once that happens people forget they were born this or that, Muslim or Hindu, Bengali or Punjabi: they become a family born of the same pool of blood. That is what *you* have to achieve for India, don't you see?

I can still see her as though it had happened today, her eyes bloodshot, threads of phlegm hanging from her lips, while she lies ranting in her bed. And yet, when I look at her, lying crumpled in front of me, her white thinning hair matted with her invalid's sweat, my heart fills with love for her – love and that other thing, which is not pity but something else, something the English language knows only in its absence – ruth – a tenderness which is not merely pity and not only love. It comes over me so powerfully that even now I can feel the anger that exploded in my head once when I told Ila what she had said, and Ila, drawing on her cigarette, made some offhand remark about warmongering fascists. I remembered how I shouted at her and told her what Tridib had once said: that she was *not* a fascist, she was only a modern middle-class woman – though not wholly, for she would not permit herself the self-deceptions that make up the fantasy world of that kind of person. All she wanted was a middle-class life in which, like the middle classes the world over, she would thrive believing in the unity of nationhood and territory, of self-respect and national power; that was all she wanted – a modern middle-class life, a small thing, that history had denied her in its fullness and for which she could never forgive it.

Early next morning my grandmother asked that I be sent to her room. When I sat down beside her I saw that her eyes were bloodshot and her face pale and more strained than ever.

Shall I tell you why Ila lives there? she said, propping herself up on her elbow.

I pleaded with her to lie down, to rest, but she cut me short.

Shall I tell you what Ila's gone there for? she said. She was shivering now, her eyes burning in her face. She's gone there because she's greedy; she's gone there for money.

I couldn't help smiling then.

Why should she go there for money? I said. Her family has much more money here than they'd ever have over there. She's the only grandchild in the family and you know how rich they are. If she stayed here she would have more money than she could count in a lifetime. And she would have houses and servants and cars too. She has nothing over there. She lives in a tiny room in a house she has to share with five other students; she has to cook and clean and do all kinds of things that a dozen servants would rush to do for her here . . .

It's not just *money*, my grandmother cried. It's things: it's all the things money can buy – fridges like the one Mrs Sen's son-in-law brought back from America, with two doors and a spout that drops ice-cubes into your glass; colour TVs and cars, calculators and cameras, all those things you can't get here.

But she doesn't *have* things, I retorted, trying to keep my voice in control. You know that. She has to live on pocket money; she doesn't have the money to buy things like that. Besides, she doesn't want things. She spends her spare time going on demonstrations and acting in radical plays for Indian immigrants in east London. You know that – when she was here last, you asked me yourself: Has Ila become a communist?

She's a greedy little slut, my grandmother said, pounding on the bedclothes with a fist she had not the strength to clench properly. I can't understand why you're defending her. You tell me then, since you know her so well: why *does* she live there, if it's not for the money and the comforts?

By that time I was so angry that I did tell her.

The year before, Ila had come to Calcutta in summer, at almost exactly the same time that Robi and I came back from Delhi for the university's summer vacations.

Ila's trip was very sudden. She had made up her mind two days after her college in London closed for the vacations. Then she had rung her father in Bratislava and he had rung his travel agent in London and four days later she was in Calcutta.

It was so sudden that even my parents didn't know.

When the Kalka Mail from Delhi got in at Howrah Station they were waiting, as they always were, under the old clock that no one had ever seen working, on platform 9: my mother in a sea-green sari, flushed with pleasure at the thought of having me back for the summer; my father bustling, looking after our luggage, organising. We dropped Robi at their house in Ballygunge Place, where he was to spend a few days before going off to visit his parents in Darjeeling.

After I had banished my four-month-old, college-starved hunger with an hour-long meal, my mother, in her usual anxiously circuitous way, was trying to find out what I would like, *really* like to eat for dinner, when my grandmother declared grimly: You'd better forget about his dinner. You're not likely to see him this evening.

98

Why not? my mother cried, turning to her in alarm. But I've already made . . .

Because, my grandmother said, her eyes boring into mine; because Ila is here.

I waited, not daring to believe what she had said.

Ila's here! said my mother. How do you know?

She rang yesterday, said my grandmother. Queen Victoria had asked her to enquire after my health.

Why didn't you tell us? my mother said.

Because I thought you'd like to have him here for lunch, my grandmother said.

How is she? I asked her. Did she say?

I'm sure she's fine, said my grandmother. Perhaps she's even better than she was when she came here last year – with her hair cut short, like the bristles on a toothbrush, wearing tight trousers like a Free School Street whore.

I wonder why she's come now, my mother said quickly, changing the subject. Why in this heat?

Because, Ila told me an hour later, when we were sitting in her room in their Elgin Road house; this is when I have my holidays too, you know, and besides I haven't been back for a year.

Anyway, she laughed, watching me as I mopped my sweating face with a handkerchief, the heat bothers you much more than it does me.

And of course she was right: the heat hadn't touched her.

She looked younger with her hair cut, boyish in a way, and she was thinner too; her arms were like wands, and the dimple was never quite gone from her cheek. She looked improbably exotic to me, dressed in faded blue jeans and a T-shirt – like no girl I had ever seen before except in pictures in American magazines.

There she is, in the green afternoon darkness of that shuttered, high-ceilinged room, not quite sitting, but draped over a leather armchair, her legs thrown over the back so that the top of her jeans has crept away from her T-shirt and left the hollow of her stomach glowing in the darkness; her body cradled lazily in the seat, her head flung back over the arm, so that her small breasts have thrust the thin cotton of her T-shirt into two gentle points which harden with her breathing, and then swell away again into dark circles, one of them dotted with a tiny black mole. She flops about in the chair, heedless of her body, childlike, and I, bracing the muscles in my thighs to contain the dull, swelling ache in my groin, have to roll over on my stomach and look at a magazine, though that makes the pain much worse, like the throbbing of a tourniquet, as though something were about to burst in my balls. I push myself away from her, along the floor, for I cannot let her see me like this, not for shame, but merely to preserve my friendship with her, for I know that between us there lies a chequerboard of relationships in which I have been given the place of a cousin, a favourite perhaps, but still a cousin and nothing more.

The day before Robi was to leave for Darjeeling, we spent a long sleepy day in their house, lolling about in her room, looking for cool spots on the floor, reading and quarrelling. When the afternoon had dragged itself out and the sun had set, Ila threw open the shutters. The sight of the cars inching along the road below seemed to act on her like a tonic.

Come on, she said, tugging at my hand; let's go out somewhere. We can't lie about all day like this. Besides, Robi's leaving tomorrow. I think we should give him a party.

Robi stirred torpidly on the floor and dropped the book he had been reading. A party, he said. In this heat?

Yes, said Ila. Let's go somewhere and have fun.

Robi and I exchanged a long, doubtful look.

I haven't got enough money, I said.

I've got money, she laughed. I'll give you a treat.

But where can we go? said Robi.

I'll tell you what, said Ila; let's go to the Grand Hotel. I've heard they have a nightclub there.

What are we going to do in a nightclub? said Robi.

We can drink a few beers, said Ila. And watch the cabaret – that kind of thing.

Drink! cried Robi. In a place like that?

What's the matter? she said sharply. You do drink don't you? What about that story you were telling me about the send-off you got from your pals in college? You *are* a little hypocrite.

Judgements of that kind came very easily to Ila, because to her morality could only be an absolute. She could understand and admire someone who never ate meat on principle, but a person who was a vegetarian only at home was, to her, the worst kind of hypocrite. She knew that Robi was quite happy to risk expulsion occasionally by smuggling bottles of rum into his room and drinking the night away with his friends, and because she could not see that he would do those things in college precisely because there was a certain innocence about those exploits in those circumstances, the kind of monasticism that honours the rules of the order in their breach, she could not understand why Robi would feel himself defiled, drinking in a nightclub, surrounded by paunchy men with dark-pouched eyes. She could not understand the real nature of his prudishness because context had no place in her judgements.

It's just petit-bourgeois nastiness, Ila had said to me once about Robi. It's a mystery to me how he's become such a legend in your college: I thought students were meant to be defiant of narrow-mindedness. But undergraduates respect muscles, I suppose, and he's got plenty of those.

I had been puzzled too when I first discovered how much deference Robi commanded in college. It was hard to understand, for he did not excel particularly in any of the spheres which were held to confer distinction in that milieu: he was not unusually good at sports, just about good enough to keep a place in the college cricket eleven; he was good at his studies but not brilliant; he was not clever, not well dressed, not talented, nor in any way unlike a dozen others in our college, and yet, without asking for it, barely seeming to notice, he commanded a respect immeasurably greater than the best sportsmen and the most brilliant students.

It took me time to see that this respect was really a tribute to the superhuman simplicity of his view of the world: to the fact that he had no hesitation in making judgements – because there were whole domains of conduct within which he would not admit the possibility of argument – and no fear of defending them, because of his abundant physical courage. Once, for example, there was a great uproar in our college because a student had been expelled for some minor misdemeanour – for asking a girl up to his room for a cup of tea or some such thing. The students' union was unanimous in calling for a strike. But Robi, alone in the whole college, refused to go along with everyone else: he didn't argue or make speeches, he merely refused to attend the union meetings. And when some of the union's leaders threatened to give him a beating, they found to their surprise that he was relieved at the prospect of settling the issue by a straightforward physical contest. Such was his standing in the college that eventually the leaders gave in and the strike was called off.

Later, I asked him: Why *wouldn't* you join the strike? Tell me, just as a matter of interest.

He wouldn't answer, so I asked him again, and then

reluctantly he said: Because a rule's a rule; if you break one you have to be willing to pay the price.

But is it a *good* rule? I asked. He only smiled, and no matter how hard I tried I could not get him to answer my question.

I understood then that he *could not* answer: that his authority grew out of that subterranean realm of judgement which we call morality, the condition of whose success is that its rulings be always shrouded from argument. I understood why his opinions always prevailed against his peers': because while they had to find their way through a fog of ordinary confusions, in every difficult situation Robi had an intuition which led him directly to what he knew he *ought* to do, even if he did not know why. And they followed him since he, uniquely, was willing to defend those inconvenient, often ridiculous, scruples which they could only too easily be persuaded to forget. That was why they, and I, both admired him and feared him, and that was why his courage, even when it manifested itself physically, was moral in the purest sense.

Come on, enjoy yourself for once, said Ila. You'll be going away soon anyway, so you can forget all about it afterwards.

But why do you want to go to the Grand Hotel? said Robi.

Because it's the poshest place in the city, of course, said Ila, tipping her head back. Isn't that the best possible reason?

I don't want to go to a place like that, Robi said.

But once Ila had made up her mind she had to have her way. She bent down in front of him and touched her forehead to his feet.

Please, Robi-kaku, she said. Please, just this once. If you don't like it, we'll leave. I promise.

So we went: Ila resplendent in a silk blouse and a

skirt, Robi and I grimly insistent on not changing out of our usual student uniform of kurta and crumpled trousers.

When we reached the entrance of the Grand Hotel and saw the beturbaned doorman's dead-fish eyes flicking disdainfully over us, both Robi and I would have kept on walking, all the way down Chowringhee. But Ila was right behind us, and with a rustle of silk she shepherded us through the corridor, into a chandeliered hall. She led us to the reception counter and in the plummiest of her English accents she asked them to show us the way to the nightclub. Suitably awed, they sent a liveried attendant to show us the way. He led us down another corridor to a large, ornate door. He pushed the door open, pocketed Ila's tip, and stood aside, bowing.

We heard the hum of an electric guitar echoing out of the darkness, somewhere inside the cavernous room.

I'm not going in there, said Robi. He pulled his hand out of Ila's; he was sweating.

Oh come on, Ila said in exasperation. Come on, Uncle Robi. You've made your point: we're willing to accept that you're just a poor peasant horrified by the badness of the big city. So now you may as well relax and enjoy yourself.

She took his hand again and he let himself be led in.

It was so dark inside that the waiter had to lead us through the clusters of empty tables with an electric torch. I felt the touch of something moist and strangely furry on my face. Instinctively, my arm rose to fight it off. I felt it again, on my forearm, and jumped backwards, knocking over a chair.

What are those things? I cried, my skin tingling. Something touched me.

It's only the decorations, sir, said the waiter. He brought us to a halt at an empty table and pulled back a chair for Ila. We sat down, and when our eyes had grown accustomed to the darkness, we saw that every available space was covered with nodding palm fronds. There were catamarans painted on the walls and clusters of coconuts were dangling from the roof. Ila pointed at the band, on a platform beside the dance floor; it consisted of four men in dark suits, bow ties and straw hats.

She giggled: I think it's meant to be a beach.

Clasping her hands she looked at the two of us, smiling. All right, she said, shall we ask for some beer?

I nodded when she turned to me, but Robi said nothing.

Can't you just pretend that you're in college? she said. If it makes you feel less of a hypocrite?

Robi raised his hand abruptly and signalled to the waiter. When the waiter came, he said: Get us three beers, please.

He put his hands flat on the table and turned to look at Ila, swivelling his broad, powerful shoulders.

Do your Trotskyite comrades know, he said, how you spend your time when you're not demonstrating for the revolution?

She smiled, and tapped his cheek with her forefinger. You can't demonstrate for a revolution stupid, she said. And yes they do know, and they don't care because Trotskyists aren't joyless little clerks like you're getting to be.

She was angry with herself as soon as she said it.

Oh come on, Robi, she pleaded. It's your last evening here. Let's not quarrel.

That made Robi angrier still, but as always, when he was really angry, he could not think of anything to say. Then our bottles of beer arrived, and he busied himself pouring them out. When our glasses were full, he raised his and drained half of it in one long swallow. Then he leant back, wiping his mouth, breathing hard, and stared into it.

To my relief, there was a loud roll on the drums and

the leader of the band announced into the microphone: Now, Ladies and Gentlemen, we have Miss Jennifer here, to sing for you. Please give her a hand.

Miss Jennifer swam out of the darkness, bowing and bobbing, a paper-pale, matronly woman, in a skin-tight crimson sheath covered with silver spangles.

Hi folks! she trilled in a thin, high voice, full of professional gaiety. Hi there! Come on now then, get yourself ready, you all, for a whole bagful of fun.

The spotlights spun, her spangles erupted into flashes of colour and she strutted down to the table next to us.

Now then, she said huskily into the microphone. Who have we got here?

The two middle-aged businessmen who were sitting at the table wriggled in shy delight. She patted their cheeks, but when they stretched their hands out to touch her, she slapped them away and danced out of reach, noisily clicking her tongue.

My, my, she said, looking at them through her eyelashes. Aren't we naughty today?

If she comes here, Robi said into his glass, I'm going to knock her teeth in.

But instead she walked into the middle of the dance floor, flung her arms dramatically outwards, like a diver on a high board, and cried: All right folks – let's dance with Ol' Blue Eyes – let's dance with a stranger tonight.

Yes, gasped Ila, that's it. Let's dance, that'll cheer us up.

Come on, she said, tugging at my hand. Get up, let's dance.

But I was clumsy and self-conscious on my feet at the best of times. And when I looked at the empty expanse of the dance floor, at plump Miss Jennifer swaying in the middle, and the hungry eyes of the businessmen staring at her, I knew that I would never be able to step on to that floor.

No, I said, shaking my head. I couldn't, not here.

She turned away disappointedly. Robi? she said. Wouldn't you like to dance?

I can't dance, he said, raising his head to look at her. And even if I could, I wouldn't in a place like this. I think you should sit down, for you're not going to dance either.

At first she was merely surprised.

I'm not going to dance? she said. Why not?

Because I won't let you, said Robi evenly.

You won't let me? she said. The muscles of her face went slowly rigid.

You won't *let* me? she said. Why, who do you think you are?

Robi folded his arms across his chest. It doesn't matter who I am, he said. I won't let you.

She turned to look at me now, her lips going thin and bloodless. Does he think, she asked me, that I'm one of his college freshers or something? Does he think because he's got a lot of muscles he can stop *me*? Does he think *I'm* scared of a college bully? Well, let's see him stop me.

She kicked her chair back and rose to her feet.

I put out my hand and tugged at her skirt. Ila, please don't, I said. You don't know him. Please sit down and let's go home.

She gave my hand a stinging slap. I'm going to find out, she said. Let's see what he does to stop me.

I jumped to my feet and stood in front of her. Ila, please, I said. What are you going to do?

She pushed me aside. I'll tell you what I'm going to do, she said. I'm going to go over to those two businessmen over there, and I'm going to ask the thin one to dance with me.

She turned on her heel and walked away.

Pivoting in his chair, Robi watched her walk up to the two businessmen. We saw her smiling at them, then she

107

bent her head gracefully to talk to the thinner of the two, and he started to his feet. We watched as his face creased into a smile and then clouded over with a leering, greedy suspicion. Then she smiled again, and he, nodding eagerly, stepped out to take her hand.

I heard the scrape of Robi's chair and stepped sideways to stop him. He elbowed me away and reached them with three long strides. He caught hold of the neck of Ila's blouse with one hand and wrenched her away from the businessman. Then he opened the palm of his hand and planted it squarely in the middle of the man's chest. Arching his shoulder back, he swivelled, suddenly, with so much force that the man staggered back for a good five feet or so, taking his chair with him.

The singer dropped her microphone and the band froze into a silvery tableau under the spotlight. There was a moment of complete silence. Then, like a reel of film coming unstuck, everyone sprang to life, and a crowd of waiters surrounded us.

The only person who was perfectly calm was Robi. He held his hands open in front of him and said, in a quiet, mild voice: Don't touch me. We'll pay and we'll leave right now, but don't touch me.

He took out his wallet and handed one of the waiters a fifty-rupee note. Then he put his arm around Ila and led us out. The waiters followed us all the way to the pavement.

Ila did not say a word until we had walked as far as the museum. At the corner she stopped and leant against the wrought-iron railings.

Have you gone mad? she said to Robi, spitting the words through her teeth. What did you think you were doing?

Look, Robi said. It's over now, let's just forget it.

We won't forget it, she said; she was screaming now, but with her voice very low, in that way women have. We will not forget it. Just tell me: what did you think you were doing?

Listen, Ila, Robi said, shaking his head. You shouldn't have done what you did. You ought to know that; girls don't behave like that here.

What the fuck do you *mean*? she spat at him. What do you mean 'girls'? I'll do what I bloody well want, when I want and where.

No you won't, he said. Not if I'm around. Girls don't behave like that here.

Why not? she screamed. Why fucking well not?

You can do what you like in England, he said. But here there are certain things you cannot do. That's our culture; that's how we live.

She stared at him, wide-eyed, speechless. Then she spun around to face me. Do you see now? she cried. She bit her lip fiercely and the tears came pouring out of her brimming eyes.

I put my arms around her and pulled her towards me. She rubbed her face into my kurta, sobbing, saying over and over again: Do you see now? Do you understand? – and I, uncomprehending, repeated after her: See what? Understand what? while trying to stop the flow of her tears with the back of my hand.

Then she pushed me away and waved at a taxi. It stopped, and she darted into it, rolled down the window, and shouted: Do you see now why I've chosen to live in London? Do you see? It's only because I want to be free.

Free of what? I said.

Free of *you*! she shouted back. Free of your bloody culture and free of all of you.

The taxi started moving and I began to run along with it.

You can never be free of me, I shouted through the open window. If I were to die tomorrow you would not be free of me. You cannot be free of me because *I am within you* . . . just as you are within me.

Then the taxi picked up speed and disappeared along Chowringhee.

So that was what I told my grandmother as she lay in her sickbed, glaring at me; I told her that Ila lived in London only because she wanted to be free.

But I knew I had made a mistake the moment I said it; I should have known that she would have nothing but contempt for a freedom that could be bought for the price of an air ticket. For she too had once wanted to be free; she had dreamt of killing for her freedom.

It's not freedom she wants, said my grandmother, her bloodshot eyes glowing in the hollows of her withered face. She wants to be left alone to do what she pleases; that's all that any whore would want. She'll find it easily enough over there; that's what those places have to offer. But that is not what it means to be free.

I got up then and went back to my room. Staring out of my window, at the darkness of the lake, I saw Ila's face again, as I had seen it that night in the taxi, wet with tears, twisted with anger and hatred, and I thought of how much they all wanted to be free; how they went mad wanting their freedom; I began to wonder whether it was I that was mad because I was happy to be bound: whether I was alone in knowing that I could not live without the clamour of the voices within me.

I went to see my grandmother again next morning.

She had a nurse now, and the moment she saw me entering the room she asked the nurse to turn her over so that she would be facing away from me. I addressed a few general remarks to her back but she wouldn't answer.

The nurse was embarrassed. She said to my grandmother,

in her most cheerful voice: Come on now, why don't you answer his questions? He's your grandson, after all.

I could not see the expression on my grandmother's face when she said that, but I could imagine it. She reached for the bedpan that was kept on a low table beside her bed and tried to fling it at the nurse. But she was so weak that she barely managed to tip it on to the floor.

The nurse was shaken: she had only been with my grandmother a couple of days. She had taken her to be a gentle thing.

You should go now, she said to me, the patient is upset.

I slipped quickly across the room. But when I opened the door, I heard my grandmother's voice issuing from the bed. It was her old voice, the strong voice I remembered, not the voice she had developed during her sickness.

Why do you always speak for that whore? she said.

I spun around. Who are you talking about? I said, staring at the back of her head.

That memshaheb whore, she said. Ila. Why do you always defend her? What does she mean to you?

The nurse darted across to wipe the spittle from her mouth and I slipped out of the room.

That evening my grandmother's condition worsened. We heard her through the walls of our rooms, labouring for her breath, all through the night. When I went to see her next morning she was lying in a tiny exhausted heap on her pillows. As soon as I entered her room she fixed her red-rimmed eyes on me and said: Why don't you answer me? Tell me: what does that English whore mean to you?

The nurse hurried over before I could say anything and bundled me out of the room.

For a few days after that her condition deteriorated steadily. Arrangements were made for setting up an oxygen tent over her bed. We had a doctor sleeping in the house at night now, as well as a nurse. Sometimes during the day, the nurse would allow us to watch her labouring for her breath inside the oxygen tent. But none of us was allowed to speak to her. The doctors wanted to move her to a hospital but she had enough strength left to tell them that she would rather die at home than in an institution.

Then, slowly, she recovered. The oxygen tent was removed and my mother began to spend a lot of time sitting beside her bed. But neither my father nor I were allowed into the room.

My holidays were almost over now. Since my grandmother's condition had improved my parents decided that I ought to go back to Delhi: my final year examinations were only three months away and I had hardly studied at all during the holidays. I had prepared myself to stay on, but I was only too glad to take their advice.

The day I was to catch the train, my mother took me into my grandmother's room to take my leave of her. She was sitting up in bed and she seemed better than she had been in a long time. To my relief she talked quite cheerfully about my college and the forthcoming examinations. I touched her feet when it was time for me to leave, and, as always, she pulled my head to her breast, to bless me. I heard the quiet, familiar murmur of her blessings. Then she lowered her mouth to my ear, so that I could feel the heat of her breath on my face.

Why have you let that whore trap you? she whispered. I know it's she who's sent you into the arms of those whores you go to in Delhi. Do you think I don't know? Did you think I would allow it?

I jerked my head out of her hands. She met my gaze and smiled. I could not believe that this withered, wasted, powerless woman was the same person that I had so much loved and feared.

For two months my parents wrote to me every other day with news of my grandmother. Her condition improved for a while after I left Calcutta. Then, for no reason that doctors could perceive, it became very serious for a week or so. Again she recovered miraculously till she was well enough to read and even write a few letters.

Then for a whole week my parents' letters stopped. I did not have time to think about anything but Indian history then, so I did not worry, except in passing.

In their next letter my parents wrote that my grandmother had died and that she had been cremated the day after her death. They had decided not to send me a telegram in case I decided to rush off to Calcutta. They didn't want to disturb me when my examinations were so close.

I wished desperately that day that Robi, who had been gone for almost a year, was still in college. I could think of no one else I wanted to talk to, so I wandered out of the college, down the road to the Maurice Nagar bus stop. An empty 210 came along after a while and I climbed into it. I got a window seat and stared out, watching the parks on Ring Road and the walls of the Red Fort go by. When the bus reached the Central Secretariat, I crossed the road and took another 210 back. At Mall Road I decided to get off and walk. It was already dark then, the roads deserted, the whole university silent under the pall of the examinations.

Walking along the deserted avenue, I found myself crying, not so much in grief as anger that my parents had not informed me in time, so that I could be there when they cremated her. I climbed up the steep road that led to the monument on the Ridge, and sitting there, on the grass, I found my anger ebbing away. There seemed to be something fitting, after all, in the manner in which I had learnt of my grandmother's death: she had always been too passionate a person to find a real place in my tidy late-bourgeois world, the world that I had inherited, in which examinations were more important than death.

Two days later a peon brought me a message from the dean of our college. He wanted to see me urgently. I put away my textbooks and hurried off to his offices. He was a small, self-important little man whom nobody liked. But nobody took the trouble to particularly dislike him either: he didn't seem to warrant it.

He signalled me to a chair when I entered his office. When I had sat down he tapped a sheet of paper that was lying in front of him, on his desk, and said: I'm sorry to disturb you at this time, but there is a very serious matter at hand. Expulsion, if not rustication, is also possible. This is a very serious matter. After all, there is the medical angle to be considered.

Ridiculous though he was, I was alarmed by the tone of his voice: he had the power to destroy whatever chances I had of an academic career.

What exactly is the matter, sir? I said.

We have received information, he said, tapping the sheet of paper again, that you have been visiting prostitutes in houses of ill repute. It says that for your own good you should be expelled forthwith and sent back to Calcutta.

I was so taken aback that for a while I could only stare at him dumbly. Then I managed to say: Who has given you this information, sir?

Your own grandmother, he said, handing me the sheet of paper. You can see for yourself.

The letter was just three lines long. The writing was very shaky, but unmistakably my grandmother's. It said that she knew I visited whores in Delhi, that she had spoken to me and I had shown no signs of repentance, and that as a schoolteacher herself she thought that my college, if it had any self-respect at all, would see to it that I was sent home.

I was so shaken by the sight of her resurrected hand, reaching out to me after her death, as it had all through my childhood, that it was some time before I could collect myself enough to offer an explanation to the dean. I told him, looking him in the eye, that in all my years in college I had visited no place more disreputable than the Chanakya cinema and the Khyber restaurant at Kashmeri Gate; I said that my grandmother had been very ill indeed when she wrote that letter, and that in her illness her mind had become prey to delusions.

The situation was so fantastic that soon the dean lost faith in the letter and let me go. But he warned me that he would be keeping an eye on me during my last few weeks in college.

When I got up to go, I cast a glance at the letter. She had even written the date in the top right-hand corner, as she always did. Later, thinking back, tallying the dates, I realised that she had written the letter the day before she died.

I have never understood how she learnt of the women I had visited a couple of times, with my friends; nor do I know how she saw that I was in love with Ila so long before I dared to admit it to myself.

At some time late in my first autumn in London, when the trees of the Embankment were already bare, I realised I could no longer hide the truth from myself.

I would find myself wandering through Soho or around Trafalgar Square, and I would pretend to myself that I was walking for the mere pleasure of it, discovering the city. But soon I would find myself walking along the Embankment. I would lean on the parapet and gaze across the dark breadth of the Thames at the concrete hillocks of the South Bank; I would stop to run my hands over the cast-iron lamps, over the pouting lips of the moulded fish, and often, to my surprise, I would discover that somewhere at the back of my throat I was softly humming the tune of an old Hindi film song – *beqaraar karke hame yun na jaiyen* ... I don't know why it was that tune: I hadn't seen the film, nor ever possessed the record, but it was always that one and no other. It would appear unannounced, for no apparent reason, and though it was always the same tune there were times when it sounded quite different. At times it was a happy, lilting kind of tune, and then, whether it was a wet, cold night or a cool, crisp one, I would find myself marching cheerfully along the deserted Embankment, singing out loud when the cars went roaring past me in packs. I would walk across to the other pavement, take a pencil out of my pocket and hold it beside me so that I could hear it clicking against the railings as I walked, drumming in time with the tune. But there were times when the tune became eerily sombre: I would find myself shying away from the patches of shadow on the pavements, and the dark masses of the tall buildings that lined the Embankment would begin to seem somehow menacing. I would try to keep to the pools of light under the lamps, and I wouldn't look down at the silky blackness of the Thames; I would lower my head and hurry, with my chin buried in my scarf, not daring to look at the other overcoated figures walking past me. On nights like that I would pray for the tune to go away, to leave me alone. At times I would even think that I had beaten it, that it had gone: I would drop on to a bench and listen hard, to make sure, and then, invariably, I would hear it again, buzzing softly at the back of my throat.

Sooner or later on those evenings I would find myself standing at Lambeth Bridge. I would look across the bridge at the weathered red-brick castellations of the Palace, and in genuine surprise I would say to myself: Why, here I am, at Lambeth Bridge. Since I've come this far I may as well walk to Stockwell and visit Ila.

Then I would walk half-way across the bridge, lean on

the railing and think of reasons why I should not go on: that it was too far, the rain would get worse before I got there, I had already been there twice that week, Ila wouldn't be at home anyway . . . I would carry on this argument with perfect disingenuousness, as though I were merely eavesdropping on a conversation between two old friends. All the while the sceptical part of my mind, the part that knew perfectly well why I happened to be on Lambeth Bridge, would be silent: I would not allow myself to listen to it.

But once I had decided — especially if it happened to be after a period in which I had successfully kept myself away from Stockwell for more than three days — a great weight would lift from my heart, and I would hurry across the bridge and walk, faster and faster, till I was almost running, all the way to her house in Stockwell.

As I walked, to drown the buzzing of that tune, I would play with numbers in my head. I would try to work out how many miles I had walked and how much time it had taken me: six and a half miles, I would say to myself, or 11,440 yards, or, better still, 34,320 feet, or 10,461 metres. The numbers would occupy and exhaust my mind so that I could abandon myself to the marvellous happiness that was driving me on, faster and faster, towards Stockwell.

Later, sometimes I would look at the advertisements for diamonds and jewellery in the British Sunday magazines, or I would read their accounts of film-star romances, and I would wonder why it so happens that it is in this state, the state we call love, that people are most driven to enumerate and quantify, when the state itself, or so those very magazines tell us, is the obverse, the antithesis, of the notions of number and quantity. I would wonder what the circumstances could be that would prompt a man to tell a journalist exactly how much money he had spent, down to the last pound or dollar, on buying a car or an island for the woman he loved; I would wonder why the advertisements hinted so carefully at the exact price of the jewellery they urged men to buy for their girlfriends and lovers; why a girl had attempted suicide exactly nine times to get back the man she loved; why I had been driven to count all the yards that I had walked when I went to see Ila. I could think of no answer, except that it is because that state, love, is so utterly alien to that other idea without which we cannot live as human beings – the idea of justice. It is only because love is so profoundly the enemy of justice that our minds, shrinking in horror from its true nature, try to tame it by uniting it with its opposite: it is as though we say to ourselves – he bought her a diamond worth exactly so much, or she gave up a career that would have earned her precisely so much, in the hope that if we apply all the metaphors of normality, that if we heap them high enough, we shall, in the end, be able to approximate that state metaphorically. And yet between that state and its metaphors there is no more connection than there is between a word, such as mat, and the thing itself: they are utterly indifferent to each other, so that we may heap the metaphors – the diamonds, the suicides, the miles, the suffering – till the end of our abilities, and yet find no trace at all of the state itself. And equally we may find the opposite.

Perhaps those miles and yards were my own living metaphors, my attempt to claim a share of justice. For I had already thrown everything else I had on the scales; not insubstantial things, after all, for I was a human being too, with my own worth and weight, not ugly, not without substance, educated, and with other qualities too, like patience and good humour – what more could a human being *have*, in fairness – I had thrown in all of that, everything I had, and by not so much as a tremor had the scales acknowledged their weight.

That was why I walked those miles, in the hope that the sheer force of those numbers would speak to Ila, tell her all the things I dared not say for fear of losing even her friendship; that somehow the weight of those accumulated yards would tip those inscrutable scales towards me. But when Ila did happen to be at home, she would open the door and say: Nice to see you, come in, but I hope you're not expecting any dinner, and I would tell her, smiling brightly: I've walked eight miles, it took me exactly two hours and ten minutes, and she would arch her eyebrows in surprise and say: Why? Is it some kind of health kick?

The people Ila shared her house with spent their evenings in the kitchen whenever they were in. They consisted of a bearded Irish computer scientist, a girl from Leicestershire who had dropped out in her second year at the North London Polytechnic to work with the Fourth International, and a morose young Ghanaian who was very active in the Anti-Nazi League. They would spend their evenings sitting around the deal table in the kitchen drinking mugs of tea, or sometimes, when they could afford it, beer. Their conversations were almost always severely practical. For hours on end they would argue about which kind of pen was better for drawing posters with, or over how they ought to make the arrangements for lunch or tea at their next picket. There were no explosive arguments nor any shouting as there would have been among like-minded people in Calcutta or Delhi. When they did argue, it was usually about small points of tactics and strategy, and the arguments usually consisted of a series of increasingly oblique statements, loaded with references to a long history of personal political decisions. These dialogues were so controlled at first I did not recognise them as arguments at all. But in fact there was a frightening quality about them; a seriousness of intent that was all the more deadly for being so quiet.

Ila often seemed to be as ignorant and uninterested in the backgrounds of those arguments as I was. Indeed it was soon evident to me that she played a bit role in their collective political life: it was often apparent that they had made their decisions long before they asked her for her opinion. They were all clearly very fond of her, but they seemed to regard her as a kind of guest, a decoration almost. Nor did they seem to resent in her the signs of cosmopolitanism they were always so quick to criticise in themselves and their other comrades. In a way they were proud of her: they would often ask about her family's wealth, how many servants she had 'at home' in India, and so on, and they would listen intently as she told them – with many exaggerations, usually. They would talk of her as 'our own upper-class Asian Marxist'. This seemed to please them: they had an acute sense of history and perhaps they saw Ila as a link with the Fabians. Or perhaps the thought that their lives and ideas might have some influence on another continent was some compensation for their impotence at home. At any rate they, who were not otherwise friendly people, were tolerant, even encouraging, towards Ila's friends. As a rule they were dismissive, even suspicious of outsiders. But 'Ila's friends' were a special case: even when they did not pay them much attention, they seemed quite happy to have them sitting around their kitchen table.

Often I would find Nick Price in the kitchen when I arrived. He was always very well dressed. I would ask him the secret of his sartorial success and he would explain that his shirt was from Turnbull & Asser and his jacket from Armani, and smile when he saw that the names meant nothing to me. He should have seemed incongruous in that kitchen, but in fact he fitted in much better there than I did. There was a practical, do-it-yourself side to his nature which meshed neatly with the ambience of that house: he was genuinely interested in poster paints and printing ink. From their conversations I discovered that he often spent the whole day in their house – he certainly had the time, for he had still not taken, or found, a job. He would run the occasional errand for them and help them at whatever they were doing – like proof-correcting pamphlets and painting posters. He even went to their demonstrations and stood with them in their pickets. I gathered that he had become something of a minor celebrity among them, because he always went dressed in a suit and a tie, and so, since he made a good impression, he was often deputed to deal with the police when there was trouble. And since politics, in any sense that I could understand, was never talked about in that house, there was never any reason for him to disagree with them anyway.

On one such evening, when I had walked all the way from Charing Cross to Stockwell, Ila looked at me, sitting beside Nick, and wrinkled her nose at my grubby blue anorak and fading corduroy jeans. She said: We should do something about getting you some proper clothes.

I reminded her that my fellowship, while perfectly adequate for my needs, wasn't quite generous enough to provide me with a new wardrobe, but she shrugged aside my objections and said: I know just the place where you could do your shopping.

Where?

You wouldn't know it, she said. It's a place where there are lots of cheap retail shops run by Indians and Bangladeshis.

Where is it? I said.

It's a place called Brick Lane, she said.

She cut herself short when she saw my face.

What's the matter? she said, raising her eyebrows. Have you heard of it?

I shook my head quickly and asked her when we could go. We arranged to meet two days later at lunch-time, in the Kembles Head.

I arrived late. I saw Ila at once, in the far corner of the room. And then I saw Nick, sitting beside her. He was wearing a tweed jacket and silk tie, she a pullover and jeans. She said something to him, but he was reading the *Financial Times*, which he had folded into a small square. He turned away from her, very slightly, and she slumped back again, raising her face to the ceiling. They were sitting apart, a good distance from each other, at different ends of a long wooden seat. They could have been strangers – it ought to have been easy to take them for that – but I could tell at once, from the way the crowd had arranged itself around them, that even they could sense that the two of them had come there together. I wanted to stand at the bar and watch them, not for a minute but for hours; I wanted to learn the language of their affinity. But the man behind the bar wanted to know what I would like, and by the time the warm, tawny beer had trickled out of the brass spigot and filled my glass, Ila had already seen me.

Where have you been? said Ila when I went up to their table, and Nick shook his hair out of his eyes with a toss of his fine golden head and held out his hand, smiling. I began to recite an explanation, but Ila interrupted me.

Nick decided to come along too, she said, with a faint trace of apology in her voice. Can you guess why?

She looked at me solemnly for a moment and then her face crumpled into laughter. She said: He's thinking of going into business. The import-export business – trading in ready-made Indian garments.

She made room for me beside her and for the next quarter of an hour Nick explained the details of his scheme. I was barely listening, but I understood that it had some- thing to do with Ila and her family investing some money at the Indian end and Nick doing the wholesaling in London.

Ila must have noticed that I was bored, for after a while she cut him short and said to me: You're really excited, aren't you? About going to Brick Lane?

I nodded and, watching me curiously, she said: Why? What's so interesting about Brick Lane?

I'll tell you when we get there, I said. Come on, let's go.

The first surprise that was waiting for me was that it wasn't a lane at all. I had thought of it as long, narrow and curving, a little like the lanes I had seen in Oxford – flanked by grey stone walls that had the ends of creepers trailing over them – but with cars and neon lights, of course, as well as a few boutiquey shops. I'd thought of small, red-brick houses jostling together, cramped, but each with its own little handkerchief-garden and flowers on its window sills.

I had no means of recognising the place I saw; it did not belong anywhere I had ever been. I walked ahead of Ila and Nick in a trance, looking at the Bengali neon signs above the shops that lined the lane, staring into display windows lined with the latest Bengali film magazines, reading the posters that had been slapped on those walls of aged London brick – stern grey anti-racism posters issued by an iridescent spectrum of the left-wing, buried now under a riot of posters advertising the very newest Hindi films – listening to quick exchanges in a dozen dialects of Bengali as people hurried past me, laughing and chattering, with their fingers curled into the sleeves of their anoraks, like shoppers at Gariahat on a cold winter's morning. I stopped to sniff the fragrance of rosogollas wafting out of a sweet-shop and waved to Ila and Nick to hurry. She laughed when she saw me gazing greedily into the shop. Exactly like that sweet-shop at the corner of Gole Park, she said, isn't it. And so it was, with exactly the same laminated counters and plastic tables; exactly the same except that it was built into a terrace of derelict eighteenth-century London houses, and there was no paan-shop at the corner, and no Nathu Chaubey, but instead, as Nick pointed out, hanging over it was the great steeple of Hawksmoor's Christchurch Spitalfields.

You see, Ila said to me, laughing. It's all new to you, I've always told you. You know nothing about London.

Nick pointed at a large chapel-like building with a sign that said: London Jamme Masjid.

Do you see that mosque? he said. That used to be a synagogue when this place was a Jewish area – up until the war and after.

That was when your uncle lived here! I said. Your uncle Alan.

My uncle? he said in surprise. Did he live here?

Yes, I said. I'll show you where he lived.

I quickened my pace and walked ahead of them, looking up at the street signs on the walls at the corners. I led them past a great brewery that was leaking the smell of fresh beer in dribbles into the lane, like a pub on a Saturday evening, under a railway bridge to the far side of Brick Lane. The lane was quiet here; there was none of the noise and bustle that we had passed through. Most of the shops along the pavement were boarded up or abandoned, the glass in the windows broken so that we could look in at the bowels of the crumbling buildings, upon wildernesses of shattered plywood partitions, broken bottles and decaying cardboard boxes. Most of the shops that were still in business were selling Indian-made leather clothes, of the kind that are hawked to tourists at Janpath in Delhi – black leather jackets and suede handbags and belts. Eventually I found the street sign I had been looking for.

There, I said to Nick, pointing triumphantly at the house

on the corner. That's where your uncle Alan lived at the beginning of the war.

His face lengthened in fastidious disbelief as he examined its crumbling masonry and the signboard of the Taj Travel Agency on the ground floor.

Look, he said, you've got it wrong. That couldn't have been it. He wasn't poor, you know – my grandfather had left him quite a lot of money. He could have lived anywhere he liked.

He frowned in a way that seemed to suggest that I had deliberately cast a slur on his family. I shrugged: I could not see any point in explaining that perhaps he had lived there not because he *had* to but because he wanted to; that perhaps he had preferred to spend his money on obscure little journals rather than cars and houses. Even I found people like that hard to believe in.

There were only two big windows on the first floor of the house. One of them was boarded over with wooden planks. But the other was open, and through it we could see the edges of brightly coloured curtains, made of the kind of synthetic cloth that looks like velvet.

That was the window of Dan's bedroom, I decided. It was easy to see how the window panes might have been blacked out with ink-blackened newspapers. It was this window that Dan had opened that September night in 1940, when he'd grown tired of trying to sleep on the mattresses below the stairs, with the others. He was something of an insomniac and sleep always came harder when he was not in his own bed. It was much safer below the stairs, of course, but now he needed sleep. He had hardly slept at all that week and he had to get back to work at the press tomorrow, as usual.

But it wasn't any easier upstairs. The drone of the plans seemed much louder up there. And every time a bomb exploded somewhere in the neighbourhood, a screw that had come loose in his steel bed would rattle eerily. He'd told the others about it and one morning they had helped him take the old bed apart, but they hadn't found it. It was still there, rattling away. He climbed out of bed, lit a cigarette, and opened the window just a little, making sure that the glowing tip of his cigarette was well hidden behind his back. The fresh air was a relief for the night was warm and still.

Downstairs they were all asleep. They had had a tiring day, for they had gone to a demonstration outside the Savoy Hotel, to demand that the hotel's cellars be turned into an air-raid shelter for East Enders. They had come back to Brick Lane flushed with triumph, glad they'd done something. But then, later, when they were eating their dinner, Dan had turned on the radio and caught the National Prayer Day service. They'd listened in silence for a moment, and then Francesca had begun to cry, so Dan had turned it off. And now the three of them were fast asleep, on the mattresses they had laid out below the stairs when the bombing began.

Dan flinched as a high-pitched metallic shriek tore the air, but then it went suddenly silent, so he relaxed and drew on his cigarette. If it had happened a little later in the Blitz, when the city had developed its collective wisdom about bombs, he would have known, because of that silence, that it was going to be close. He would have thrown himself flat on the floor, and if he had he might have lived, even though the bomb hit the pavement just in front of his window, carving out a ten-foot deep pit, and pulling down a large part of the front of the house with it – that part where the Taj Travel Agency's display windows now stood. But it happened too early, just a few days after the bombing had begun. He was standing right beside the window when the blast shattered the panes into fine, sharp splinters and blew them into the room like a curtain of needles. When the men from the Heavy Rescue Services carried his body out, every last inch of it was tattooed with the fine, clean perforations of the scalpel-sharp slivers of glass that had been blown through him by the blast.

The stairs were the first part of the house to collapse. The wood gave a long, wrenching groan when the blast shook the foundations. That momentary pause gave Tresawsen time to push Mike clear of the stairs and throw his body over Francesca's. Then a beam fell upon him, killing him instantly, breaking his spine.

Francesca was pinned under his body, rigid with shock but otherwise unhurt, until they dug her out. A month later she was sent to an internment camp for enemy aliens on the Isle of Wight. Mrs Price never heard of her again. As for Mike, he survived, but he had already signed up for the Navy and he was called up a month later. In 1943 Mrs Price read his name in the casualty list in *The Times* and learnt later that his ship, a minesweeper, had been torpedoed by a U-boat, not far from Lowestoft harbour.

Two days later, when Tridib came to Brick Lane with Mayadebi and Mrs Price to collect Tresawsen's things, he found a picture of the four of them together, stuck on the kitchen wall: it had been taken in a park, and all of them were laughing, Dan standing a little apart, and Mike with his arms around Tresawsen and Francesca.

How sad, said Ila. They must have been wonderfully happy in that house.

How do you know? I said, surprised by the note of certainty in her voice.

Because we live like that too, she said. In Stockwell.

I thought she was joking, at first. But when I looked at her I knew she had meant it exactly as it had sounded. I began to marvel at the easy arrogance with which she believed that her experience could encompass other moments simply because it had come later; that times and places are the same because they happen to look alike, like airport lounges.

Do you think anybody could really be 'wonderfully happy' at a time like that? I snapped at her. Don't you think it possible that they quarrelled a lot – for example, over the Nazi-Soviet Pact?

Ila was unshaken, serene. Of course they quarrelled, she laughed. It's part of the fun of living like that – you're too earnest. And in any case, you've never lived like that – you can't know.

What do *you* know of how I've lived? I said.

Well, she said quietly, I know, for example, that you've spent your whole life living safely in middle-class suburbs in Delhi and Calcutta. You can't know what this kind of happiness means: there's a joy merely in knowing that you're a part of history. We may not achieve much in our little house in Stockwell, but we *know* that in the future political people everywhere will look to us – in Nigeria, India, Malaysia, wherever. It must have been the same for Tresawsen and his crowd. At least they knew they were a part of the most important events of their time – the war, and fascism, all the things you read about today in history books. That's why there's a kind of heroism even in their pointless deaths; that's why they're remembered and that's why you've led us here. You wouldn't understand the exhilaration of events like that – nothing really important ever happens where you are.

Nothing really important? I said incredulously.

Well of course there are famines and riots and disasters, she said. But those are local things, after all – not like revolutions or antifascist wars, nothing that sets a political example to the world, nothing that's really remembered.

She seemed immeasurably distant then, in her serene confidence in the centrality and eloquence of her experience, in her quiet pity for the pettiness of lives like mine, lived out in the silence of voiceless events in a backward world.

I began to shout at her, saying that she made me laugh, she and her pathetic little welfare-pink friends, that she knew nothing at all about courage and politics, that *I* could understand people like Tresawsen better than she could, because I could conceive of a time when politics was serious.

Serious? she said, her voice growing sharp. God, you're so naïve: everybody knows what those thirties lefties were doing in those bars in Berlin. They probably spent all their time fighting over each other's beds – not the Nazi-Soviet Pact. But you wouldn't guess because you know nothing about England.

I gave up then, for of course she was right: I knew nothing at all about England except as an invention. But still I had known people of my own age who had survived the Great Terror in the Calcutta of the sixties and seventies, and I thought I had at least a spectator's knowledge of their courage, something that Ila, with her fine clothes and manicured hands, would never understand.

And yet that was not the truth either, for I had been with Ila once when she had come out of her hairdresser's shop, her hair all new and curled, and marched straight off to Brixton with her little crew of friends, to confront a gang of jack-booted racists armed with bicycle chains.

As for me, I knew I would not have dared.

Nick was bored by our pointless argument.

Come on, he said. Let's go and have a look at that house.

He led us across the road and pushed open the greasy glass doors of the Taj Travel Agency. The door opened into a very large, dank room, so large that it was evident at once that they had torn down a wall and joined two rooms. A long Formica-topped table ran down one side of the room, behind which sat a row of girls, some in churidars and some in skirts. A little bell pealed tinnily as soon as Nick pushed the door open. One of the girls frowned at us as we walked in and gestured at the chairs in front of her desk. But before we could sit down a middle-aged man in a brown suit called out in Bengali from the other end of the room: Send them here, Zeenat, I'll deal with them.

He examined us as we walked up to his desk, and when we had sat down he said expressionlessly, in a glottal London voice: Wha' can I do for you?

Ila, instinctively adopting the manner of the Indian grande dame, said: We'd like a little information please.

The man behind the desk was not impressed. He looked her over, and said: How many of you travelling? We only do groups.

We're going to Calcutta, I said to him in Bengali, smiling my most ingratiating smile. Could you give us some idea . . . ?

All business in English here, he snapped at me. And I can't tell you anything until you let me know how many of you are travelling.

You're not being very friendly, Nick said. Are you now?

Not my job to be friendly, he said.

Tell me, I said quietly. Was there ever a staircase in here?

What? the man exploded.

Just wanted to know whether there was ever a staircase in here that was blown up by a bomb.

Get out, he said. You've wasted enough of my time.

Now look here, Nick began.

If you don't look sharp, he said, I'm going to throw you out.

I don't like this place, Ila said loftily. I'm going anyway.

We got up together and walked to the door while the man glared at our backs.

Bet he's running a sweat-shop upstairs, Nick whispered loudly as we were going out.

I heard that, the man bellowed, but before he could say anything else we were outside. When we had crossed the road, I turned back to take a last look at the house, trying to see it with a great hole gouged out of its side, as Tridib had.

Nick stopped too, and looking back at the Taj Travel Agency he said: You've got to hand it to people like that though: they come over with next to nothing, and before you know it they've built up thriving little businesses. Now if I could get my hands on a little capital, I'd go into the futures market. Friends of mine have made killings there – it's all a question of knowing what to buy when.

For once I allowed myself to show my irritation.

Shouldn't you think of getting a job first? I said. Before you start making a fortune on the futures market?

He took my question seriously, or at least he pretended to. The trouble is, he said, there's not enough money in jobs here. It's stupid really. Chartered accountants have to start at fifteen thousand pounds or something. In America or Kuwait they'd get two or three times as much.

So, then, why did you give up your job in Kuwait? I asked.

Got sick of it, he said, wrinkling his nose. It wasn't really a properly professional outfit. Outdated management practices. I thought of setting up something on my own there, but the trouble is, you have to have an Arab business partner, and they always interfere.

So you mean you just chucked up your job one fine morning and came away? I said. I must have sounded sceptical, for he turned to give me a long, cool look.

Yes, he said. That's what I did.

Really? I said. Well if I were you, I'd think of getting a job before I thought of the futures market.

Abruptly, Ila thrust a hand through Nick's arm. I stole

131

a quick glance at her: her lips were white; she was very angry.

Nick and I have to go now, she said. I think you're old enough to do your own shopping.

She turned on her heel and led him away, leaving me standing where I was, speechless. After they'd gone a hundred yards or so, she left him and came running back towards me.

I don't like you being rude to my friends, she said, when we were face to face. You'd better telephone before you come to Stockwell again. I may not be in.

A fortnight passed before I saw Ila again.

We met on Christmas Eve at 44 Lymington Road; Mrs Price had invited us to join her and Nick and May at a small family dinner.

Ila came very late. She burst in upon us when Mrs Price and May were about to serve dinner. She was smiling, radiant, dressed in knee-length leather boots and a short skirt. She said a quick word of apology to everyone in turn, and to my relief, when she came to me, she was smiling.

Where have you been all these days? she whispered. Why haven't you come to see me?

Then she turned away to admire the table. It had been beautifully laid: the silver and glass sparkled in the candle-light and a huge bowl of fruit glowed gently in the centre of the table. After we had sat down and May had served us our soup and Nick had poured us wine, Ila, looking as though she would burst, clapped her hands together and cried: I've got good news. You'll never believe it.

My heart went cold as I watched her turn her glowing face towards Nick.

I've got a job, she cried.

Wonderful! said May. With whom?

132

With the Save the Children Fund, said Ila. It won't pay much, but it's something.

Breathless with relief, I said: But I thought you hated children.

Well I don't actually have to see the little creatures, she said. I only have to save them, and that's not too hard if all it means is filling in ledgers and pushing files.

We laughed, Nick proposed a toast and we all drained our glasses. Then Mrs Price raised her glass shakily, her small, lined face wrinkling into a smile, and said: Since we're more or less evenly matched here, if you don't count an old biddy like me, I think we ought to drink a toast to Mr Justice Chandrashekhar Datta-Chaudhuri, and my father, Lionel Tresawsen, for we wouldn't be here together now if it weren't for them.

We raised our glasses again, but solemnly this time. Nick drained his glass again, and then, twirling it between his fingers, slurring his words slightly, he said: Now Grandpa Tresawsen had a good time. How wonderful it must have been to go around the world like that: like some great Dickensian show on a stage. There's never been anything like it before and there'll never be anything like it again.

He turned to me and shrugged, making a rueful face.

And what did *I* get? he said. Bloody old Kuwait. That's what comes of being born too late.

Well, May said lightly, reaching for our plates; I think you might allow for the possibility that grandfather Tresawsen would have made a little more of Kuwait than you did.

Kuwait! Nick snorted. You wouldn't say that if you knew what it's like out there. It's a bubble that's going to burst any day now. That's why I got out while there was still something to get out of.

May banged the plates down on the table and looked at him for what seemed like a very long time. Then she

133

leant towards him and said: Nick, isn't it time you stopped lying about this Kuwait business? I was willing to go along with it when it was just a lie meant for other people. But you've begun to believe it yourself, and you shouldn't, you really shouldn't. You ought to be able to stand up and tell the truth; you were brought up to tell the truth, just as I was. You should be able to look people in the eye and tell them what you told us: you ought to be able to say that your boss didn't like you, that he concocted charges of embezzlement against you. If he did concoct them, that is.

Nick stood up, swaying on his feet. He threw his napkin on the table and hissed at May.

You're a liar and a bitch, he said. It doesn't surprise me that you never got married. Who'd want to put up with that fake honesty and those staring eyes every day at breakfast?

Then he turned to Mrs Price and said that he was going up to his room; that he didn't want any dinner. But Mrs Price was fast asleep, with her chin buried in her neck. He marched out of the room without another word, and a moment later Ila ran out after him.

May did not seem to notice; she was staring blankly into the flame of a candle. Oh God, she whispered. What have I done?

Nick and Ila came back together, a quarter of an hour later. We woke Mrs Price and May brought in the turkey and carved it. Mrs Price talked to me for a while about Calcutta, but nobody else said a single word. When we had finished our turkey, May blew out the candles as though she were sleep-walking through a ritual, and brought in the Christmas pudding and lit it. But only I applauded when the brandy flared up into a clean blue flame.

After we had eaten our portions and cleared the plates

away, Mrs Price led us back to her drawing room and poured out glasses of brandy for all of us. I emptied my glass as quickly as I could and got up to go.

Thank you very much, I said to Mrs Price, trying not to sound awkward. It's been a wonderful evening. A real English Christmas – nothing could have been better. It was lovely. But I'd better go now, or I'll miss the last tube home.

She smiled, squinting at me short-sightedly, and stretched out her hand. I'm glad you enjoyed yourself, she said. You must come again.

While I was fetching my scarves and overcoat, May went to the window and looked out at the garden.

I don't think you'll be able to go just yet, she said. Have you seen what it's like outside? There's a blizzard blowing out there. You'll freeze.

I went to stand beside her, wrapped up in my scarves and overcoat. I could not see very far: there where whirlpools of snow blowing against the window.

You'd better stay, said May. I think we'll all have to stay. I can't face going back to Islington in a storm.

She looked at me, pleading, as though to tell me that she wouldn't dare stay if I went.

All right, I said. I'll stay.

But where will I put all of you? said Mrs Price. There won't be room for two people in your old room, May. Nor will there in Nick's.

I know! May said brightly. The two of them can sleep in the cellar – on the old camp beds. There's that old heater down there, too, so they won't be cold, and Nick and I can give them our sleeping bags. They ought to be quite comfortable.

That's fine by me, said Ila, giving me a tight conspiratorial little smile. I nodded my assent, my heart bursting with hope.

Well then, you arrange it, said Mrs Price. As for me. I'm eighty years old, and I'm going to bed.

May hurried out of the room and we followed. She threw open a door that was tucked away behind the suitcase and switched on a light. It smelt slightly damp, but not musty: it was much cleaner than I had expected. There were stacks of paperbacks in one corner of the cellar, and suitcases and trunks were piled up high in another. May showed us the camp beds, tucked away behind the suitcases, and Nick and I dragged them out. It took us a while before we got the knack of opening them. But once they had been laid out properly they looked quite comfortable. Nick and Ila went upstairs and fetched sleeping bags, towels and nightclothes and soon the cellar began to look warm and inviting. Then May and Nick said goodnight and left.

Ila turned to look at me after they were gone.

So here we are, she said, smiling. We're back under our old table, playing houses.

I nodded and threw myself down on the edge of one of the beds. My knees were shaking and the palms of my hands were wet. Ila turned her back on me and pulled off her jacket and sweater, talking in a low voice all the while, about May and how she had ruined the evening.

She was in a thin blouse now; I could see the outline of her breasts and even the shadow of the mole above her nipple.

It's hot in here actually, she said, undoing the buttons of her blouse. I don't think I'm going to need any nightclothes.

She turned to reach for a towel and her eyes fell on me, crouched on the edge of the camp bed.

Why, you're staring, she laughed in surprise. I'll have to turn my back on you again.

She turned away and shrugged off her blouse. I could

smell her now: she smelt of soap and fresh sweat. I could see the soft skin of her waist curving gently into her belt.

She wrapped the towel around herself and kicked off her skirt. I could see the slanted grain of the down running down her legs. At that moment, draped in a towel, from her armpits to her thighs, her weight resting on one leg, her skin shimmering like soft, dark silk, she seemed to belong to a wholly different species of being from the women my friends and I had visited – more perfect than any human form could possibly be.

I could not sit still any more. I stole up behind her and put my hand on her bare shoulder.

Take your hand away, she giggled. It's cold.

She spun around, and I don't know what she saw on my face but the laughter died on her lips.

Oh, what's happened? she cried. Why are you looking at me like that?

She stepped back to look at me and then she ran into my arms and hugged me.

You poor man, she said.

Her voice was full of pity.

You poor, poor man.

She reached up and ran a hand over my face. It was only then that I felt the tears running down my cheeks.

I didn't know, she said. You were always the brother I never had. I'm sorry. If I'd known, I wouldn't have behaved like this. Really, believe me.

It doesn't matter, I said.

She came and sat beside me and ran a finger over my neck and back. I'm sorry, she said. I'm really, truly sorry.

You've got nothing to be sorry for, I said. It's no one's fault but mine.

We heard the sound of a door shutting somewhere upstairs. Ila leapt to her feet.

I've got to go now, for a bit, she said, her voice light

with relief. I'm going up to have a chat with Nick; he's very upset.

I felt the warmth of her body over mine as she leant to kiss me on my chin.

Go to sleep, she said. I'll be back in a couple of minutes.

A moment later I heard her tiptoeing softly up the staircase.

I lay on my back, staring up at the ceiling, and as the hours passed I saw Ila again and again as she was when she stepped out of that car at Gole Park, eighteen years ago; on that morning when she wrenched me into adulthood by demonstrating for the first time, and for ever the inequality of our needs. And when she did not come back to the cellar that night, I knew she had taken my life hostage yet again; I knew that a part of my life as a human being had ceased; that I no longer existed, but as a chronicle.

Coming Home

Coming Home

In 1962, the year I turned ten, my grandmother retired, upon reaching the age of sixty. She had taught in a girls' high school since 1936. When she'd first joined, the school had had only fifty pupils and the premises had consisted of two sheds with tin roofs. During the monsoons she had often had to teach standing in ankle-deep water – once, or so she claimed, it had been so bad that a girl had actually managed to spear a fish with a compass during a geometry lesson. But over the next two decades the school had grown into a successful institution and had acquired a big building near Deshapriya Park. For the last six years before she retired, my grandmother had been its headmistress.

She had been looking forward to her retirement although she'd grown very attached to the school in the twenty-seven years she had spent there. But she no longer had the stomach for staff-room intrigues and battles with the board, she would tell my parents; she was growing old, she had earned her rest. And besides, my father's career was going well, so she had no real worries left.

There was a farewell ceremony on her last day at school, to which my parents and I were invited. It was a touching ceremony in a solemn kind of way. The Calcutta Corporation sent a representative and so did the Congress and the CPI. There were many speeches and my grandmother was garlanded by a girl from every class. Then the head girl, a particular favourite of hers, unveiled the farewell present the girls had bought for her by subscription. It was a large marble model of the Taj Mahal; it had a bulb inside and could be lit up like a table lamp. My grandmother made a speech too, but she couldn't finish it properly, for she began to cry before she got to the end of it and had to stop to wipe away her tears. I turned away when she began dabbing at her eyes with a huge green handkerchief, and discovered, to my surprise, that many of the girls sitting around me were wiping their eyes too. I was very jealous, I remember. I had always taken it for granted that it was my own special right to love her; I did not know how to cope with the discovery that my right had been infringed by a whole school.

Later we were served a meal in the staff room. The teachers had decided to give her a surprise.

When she was headmistress my grandmother had decided once that every girl who opted for home science ought to be taught how to cook at least one dish that was a speciality of some part of the country other than her own. It would be a good way, she thought, of teaching them about the diversity and vastness of the country. As a farewell surprise, the home science department had arranged for us to sample the results of my grandmother's initiative.

After we had been led into the staff room the girls came in, one by one, bearing dishes on trays. My grandmother was delighted; she understood at once what was in store for us. She had taken so keen an interest in this project that she knew each girl's speciality by heart. There's Ranjana (or Matangini), she would say, clapping her hands as they entered the room – Ranjana's doing Kerala, so avyal is what you'll get. Or: That's Sunayana, she's our Tamil for this term, wait till you taste her uppama, you'll want to be Tamil yourself. But then, in her mounting excitement, she began to make mistakes. There's a nice Gujarati mutton korma for you, she said, and then, leaping to her feet, she cried: Ah, there's my dear dahi-bara, you wait and see what a plump and juicy Punjabi she is!

As it happened, the girl who had made the dahi-baras was unusually fat. She burst into tears, dropped her plate of dahi-baras with a loud splash on the Sanskrit teacher's silk sari and ran out of the room.

We ate the rest of our meal in silence.

That was the only false note, however, and afterwards, since there would not have been room for the Taj Mahal in a taxi, the headmistress lent us one of the school's buses to go home in. The whole school lined up to wave as we steamed out through the gates. My grandmother waved back, tears streaming down her cheeks.

I remember very well the first day of her retirement. She spent the morning clearing away all the old files and papers that had accumulated in her room over the years. In the evening, we were invited to have a look. It was transformed. The files and papers were gone and the room was bathed in the gentle white glow of the Taj Mahal. She was very happy that night. At dinner, smiling her real smile, warm and impish, not the tight-lipped headmistress's smile that we had grown accustomed to, she told us funny stories about her early days in the school.

But her happiness did not last very long.

One afternoon, a few days later, I came home from school and found that both she and my mother had locked themselves into their rooms. That night I overheard my mother complaining tearfully to my father that she'd been nagged all day long – about her cooking, her clothes, the way she kept the house. My grandmother had never paid any attention to these matters before.

Soon she began to worry about other things too.

One afternoon my friend Montu and I were walking

143

back together from Gole Park, where the school bus had dropped us, when he stopped dead on the street and pointed up at our flat. Look! he cried, There's a man with a turban in your grandmother's room!

Montu was my best friend at that time. He and his family lived in the building next to ours, but our flats were so close we could talk to each other from our respective balconies. His name wasn't really Montu. It was Mansoor and he was from Lucknow. But he had grown up in Calcutta – his father was a teacher in the Ballygunge Science College – and when they'd moved to Gole Park from Park Circus, someone had shortened his name to Montu. There was very little we did not know about each other's families. He knew perfectly well that it was quite unprecedented for my grandmother to let any man into her room, let alone a stranger in a turban.

Liar! I said. But when I looked up, I saw he was right: there was an unmistakably turbaned head framed in my grandmother's window.

I sprinted down the street and up the stairs, jammed my finger into our doorbell and kept it there till my mother opened the door.

Who's that in Tha'mma's room? I whispered breathlessly. She raised a finger to her lips and gave me a warning tap on the shoulder, but ignoring her, I ran straight into my grandmother's room.

She was sitting on a chair in front of the open window with her head wrapped in a wet sari.

Speechless, I withdrew backwards, step by step, and fled to look for my mother.

What's Tha'mma doing? What's happened to her head?

My mother made me sit down and explained carefully that my grandmother had started on a course of Ayurvedic treatment and that the doctor had given her various herbal oils, with instructions to keep her head tied up all morning.

But why? I asked. What's happened to her head?

My mother frowned at me sternly.

Tha'mma thinks she's going bald, she said.

Then her composure dissolved and she began to laugh. She had to hold a pillow over her face so that my grandmother would not hear her.

I did not go out to our balcony that evening; I didn't see how I could begin to explain to Montu that my grandmother had tied up her head because she was afraid of going bald.

Fortunately she did not persist with that treatment for very long. Her vanity was not really strong enough to keep her sitting in a chair for hours on end with a wet sari wrapped around her head. And in any case she had a full head of thick silver hair.

Instead she took to visiting her school again. She would leave in the afternoon and come back a couple of hours later, bursting with the horror stories she had heard in the staff room: how the new headmistress was planning to dig up the rose beds she had planted, in order, if you please, to lay down a basketball court; how the wretched woman had insulted poor Mrs So-and-so in a staff council meeting and so on. After a dozen or so of these visits the new headmistress rang my father at his office and told him that if he could not think of some way of keeping his mother away from the school she would instruct the chowkidars not to let her in the next time she came.

I do not know what my father said to her, but she did not go back again till Founder's Day.

After that, for a few weeks, she spent all her time alone in her room. Once I pushed open her door and saw her sitting by the window staring blankly at her cupped hands. I shut the door quickly. I knew what she had in her hands. Time – great livid gouts of it; I could smell it stinking.

We left her to herself for a while and soon she began

145

to spend more time with us. She would sit with us in the evenings with a book or a half-finished letter on her knees and talk about our relatives or my father's work or my homework much as she used to before – but even I could tell that she was merely making an effort now; it was plain that she no longer cared.

I was puzzled and worried by the change in her and in my own way I began to make an effort to combat it. I had always resented the tyranny she had exercised over everything to do with my schoolwork, but now, of my own accord, I began to ask her for help with my homework. And on those occasions when I could persuade her to sit with me at my desk as she used to before, I found myself devising small ruses – like spilling ink on my textbooks – to keep her attention from straying. Sometimes my ploys would work and she would jerk herself out of her trance and rap me on my knuckles with the thin edge of a ruler. But then, soon, her mind would wander off again and I would sit doodling in my exercise book while she gazed out of the window. But for all that, her eyes had lost none of their glitter nor her walk its old rhythm or energy.

There's something stirring in her head, my mother whispered to me one day, watching her with narrowed eyes. I can tell from the look on her face. We have to be careful.

1962 was an exciting year for us. A couple of months after my grandmother retired my father became General Manager of his firm. The appointment was unexpected because there were many older and more experienced executives in the firm. It was a promotion such as he had not dared dream of. But my grandmother, who had always been very quick to tell our relatives about every small sign of success in my father's career, seemed hardly to notice this unforeseen and spectacular advancement. I heard her making a couple of calls once, but that was all. I remembered clearly how she had spent hours ringing everyone she knew when he'd been promoted from the position of Assistant Manager, Personnel, to Manager, Marketing, and I could not help noticing how brief her calls were this time.

Soon after my father's promotion we moved to a new house on Southern Avenue, opposite the lake. To me, after our cramped little flat in Gole Park, our new house seemed immense: it seemed to have more space than we could possibly use – rooms upstairs, rooms downstairs, verandas, a garden as well as a roof big enough to play cricket on. Best of all, as far as I was concerned, I still had Montu and my other friends close at hand because our new house was only a few minutes' walk from Gole Park.

I took it upon myself to introduce my grandmother to the house. I led her around it several times pointing out hidden lofts and unexpected doors and passageways. She made a few approbatory noises, but since they all sounded the same I knew soon enough that she was only pretending to be interested for my sake.

As we settled into our new house, it gradually became evident that the balances within our family had subtly but irrevocably shifted. In our old flat my grandmother had always been careful to maintain a titular control over the running of our household: now she didn't seem to care any more. It was to my mother that I had to go now when I was hungry and wanted the keys to the cupboard in which the dalmuth was kept, or when I wanted money to buy peanuts at the lake.

My grandmother's enveloping, placental presence was slowly withdrawing from the rest of the house and concentrating itself within the four walls of her room.

She had the best room in the house. It was very large and its walls were lined with tall shuttered windows. The few bits of furniture she had collected over the years seemed to be adrift in the vast spaces of that room, like leaves in a lake. I still occasionally took my homework to her. Usually when I went into her room, I would find her sitting in an armchair beside an open window – a shrunken, fragile little figure, gazing out across the lake. I would pull up a chair and sit beside her, scratching noisily in my exercise book to attract her attention.

One evening, when she seemed particularly distracted, I threw my exercise book down in frustration and cried: Tha'mma, why do you always stare out of the window like that? Don't you like this house?

She glanced at me in surprise and patted my shoulder. It's a nice house, she said, smiling. It's a nice house for a child, like you.

But then a frown appeared on her forehead and she bit her lip and said: But you know, it's very different from the house Maya and I grew up in.

How? I asked.

And so, over months of such evenings, she told me about the house she had grown up in – in Dhaka.

It was a very odd house. It had evolved slowly, growing like a honeycomb, with every generation of Boses adding layers and extensions, until it was like a huge, lop-sided step-pyramid, inhabited by so many branches of the family that even the most knowledgeable amongst them had become a little confused about their relationships.

Their own part of the house was quite large, and in my grandmother's earliest memory it was very crowded. Theirs was a big joint family then, with everyone living and eating together: her grandparents, her parents, she and Mayadebi, her Jethamoshai – her father's elder brother – and his family, which included three cousins of roughly her own age, as well as a couple of spinster aunts. She remembered her grandfather, although she had only been six when he died: a thin, stern-looking man with a frown etched permanently into his forehead. In his presence everyone, including her father and Jethamoshai, spoke in whispers, with their heads

148

down and their eyes fixed firmly on the floor. But when he left the house for the district courts, where he practised as an advocate, the house would erupt with the noisy games of the five cousins. Every evening the five children would be led by their mothers into his study, where they would each have to recite their alphabets – Bengali first and then English – with their hands held out, palm downwards, and he would rap them on the knuckles with the handle of his umbrella every time they made a mistake. If they cried they were rapped on their shins.

Still, terrifying though he was, he did manage to keep the house together. After he died, Jethamoshai, as the eldest son, tried hard to step into his place, but without success. He was an odd man, Jethamoshai; in some ways he was an oddly lovable man, but in others he was even more frightening than his father. He was thinner, for one, cadaverous in fact, and he had very bright, piercing eyes, set deep in the hollows of his long, gaunt face. But he had odd 'notions' – he liked to eat standing up, for instance, because he thought it was better for the digestion: no animal has a better digestive system than the cow, he used to say, and look at them, they eat standing up. He was undeniably eccentric, and the children found it hard to take him altogether seriously. For example, after his father died, he insisted that the children recite the alphabet every evening to him too, while he sat exactly as his father had, with the handle of his umbrella poised over their knuckles. But although he looked every bit as stern as his father, he had an odd trick of blowing through his lips, exactly like a tired tonga-horse, when he was listening. So, often, either she or Mayadebi would burst into laughter, half-way through their recitation. This would infuriate him and he would begin to pound out a drum roll of raps on their knuckles, whereupon they would begin to scream their lungs out, and then he would lose his temper altogether and start kicking them in the shins. The children usually enjoyed this production hugely because Jethamoshai wasn't really strong enough to hurt them, and besides his face became very funny when he was really angry. But of course their mother would be furious: she didn't understand that he didn't mean badly – it was just that he had no control over his temper at all. Often, after he had lost his temper, he would secretly buy the children halwa and shandesh as a kind of apology. But their mother didn't know this, and within a month or so of her father-in-law's death she was no longer on speaking terms with Jethamoshai and his wife and family.

It did not take long for the quarrels to get worse. The two women began to suspect each other of favouring their own children above the rest, of purloining the best little tid-bits of food for them from the common larder and so on. In the privacy of their rooms they would both berate their husbands, calling them unmanly and incapable of protecting the interests of their own children. Soon the two brothers were quarrelling too. And since they were both lawyers their quarrels took a peculiarly vicious, legalistic form, in which very little was actually said. Instead, they would send each other notes on legal stationery. My grandmother, since she was the elder, would always have to carry these, and she came to dread those missions for she would have to wait beside Jethamoshai's chair while he read them over and over again until the veins in his forehead began to throb with anger.

Those were terrible days for the children – spent cowering, in the background, listening, while their mothers quarrelled in whispers behind locked doors or lay crying in their bedrooms. When the cousins played now, it had to be in secret so that their parents would not see them together.

Soon things came to such a pass that they decided to

divide the house with a wooden partition wall: there was no other alternative. But the building of the wall proved to be far from easy because the two brothers, insisting on their rights with a lawyer-like precision, demanded that the division be exact down to the minutest detail. When the wall was eventually built, they found that it had ploughed right through a couple of doorways so that no one could get through them any more; it had also gone through a lavatory, bisecting an old commode. The brothers even partitioned their father's old nameplate. It was divided down the middle by a thin white line, and their names were inscribed on the two halves – of necessity in letters so tiny that nobody could read them.

They sprang from notoriously litigious stock.

They had all longed for the house to be divided when the quarrels were at their worst, but once it had actually happened and each family had moved into their own part of it, instead of the peace they had so much looked forward to, they found that a strange, eerie silence had descended on the house. It was never the same again after that; the life went out of it. It was worse for my grandmother than Mayadebi, for she could remember a time when it had been otherwise. She would often look across at her cousins on the other side and wonder about them, but so much bitterness lay between the two families now that she could not bring herself to actually speak to them.

In later years it always made my grandmother a little nervous when she heard people saying: We're like brothers. What does that mean? she would ask hurriedly. Does that mean you're friends? As for herself, having learnt the meaning of brotherhood very early, she had not dared to take the risk of providing my father with one.

And yet, those very women, my grandmother's mother and her aunt, the accumulated spleen of whose quarrels had probably shortened their lives by several years, became close, though silent, allies when it came to the business of their daughter's marriages. For example, their aunt played a central role in arranging Mayadebi's marriage to the Shaheb. It was she who first learnt of it when old Mr Justice Datta-Chaudhuri came to Dhaka on tour with his son (then an eminently eligible stripling of eighteen), and since she had already married off her own daughters, she made sure that the old judge got to hear of Mayadebi (whose beauty was already famous in the city). Once that had been accomplished the rest was easy, for their horoscopes, as well as every other circumstance, were eminently well suited. The pact was quickly sealed, and within six months Mayadebi was married. When she left, their mother gave her strict instructions not to forget to send her aunt half a dozen saris from Calcutta.

But there, at home in Dhaka, they never so much as exchanged a single word across that wall.

As for my grandmother, she had been married off four years before Mayadebi. My grandfather was an engineer with the railways, in Burma; my grandmother spent the first twelve years of her married life in a succession of railway colonies in towns with fairy-tale names like Moulmein and Mandalay. But later, all she remembered of them was hospitals and railway stations and Bengali societies: to her, nothing else in that enchanted pagoda-land had seemed real enough to remember.

My father was born in Mandalay, in 1925. My grandmother used to take him back to Dhaka every year for a couple of months to stay with her parents. Their part of the house was much emptier now because her cousins (of whom there were three, two boys and a girl) had scattered to various parts of the subcontinent. After Mayadebi got married and went to live in Calcutta only those four elderly people – her uncle, aunt and her parents – were left in the house. They had very little to quarrel about now, but the passage of time had in no way diminished that ancient bitterness. My grandmother did what she could to make them forget the past, but they had grown so thoroughly into the habits engendered by decades of hostility that none of them wanted to venture out into the limbo of reconciliation. They liked the wall now; it had become a part of them.

When my father was about six, both my grandmother's parents died, within a few months of each other. My grandmother returned to Dhaka only twice after that, and then only to make sure that the rooms she and Mayadebi had inherited were still intact. On both occasions she decided to go across and talk to her uncle and aunt, but the house was full of painful memories now and both times she fled back to Mandalay after spending barely a day in Dhaka.

And then, in 1935, my grandfather caught a chill while supervising the construction of a culvert somewhere in the Arakan Hills. He died of pneumonia before they could bring him back to Mandalay.

My grandmother was thirty-two when he died. She had no savings and she had never worked in her life but that merely made her all the more determined to see her son through school and college. Luckily she still possessed a scroll to prove that she had been awarded a bachelor's degree in history by Dhaka University. On the strength of that, a sympathetic railway official managed to arrange a job for her in a school in Calcutta – the school she was to work in for the next twenty-seven years.

She had no time to go back to Dhaka in the next few years. And then, in 1947, came Partition, and Dhaka became the capital of East Pakistan. There was no question of going back after that. She had never had any news of Jethamoshai and her aunt again.

In the years that followed, living in Calcutta in a one-room tenement in Bhowanipore, she would often think back on Dhaka – the old house, her parents, Jethamoshai, her childhood – all the things people think about when they know that the best parts of their lives are already over.

But do you know? she said, looking out across the lake, half smiling. In all that time there that was only thing I ever really regretted about Dhaka.

What? I asked.

She smiled: That I never got to see the upside-down house.

What was that? I said.

She began to laugh.

When the house was divided, she said, Maya was very little and she didn't remember the other side at all. So, later, often, to frighten her when she wasn't going to sleep or something like that, I would make up stories about that part of the house. Everything's upside-down over there, I'd tell her; at their meals they start with the sweets and end with the dal, their books go backwards and end at the beginning, they sleep under their beds and eat on the sheets, they cook with jhatas and sweep with their ladles, they write with umbrellas and go walking with pencils . . . And Maya grew to like these stories so much that every night I'd have to make up a new one or she wouldn't go to sleep. One night I'd tell her how today Jethamoshai had been brought his tea in a cup and he'd lost his temper and blown through his lips and shouted: Why did you bring it to me like that? Don't you know that tea is meant to be drunk out of a bucket? And the next night I'd have to make up a new one, so I'd say: Today Jethamoshai screamed at one of our cousins because he'd forgotten to bathe in the kitchen. Nonsense like that. And when I'd finished, I'd make a ghastly face and say: If you don't go to sleep right this very minute I'll drop you over the courtyard wall, and then you'll have to become upside-down too. That was usually enough to make Maya shut her eyes and drop off to sleep. But you know, the strange thing was that as we grew older even I almost came to believe in our story. Often, when we were quite grown up, going to school and everything, we would sit in the patch of garden in front of their part of the house, and watch Jethamoshai's door and try to imagine what was going on inside. It's afternoon now, Maya would say, so they must be eating their breakfast, or some other silly thing like that, and we would both double up with laughter and hang on to each other's necks. But sometimes, you know, when our parents were angry with us or we were feeling bad about something, we used to sit out there and gaze at that house. It seemed a better place to us then and we wished we could escape into it too.

But now, she said sadly, ruffling my hair, it's all gone. They're all dead and I have nowhere to invent stories about and nowhere to escape to.

Soon our brief Calcutta winter set in. The lakes were wonderful in that season and my grandmother took to accompanying me when I went out in the evening for my game of cricket. To my relief, she had the good sense to leave me and go off by herself once we were through the gates, but sometimes, when I was fielding at fine-leg or deep-square-leg, I would see her, a little white daub on the far side of the lake, walking briskly, stopping every once in a while to exchange a few words with the other elderly people who came to walk there in the evenings. My parents were pleased about her walks. I overheard them saying she had become easier to cope with now that she was going out of the house regularly and meeting people her own age. Soon she took to staying on in the park till long after our cricket game. I'd often look for her before going home and usually I would find her sitting on a bench, under one of the lake's huge trees, chatting with her new friends.

At dinner, my father, smiling good-humouredly, would

ask her what they had talked about: did they have any views, for instance, on the recent war with China?

Oh, we're not interested in anything as current as that, my grandmother would reply. The past is what we talk about.

It turned out that many of the elderly people who went to the park had come across the border from the east too, during or just before Partition. Most of them had settled, just as my grandmother had done, in our part of Calcutta, which was then still undeveloped. So it was not really much of a coincidence that my grandmother often ran into people she had known or heard of, in Dhaka, when she went on her walks by the lake.

On one of those evenings my father came home exhausted after a series of long meetings at his office. It was not often that he came back as tired as that, and every time it happened a pleasurable sense of crisis would invade our house. It often seemed to me later that those were the moments in their lives that my parents most looked forward to: my father because it was at that those times, tired, fussed over and cared for, that he tasted most fully and richly the subtle rewards of a life that had never strayed from convention by so much as a displaced hair; my mother because it was then that she could best display her effortless mastery of the household arts – for instance, her ability to modulate the volumes and harmonies of our house down to a whisper, while making sure that its rhythms kept ticking over, in perfect time, in much the way that a great conductor can sometimes produce, within a vast tumult of music, one perfect semibreve of silence.

On evenings like those my mother would read the tell-tale signs upon my father's drawn face as soon as he stepped out of the car. She would usher him at once to their room upstairs, and then she would come down again and tiptoe swiftly around the house: the servants would be told to turn off the transistor in the kitchen, the windows of the rooms that faced the traffic would be quickly and silently shut and I would be warned not to play with my cap guns. When silence had fallen on the house she would go back upstairs and lay out a clean, fresh kurta and a pair of pyjamas, and gently nudge him into the bathroom. While he was bathing she would hurry down again to the kitchen and make a cup of tea, exactly as he liked it, hot, sweet and milky, take it upstairs to the veranda that looked out over the garden, and put it on a table beside his easy chair. Then, when he came out, bathed and cool, she would sit beside him while he drank his tea, and talk to him in a quiet, soothing monotone about everything that had happened in the house that day.

It was on an evening such as that that my grandmother burst in upon us and cried: You'll never believe who I met in the park today!

My mother was not pleased by this intrusion, and she tried to indicate that, whatever it was, it would keep till dinner-time. But there was no stopping my grandmother.

I met Minadi, she said breathlessly. You don't know her; her family used to live down the lane from us in Dhaka. She's always up on all the news about the whole world; she's been like that since we were schoolgirls. Anyway, we were talking about this and that, catching up – it's the first time I've met her in years – and suddenly she slaps my hand and says: Do you know that your cousin, one of your Jethamoshai's sons, is living right here in Calcutta with his family? Somewhere in Garia if I'm not mistaken? Of course she knew I wouldn't know; she knows everything about everyone. But anyway, I said no, we had lost touch, I had no idea where he was; and how had she found out? She said her maidservant had mentioned the name once, a long time ago – about a year or so. So naturally, being Minadi, she'd asked her a few questions and she'd found out soon enough that it *was* him – my cousin, Jethamoshai's son. But it's lucky for me that she's such a walking daily gazette of other people's affairs, because now she's going to find out exactly where he lives so I can go and visit him.

Running out of breath she stopped to give us an eager sparkling look.

My father, at a loss to know what she wanted him to make of this, remarked mildly that after all those years they probably wouldn't even recognise each other.

My grandmother frowned. That's not important, she snapped. It doesn't matter whether we recognise each other or not. We're the same flesh, the same blood, the same bone, and now at last, after all these years, perhaps we'll be able to make amends for all that bitterness and hatred.

Then, in that particular tone of hers which nobody argued with, a voice we had not heard for some time, she said to my father: Don't forget to have the car ready on Sunday. Minadi's promised to send her maidservant to lead us to his house.

At that, my mother gave a little cry of surprise and opened her mouth to say something, but my father shook his head at her, and she sat back in silence.

It was not as though she disapproved of what my grandmother was planning to do. On the contrary, she would have done the same herself, only she would have done it sooner, because for her, relatives and family were the central points which gave the world its shape and meaning; the foundations of moral order. But my grandmother on the other hand had never pretended to have much family feeling; she had always founded her morality, schoolmistress-like, in larger and more abstract entities. On the whole, for all but a few exceptions, she was extremely wary of her relatives; to her they represented an imprisoning wall of suspicion and obligations. Usually when she spoke of them, it was to remind us that it was all very well for Uncle So-and-so to smile and grin at us whenever he saw us now, but we ought not to forget that he had been quick to turn the other way during her hard years. She chose to forget that in those years it was she who, in the fierceness of her pride, had severed her connections with most of her relatives, and had refused to accept any help from them at all, even from Mayadebi, her own sister; that she, being, as she was, too formidable a woman for people to thrust their help upon without being asked, had never had the generosity to ask of her own will. The price she had paid for that pride was that it had come to be transformed in her imagination into a barrage of slights and snubs; an imaginary barrier that she believed her gloating relatives had erected to compound her humiliation.

It was only natural that my mother was surprised at this sudden onrush of family feeling in her. Nobody had ever heard her speak of any of her relatives – not even Mayadebi, whom she loved – with the missionary warmth that she had in her voice now, while speaking of the children of a man whom her parents had hated more than anyone else in the world.

I don't know what's got into her head now, my mother said later, worriedly; but I'm sure it's nothing to do with her cousin – there's something else inside her, rattling around.

Duly on Sunday the car arrived, and soon afterwards so did the woman who was to lead us to my grandmother's cousin's house. She was dumpy and middle-aged with a large round face and prominent eyes.

What's your name? My grandmother said, looking her up and down without enthusiasm.

Mrinmoyee, said the woman, shifting a wad of paan from one cheek to the other.

Oh, 'Mrinmoyee' is it? mimicked my grandmother, thrusting her chin forward – she was always savagely cutting maidservants who had names which struck her as being pretentious for their station.

But now my father, intervening hastily, broke in to ask Mrinmoyee whether she was sure she knew exactly who we were looking for. He said the name aloud, watching her closely.

Mrinmoyee nodded, chewing slowly on her paan. Yes, she said, in a thick Noakhali accent. Yes, that's the one. Nidhu-babu they used to call him – he used to be a ticket clerk at the Shonarpur railway station near where my brother lived. But after he retired he went off to Garia.

She stopped and gave my father a long, considering look. Of course, she said, you must know that he died last year, of a pain in the chest?

My grandmother gasped and sank into a chair, stunned; but it was clear that she was less grieved than disappointed. She was silent for a while, covering her eyes with her hands. Then she stood up and announced: It doesn't matter – we'll go anyway. Maybe his wife will be able to give us some news of the rest of the family.

No, Ma, listen, my father began, but she cut him short. Yes, I've decided, she said, leading us out. Come on, let's go.

So my father reluctantly started the car and we all climbed in.

We turned off Southern Avenue at Gole Park, and found, inevitably, that the gates of the railway crossing at Dhakuria were down. We had to stew in the midday heat for half an hour before the gates were lifted again. We sped off past the open fields around the Jodhpur Club and down the tree-lined stretch of road that ran along the campus of Jadavpur University. But immediately afterwards we had to slow down to a crawl as the road grew progressively narrower and more crowded. Rows of shacks appeared on both sides of the road now, small ramshackle structures, some of them built on low stilts, with walls of plaited bamboo, and roofs that had been patched together somehow out of sheets of corrugated iron. A ragged line of concrete houses rose behind the shacks, most of them unfinished.

My grandmother, looking out of her window in amazement, exclaimed: When I last came here ten years ago, there were rice fields running alongside the road; it was the kind of place where rich Calcutta people built garden houses. And look at it now – as filthy as a babui's nest. It's all because of the refugees, flooding in like that.

Just like we did, said my father, to provoke her.

We're not refugees, snapped my grandmother, on cue. We came long before Partition.

Mrinmoyee suddenly thrust her head out of the window and pointed to a two-storey concrete building. That's the one, she said. That's where they live.

My father brought the car slowly to a halt, inching it carefully off the narrow road and on to the gravel. He opened his door to climb out, but then, glancing suspiciously at the shacks and shanties on either side of the road, he announced that he was going to stay in the car; he had heard that cars were often stripped down to their chassis in places like this.

Turning to me he said: Stay here with me. I don't want you to go up there.

There was a harsh, insistent note in his voice; I knew that he was angry with himself for having brought me there. But now I was determined to go too, so I slipped out quietly when he wasn't looking.

Mrinmoyee led us into the building and up two dark flights of stairs. We had to stop several times to make way for groups of children who went swarming past us, chasing each other up and down the staircase, their shouts and laughter booming down the stairwell. The stairs were slippery with dirt, the bare cement walls blackened with soot and wood smoke, the wiring strung up in bright festoons, the copper exposed at the joins where the insulating tape had worn off. It was a long, matchbox-like building, not large, although it was evident from the barrack-like partitions that divided its corridors that dozens of families inhabited it.

Mrinmoyee led us to a door on the second floor and called out: Anybody in? We heard feet shuffling inside, and a moment later the door swung open.

My mother and grandmother were taken aback by the appearance of the woman who stepped out. They had been expecting someone very old, with a bent back perhaps, and a face like a raisin. The woman standing in front of us was no more than middle-aged, with thick spectacles, a broad chin, and very black hair – so black, my grandmother said later, that she must have used an industrial dye.

She looked at us in surprise, recognised Mrinmoyee, and raised a puzzled eyebrow in our direction.

They wanted to meet you, Mrinmoyee said placidly, and my grandmother quickly broke in and explained that we were relatives.

The woman understood at once who we were and how we were related to her dead husband. She smiled and patted me on the head when, in response to my mother's proddings, I bowed down to touch her feet. But then she glanced at her crumpled sari and, gesturing with her thumb and forefinger, she said: Just one minute.

She disappeared inside, shutting the door behind her. When she opened it again, five minutes later, there was a thick layer of powder on her face, and she had changed into a brilliantly white nylon sari.

She ushered us into the room, apologising loudly for its smallness, the lack of chairs, explaining that she was soon going to move out, with her son, to a much bigger, better flat, it was a pity we had come at exactly this very moment, we had caught her in the middle of her packing . . .

The room was so dark there was neon light glowing inside, although it was midday. A large framed picture of Rabindranath Tagore hung on one of the walls. Under it, on a length of rope, strung up between the corners of the room, hung a dishevelled curtain of drying saris, dirty petticoats and unwashed trousers and underwear. My mother and grandmother seated themselves gingerly on the edge of a bed that was pushed up against the far wall. Our relative sat down beside them and motioned to Mrinmoyee to squat on the floor.

There was no place for me to sit, so I slipped back outside to the long, veranda-like corridor. Raising myself on tiptoe, I leant on the low railing that ran along it and looked down. I could not see the road; the corridor faced in the other direction. There weren't any more houses behind the building we were in. The ground fell away sharply from the edges of the building and then levelled out into a patchwork of stagnant pools, dotted with islands of low, raised ground. Clinging to these islands were little clumps of shanties, their beaten tin roofs glistening rustily in the midday sun. The pools were black, covered with a sludge so thick that it had defeated even the ubiquitous carpets of water hyacinth. I could see women squatting at the edges of the pools, splashing with both hands to drive back the layers of sludge, scooping up the cleaner water underneath to scrub their babies and wash their clothes and cooking utensils. There was a factory beyond, surrounded by a very high wall. I could see only its long, saw-toothed steel roof and its chimneys, thrusting up smoke that was as black as the sludge below. Running along the factory wall was a dump of some kind; small hillocks of some black and gravelly substance sloped down from it towards the sludge-encrusted pools. Shading my eyes, I saw that there were a number of moving figures dotted over those slopes. They were very small at that distance, but I could tell they had sacks slung over their shoulders. They were picking bits of rubble off the slopes and dropping them into their sacks. I could only see them when they moved; when they were still they disappeared completely – they were perfectly camouflaged, like chameleons, because everything on them, their clothes, their sacks, their skins, was the uniform matt black of the sludge in the pools.

Our relative spotted me leaning on the railing and ran out.

Don't look there! she cried. It's dirty! Then she led me back inside.

I went willingly: I was already well schooled in looking away, the jungle-craft of gentility. But still, I could not help thinking it was a waste of effort to lead me away. It was true, of course, that I could not see that landscape or anything like it from my own window, but its presence was palpable everywhere in our house; I had grown up with it. It was that landscape that lent the note of hysteria to my mother's voice when she drilled me for my examinations; it was to those slopes she pointed when she told me that if I didn't study hard I would end up over *there*, that the only weapon people like us had was our brains and if we didn't use them like claws to cling to what we'd got, that was where we'd end up, marooned in that landscape: I knew perfectly well that all it would take was a couple of failed examinations to put me where our relative was, in permanent proximity to that blackness: that landscape was the quicksand that seethed beneath the polished floors of our house; it was that sludge which gave our genteel decorum its fine edge of frenzy.

Our relative made us tea and served us Thin Arrowroot biscuits, prettily arranged in a flower pattern on a plate.

While we were sipping our tea she and my grandmother had a long conversation. She told my grandmother that her late husband had gone back to Dhaka a few years before he died in the hope that he would be able to persuade his father to move to India.

You mean he was still there then? my grandmother cried, leaning forward.

She nodded. Yes, she said. Still living in the old house.

Her husband had tried to get his brothers and sisters to go back to Dhaka with him, to bring the old man to India, but they hadn't shown much interest. They were scattered all over anyway – one of them was in Bangalore, one in the Middle East, and the other God knew where. So her husband had gone back to Dhaka alone. He had thought they might even make a little money by selling the house if their father could be persuaded to move to Calcutta. But when he went there he found that the whole house had been occupied by Muslim refugees from India – mainly people who had gone across from Bihar and U.P.

My grandmother gasped in shock.

Our house? she said. You mean our house has been occupied by refugees?

Yes, said our relative, smiling benignly. That's what I said. The house was empty after Partition, everyone had left but my father-in-law, and he didn't even try to keep the refugees out. What could he have done anyway? As soon as he got to Dhaka my husband realised that he wouldn't be able to reclaim that house – no Pakistani court was going to evict those refugees. And the old man didn't care anyway – there was a family living there who looked after him, and that was enough as far as he was concerned. He was – you know – not quite all there; he didn't really care what happened.

Poor old man, my grandmother said, her voice trembling.

Imagine what it must be like to die in another country, abandoned and alone in your old age.

Oh, he may not be dead yet, our relative said brightly. Didn't I say so?

What do you mean? said my grandmother. Are you saying he may still be alive? But he'd be over ninety . . .

Our relative smiled and bit into a Thin Arrowroot biscuit, decorously covering her mouth with the back of her hand as she chewed.

Well he was certainly alive last month, she said. He wrote to me, you see – just a postcard, but it was definitely in his handwriting. I'd written to him after my husband died, just in case, at the old address – although we hadn't heard from him in years. But that was months and months ago, and when we didn't hear from him I just thought, well . . . But then, last month, there it was, a postcard . . .

Can I see it? my grandmother said eagerly.

Our relative nodded, picked a postcard off a shelf and handed it to my grandmother.

My grandmother stared at it as it lay in her open palms, like an offering.

There's the address, she mumbled to herself; 1/31 Jindabahar Lane – it's still the same.

She had to raise her hand to wipe away the tear that was rolling down her cheek.

I can read his handwriting! she said. He's written: 'He should have stayed.'

Taking a deep breath, she handed the postcard back. Then she rose to her feet, thanked our relative and said it was time for us to go now, my father would be waiting. Our relative insisted politely that we stay a while longer, but my grandmother declined, with a smile. So then our relative said she would come down with us to see us off, and on the way down she took my mother's arm and they hung back, whispering. It was a while before they came

166

down and my father was beginning to get impatient. But before starting the car he thanked our relative profusely and asked her to visit. I turned back to look as we pulled away, and saw her, framed by the concrete doorway, waving.

What was she saying to you on the stairs? my grandmother asked my mother.

My mother laughed in a puzzled kind of way, and explained that evidently she'd known all about us, even though we'd never met her before – she'd known exactly what my father did and where we lived. She had talked about her son: he was twenty-five now and had passed his matric, but he hadn't been able to find a job. He was going to the bad, she'd said, doing nothing all day long, except hanging around the streets with gangsters. Could my father find him a job? she had begged.

Poor thing, my mother concluded. We should do something to help her.

Why? retorted my grandmother. Did anyone do anything to help me when I was living like that? Don't get taken in by these stories. Once these people start making demands it never ends. Anyway, she looks quite capable of managing by herself.

My mother kept quiet; she knew better than to argue with my grandmother on that subject.

It's not *her* I'm worried about, my grandmother said with a vehement shake of her head. I'm worried about *him*: poor old man, all by himself, abandoned in that country, surrounded by . . .

She allowed the sentence to trail away. When she spoke again we were almost home, and her voice was soft and dreamy.

There's only one worthwhile thing left for me to do in my life now, she said. And that is to bring the old man home . . .

And her eyes grew misty at the thought of rescuing her

uncle from his enemies and bringing him back where he belonged, to her invented country.

It must have been at about this time that May received her fourth letter from Tridib. She found it lying on the carpet, with the gas bill, when she got home from college and opened the front door. She knew it was from Tridib at once, because of the stamps. But apart from that it wasn't at all like the other letters she had had from him. The others had been very thin, postcards really. But she could tell from the weight of the envelope that this one was several pages long. She was mildly intrigued, but she decided to save it up for later. She took it into the kitchen, unopened, and handed her mother the gas bill. Mrs Price noticed the envelope, and May, seeing that she had noticed, mumbled something about Tridib having written again. Mrs Price nodded vaguely in acknowledgement and turned away to check the kettle.

May heard Nick's key turning in the front door and ran up to her room with the letter. They had quarrelled that morning, as usual, about the washing-up or something, and she didn't want to wear herself out by quarrelling with him again. She had to be at her best that evening: she was rehearsing in a church in Kilburn with a quintet a friend of hers had got together. She slammed the door shut, flopped down on her bed, and tore the top off the envelope with her teeth. The letter slipped out of her hands: it was even longer than she had thought.

By the time she had finished reading it her face was beaded with sweat. Raising her knuckles, she found that her cheeks were burning, almost feverish. She jumped off her bed and ran down to the bathroom. Gently, almost furtively, she shut the door behind her and leant on it to catch her breath.

He had her picture on his desk, he'd written. He liked

to have it in front of him every time he wrote to her. But it was awful having it there in a way, looking him in the face: there were so many things he wanted to write about, but every time that picture caught his eye, he found himself thinking of Lymington Road and Hampstead. But that wasn't quite right either, not really accurate. He didn't 'think' of Lymington Road; he could see it, quite clearly, as though he were there, with her, sitting under the cherry tree in the garden.

A September evening, for example, the end of a lovely day. There had only been one short Alert during the day, and that was around midday. It was twilight now, and the sun was already dipping behind the houses on the other side of West End Lane; soon he would have to go back to number 44 – soon, but not quite yet. So while there was still time he might as well go down to the corner and take a look at the house which had been hit by a bomb yesterday.

It was the block of flats on the corner of Lymington Road and West End Lane; a building called Lymington Mansions. He had always liked it, with its gables and its cheerful façade of red brick. But a lot of it was gone now, especially the upper parts: it had taken a direct hit. He could see a window flapping in the breeze on the first floor; it looked as though the whole frame were flapping on hinges. But there wasn't any rubble anywhere; it had all been cleared away.

He ought to go back to number 44 now; it was getting late . . .

On an impulse he sprinted across the road, forgetting to look to his right and left as he had been taught. And sure enough, there was a screech of rubber somewhere to his right, followed by a furious blast on a horn. He didn't dare look back till he had reached the safety of the pavement. A man with a big, red face was climbing out of a little Morris, glowering at him, shaking his fist.

He turned on his heel and ran as fast as he could, without looking back again. He didn't stop till he had crossed another big road and found a narrow deserted lane to hide in. He wasn't sure where he was, but he guessed he had run past Brondesbury Station. He had come a long way from West End Lane anyway, he was safe from the man in the Morris.

Leaning against the wall, he looked for a place to rest. There was a row of small shops running down the other side of the lane. They were all shut now. On his side there was a high wall – no, not quite a wall, it was actually the side of a large building. It was a long, blank stretch of red brick – nowhere to sit, not even a doorway. He was about to go back the way he'd come when something caught his eye – a black patch in the wall, near the end of the lane. It looked like an opening of some kind, but it wasn't a door, he could tell; it looked more like a hole.

He couldn't tell exactly what it was, so he decided to take a look.

It was exactly as he had thought – a section of the wall had been knocked out, leaving a jagged, triangular breach. There was something intriguing about the darkness and the smell of dust inside. He took a quick look up and down the lane, and when he was sure no one was looking he climbed in. There was no reason why he should not be seen climbing in, but somehow it was that kind of place.

He was inside a high, warehouse-like building. Puzzled, he looked around, trying to decide what it was. Then he saw long, curved rows of seats, all looking in the same direction, and he knew at once that it was a cinema. But now the empty seats were looking towards a hole in the wall, for a large part of the front of the building, where the screen had once hung, had been blown out – he could see two roofs through the hole. The bomb had probably exploded somewhere there, near the screen – perhaps it had looked like a part of the film. There was a deep pit in the floor there and a couple of seats were poised on its edge, crazily tilted, as though they had just tipped their occupants in.

Turning around, he saw that the gallery, projecting out over the back rows on the ground floor, was still intact. It looked as though it hadn't been damaged at all. He found himself making his way instinctively towards it; he loved to sit in the gallery when he went to see films. He was glad this hall had one; sometimes they didn't. He jumped easily over the few twisted seats that barred the aisle. There wasn't any rubble; it had been swept neatly into the corners.

The aisle led him to a door at the back of the hall. He put his ear to the door, and when he didn't hear anything on the other side, he pushed it open, gingerly. It opened into the foyer. The ticket booth was untouched – it looked as though its lights might come on any minute. He let the door go and it swung back into place, shutting out the reflected twilight. It was suddenly very dark in there. He had to feel his way along the wall towards the spot where he thought the stairs to the gallery might be. It seemed much further away than he had expected, but just when he thought he was lost, he stubbed his foot against the stairs. Going down on his hands and knees, he crawled up feeling cautiously ahead of him – he didn't relish the thought of falling through a hole in the staircase. He felt his way around a bend in the staircase and up another flight of stairs, and then he was there, right at the entrance to the gallery, and he could see again, because the twilight was shining in gently, through the hole near the screen. The gallery was undamaged, untouched; it sloped gently away from him, the blue upholstery of the seats shimmering, like velvet, in the twilight. He fell into one of the seats, and tried to fold himself up in it – it was fun doing that in cinemas; sometimes he could even touch his nose with his knees. But today he didn't try; instead he leant back and looked up. It was oddly exhilarating to sit back in a plush seat in a cinema and find a twilit sky looking down on you.

He got up, went down to the bottom of the gallery, lay on his stomach, and peered through the gaps in the wrought-iron balustrade. The twisted seats below looked odd from up there – like plants curling up towards the sunlight. He turned his head and found that he could see the pavement through the breach in the wall that had let him in.

As he lay there, looking out at the road, whistling through his teeth, a shadow crossed the breach in the outer wall. Startled, he stopped whistling and watched warily, ready to run. A woman in a blue skirt went by and then, a moment later, came back again and stood still, framed by the jagged arch in the wall. She glanced down at her feet in irritation, and following the direction of her gaze he saw that she was holding a small white and tan spaniel on a lead. It had stopped to shit on the pavement. The woman made a face, reached into her handbag, took out a cigarette, and lit it. She drew on it hard, sucking in her cheeks, and then, throwing her head back, she let the smoke curl gently out of her nostrils.

And then, while she was drawing on her cigarette again, another pair of feet appeared, a man's this time, on the pavement on the other side of the lane – though from his vantage point they seemed to be hanging at the top of the arch-like breach, like a cloud in a painting. The feet came to a halt, seemed to hesitate and then turned and crossed the lane. Now he could see the man: he was wearing a blue uniform and a cap, obviously an airman of some kind, maybe even a pilot. He had a thin moustache and there was an unlit cigarette in his mouth.

The woman turned away quickly when she saw the man

walking towards her. She tugged at the dog's leash but it would not move; it ground its heels into the pavement and began to whine. The man paid no notice. He went up to it, bent down to give it a pat on its head, and then straightened up again, smiling, and said something to the woman, gesturing at his unlit cigarette. The woman nodded, and reaching into her handbag she took out her lighter and handed it to him. The man lit his cigarette, cupping his hands around the flame, and gave it back to her. Then he took the cigarette out of his mouth, grinned, and said something into her ear, nodding in the direction of the breach in the cinema's wall. At first the woman's head snapped back and she opened her mouth in outraged surprise. But then she looked at him again, properly, and her face softened. She tossed her head, still looking at him, and giggled. The man in the uniform laughed and slipped his arm through hers. She picked up the dog, and with a quick glance up the lane they stepped through the breach.

Once they were in they looked around for a moment, blinded, their eyes searching the darkness. The boy got a good look at their faces now. Her face was very white, her lips a brilliant red; he was much taller than her and heavily built, but she looked much older than him.

The man put an arm around her waist and pointed, down the aisle, to a spot almost directly below the boy. She giggled again, and shook her head, but she let him take her elbow and lead her forward. She was wearing high heels and she kept stumbling on the tattered carpet and twisted chairs in the aisle, but the man seemed to know his way around the hall, and he managed to keep her from falling.

By the time they reached the clean patch in the carpeted aisle, below the boy, they were both breathing heavily. The man let go of her arm suddenly, spun her around and gave her a kiss on the middle of her forehead. He took the dog out of her hands, put it down on a seat, and twisted its lead around the armrest.

Then he spun around, and at once the woman caught hold of his collar and pulled his head down towards hers and pushed her mouth up against his. She was clasping his head so hard her knuckles were white with the effort. But the man managed to jerk his head away, and then, smiling, he worked one of his hands free, holding her pinned to his chest with the other, and reached down and tugged at her skirt. Parting her legs the woman rose on tiptoe, pushing her lips against his ears. He laughed and raised her a few inches off the ground with a great heave of his shoulders, and pushed his hand gently up her thighs and into her skirt. The woman pecked at his ear, and in response he pushed his hand all the way up her skirt and held it there. She gave a tiny scream, clenching her teeth, and the small of her back began to twitch. The man let her down then, pulled his hand out of her skirt and lifted it to his nose, rubbing his fingers together. He sniffed the tips of his fingers, smiling, and then held them against her nose. She turned her head away with a grimace, so he kissed his fingertips and laughed. She began to laugh with him too, and he pulled her towards him and thrust his mouth down on hers, and she, squeezing a hand between their bodies, contrived to push it under his belt and into his trousers. His shoulders snapped back, and he took hold of her arm for a moment and held it where it was, inside his trousers. Then he stepped back, loosened his belt, put an arm around her shoulders and lowered her to the floor.

Suddenly the dog began to bark. It was a shrill, ugly sound. The boy looked quickly up at the breach in the wall and saw a man in a black hat walking past. The man in the hat stopped when he heard the dog, and peered in. Now the boy was frightened for the man in the uniform and the woman in the blue skirt; he wished they would stop the dog barking.

The woman sat up and gave the dog a slap on its nose. It whined and stopped barking, and the man in the black hat shook his head and went away.

The woman was in a hurry now; the boy could tell from the sound of her breathing. She reached quickly for the bottom of her pullover and pulled it over her shoulders along with her blouse. Then she sat up briefly, reached behind, and suddenly her brassière fell away. Her breasts were heavy and full, reaching down half-way to her stomach, the skin very pale and a little wrinkled, as though she had just spent hours in the sea. The boy could see the nipples; they were brown and round, like the tuppenny pieces he took to the newsagent's every morning. In the centre they were hard and pointed, and very dark, like raisins; he longed to reach down and touch them and roll them between his fingers.

The man in the uniform put his hands on them and the woman's body seemed to shiver, and her torso arched upwards. She wasn't smiling any more; she was sweating, and the drops were carving furrows in the white make-up on her face.

She undid the clasps of her skirt and the man pulled it off. Then he pulled off her white underwear too, put his hand on the damp shadow between her legs and ran his thumb over it, gently, smiling. She groaned and thrust her hips against his body, but she was cold now, her breasts and stomach were dotted with goosepimples, and she tried to pull him quickly down on top of her. But he twisted out of her reach and sat back, balancing on his toes and knees, and pushed his trousers down, to his ankles.

The woman reached out towards the man, and looking down, at her outstretched arms, it seemed to the boy that she was reaching for him, and suddenly he found himself

175

writing, his pelvis pinned against the wooden floor of the gallery.

When he looked down again, the man was on top of her, his hips between her parted thighs. He was still wearing his cap and his jacket, only his buttocks were bare. The boy could see the sweat rolling down the sides, beading the line of dark hair that divided them.

Then the dog began to bark again, and the boy quickly looked up at the breach. There were two pairs of feet walking past this time, on the other side of the lane. He held his breath, wondering whether there was any chance of their not hearing the dog, or the noise the two of them were making. The sounds of their lovemaking seemed impossibly loud now, a fierce, panting kind of sound, along with the rhythmic, sweaty slapping of their bodies. He could feel his knees trembling, with apprehension, with a longing that he couldn't understand, and with a fierce, bursting pain that was running through his body and gathering in his groin. But he knew that he didn't want them to be found by those other people outside; he knew he was on their side. He wished he could think of a way of warning them.

The two pairs of feet on the pavement went away, without stopping, and the boy was so glad, for them, and himself, that he almost giggled. And then, down below, he heard the man choke while his whole body went rigid. Then the woman screamed, very softly, and her feet kicked the air, and her back rose off the floor, lifting the man.

The boy got to his feet quietly then, and managed to slip out without being seen.

May splashed water on her face and watched herself as it dripped into the basin.

It was all so long ago, the letter had said, that he didn't know any longer whether it had really happened or he had imagined it.

But he did know that that was how he wanted to meet her, May – as a stranger, in a ruin. He wanted them to meet as the completest of strangers – strangers-across-the-seas – all the more strangers because they knew each other already. He wanted them to meet far from their friends and relatives – in a place without a past, without history, free, really free, two people coming together with the utter freedom of strangers.

But of course, if that was to happen, she would have to come to India. They would find a place like that some-where; he was an expert on ruins.

May seated herself on the rim of the bathtub and touched her face again – it was still hot.

It was hot because she was angry, she decided. And no wonder she was angry – anyone would be if they'd got a pornographic letter from a man they'd never met, would never meet. She was shaking now, with anger: what right had he to write to her like that? Really, what right? It was an intrusion, a violation of her privacy; that was why she was trembling. It was like seeing a flasher. It was incred-ible, mad; only a madman would think of writing a letter like that.

She heard Nick running up the stairs, past the bath-room, going into his room. Every sound in the house seemed to carry into the bathroom with an unnatural clarity – she told herself that she ought to remind her mother to do something about it; it wasn't right in a house like theirs, not decent, really . . .

She opened the bathroom door and went back to her room. Stuffing the letter back into its envelope, she tucked it away under her clothes, in a drawer. Then she fell on her bed and began to wonder why she had bothered to hide it. It wasn't any fault of hers if someone she didn't know wrote her a pornographic letter. Why shouldn't her mother find it? It was her fault as much as anybody else's.

She glanced at her watch and saw that it was time to leave for her rehearsal. On her way out she went into the drawing room to tell her mother she was going out and would be back late for dinner.

Mrs Price was sitting in an armchair, reading. She took off her spectacles to look at May, nodded, and said absently: Don't be too late, will you, dear.

Of course not, May answered. You know I won't.

She had turned to go when Mrs Price said: Oh yes, and what did Tridib have to say in his letter?

Before she knew it, May found herself saying: Oh, nothing very much. He's invited me to visit India.

Mrs Price smiled, looking mistily up from her book. Yes, she said. It's a good idea, you ought to go.

May gave her a quick smile and hurried out of the house. It was only when she was walking down Lymington Road that she found herself wondering why she had bothered to lie to her mother when she had promised to herself that she wouldn't.

The rehearsal seemed to go on for ever.

Afterwards, while they were drinking tea, the clarinettist, who was doing research on something to do with modern French music, talked about Messiaen and the Indian influences on his music. She was surprised; she'd thought it was all bird-calls and stuff like that. It seemed eerily coincidental somehow.

Later, on her way home, walking down the Kilburn High Road, she caught herself thinking about Messiaen again. She didn't have anything of his at home; perhaps she could drop into a record shop tomorrow and have a look.

A little farther down the road, waiting to cross the street, she found herself dawdling outside an Indian restaurant. The Taj Mahal Curry Palace. It had a picture of the Taj Mahal in the window. Staring at it, she found herself wondering whether her mother wasn't right after all –

perhaps it wouldn't be such a bad idea. There was the Messiaen to find out about; nothing to do with Tridib.

She touched her face and found that it was hot again. She turned abruptly, and hurried across the road.

My father, who was a boyish sort of man in some ways, used to take a great delight in carrying good news to people. Like a child with a bar of chocolate, he would draw out the pleasure by asking teasing questions or by pretending that he had forgotten the news, and then, suddenly, he would spring his surprise and lean back to savour the moment, rubbing his hands. That moment would give him so much pleasure that sometimes, in his eagerness to savour it, he would fail to distinguish between news that was really good and that which was merely unexpected.

One evening in March 1963, he came home from work with that unmistakable look of mischief and anticipated pleasure written large on his face. My mother noticed it when she took him his cup of tea. She asked him what the matter was, but he shook his head, smiling enigmatically, and told us to wait – we would find out at dinner.

My grandmother was late for dinner that evening. She was out walking in the park. I could sense my father's growing impatience as we sat out in the garden, waiting for her to come back so that we could go in and eat our dinner. When at last he heard the creak of the gate and saw her walking up the path, he leapt out of his chair and began to scold her: she oughtn't to stay out in the park so late, and didn't she know it wasn't safe, and so on. My grandmother was taken aback. And didn't *he* know, she retorted, that she hadn't been born yesterday?

By the time we were sitting around the dinner table, my father was too impatient to play his usual guessing games.

I have some news for you, he said to my grandmother.

News? said my grandmother apprehensively. What news?

Rubbing his hands together, my father told her that the Shaheb had been given a new posting and a promotion – one of the most challenging assignments in his profession.

My grandmother snorted and reached for the dal.

Impossible, she said with a little toss of her head.

Why? My father was indignant.

Who would promote *him*? my grandmother said, her profile growing spiky with contempt. He drinks; he's a drunkard.

My father shook his head furiously and said she had no idea what she was talking about; the Shaheb wasn't a drunkard at all – he just had the occasional drink, and that was only normal in his line of business. It was well known that he was an extremely competent man, and if he hadn't risen quite as high as he should have, it was only because certain cliques in his ministry were trying to do him down. It had nothing whatever to do with drink; she was wholly mistaken. And so on.

But it was apparent from my grandmother's face that she was not persuaded by my father's arguments. That wasn't surprising, for my grandmother's contempt for the Shaheb had nothing to do with drink at all, as my father thought: it was founded on the same iron fairness which prompted her, when she became headmistress, to dismiss one of her closest friends – a good-natured but chronically lazy woman – from her job in the school: at bottom she thought the Shaheb was not fit for his job, that he was weak, essentially weak, backbone-less; it was impossible to think of him being firm under threat, of reacting to a difficult or dangerous situation with that controlled, accurate violence which was the quality she prized above all others in men who had to deal with matters of state. She knew instinctively that it was Mayadebi who took his decisions, who virtually did his work for him, who had politicked and manoeuvred with all her resources to salvage something of his career, and therefore, imagining him to be nothing but a dim irradiation of her sister, she could not help being a little contemptuous of him.

It was not that she disliked the Shaheb: she merely distrusted and despised him in a mildly amused sort of way, and she would have done neither, as she often said, if he were only doing something else, something less important, though what that something was I was never sure, for she certainly would not have been any more tolerant of him had he been a schoolteacher or even a revenue inspector: perhaps she would have liked him best if he had been a hotelier, or maybe an artist, for professions such as those were synonymous in her mind with the most detestable kind of cosmopolitanism.

My father spent a good half-hour trying doggedly to persuade her that the Shaheb was a very able man and deserved to be at the top of his profession. When he finally gave up, my grandmother said quietly: You still haven't told me where he's been posted.

My father slapped his forehead. Oh yes, he cried. I forgot that was the real news.

Why? said my grandmother. Where is he going?

You wouldn't ever be able to guess, my father said.

Where is it?

Not far from here, he said, his eyes twinkling mischievously.

My grandmother thrust her plate away. She seemed disturbed now, possibly even a little frightened.

Where? she pleaded. Tell me.

He's going to Dhaka, my father announced triumphantly. He's been made Councillor in the Deputy High Commission there.

My grandmother gave him a long, blank stare, then she pushed her chair back and went slowly up to her room.

When I followed her up a little later I found that she had locked the door.

Nobody mentioned Dhaka again to her over the next few days, but once I heard my mother saying wistfully to my father that it *would* be nice if she went off to Dhaka for a holiday – it would give everyone a rest.

A week later there was a letter for my grandmother. It was from Mayadebi. My father turned it over and he and my mother exchanged glances. Then he handed the letter to me and told me to take it up to my grandmother's room.

I sprinted up the stairs and into her room, waving the envelope like a flag: Tha'mma, Tha'mma, there's a letter for you.

Her forehead wrinkled into a frown of anxious expectation, and she touched her gold chain before she took the letter from me. I sat down to watch her, while she put on her spectacles and tore open the envelope. But she happened to look up and see me, and she put the letter down and told me firmly to leave the room.

At dinner that evening my parents were careful not to mention the letter. For a while my grandmother talked nervously about politics, the state of education, the Prime Minister's speech in Parliament and so on. And then, without a pause, in the same flat voice, she said: Maya's invited me to visit her in Dhaka.

My parents looked up, smiling, and my father sighed and said: Yes, of course, I knew she would.

My grandmother was chewing her lip now and looking down at her plate. Softly, she said: I don't know if I should go.

My parents exchanged an astonished glance.

Of course you must go, Ma, my father said.

Why, said my mother, even a few months ago you were saying that it was the one thing you really wanted to do.

I know, my grandmother said uncertainly. But now . . . .

I don't know. I feel scared. Do you think it will be wise after all these years? It won't be like home any more.

The cham-chams and all the other sweets will be the same, my mother said encouragingly. And so will all the fish. And there'll be all those lovely Dhakai saris to buy.

And imagine, added my father, you'll get to fly in an aeroplane for the first time. It'll be a lovely holiday.

This stung my grandmother. Glaring at my father, she said: If I go it won't be for a holiday. You ought to know I don't believe in luxuries like that. I haven't taken a holiday all my life and I'm not going to start now. If I go it will be for the sake of Jethamoshai. Since I am the only person in the family who cares, it is my duty to see if I can bring the poor old man back.

So you *are* going then? my mother asked anxiously.

At that my grandmother's uncertainty returned. I don't know, she said. I really don't know . . .

Over the next few months my parents tried often to push her gently to make up her mind. But every time they brought up the subject my grandmother would either shake her head or simply get up and leave the room.

Then, in June, after three months had passed, our phone rang late one evening. My father happened to answer it. He listened, and then told me to fetch my grandmother – it was a trunk call for her from Delhi. From Mayadebi.

A trunk call from another city was a very exciting matter: a kind of minor miracle, but also cause for anxiety until one found out whether the news was good or bad. I ran up the stairs so fast that when I got to her room I was too breathless to explain. Instead I simply grabbed her hand and dragged her down the stairs.

My parents and I hovered around as she stuck a trembling finger in one ear and raised the instrument to the other. We heard her say: Yes, yes, I don't know, I can't make up my mind, when are you leaving? There was a short pause as she listened to Mayadebi. Then, at the top of her voice, she began to explain that their uncle was still alive, still living, in Dhaka, in their old house; that she, Maya, must go and look him up as soon as she reached Dhaka, something had to be done about bringing him to India . . . She ran out of breath and listened again, for a bit. I don't know, she said in response to a question. No, really, I can't decide – it's not for myself, I'm worrying about Jethamoshai. Then again she listened, smiling now, and at last she said: All right, I'll come, I give you my word.

Mayadebi, the Shaheb and Robi had flown into Delhi last week, she explained to my parents after she had put the phone down. They were leaving for Dhaka a couple of days later – they weren't going to be able to stop in Calcutta – they didn't have enough time.

But are you going to Dhaka too? my father said. That's the important thing.

My grandmother shrugged helplessly. What else can I do? she said. It's out of my hands now; everything seems to be pointing in that direction.

When will you go then?

If I go, she said, it will have to be in January next year. I must give them some time to settle down in their new house.

A few weeks later, at dinner, my father, grinning hugely, pushed an envelope across the table to my grandmother. That's for you, he said.

What is it? she said, eyeing it suspiciously.

Go on, he said. Have a look.

She picked it up, opened the flap and peered into it. I can't tell, she said. What is it?

My father burst into laughter. It's your plane ticket, he said. For Dhaka – for the third of January, 1964.

That night, for the first time in months, my grandmother seemed really excited. When I went up to see her, before going to bed, I found her pacing around the room, her face flushed, her eyes shining. I was delighted. It was the first time in my eleven-year-old life that she had presented me with a response that I could fully understand – since I had never been on a plane myself, it seemed the most natural thing in the world to me that the prospect of her first flight should fill her with excitement. But I couldn't help worrying about her too, for I also knew that, unlike me, she was totally ignorant about aeroplanes, and before I fell asleep that night I resolved that I would make sure that she was properly prepared before she left. But soon enough it was apparent to me that it wasn't going to be easy to educate her: I could tell from the direction of the questions she asked my father that, left to herself, she would learn nothing about aeroplanes.

For instance, one evening when we were sitting out in the garden she wanted to know whether she would be able to see the border between India and East Pakistan from the plane. When my father laughed and said, why, did she really think the border was a long black line with green on one side and scarlet on the other, like it was in a school atlas, she was not so much offended as puzzled.

No, that wasn't what I meant, she said. Of course not. But surely there's something – trenches perhaps, or soldiers, or guns pointing at each other, or even just barren strips of land. Don't they call it no-man's land?

My father was already an experienced traveller. He burst out laughing and said: No, you won't be able to see anything except clouds and perhaps, if you're lucky, some green fields.

His laughter nettled her. Be serious, she snapped. Don't talk to me as though I were a secretary in your office.

Now it was his turn to be offended: it upset him when she spoke sharply to him within my hearing.

That's all I can tell you, he said. That's all there is.

My grandmother thought this over for a while, and then

she said: But if there aren't any trenches or anything, how are people to know? I mean, where's the difference then? And if there's no difference, both sides will be the same; it'll be just like it used to be before, when we used to catch a train in Dhaka and get off in Calcutta the next day without anybody stopping us. What was it all for then – Partition and all the killing and everything – if there isn't something in between?

I don't know what you expect, Ma, my father retorted in exasperation. It's not as though you're flying over the Himalayas into China. This is the modern world. The border isn't on the frontier: it's right inside the airport. You'll see. You'll cross it when you have to fill in all those disembarkation cards and things.

My grandmother shifted nervously in her chair. What forms? she said. What do they want to know about on those forms?

My father scratched his forehead. Let me see, he said. They want your nationality, your date of birth, place of birth, that kind of thing.

My grandmother's eyes widened and she slumped back in her chair.

What's the matter? my father said in alarm.

With an effort she sat up straight again and smoothed back her hair. Nothing, she said, shaking her head. Nothing at all.

I could see then that she was going to end up in a hope-less mess, so I took it upon myself to ask my father for all the essential information about flying and aeroplanes that I thought she ought to have at her command – I was sure, for example, that she would roll the windows down in mid-air unless I warned her not to.

It was not till many years later that I realised it had suddenly occurred to her then that she would have to fill in 'Dhaka' as her place of birth on that form, and that the prospect of this had worried her in the same way that dirty schoolbooks worried her – because she liked things to be neat and in place – and at that moment she had not been able quite to understand how her place of birth had come to be so messily at odds with her nationality.

My father could see that she was worrying over something. But Ma, he said, teasing her; why are you so worried about this little journey? You've been travelling between countries for years. Don't you remember – all those trips you made in and out of Burma?

Oh *that*, my grandmother laughed. It wasn't the same thing. There weren't any forms or anything, and anyway travelling was so easy then. I could come home to Dhaka whenever I wanted.

I jumped to my feet, delighted at having caught her out – she, who'd been a schoolmistress for twenty-seven years.

Tha'mma, Tha'mma! I cried. How could you have 'come' home to Dhaka? You don't know the difference between coming and going!

I teased her with that phrase for years afterwards. If she happened to say she was going to teach me Bengali grammar, for example, I would laugh and say: But Tha'mma, how can you teach me grammar? You don't know the difference between coming and going. Eventually the phrase passed on to the whole family and became a part of its secret lore; a barb in that fence we built to shut ourselves off from others. So, for instance, when we were in our teens, often, when Ila was in Calcutta and we happened to meet an acquaintance who asked: When are you going back to London? we would launch into a kind of patter: But she has to go to Calcutta first; Not if I'm coming to London; Nor if you're coming to Calcutta . . . And at the end of it, sobbing hysterically with a laughter which must have seemed as affected as it was inexplicable to those who heard it, I would say: You see, in our family we don't know whether we're coming or going – it's all my grandmother's fault. But, of course, the fault wasn't hers at all: it lay in language. Every language assumes a centrality, a fixed and settled point to go away from and come back to, and what my grandmother was looking for was a word for a journey which was not a coming or a going at all; a journey that was a search for precisely that fixed point which permits the proper use of verbs of movement.

In November, when my grandmother was already busy with her preparations for the trip, there was another bit of news. Mayadebi had written to say that May, her old friend Elisabeth's daughter, was coming to India for a holiday in December. She would be going to Delhi and Agra first, and then to Calcutta, where she would spend a few days before flying out to Dhaka with my grandmother. Mayadebi wanted to know whether she could stay with us while she was in Calcutta – she was sure she would be better looked after in our house than she would be in theirs in Ballygunge Place where Tridib's bedridden grandmother did the house-keeping.

My grandmother handed the letter to my father, and he wrote at once to say that we would be glad to have May.

A fortnight later Tridib came to see us. He made a little desultory conversation with my parents, and then he announced that he would be going to Dhaka too, with May and my grandmother.

It seems a good time to go, he said, since everyone is going.

Then he turned to me and said: I'm going to receive May at the station when she gets here, ten days from now. Would you like to come too?

The first time May and I talked about her visit to Calcutta was on the day after Ila's wedding.

The London part of Ila's wedding was very simple: she and Nick signed a register somewhere, and in the evening Mrs Price invited a few people to dinner, including me. Nick and Ila were to leave for Calcutta the next day. Nick had decided that it would be fun to have a 'proper' Hindu wedding. The preparations were already under way in Calcutta: my mother told me on the phone that it promised to be one of the most lavish weddings she had ever seen. Ila's parents were in Calcutta making the arrangements. They had stopped by in London on their way back from Tanzania because Ila's father had decided to buy them a flat in London as a wedding present. Since he had never had a very high opinion of Ila's judgement in practical matters, he'd wanted to take a look at the house himself before buying it. Nick had done a lot of preliminary research, and eventually they had settled on a two-bedroom flat on Clapham Common. Nick was very happy with it, and in fact so was Ila, although she claimed to be indifferent. Since Ila was working and could not spare the time, Nick had bought curtains and furniture and set up the flat so that they would have a place to move into as soon as they returned from their honeymoon. They were planning to go to Africa for their honeymoon; they were going to spend a week or so with Ila's parents in Dar-es-Salaam, and after that they were going to drive around Kenya and Tanzania in Ila's father's car.

I remember very little of that evening at Mrs Price's house. I remember I was carrying a present. It was a minute silver salt cellar which I had wrapped in coloured paper. I had bought it in an English shop of the kind which has a black signboard with very precise Times Roman lettering and a little gold monogram which says: By appointment to . . . It was the cheapest thing in the shop, although it had cost all of twenty pounds – every penny I had saved in my six months in England. And I almost lost it on the way to Mrs Price's house.

I arrived early at the West Hampstead tube station, so I found a pub and bought myself a half-pint of beer, to pass the time. But then I got into a conversation with a Lebanese journalist; we bought a few rounds of beer for each other and when next I looked at my watch I discovered I was more than an hour late. I jumped to my feet, rushed out of the pub and began to run towards Lymington Road. I had not gone far when I heard the sound of feet pounding heavily after me. Looking around, I saw the Lebanese journalist panting up the road, waving. I stopped, and when he caught up with me he dropped the little paper-covered object into my hand and said: It had rolled into the ashtray.

Ila was very amused when I handed it to her. What is it? she said. Let me guess – it's a miniature tiepin studded with diamonds; or, no, it's a gold plate for feeding pet ants; or, yes, I know, it's a thimble for a baby's little finger . . .

Someone else came in and she turned away. I leant against a wall and watched her. She was smiling radiantly; laughing that wonderful tinkling laugh of hers as she spun around the room in a blaze of crimson silk, talking to her guests. I had never seen her as happy as she was that evening.

After a while May handed me a glass of wine and led me into the drawing room. It was full of people I didn't know. May started to say something, but there was a crisis in the kitchen and someone called her away. I found another glass of wine, sank into an armchair and shut my eyes.

Then, dimly, I heard May saying: Wake up, wake up, it's time to go home now, and I felt her hand on my arm. When I opened my eyes, she was looking anxiously down at me. There was no one else in the room.

I started groggily to my feet. I tried to speak but my throat felt like sandpaper and my voice had gone hoarse. Where's Ila? I managed to say. Where is she?

May laid a steadying hand on my shoulder. Ila's gone home with Nick, she said. They've got to pack – for tomorrow. And Mother's gone to bed, and I'm about to go home myself.

I fell back into the armchair, biting my knuckles: I knew I had meant to say something to Ila before she left, I had been rehearsing it in my mind for days, but now I couldn't remember what it was.

What will you do? May said.

I'd better get back to Fulham, I said, struggling to my feet.

May watched me quietly, arms folded across her chest, as I fetched my coat and scarf. When I said goodbye to her, she answered drily: I'm not wholly persuaded that it would be wise for you to go home right now, given your present condition.

Holding on to the mantelpiece, I said: I'm fine, really.

I have a plan which is in some respects superior to yours, she said, smiling. I think you should come home to Islington with me. I could make up a bed for you and give you something to eat. And tomorrow morning you can wend your way home, a renewed son of Bengal. I do beseech you to give this possibility some consideration, because you'll only waste my morning if you try to make your way to Fulham right now – I'll have to spend hours tomorrow, ringing all the hospitals to make sure you haven't ended up in one of them.

I felt I ought to offer some counter-argument, but I found, to my relief, that I couldn't think of any.

All right, I said. I'll do as you say – if you're sure it won't mean too much trouble for you.

Good, she said. I'm glad you've decided to be sensible.

Since we had already missed the last tube, May decided to ring for a radio cab. It arrived within a few minutes, and she led me out of the house, locking the door behind her.

Once we were in the cab, I found myself breathing hard, my throat constricted by the kind of breathlessness that precedes hysteria. I rolled the window down and stuck my head out of it. The air was cold, sharp with the smell of vinegared chips and fish frying in a late-night takeaway. My ears went numb and my eyes began to water, but the sting of the air woke me; my body began to tingle the way it did after a mustard-oil massage on a winter morning: I could feel the skin, the hair, on my scrotum and my thighs, coming alive. It was as though a part of my body had discovered, in my drunkenness, a means of pricking me on to look for a means of mourning Ila's marriage.

I felt a touch on my arm; May was looking at me, anxiously. Are you all right? she said. Shall I tell him to stop?

No – I shook my head. Then I picked her hand off my arm and rubbed it between mine.

Well, well, she said drily, drawing her hand back.

I leant across, slipped my arm around her shoulder and kissed her, running the tip of my tongue over her earlobe.

For a moment she was too startled to speak; then she gasped and her body went rigid. She put her hands on my chest and pushed me back.

You're stinking of drink, she said, grimacing. I hope you're not going to make any trouble.

I caught the driver's eye in the mirror. He was a young West Indian. He was watching me, his eyes flicking from the road to the mirror and back again, expressionless. His hand snaked out to the dashboard when he caught my glance. He toyed with something and let it fall back with a clink. It was a knuckleduster: he smiled when he next caught my eye.

By the time we reached her house May was worried; I could tell from the awkwardness of her gestures as she paid off the driver. But I was merely curious; it didn't occur to me that she was afraid, and that her fear might have had something to do with me.

Please don't make a noise going up the stairs, she said, spacing the words out, speaking slowly. The landlady gets *very* annoyed if she's woken up.

I'll be quiet, I said. I reached out and ran a finger through her hair.

Stop that! she cried, jerking her head away. What do you think you're doing?

Shh! I said. You'll wake the landlady.

She tiptoed up the stairs, opened her door, and shut it quickly behind me.

Now you go over there, she said, pointing to her bed. Get into bed and go to sleep at once. I'm afraid I can't give you anything to change into, so you'll have to go to bed as you are.

At once? I said, grinning. I know you don't mean that; not really. Please, she said. Her voice was hoarse now. *Please* go to bed.

I turned to look at the bed: it was small and narrow, piled high with quilts and blankets and covered with a green bedspread.

All of a sudden, an idea occurred to me.

But if *I* sleep over there? I said, with drunken cunning. Where will *you* sleep?

I'll be all right, she said quickly. Don't worry about me.

But I can't *help* worrying about you, I said. Where *will* you sleep?

She went over to the bed and drew the covers back.

193

It was perfectly made up, with clean new sheets and pillowcases, but it looked curiously unused. There were sachets of pot-pourri under the quilts, and the sheets smelt mustily of lavender and roses.

I don't sleep on the bed anyway, she said, picking out the sachets of pot-pourri.

Oh really? I said. So if you don't sleep here, whose bed do you sleep in?

She flashed me a quick, bright glance. I sleep over *there*, she said, pointing across the room, at the floor.

Where? I said.

Without answering, she opened a cupboard and took out a thin mattress, a couple of blankets and a sheet, and carried them across the room. Kneeling, she unrolled the mattress and spread it out on the floor. It was very thin; not much more than a sheet.

You *can't* sleep there, I said in astonishment. I don't believe you do. Why've you got a bed then?

Oh, that, she said. That's for people to see – so that they won't think me odd.

But you don't even have a pillow, I said.

No, she said wryly. That was the hardest bit to get used to.

Why do you do it? I said. It must be horrible sleeping down there.

It's not too bad, she said briskly. 'No big deal' as they say on television. After all, this is how most people in the world sleep. I merely thought I'd throw in my lot with the majority.

She sprang up and dusted her hands. All right, she said. Now go to bed – please.

Can I mortify my flesh too? I said. Can I sleep over there with you?

She began to laugh, the tension draining out of her face. You're going to feel really stupid about all this tomorrow morning, she said. I'm longing to see the look on your face when I remind you.

Please May, I said.

You idiot, she said, laughing. You're just drunk; you don't really want to – I'm old enough to be your spinster aunt.

I do, I said. I really do.

Well, we'll see if you can bring yourself to say that when you're sober, she said. And as for now, you'll just have to go without, won't you?

She pushed me gently towards the bed. Now, please go to bed, she said.

You're laughing at me, I said, knocking her hand away. You shouldn't laugh at me.

I reached out, took her face in my hands and pulled her towards me.

Please don't, she said, her eyes widening with fear. Please.

Why not? I said. I kissed her on her open mouth, and slid my right hand quickly down her neck, into her blouse and under the strap of her brassière.

Stop! she cried, clawing at my face.

Why? I said. I pinned her against my body with my left hand, holding her tight, so that she couldn't get her hands free. My right hand was deep inside her dress now, cupped around her breast.

With a tremendous effort, teeth clenched, she squirmed out of my grasp, threw herself backwards, and fell on the mattress. There was a ripping sound as her dress tore open and I was left clutching the air. When I looked down at her, she was crouching on the mattress, and her breast was hanging down, out of the rent in her dress, flapping against her ribs.

You bastard! she screamed. She flew off the bed and across the room and suddenly the lights went out. I heard her going across the room, to the bathroom, and I slunk over to the bed and crept in. I was asleep within a moment.

When I woke up next morning my head was throbbing and my mouth tasted of sour bile. I could hear plates rattling in the kitchen. I raised my head and saw May standing at the wash basin; she had changed into a pair of faded brown corduroy jeans and a white pullover, and her grey-streaked hair was tied in a ponytail with a rubber band. Her mattress and blankets were neatly rolled up, standing in a corner.

I was about to call out to her when an image of her, crouching on the mattress, trying to shield her naked breast, flickered before my eyes. I fell back on the pillow and shut my eyes, and slowly everything I had done and said the night before came back to me, in minute, ghastly detail.

She must have known I was awake; seen the sweat on my face. I heard her voice, low and gravelly, above me, saying: Well? Do you think you're ready to eat something now?

When I opened my eyes, she was looking down at me, her face calm, grave.

May . . . I began. I could not look at her; I let my head fall.

Yes? she said coolly. I knew she was waiting.

I don't know how . . . I began again. I raised my head with an effort; she was still looking at me, her gaze steady, unwavering.

I'm afraid you'll have to think of some way of saying it, she said. That's absolutely the very least I expect.

I'm sorry, I said. What else can I say? Is there anything I can do to show you how sorry I am?

She was still looking at me steadily, but now there was a twitch at the corner of her mouth.

Not feeling quite such a he-man now, may we surmise? she said.

Yes.

Her lips twisted into a smile and she stretched out a hand and rapped me on the back of my head.

Go on, she said. Get out of bed and wash your face. Then I'll see about making you some breakfast.

By the time I was out of the bathroom, a plate of fried eggs and toast and a glass of orange juice were waiting for me on her table. I was very hungry now; I remembered I had eaten nothing the night before. But May was still busy in the kitchen so I stood behind a chair and waited.

Don't wait for me, she called out. Go on – eat. You must be hungry after all your exertions.

But what about you? I said awkwardly. Aren't you going to have any breakfast?

I wouldn't worry about that if I were you, she said. In fact, if I were you, I would address myself to the toast and eggs before they get cold and squishy. The bread is that wholewheat stuff we're told we ought to eat nowadays – the trouble is it transmutes itself back into dough if it's left to itself for more than a minute.

Without another word, I sat down and began to eat. Soon, she finished putting away her plates and stood leaning on the wall, watching me eat.

Some more toast? she said.

Yes, I said. But what about you? Aren't you going to eat anything?

She handed me another slice and shook her head.

Have you had your breakfast already then?

No.

I was puzzled now. So then? I said.

I'm not going to eat any breakfast today, she said.

Why not?

She laughed. Evidently, she said, in Calcutta they don't know the old adage about curiosity and cats. The answer to your question is: I'm not going to eat any breakfast today because this is a Saturday.

What does that mean? I said, mystified.

I don't eat anything on Saturdays, she said. It's what you might call my fast day.

Your fast day? I said. Do you mean you fast every Saturday?

She nodded: That is exactly what I mean. But why? I said.

This is beginning to sound like a catechism, she said. Well, I fast because it occurred to me a few years ago that it might not be an entirely bad idea to go without something every once in a while: who knows what the future has in store for me – or you, or, for that matter, the human race? We may as well try and prepare ourselves. And since, as far as I'm concerned, most days of the week are pretty much alike, I thought it might as well be Saturday. Your toast's going cold again; I feel I ought to warn you.

I can't understand it, I said. I think you're joking.

Oh please, she said. Don't go on about it – it's not worth the bother.

She went into the kitchenette and came back with a carton of orange juice.

I don't know whether you have any plans for the day, she said, filling my glass. But as for myself I have to be out on streets collecting money for one of my several worthy causes. I've been assigned to the corner of Oxford Street and Regent Street – which is the prestige beat amongst us Good Workers, I'll have you know – one of the most lucrative. You can come with me if you like.

What are you collecting money for?

For famine relief, she said. In Africa mainly. But who knows? Even you may benefit from it some day.

All right, I said, licking honey and butter off my lips. I'll come with you. I may not be of much use, but I'd like to.

It'll be very crowded, she said, and not particularly pleasant. I warn you.

Oh, I'm used to crowds, I said.

Well, we'll see, she said. You may find this particular kind of crowd a little overpowering.

As it turned out, she was right. The moment we stepped out of the underground station at the intersection of Oxford Street and Regent Street, with our posters under our arms and collection boxes in our hands, I found myself awash, floundering in the torrent of shoppers, hurrying past, laden with plastic bags and packages. Before I knew it, I was swept away, and when I looked around all I could see was the tall windows of the department stores, glittering with lights and mannequins, and the stream of shoppers, stretching all the way down the street. Then I heard May's voice and saw her, at the corner, laughing at me, and waving. It took a while before I could get back to her; I had to work my way around the stream, keeping my back to the shop windows.

So you're used to crowds, May said, laughing.

She showed me how to hang the posters on the railing that divided the pavement from the road. Then she tapped my collection box and said: Go on – good hunting.

I stood at the edge of the flowing crowd and held out the box, hopefully. But after a quarter of an hour nobody had yet stopped to drop anything into it, and I began to wonder whether they could even see me. I stood back against the railing, in dejection, and watched May.

It was clear at once that she was skilled at the job; her usual tentative and rather shy manner had vanished, her voice had become loud and commanding. She would pick an individual in the crowd, catch his or her eye, step up and thrust out the box. Invariably, they dropped something into it.

I went back again to try out her technique, and soon people began to drop coins into my box too. A couple of hours later, with my box half full, I worked my way back to May's side and sat down, using the box as a seat.

Tired already? May said.

Taking a break, I told her. Can't we go somewhere and have a coffee?

No, she said. We've got work to do.

Tell me, I said, you must be quite senior in the Good Works hierarchy. You ought to be deciding where the helicopters go and things like that, shouldn't you? Surely you don't *have* to do this kind of legwork any more. This must be for rank novices.

I like doing this, she said. It seems, well, somehow useful.

She looked down at me and smiled, a wry, gentle smile that softened the harsh lines of her face.

Do you know, I said, that's exactly how you used to look when I first met you. Do you remember? I was looking up at you then, just as I am now.

You had to look up at everyone then, she said, thrusting her collection box at a woman with a purple hat.

But do you remember? I said.

Yes, of course, she said. It was at Howrah Station, wasn't it?

She had arrived on the Frontier Mail. My father, Tridib and I had gone to meet her.

I was very worried on the way to Howrah. How will you know her? I kept asking Tridib – you don't even know what she looks like now, you haven't seen her since she was a little baby.

But Tridib wasn't worried. I'll recognise her somehow, he said, you wait and see.

But of course I did worry: I didn't know they'd exchanged photographs. Secretly, I was sure it would be I who'd recognise her first. This was because I had developed a theory about her name. Her name had puzzled me at first: I'd wondered why she had been named after a month. Then I read somewhere that English buttercups flowered in May. The rest was easy: obviously she was called May because she looked like a buttercup. I was certain I would recognise her first: I was the only person there who knew what to look for.

We were waiting on the platform when the Frontier Mail steamed in. A huge crowd spilled out of it and swept down the platform. We waited for half an hour, but there was still no sign of her. Tridib was less sanguine now; he was beginning to bite his fingernails. I was close to tears.

It turned out exactly as I had expected: I saw her first. She was standing patiently beside a tea-stall with her suitcase between her legs. I was stunned: she did not look remotely like anything I had expected. She saw me staring at her and waved tentatively. Then my father saw her too and waved back.

She picked up her suitcase and came running up to us. Dropping it on the platform, she shook hands with my father, and then looked down at me, from what seemed like a great height, and ruffled my hair, smiling, so that her blue eyes shimmered like water in a breeze.

I was no longer disappointed: I did not mind that she didn't look at all like a buttercup – to me she was exotic enough.

Straightening up, she looked over my head and stepped back. I knew she had seen Tridib, so I didn't turn, for I wanted to watch her face when she greeted him. She did not recognise him at first – I could tell, because she smiled in a general, inclusive kind of way, as though she had understood he was with us and was smiling for the sake of politeness. Then her smile faded away and her eyes widened. Raising a hand, she pointed at him and said: You're not, you're not . . .

I slipped away to one side so I would have a better view of the two of them.

Tridib was nodding at her, shyly; I could tell he was trying to smile. I didn't blame him: the moment seemed so unbearably poignant I was sure in his place I would not have been able to smile either.

I can still see what May did next as though it were a film running through my head in slow motion; I remember how the noise and bustle of that busy platform seemed to evaporate; I remember the face of a man standing behind the tea-stall, gaping, with his mouth wide open; I even remember my father's eyes growing large with disbelief.

She stepped up to Tridib and kissed him on both cheeks.

A battery of whistles shrilled out from every corner of the platform; a chorus of voices shouted – Again! Again! Tridib's spectacles misted over and he looked as though he would burst with embarrassment.

Oh, I'm so sorry, May said. She was blushing. It's obviously not the right thing to do here.

No, no, Tridib stammered. Thank you very much . . .

What are you staring at? my father snapped, waving his hands at the people who had gathered around us. Then he picked up May's suitcase and shepherded us out of the station.

On the way back to our house Tridib told us how long ago, in London, Mrs Price had called him into the house one morning when he was sitting out in the garden and told him to go into the drawing room and take a look at May. Puzzled, he had gone up to her cradle and looked in. When he saw her, his hair had stood on end and he'd almost wet his trousers. He had run out of the room screaming: she had turned into an insect, her face had gone all black and shiny and her mouth had grown into a long black snout, like a pig's.

Later they had explained, laughing, that it was just a gas mask – a baby's gas mask, to protect her in case the Germans dropped gas bombs. But they hadn't been able to convince him until they took it off and showed him her face, soft, pink and quite unchanged.

I stole a glance at May and my heart warmed to her when I saw she was laughing.

But May didn't remember Tridib's story; she was too excited to listen properly.

She made a face at the stream of shoppers flowing past us and said: We've done enough for today – I think we can leave the rest of these damned souls to wallow in the mire of their complacency for the moment. Come on, I'll show you a little place around the corner where you can have a cup of coffee.

Does that mean you'll be breaking your fast too? I said.

I'm sorely tempted, she said. But I'll try and hold out a little bit longer.

We rolled up posters and breasted the quick-flowing crowd. Eventually, we made our way into a small lane off Regent Street, and May led me into a sandwich bar that had trays of salad and shrimps and salami displayed behind a misty window. Inside, it smelt of bread and mayonnaise; it was only a small, narrow room with a counter at one end, but it looked larger than it was because the far wall was a huge mirror, with a thin, ledge-like table built into it. May found a couple of high stools and we carried them across the room to the ledge at the far end. Then I went back to the counter to choose a sandwich and get myself a cup of coffee, and when I came back May was looking into the mirror, laughing silently.

What's happened? I said.

She shook her head: I was thinking of that silly story about me in a gas mask, when I was a baby.

She hadn't heard Tridib telling it, but she'd laughed anyway – she remembered that – she'd laughed because she was light-hearted with relief. She had been frightened all day, on the train. In fact, she had been frightened ever since she arrived in Delhi. She couldn't remember why; there wasn't any real reason. But she remembered her fear, how she had shut herself into her hotel room – it was like that time when she was a little girl, and she'd found herself alone at the deep end of a swimming pool. She was frightened because she was alone, because she didn't know what to do. A woman with a mangled hand had asked her for money one morning, and she'd stood there paralysed wondering what to do. All she could do was give her money, and that wasn't doing anything at all; it was an act of helplessness. She wasn't used to being helpless; she was used to doing things. She always had been.

She had thought it would be a good idea to go to Delhi and Agra first; it would let him, Tridib, know she hadn't come to India in answer to his summons, as it were. But now she couldn't bring herself to go to Agra. She locked herself into her room in her hotel in Delhi, and lay in bed wondering why she'd come. Of course, there wasn't a reason, no good reason at all that she could think of, except curiosity – curiosity about what lay beyond West Hampstead, a curiosity that had come to be focused on this man whom she'd never met. But lying there, frightened, in that hotel bed, curiosity seemed like no reason at all for travelling five thousand miles. It didn't seem like a reason for anything – what was curiosity, after all? She tried to think about why she'd been curious, tried really hard, but it eluded her – she didn't know what it was any longer, it had vanished.

Instead, she found herself wondering about Tridib. She tried to think of him waiting for her at the station at Calcutta, but she had no idea what the station would be like. She thought of a crowded version of Paddington, in London, and she saw him waiting for her at the bookstall. She saw herself walking up to him, putting out a hand, saying very demurely, How-do-you-do. But he didn't respond – he smiled at her thinly, looking her over with bright, piercing eyes. He looked exactly as he did in the picture he had sent her – intense, saturnine, more than a little mad. And then she was really frightened: she didn't want to meet a man like that alone, in a strange country. That was when she sent my father a telegram asking him to meet her at the station.

But then, when she saw him, looking over my head, he wasn't at all like his picture. He looked awkward, absurdly young, and somehow very reassuring. Also a little funny, because his eyes were hugely magnified by those glasses of his, and he kept blinking in an anxious, embarrassed kind of way. She hadn't been able to help throwing her arms around him; it was just pure relief. She knew at last why she had come, and she was glad. It had nothing to do with curiosity.

She was given our guest room – a large, airy room which looked out over the garden. I used to slip in there whenever I could. I would sit on the bed and watch her – writing letters, playing her recorder, brushing her hair. I loved the smell of her: the smell of shampoo and soap and something else, not perfume, I was sure, because I hated the smell of perfume. Something cool and breezy.

I leant over, picked at her pullover and sniffed it. She drew back, startled.

What's this now? she said. What're you up to?

I'm wondering whether you still smell the same, I told her.

And do I?

Yes, I said. You do. What do you smell of?

She sniffed her pullover herself and made a face: Sweat? Grime?

No – something else.

All right, she said, laughing. I'll confess: it's lavender water.

Later, in my adolescence, I was ashamed, nail-bitingly ashamed, of staring at her like that, sniffing at her, fingering her clothes surreptitiously. I used to squirm, thinking of how I had behaved, and then I would argue with myself, try to restore a sense of balance: she hadn't minded, I would say, she probably liked the attention; maybe she hadn't even noticed – after all, to her I was probably like a boy from Mars. But then I would be ashamed again, for I knew it wasn't the truth. The truth was that she was kind – so kind that she had not spared herself the sight of herself seen through my eyes.

One evening we went for a walk. I led her down Southern Avenue, towards Gole Park, partly because I wanted to show her our old flat, and partly because I wanted to teach Montu a lesson. In school I had bragged to him about our visitor and he had laughed and refused to believe me. On the way we encountered the 'cotton man'. He was, as usual, twanging on the instrument he used in the plying of his trade – the single-stringed tool, like a very long bow, with which he fluffed up the cotton in old mattresses and quilts. May stopped dead on the pavement when she saw him. What *is* that instrument? she asked me. I was trying to think of an answer when she said: It's a kind of harp, isn't it? I didn't know what a harp was, but she was looking so eager, I nodded anyway. She was delighted that she had guessed right. Oh please, she said, do you think you could ask him to stop and play for us a bit?

I had no choice now. I went up to him and said: This foreign lady wants to hear the sound of your machine. Can you sit on the pavement and twang on it for a bit? He was taken aback, but he nodded, squatted on the roadside and duly plucked at the string. We listened for a while to its deep, monotonous drone. May was a little disappointed. It's a rather limited instrument, she said. Isn't it? But she gave the cotton-man five rupees and he went off, twanging happily.

I don't remember any longer whether we did go to Gole Park in the end, nor whether I managed to score a point off Montu. But I do remember that when we got back home we found that the cotton-man had already been there and told my parents about his encounter with me and May. My father had laughed so much, he was hiccuping. I made faces at him, trying to get him to be quiet, but it was no use; the secret was out. I was afraid May would be angry with me when she found out; that she would not let me sit in her room any longer. But she wasn't; she merely twinkled her blue eyes at me, ruffled my hair, and said: So you played a little joke on me, did you?

She won my heart.

Years later, when I told Ila about May and the cotton-man, she curled her lip and said: Sounds exactly like her. She has a kind of wide-eyed air about her even when she's in London – like one of those worthy women who come down from small towns on weekend-return tickets.

But that wasn't what I had meant at all. To me it seemed that May's curiosity had grown out of a kind of innocence; an innocence which set her apart from all the women I knew, for it was not the innocence of ignorance, but a forthright, unworldly kind of innocence, which I had never before met in a woman, for among the women I knew, like my mother and my relatives, there was none, no matter how secluded, who was free of that peculiar, manipulative worldliness which comes from dealing with large families – a trait which seemed to grow in those women in direct proportion to the degree to which they were secluded from the world.

Often, especially during the first few days of her visit, May would take me along with her when she went out with Tridib. One morning Tridib drove us to the Victoria Memorial, which May had particularly wanted to see, in the old blue Studebaker. It was May who insisted on taking me along. I was glad to go, of course: there was nothing I liked better than to eat chaat and ice-cream at the Victoria

Memorial. On the way, leaning over the front seat, I told May about all the nice things she would get to eat when we got there. When we reached the corner of Lower Circular Road and Chowringhee, I told her to shut her eyes. She humoured me, and when the immense marble edifice was directly in front of us, I cried: May, look!

I remember she cried out – My God! – so loudly that Tridib trod hard upon the brakes and the Studebaker came to a sudden halt at the foot of the huge, black statue of Queen Victoria. We found ourselves staring up at her, like maharajas at a durbar. Tridib and I began to laugh, because it was after that statue that Ila's mother had been named, because she sat just so, with her hands planted regally on the arms of her chair, clutching her teacup like a sceptre. We started to explain the family joke to May but got lost somewhere halfway through. And then, at the same time, Tridib and I both noticed that May had turned her head, averted her eyes from the statue and the building.

She saw us looking at her and threw her door open. Come on! she said. Let's have a look at that Memorial.

We went up to the wrought-iron gates and gazed at the odd little dome and stunted minarets. Then she put a hand on my shoulder and said: Let's go, please, I can't bear it.

She had gone very pale. Tridib put his arm around her, led her back to the car and helped her climb in. He gestured to me to get in and climbed in himself, behind the wheel. He reached absentmindedly for the ignition-key, but then he let his hand drop and turned to look at May. She was staring blankly at the dashboard, crouched in her seat.

He stretched his hand out, cupped her chin in his palm and turned her face towards him. May? he whispered. What's the matter, May?

Her teeth were clenched; she would not look at him. What's the matter? Tell me.

It shouldn't be here, she blurted out. It's an act of violence. It's obscene.

Tridib laughed and tilted her face up. Her eyes were wide open now, looking directly at him.

No it's not, he said. This is *our* ruin; that's what we've been looking for.

Then she laughed too, and put her hand over his, turned the palm up and kissed it.

Yes, she said. This will do for our ruin.

Then Tridib handed me a five-rupee note and told me to go and eat whatever I wanted. He said they would wait for me.

Why do I remember this incident when I have forgotten so much else? I don't know. Because of the way they looked at each other, perhaps, the way he touched her and she kissed the palm of his hand, the way they smiled, as though there were a secret between them that I would never understand. I was jealous, achingly jealous, as only a child can be, because it had always been my unique privilege to understand Tridib, and that day at the Victoria Memorial I knew I had lost that privilege; somehow May had stolen it from me.

I remember it besides, because that day May changed that place for me. I never went back there again in that old mood of cheerful expectancy. I knew there was something else in that building now, some other meaning, a meaning I couldn't fathom, but which I knew existed, despite me. It became a haunted site: I could not go there without hearing Tridib's soft voice whispering: This is our ruin; this is where we meet. I would wonder about those words; they would ring in my head, and I would try to take them apart, see what they meant, always without success, until that afternoon in that sandwich bar, when she looked into the mirror and told me about his letter, the letter about ruins.

One evening my father decided that May ought to see Diamond Harbour. Since he was busy himself, he suggested that Tridib take the two of us there for a drive on Sunday. I don't remember what Tridib said, but I knew he was reluctant to take me.

I *will* go, I shouted at him. You can't go without me.

Then May drew me into her arms, hugged me, and said: Of course you'll come with us. I wouldn't dream of going without you.

So Tridib had no choice but to agree.

He was in one of his odd, abstracted moods when he came to pick us up on Sunday morning. He took a wrong turning within minutes of leaving our house, and didn't even notice. If I hadn't pointed out his mistake we would have ended up in Dalhousie.

You see, May said, giving me a congratulatory pat. We wouldn't have got there without you.

Soon we were out of the city, rattling along as fast as the ancient Studebaker would go. They were not talking very much, so I chattered about my friends, Montu and the rest of them, and what we got up to in school. Neither of them paid any attention to me. May stuck her head out of the window, letting the wind blow through her hair, and exclaimed over the pretty green rice fields, rippling in the breeze. Tridib was busy battling with the Studebaker's stiff old steering wheel.

After we'd been driving an hour or so, somewhere on a stretch where the road cruises high over the rice fields on a raised embankment, we saw a small, indistinct shape ahead of us sprawled out on the middle of the road. Tridib was driving quite fast now, and he had to swerve sharply. May and I craned our necks out of our windows. I caught a glimpse of a twisted animal shape, smeared with blood, and shut my eyes immediately. I heard May shout: It's a dog! It's still alive!

Oh? said Tridib, glancing at the mirror as the car picked up speed: I didn't see it.

Aren't you going to stop the car? May said, her voice rising.

Stop the car? Tridib said, puzzled. Why? What good will that do?

It's still alive, she said, shouting out the last word. We ought to go back for it.

Why? Tridib said. There's nothing we can do for it.

The car was still accelerating.

May folded her hands in her lap and allowed herself to sink back in the seat as though she were going to sleep. Her voice was very calm when she turned to Tridib and said: If you don't stop the car right now, I'm going to open the door.

Tridib shrugged, stopped the car, and turned it around. Thank you, May said, laying her hand on his arm, but he shook her hand off, his face completely impassive.

He brought the car to an abrupt halt a few feet from the dog. May jumped out and ran across the road. Tridib and I followed.

The dog was lying on its side, with one half of its back at a right angle to the other. It was whimpering and a ribbon of blood was trickling slowly out of its mouth.

It's back's broken, May said dully. It must have been hit by a car.

She grimaced, turning her head away, and a tremor seemed to run through her whole body. Then she took a deep breath, forced herself to look up again, walked over to the car and came back with the large leather handbag she always carried. Opening it, she took out a penknife and a handkerchief.

What's she going to do? I shouted in panic to Tridib. Stop her: don't let her do it.

Tridib's hand shot out and gripped her wrist. You can't

do this, he said. It's too dangerous. It can still bite; it's probably rabid.

May brushed his hand off without a word. She opened out the handkerchief, wrapped it around her left hand and knelt beside the dog. It began to snap at her now, trying to raise its head high enough to lunge at her, its blood-flecked eyes rolling wildly. She made a quick pass at its muzzle with her handkerchief-wrapped hand, but the dog jerked its head up suddenly and slashed at her hand with its foaming jaws. May managed to snatch her hand back in time, but the dog's teeth ripped a corner off her hand-kerchief. She was trembling now, and sweat was pouring off her face. She fell back on her haunches, breathing hard. The dog dropped its head back on to the road, but it kept its eyes fixed on her, and made a small rattling sound, too weak to be called a growl, deep down in its throat.

Let it be, May, Tridib pleaded. There's nothing we can do.

She threw him a look.

Can't you help a bit? she said. All you're good for is words. Can't you ever *do* anything?

Tridib rose and circled around to a position where the dog could no longer see him. Then, squatting, he edged towards it, crab-like. The dog heard him and tried to twist its head around, and failing, began to whine softly. Then Tridib lunged at it, gripped its neck and head firmly with both hands, and pinned it to the tarmac. The dog's front legs scrabbled wildly as it tried to squirm out of Tridib's grip, but it was very weak now, and Tridib was able to hold it without much effort.

May leant forward and clenched its mouth shut with her left hand, still wrapped in the torn handkerchief. Then she flicked the penknife open with her thumb, pushed its head back, pressed the blade to its jugular vein and began to hack at the skin. The knife made a dull sawing sound as it scraped against the dog's wiry hair. The front half of its body was twitching furiously now; its legs were clawing at May's feet. May made a final, determined jab with the penknife and sprang back. There was a spurt of blood from the jagged cut in its neck. Its twisted body twitched convulsively and then it lay still.

May let the penknife fall and stood up. Her hands and arms were spattered with blood. She scrambled down the side of the embankment to the flooded rice fields below and plunged her arms deep into the water. She stayed there a long time, washing her hands, her arms and her face.

Tridib and I were sitting in the car when she climbed back up to the road. She got into the car, shut the door gently, and said: Sorry about all that. She was trying to be brisk and hearty but she could not keep the strain out of her voice. Tridib started up the car, and then she added: Anyway, it's done now, so let's be off to your harbour.

Without looking at her, Tridib said: You shouldn't apologise; you did the right thing.

He turned the ignition key, and when the car began to rattle he cleared his throat and said: I want you to promise me something.

What? she said lightly. That I won't murder any more dying dogs?

No, not that, he said, smiling. He raised his chin and ran his forefinger down his neck, like a barber stropping a razor.

Promise me, he said, that you'll do it for me too, if I should ever need it.

I think she laughed, though uneasily.

It was dusk when we got back to Calcutta. Tridib dropped me at our gate and said: Tell your parents May and I are going out for dinner. I'll drop her home later.

I need a coffee too, now. May said. I've fasted enough for today.

213

She went to the counter and came back with a cup of coffee and a sandwich.

We went to that old house of theirs, she said, stirring her coffee, looking at me in the mirror.

We went straight up to his room. It was the first time we'd ever really been alone together. He switched on the light and stood in the middle of the room, just looking at me. It was such an oddly monastic room – a naked light bulb, stacks of books piled up like old newspapers on the floor, a couple of mats and pillows strewn around – nothing at all to suggest that a grown man sought his comfort there.

He went over to the window and made a great business of opening it, fumbling with the latch, pushing it open and pulling it shut again. Then he turned around – he looked like a boy, so thin, with his small, angular face and his short hair and bright black eyes. He made a rueful kind of face and said something, about how long he'd been hoping . . .

I had nothing to say. I went up to him and put my hands on his shoulders – he wasn't much taller than me – and we looked at each other for a long, long time. He was terribly shy, really painfully shy. He wanted to say something – about love or something like that – and I wouldn't let him, I didn't want to hear it.

And you? I said.

She picked the plastic spoon out of the cup and twirled it between her fingers. What about me? she said.

Were you in love with him?

I don't *know*, she said. How can you expect me to know? What right have you got to ask me that? What do you think I've been asking myself these last seventeen years? I don't know whether any of it was real, whether I was in love with him, or merely fascinated by the sense of defeat that surrounded him. I don't know whether everything else that happened was my fault: whether I'd have behaved otherwise if I'd really loved him. What do you think I've been doing ever since, but trying to cope with that guilt? I don't know, I simply don't know – how could I know when the time was so short and there were so many questions? I was so young; I didn't know what was happening to me.

And so? I said.

She turned away so that I couldn't see her eyes, even in the mirror.

All I remember, she said, is him saying – you're my love, my own, true love, my love-across-the-seas; what do I have to do to keep you with me? But it's just a whisper.

She picked up the posters and the collection boxes and rose to her feet. You take that, she said, thrusting her uneaten sandwich at me. You can wrap it up and take it home. I must go now; it's late, and I've got a meeting to attend. Besides, I've got to hand all this money in.

We left the bar together and walked down the lane, in silence. She was awkward now, uncomfortable with me, and once we were back amongst the crowds on Regent Street, she went ahead, leaving me behind. I caught up with her at the entrance to the underground station.

She stopped to look for me, the coin boxes clanging together in her hands, smiling an absurd little smile of apology when her posters jabbed people in the ribs as they streamed past her on their way down to the station. She looked worried and distracted, but the light had caught her blue eyes, and the wind had blown her grey-streaked hair across her face, and suddenly she seemed much younger, very much more like the May I had looked up at all those years ago on that platform at Howrah Station.

I don't know why I've told you all this, she said, when I reached her. I've never told anyone else ever before.

Of course not, I said. There was no one else you could tell. No one knew Tridib like I did.

A poster dropped out of her arms and I picked it up and tucked it into her armpit again.

Well, she said, flustered. I must go now; I'm late. The meeting's probably started already.

Wait, I said. I had to clear my throat before I could go on.

May, I said. About last night: I'm really sorry. I don't know what else I can say.

That's all right, she said gruffly. I was a bit scared at the time, but I didn't really mind – not much, anyway. I was amazed, actually – that anybody should think of *me* like that.

Really? I said.

Yes, really, she said, smiling.

She gave my hand a squeeze, her coin boxes rattling, and then she was gone.

A few days before I flew back to Delhi, I went to Lymington Road one last time to say goodbye to Mrs Price.

One morning, earlier that week, there had been a knock on my door, not long after dawn.

It was September again now: the short English summer was long gone. It was very cold in the mornings in the ramshackle house in Fulham where I had taken a room. I heard the knock through several layers of blankets. Ignoring it, I turned over and tried to withdraw my extremities from the chilly edges of the bed. The small gas fire in my room had gone out; it worked on five-pence coins, and my stock had run out hours ago. The knocking would not go away, and eventually I had to get out of bed. The room was like an refrigerator, ludicrously so, the window frosted over like an ice-tray. I pulled on my overcoat and hobbled over to the door.

It was Kerry, the American girl who lived in the room next to mine. She was an art student from Seattle and she was spending six months in London before going on to Rome and Paris. We had become good friends in the few months we had spent in the house. There were about half-a-dozen other people in the house, students and itinerants of various kinds, but most of them kept to themselves and few stayed longer than a month. Kerry and I had first met late one July night, on the landing outside our rooms. We had both burst out of our rooms upon hearing a series of loud thuds in the third room on our floor, where a bearded young Scandinavian had recently moved in. It was an oddly disturbing, rather sinister sound, like the cracking of a whip. It was punctuated by long, low moans. I suggested we call the doctor, but Kerry smiled at me wisely and shook her head. No point in doing that, she said. They seem to be enjoying themselves in there. I listened again, and it was obvious soon that she was right. So, instead, she and I went down to the kitchen where she brewed a pot of rosehip tea. She took me to be Chinese at first, perhaps because of my eyes, and though she tried to sound enthusiastic when I explained I was Indian, it was clear that she was disappointed in some way. Later I discovered that she was interested in China because she was on a diet which forbade the consumption of milk and dairy products; having read somewhere that the Chinese didn't like milk, she had conceived an immediate empathy with that country. Eventually I succeeded in persuading her that I didn't like milk either, and we became good friends.

Now Kerry was dressed in an ultramarine track suit, and in between knocking on my door she was jogging up and down our landing, her bunched fists pounding on her thighs. She was a good eight inches taller than I, and considerably more powerfully built, with a large, square-jawed face.

217

Hi! she said. There's a call for you downstairs. A lady.

She began to giggle, looking at my overcoat. Jesus! she said. You poor little guy; you're really cold, aren't you.

She stopped jogging long enough to give me a hug.

You shouldn't be living in a primitive country like this, she said. You need to be in some place with central heating and hot water, like the States.

You're right, I said, and followed her as she sashayed down the stairs into the kitchen, where our payphone hung on the wall. She taught me that wonderful word, sashayed, and now, when I think of her, I always see her sashaying along the seaside, somewhere near Seattle.

It was Ila on the phone: it was the first time she had rung me since she and Nick had returned from their honeymoon, some three months before.

What took you so long? she said.

I began to explain, but she cut me short.

Listen, she said, her voice softening. I woke up yesterday and realised that you're due to go back home in a week or so, aren't you?

Yes, I said. I added something about coming and going.

Never mind about that, she said breathlessly. Have you packed? Have you made all the arrangements? You must have thousands of things to do. What can I do to help?

Stung by the note of urgency in her voice, I said: You've known for months I'd be leaving next week – why the big surprise?

That's true, she acknowledged. I suppose I did know. But I hadn't actually thought about it, about what it would mean for you. I woke up yesterday and remembered, and then I thought of all the things *I'd* have to do if *I* were going home, and I got into such a panic just thinking about it, I decided I must ring you, absolutely at once. But I couldn't catch you at home yesterday, so I thought I'd ring early this morning.

I couldn't help laughing. I was sure she was telling me no more than the bare truth, for it was true that in those rare moments when the clouds of her self-absorption parted, she was granted glimpses of such startling clarity into the practical exigencies of other people's lives that for a while they assumed an urgency in her mind that was no less pressing than it would have been had they been her own. I could quite easily believe that she had ruined Nick's egg that morning, and even perhaps poured sugar in her muesli in her anxiety about my departure.

Have you paid all your book-club bills? she said. Returned all your credit cards?

I laughed: she knew perfectly well I didn't have a credit card.

What about having your things shipped? she said. Have you arranged all that? Let me help; I know exactly what to do.

I don't have much luggage, I said.

Oh, she said. So there's nothing I can do?

I thought of her then, with the phone in her hand, scratching her chin, crestfallen, and suddenly the resolve I had made, to wound her a little by excluding her from this last intimate act of departure, crumbled, like all the plans I had ever made for avenging myself upon her.

Yes, I said, there *was* one thing she could do to help me – I wanted to visit Mrs Price to say goodbye, and maybe she could arrange it, perhaps even come with me. She responded with a sigh of relief. Yes, of course, she said; she would like to, nothing better. She would talk to Mrs Price and ring me back.

And so it was arranged that on my last Saturday in England, three days before I caught the Thai Airways flight back to Delhi, Ila and I would go to tea with Mrs Price. And Nick? I asked, when she rang me up to tell me. Wouldn't Nick like to come too? She had already thought of that. Nick would come to Lymington Road later, she said; he would meet us there. She laughed: she wanted to have me to herself for a little while, before hubby arrived.

Where shall we meet, then? I asked, and while she was trying to think of a place, I said quickly: What about Trafalgar Square, on the steps of St Martin-in-the-Fields? She burst into laughter. Anyone would think you were writing a script for a bad film, she said; but then she added: All right. I'll meet you there.

I arrived early at the church of St Martin-in-the-Fields: I wanted to take a last, long look at Trafalgar Square, a look that would be long enough to keep it alive in my mind for years. I found myself a clean place on the steps, near one of the pillars, where the tourists would not trip over me, and no sooner had I sat down than the clouds in the sky parted, as if to my command, and a great, golden shower of sunlight poured into the square. The traffic became a blur, a frame for the white canvas of the square; for the tourists' clothes as they sat eating their sandwiches and feeding the pigeons at the foot of Nelson's Column, as they swarmed over the great stone lions and danced on the parapets of the fountains. In exultation, the organ of St Martin-in-the-Fields boomed out the first rising notes of a Bach toccata, and at the same moment I saw her, Ila, picking her way through the crowd that had gathered at the steps of the National Gallery. She was wearing a long coat of thick, silver-tipped fur. Her head was thrown back against the collar, her face a dark smudge against the shimmering silver. She was walking slowly, looking down at the pavement, preoccupied, oblivious of the people who stopped to stare at her. I pushed myself back against the pillar, willing her not to see me; I wanted to watch her walking, unselfconscious, for as long as possible. She stopped at the zebra crossing, beside a group of rainbow-haired punks. She seemed to remember something, and, reaching into her pocket, she took out a pair of sunglasses and put them on. Then she walked slowly across the road, her hands deep in the pockets of her coat. She looked up at the church, spotted me and smiled. A couple of tourists standing beside me gasped. She was so improbably, absurdly beautiful, I began to laugh. Still laughing, I went down the stairs, and holding her back at arm's length so that I could look at her properly, I took her sunglasses off.

She tried to snatch them back, but it was too late, for I had already seen her eyes: they were red-rimmed and swollen, as though she had been weeping through the night.

What's happened? I cried in shock. What's the matter, Ila?

Nothing's happened, she snapped. Come on, let's go, we're late already.

It took us three-quarters of an hour to get to Lymington Road. Mrs Price opened the door for us. She seemed to have grown even smaller and frailer than she was when I had met her last. She led me into the drawing room while Ila went to the kitchen to make the tea. There were sandwiches waiting for us, covered with a damp cloth, as well as a cake. She had baked it herself, she said; it was a Cornish heavy cake, her father's favourite kind. While she cut me a piece she asked me about Mayadebi and the Shaheb. I had little to tell her, except that Mayadebi was moving back to their old house in Raibajar – alone, because the Shaheb had no intention of leaving his clubs and going to live outside Calcutta. She listened carefully, but it was evident that she was already very tired; I could see that she was wondering how she was going to get through another half-hour with us. Ila noticed, too, when she came in with the tea, and as soon as we had drunk a cup of tea each, she asked me tactfully whether I would like to look around the house and the garden one last time. I nodded quickly, and Mrs Price, relieved, waved us out of the room.

Out in the hall, Ila asked me whether I would like to go out into the garden for a bit. But I already knew where I wanted to go.

No, I said. Let's go down to the cellar.

Without a word, she crossed the hall, opened the door to the cellar and switched on the light. The camp beds were still out, where we'd left them at Christmas; we had forgotten to fold them away when we left. Now they were covered with a fine film of dust. Ila settled, cross-legged, on one of the beds, and beckoned to me to sit beside her.

So here we are, she said. Back in Raibajar.

I sat on the hard edge of the camp bed and looked around the cellar – at the piles of old trunks and suitcases, the stacks of paperbacks, at the garden tools that lay rusting in a corner. Slowly, as I looked around me, those scattered objects seemed to lose their definition in the harsh, flat light of the naked bulb; one of their dimensions seemed to dissolve: they flattened themselves against the walls; the trunks seemed to be hanging like paintings on the walls. Those empty corners filled up with remembered forms, with the ghosts who had been handed down to me by time: the ghost of the nine-year-old Tridib, sitting on a camp bed, just as I was, his small face intent, listening to the bombs; the ghost of Snipe in that far corner, near his medicine chest, worrying about his dentures; the ghost of the eight-year-old Ila, sitting with me under that vast table in Raibajar. They were all around me, we were together at last, not ghosts at all: the ghostliness was merely the absence of time and distance – for that is all that a ghost is, a presence displaced in time.

So when Ila turns to me and buries her face in my shoulder, it is that other eight-year-old Ila – and I, my own other – both of us sitting under that table in Raibajar. She has her arms around me and she is crying because she has just finished telling me the story of Nick Price and Magda. She is crying her eyes out, for some reason I cannot understand. We hear the door to our secret underground room opening, and I beg her to stop crying, or they'll find us, plead with her, but she cannot keep back her sobs. And then the door shuts, mysteriously, and now, frightened, she stops, and we hold on to each other, because we know that someone is in the room with us, and we do not know who it is, or what.

But then there he is, only Tridib, looking down at us, smiling, asking what we're doing down there in the dust, and I begin to explain that we're playing Houses, that we're not in Raibajar, but in London, in Mrs Price's house in Lymington Road. I show him the way in, through the garden, past the cherry tree – he has a little trouble getting in – but once I've brought him in through the front door and shown him the drawing room, he knows exactly where to go. Of course. He knows the house much better than I do; he lived in it as a boy.

When we are in the drawing room Ila begins to cry again. What's the matter? Tridib asks her. But she won't answer; she is rubbing her fists in her eyes, sobbing. So Tridib puts his arms around us and leads us back into the garden, and makes us sit cross-legged on the grass, under the cherry tree. All right now, Ila, he says. Tell me why you're crying.

But that only provokes a fresh outburst of tears from Ila, and I, losing patience with her now, tell Tridib that it's only because of a stupid story she's thought up, about her doll, Magda, and Nick Price. I tell him the story as Ila told it to me, and because Ila is still crying, I turn upon her at the end of it, and yell at her to be quiet – not to be a damn-fool girl, it was just a story, about a stupid little doll, and there she is, crying her eyes out as though she's been living in it.

Tridib laughs and shakes me by the neck and tells me not to shout at her. Everyone lives in a story, he says, my grandmother, my father, *his* father, Lenin, Einstein, and lots of other names I hadn't heard of; they all lived in stories, because stories are all there are to live in, it was just a question of which one you choose . . .

But that does not console Ila: she only cries harder.

Tridib scratches his head, wondering what to do, and suddenly he says: Yes, come on, let's go in, down to the shelter, and we'll all listen to a story, a nice one – in fact the best in the world.

Ila's curiosity is stirred, and at last she forgets her stupid crying and we get up and follow him in through the front door. On the way he explains that it's a very special day today, the 25th of September, 1940, his ninth birthday. And that is why we're going to be told a story – it's a birthday present from Snipe, he's been promised it as a reward for all those trips down to the chemist's on West End Lane to buy Dentesive and Sanatogen and Rennie's digestive tablets. But it's special for another reason too – because they are leaving next week, Tridib, his father and his mother, they are leaving to go back to Calcutta, his father is quite well now, completely recovered. Tridib can't bear to think of leaving London behind, but it's true – they're leaving next week, they're going home.

But still, at least there's Snipe's story to look forward to tonight. Snipe has promised that it's going to be a nice, long story, a good, proper, Middle English story; he knows it well, he says, because he's been teaching it to his students for years.

Tridib thinks he's earned it: today has not been a good day for him.

Early this morning his mother told him that he was not

to leave the house today, under any circumstances. But when he asked why, she wouldn't explain: just do as I say, she said. It was so unreasonable. How could she really expect him to stay in all day long, doing nothing? Especially when there was so much going on outside.

Soon after breakfast, when his mother went to help his father shave, he slipped out of the front door, through the little wicket gate, and then, turning left, sprinted down towards the cricket field on Alvanley Gardens. There was a gun emplacement there, where square leg used to be, if you were bowling from the pavilion end. One of the men who manned the huge anti-aircraft gun had been in India with the army. He could speak a few words of Tamil, but he didn't know what they meant and wouldn't tell Tridib how he had come to learn them. He would let Tridib watch sometimes, when he and the others were polishing the gun: a huge steel-grey thing, as big as a tree. And then, two nights ago, a bomb had dug up a huge fifteen-foot crater in the cricket field, a bare fifty yards from the gun emplacement. It was at extra-cover if you were batting facing the pavilion.

He crawled under the fence and ran across the field to the crater. It had changed overnight. It had filled up with water, because of the rain. The piles of earth that had been thrown up all around it had turned into mud. He got down on his hands and knees and crawled up to the rim of the crater. He got a shock, almost fell in, and then laughed: his own face was staring back at him from the water.

Then he heard his mother's voice again, running down the road, shouting his name. He answered, without meaning to, and regretted it at once, for she came running in after him, pinched his ear and dragged him back to the house. And when she had shut the door, she turned around and slapped him, hard. She had never slapped him before. He was so shocked, he couldn't even cry.

Mrs Price heard the slap and came running out of the kitchen. Oh, poor Tridib! she said, when she saw him rubbing his cheek. She led him into the kitchen, and whispered in his ear: She didn't mean to – it's just that she's very worried today.

She was worried about the journey that lay ahead of them, Mrs Price told him. But even more than that, she was worried about the toffee tins. Toffee tins? said Tridib. Yes, she explained. Toffee tins.

Yesterday, Snipe had shown them an Air-Raid Precautions notice which said: Tins of toffees are believed to have been dropped by enemy aeroplanes. They are shaped like handbags and some have coloured tartan designs, with a puzzle, on the lid, marked Lyons Assorted Toffee and 'Skotch' and bearing the name of J. Lyons and Co.

They wouldn't have paid much attention if it hadn't been an ARP notice. But even Snipe who was usually so dismissive of rumours hadn't been able to laugh away an ARP notice. And besides, he'd point out, it made sense, in a way, to demoralise the population by getting at the children. As for Mayadebi, she had convinced herself that Tridib was going to find one of those toffee tins – he was more or less the only child left on Lymington Road; all the rest had been sent out of London. He was certain to come upon one of those tins, she'd worried, wandering around all day long, as he did. That was why she hadn't even dared to warn him about them – she was sure he'd go out to look for them if he knew.

So he had to stay at home while Snipe went off to work, and his father went to Guy's Hospital to see his specialist. Then Mrs Price went out too; to see if she could get anything special for dinner.

She was back an hour later, exhausted, having managed to buy a loaf of bread, a dozen eggs and a pound of lamb's liver. She dumped her bag on the kitchen table and sat back to look at it.

What on earth are we going to do about your birthday dinner? she said. This won't even make a proper meal.

I don't mind, Tridib answered. Snipe's giving me a nice birthday present anyway.

And then, because Mrs Price didn't know about his present, Tridib told her about the story Snipe had promised him.

But, of course, in the event he got a birthday dinner and other presents as well. Mrs Price looked in her larder and found a few odds and ends with which she managed to put together a fairly hearty meal (no boiled cauliflower leaves today, dear) *and* a Cornish heavy cake (with invisible Blackout candles, Snipe said). And he got a jacket and shirt from his mother and father and a nice old pair of brass opera glasses from Mrs Price, to watch the planes with, and best of all a brand new Bartholomew's Atlas from Snipe. So altogether he'd done quite well, even before the story. But he couldn't linger over his presents, as he'd have liked, because the Alert sounded while they were still at the dinner table.

They knew it was going to be a bad night as soon as they heard the first planes. They could tell from the noise as the planes flew over the house – in massed groups, their engines chugging along in a steady determined rhythm. Then the gun in the cricket field in Alvanley Gardens opened up, and at once the pictures on the walls and the cups on the table began to rattle. Soon Snipe led them down to the cellar, carrying May in his arms, and they sat on their beds, looking at the ceiling in the light of the oil lamp, and wondering how long the raid would last. There was a very loud explosion somewhere near by: it shook the floor of the cellar and nearly toppled the oil lamp off its shelf. May began to cry, and Tridib, just when he was beginning to wonder how much longer he'd be able to hold out without crying himself, remembering Snipe's promise: Please Snipe – the story – you promised . . .

And what of the story?

I see it in the mouths of the ghosts that surround me in the cellar: of Snipe telling it to Tridib, of Tridib telling it to Ila and me, in that underground room in Raibajar; I see myself, three years later, taking May, the young May, to visit the house in Raibajar the day before she left for Dhaka with my grandmother and Tridib; I see myself leading her into that underground room in that old house, showing her the table under which Ila and I had sat when she first introduced me to Nick; I tell her how Ila cried that day after telling me the story of Magda; and now May talks to me about Nick, and later I show her how Tridib had come into the room while Ila was still crying on my shoulder, crying for her brother Nick, and I tell her how Tridib asked me what the matter was with Ila, and I tell him, so to stop her crying he crawls into the house on Lymington Road and leads us down to the cellar, and tells us the story Snipe had once told him.

What story? May said. I tried to remember, tried very hard, but somehow it wouldn't come back to me. But later that day, back in Calcutta, in Tridib's house in Ballygunge Place, when Tridib asked me what I'd shown May in Raibajar, I said: I took her to that underground room – do you remember, where . . .

. . . Where I found Ila crying, and you sitting beside her? he said.

And to stop her crying you told us a story, remember? What was the story? said May. I want to know. Tell me.

Tridib seated himself on a mat and folded his legs.

It was a wonderful, sad little story, he said. I forgot all about the air raid while he was telling it to me.

Where did it happen? I asked. Which country?

228

Ah, said Tridib. That's the trick, you see. It happened everywhere, wherever you wish it. It was an old story, the best story in Europe, Snipe said, told when Europe was a better place, a place without borders and countries – it was a German story in what we call Germany, Nordic in the north, French in France, Welsh in Wales, Cornish in Cornwall: it was the story of a hero called Tristan, a very sad story, about a man without a country, who fell in love with a woman-across-the-seas . . .

That was on the day before they left for Dhaka: it was the last story Tridib ever told me.

And I heard his voice again, in that cellar, while Ila cried, sitting beside me on the camp bed.

She was crying very hard. I had never seen her cry like that: her whole body was racked by the effort of her sobs; at times it seemed as though she was going to retch into her handkerchief.

I put an arm around her and held her tight against me. I knew; I'd known from the moment I'd seen her eyes at Trafalgar Square that she wanted to tell me something. I knew she was waiting for me to ask her what it was, but also knew I wouldn't: I did not want to know; I did not want to offer a sympathy I did not feel.

It was a while before she stopped crying, and even after that she lay with her head against my chest, hiccuping, unable to speak.

I'm sorry, she said at last. I don't know what came over me.

I waited, in silence.

It's Nick, she said.

All right, I said. Go on, tell me. What's he done? Forgotten to buy you roses or spilt your morning tea?

You bastard, she said, pushing herself upright. Don't you dare talk to me like that.

Go on, I said. Let's get it over with. You may as well

tell me now. What happened? Did you creep back home in the still of the day and find him in bed with another woman?

She gave me a startled glance and turned away again, to look at her fingernails.

Could I ever have imagined, she said, that I, Ila Datta-Chaudhuri, free woman and free spirit, would ever live in that state of squalor where incidents in one's life can be foretold like teasers for a bad television serial? I suppose not, but there you are. Yes, you're right, more or less – you've seen it all already, on TV. That's more or less exactly what happened.

She had telephoned him at home, one afternoon, soon after they got back from their honeymoon in Africa. She used to miss him dreadfully while she was at the office; miss being with him all day long, miss his voice, the smell of him. But she'd made it a rule not to telephone him too often; she didn't want him to feel that she was being too possessive.

But that afternoon she gave in. She picked up the phone in her office, when the others happened to be out for a bit, and dialled the number, hoping he'd be at home. He usually stayed in, or so he said, since he wasn't working yet. The phone rang for a while, and just when she was about to ring off, a female voice answered – breathless, as though they'd had a playful tussle. The voice said: 'Allo, with a French kind of intonation. Ila was so taken aback, she found herself saying: Could I speak to Nick Price please? as though she were asking her bank manager's secretary for an appointment. The voice giggled and said: 'Oos speaking please?

His wife, Ila answered, and slammed the phone down.

Despite myself, I began to laugh. Oh, sad little Ila, I said. Your sins have finally come home to roost.

I wish it *were* that, she said, with a tired little shake of her head. I wish I could say to myself, why, I used to do that kind of thing too, it doesn't mean anything. But I never did, you know. You see, you've never understood, you've always been taken in by the way I used to talk, when we were in college. I only talked like that to shock you, and because you seemed to expect it of me somehow. I never did any of those things: I'm about as chaste, in my own way, as any woman you'll ever meet.

I was ashamed now. I dropped my eyes and said: Did you ask him about it?

Yes, she said. He was waiting for me when I got home. He was very calm, very cool. He had obviously thought it all out. I think he'd wanted me to find out, in a way; maybe he'd even guessed I'd ring and asked her to answer the phone. He wanted to make a point; to let me know that I shouldn't take anything for granted just because we're living in a flat my father's bought for me. And because I have a job and he doesn't.

She turned to look at me, her eyes hysterically bright, her mouth twisted into a smile.

He told me, she said, that the woman who'd answered the phone was from Martinique. He'd met her in a pub or something and he's been seeing her for a year or so, since long before we were married. He's got an Indonesian woman in line too, somewhere. And there's me, of course.

Why does he do it? I said.

She began to laugh, gritting her teeth, while tears ran down her cheek.

That's exactly what I asked him. He said he just likes a bit of variety; it's his way of travelling.

I could think of nothing to say; nothing that would console her for the discovery that the squalor of the genteel little lives she had so much despised was a part too of the free world she had tried to build for herself.

You must leave him, Ila, I said.

I can't, she said. Can't you see that I couldn't?

Why not?

She began to laugh. It was her familiar, high-spirited laugh, and I found myself laughing with her.

Don't you see? she said. I wouldn't leave him if he moved a whole bloody massage parlour from Bangkok into the house. He knows that perfectly well; he knows I love him so much I could never leave him.

And yet, I discovered soon enough that she had invented her own ways of punishing him.

Half an hour later, when Nick arrived and came into his mother's drawing room, she announced, laughing, to me and Mrs Price: Do you know? Nick's had another of his ideas. He's trying to get my father to buy him a partnership in a warehousing business.

She gave him a long look, her face going hard in a way I had never before noticed in her. Of course, she said, it takes hard work to make a success of a thing like that, and Nick, well . . .

Nick's face crumpled, and he looked down at the carpet, hanging his head.

Looking at him, I tried to think of the future as it must have appeared to him: of helpless dependence coupled with despairing little acts of rebellion. I wanted to get up then and hold him, chest to chest, his shoulders to mine. But, of course, I didn't – he did not know of the part he had played in my life, standing beside me in the mirrors of my boyhood: I knew he would not have understood.

I remembered what May had said about him in that underground room in Raibajar: He's different; he's not like us.

That was on the day before they left for Dhaka.

On 2 January 1964, the day before they left for Dhaka, my grandmother received a letter. It was from Mayadebi. It

232

had taken ten days to reach Calcutta because it had come through Delhi by the diplomatic bag.

Mayadebi wrote that she had not been able to visit their old house yet, because she had been very busy with one thing and another, and besides, the house they were living in now was a very long way from Jindabahar Lane. Also, as Indian diplomats their movements were restricted – as we would understand. But she had been making enquiries and she had had a stroke of good luck; she had discovered that one of the High Commission's drivers knew someone who lived in their old house – a mechanic called Saifuddin who had set up a workshop inside their old courtyard.

A workshop! gasped my grandmother. Inside our courtyard! What's become of the old jackfruit tree?

The driver had brought Saifuddin to see her. He was a nice man, very well spoken and polite; he was from Motihari in Bihar. He'd come to East Pakistan with nothing at all, other than a large family, and he managed to set up a thriving little business. The driver said he was one of the best mechanics in Dhaka.

She had asked Saifuddin about their old Jethamoshai, referring to him as Shri Goshtobihari Bose. He hadn't understood who she was talking about at first; apparently they knew him as Ukil-babu because until very recently he had still been drafting wills and affidavits, and even going to the High Court once in a while. But now, Saifuddin had said, he was completely bed-ridden, and his mind was wandering a lot – he often didn't recognise people he had known for years. Luckily for him, he was looked after by a family to whom he had given shelter years ago. But they were very poor – their only income was from a cycle-rickshaw. They probably wouldn't be able to support the old man for very much longer. It was providential, Saifuddin had said, that they, his relatives, had come to Dhaka now, a part of God's design. Perhaps now the old man would be able to spend his last days with his relatives, in peace and comfort, as he deserved.

So, wrote Mayadebi, my grandmother's intuition had been right: it was clear that they would have to do something for the old man. But they could decide about that once they were together in Dhaka.

In the meanwhile, perhaps she could bring a little present for Saifuddin, since he had been so helpful – maybe a nice Indian sari for his wife.

My grandmother handed the letter around with an air of quiet, unsurprised triumph: she had known all along. But once everyone else was out of earshot, she shook me gleefully and cried: Oh I'm so glad Maya hasn't been back to the old house yet – I didn't want her to be the first.

Later that evening, she announced that she wanted me to spend the night in her room: she was already missing me, she said. I was hoping she would ask me to: I liked sharing her bed and listening to her stories. But tonight there was another, more serious matter at hand too. When I had her to myself, I had decided, I would go over all my instructions about the plane once again. I had an uneasy feeling she had not been listening the last time.

So, as soon as I saw her climbing into bed beside me, I started at the top of my list: did she remember about buckling her seat belt? And keeping an air-sickness bag close at hand? Not to speak of the parachutes under the pilot's seat, did she remember? She laughed and told me to go to sleep, but I said no, I wouldn't, not without a story. So she began on one of her Dhaka stories, one about the old house and the people who lived down the lane. But her voice trailed away slowly, and when she got to Kana-babu's sweet-shop, she forgot all about me and climbed out of the mosquito-netted bed and drew her favourite armchair up to her window. When I fell asleep she was still there, staring out at the smudged blackness of the lake.

When I woke up, our house was already convulsed with the preparations for their departure: my mother was in the kitchen, supervising the packing of the three different kinds of shandesh we were sending with them; my grandmother was in a fever of excitement, choosing a sari for Saifuddin's wife, locking her cupboards and making sure she'd taken all her medicines with her. Only May seemed to be untouched by the excitement. I couldn't understand how she could sit in her room playing her recorder like that, as though it were an ordinary morning.

We left for Dum Dum airport at noon. By the time we arrived at Ballygunge Place to pick up Tridib my grandmother was giggling like a schoolgirl. She couldn't believe she was really going to fly off into the sky.

At Dum Dum, after we had said our goodbyes and they had been swallowed into Immigration and Customs, we went up to the terrace on the roof to watch their plane take off. We had to wait half an hour before we saw them, three tiny figures on the tarmac. They knew we were watching and they walked towards the plane with all the shy self-consciousness of amateur actors making an entry on a big stage. When they reached the stairs that led up to their brand new Fokker Friendship aircraft, my grandmother turned and waved in our direction, her sari a white blur against the black tarmac. We waved back, although we knew she wouldn't be able to see us. Then a hostess bowed them through a hatch-like door and they vanished from sight. But minutes later I saw a face appear in one of the windows, like a smudged cameo, and waved wildly at it, certain it was my grandmother. The door was slammed shut, the stairs were wheeled away, and the plane began to move. It turned slowly and trundled down the runway with an ungainly, waddling motion. I stopped waving: it was hard to believe that this graceless, plodding thing would actually have the temerity to thrust itself into the sky. It came to a wide apron, turned again, and pointed its nose down the runway. It was stationary for a long moment; its energy seemed to seep away. A hush fell over the airport. Then the propellers started up; in an instant they were spinning so fast they melted into the shimmer of the heat on the tarmac. I was still watching my grandmother's window – it was the third from the door at the back. I was sure I could see her, smiling, waving into the glass. Then the whole plane shook as a shudder ran down the fuselage. It began to roll down the runway, engines screaming, its silver body flashing back the glare of the midday sun. Its gracelessness was gone; the power of the engines had given the long fuselage the lean muscular taut-ness of the neck of a heron in full flight. It was shooting down the runway now; my grandmother's window length-ened into a long, white blur. Its nose lifted, very gently, and then, suddenly, unbelievably, the whole of its huge metal body was riding the sky.

As the plane circled above us, my mother allowed herself, at last, to breathe a long, deep sigh of relief: till that moment she had not really believed that my grandmother would really go to Dhaka.

My father sighed too, but in a different sort of way, and said: Yes, it's a good thing they've gone.

There was something in his voice that made my mother ask: Why? Why particularly?

He scratched his ear and said: People say there's going to be trouble here. I'm glad they've gone abroad – espe-cially May – they'll be far away from it over there.

What trouble? I asked.

My mother gave him a frown and a quick shake of the head, so he turned me around, pointed at the plane and said: Nothing. Nothing that you would understand.

We watched the plane until it disappeared over the horizon.

Years afterwards, Robi told me that the first thing my grandmother said to Mayadebi when they met at the airport was: Where's Dhaka? I can't see Dhaka.

I tried then to see Dhaka as she must have seen it that night, sitting by her window. But I hadn't been to Dhaka, and in any case her Dhaka had long since vanished into the past. I had only her memories to go on, and those put together could give me only a faint, sepia-tinted picture of her other arrivals in Dhaka, decades ago: a picture in which I could see dimly in the middle distance, a black steam engine, puffing smoke, and a long line of carriages vanishing into the right-hand corner; in the foreground a deeply shaded platform, porters and vendors, and a crowd of relatives jostling to meet the new arrivals as they step out of their carriage; in the background, perhaps, a glimpse of the minarets of a mosque. I can guess at the outlines of the image that lived in her mind, but I have no inkling at all of the sounds and smells she remembered. Perhaps they were no different from those in any of the thousands of railway stations in the subcontinent. Perhaps, on the other hand, they consisted of some unique alchemical mixture of the sounds of the dialect and the smell of vast, mile-wide rivers, which alone had the power to bring upon her that comfortable lassitude which we call a sense of home-coming.

At any rate, the one thing she was completely unprepared for was the bare glass-and-linoleum airport, so like the one she had just left. Nor was she prepared for the drive to the Shaheb's house, along a straight road, flanked by tall eucalypti and the occasional suburban bungalow.

May liked it. She said: What a pretty road, it's so much more open than Calcutta. But as for my grandmother, she kept saying: I've never seen any of this. Where's Dhaka?

The Dhaka she was thinking of was the city that had surrounded their old house.

She had talked to me often about that house and that lane. I could see them myself, though only in patches, for her memory had shone upon them with the interrupted brilliance of a lighthouse beam. So, for example, I could see Kana-babu's sweet-shop at the end of their lane with absolute clarity, I could even see the pink cham-chams stacked in their trays, the freshly pressed shandesh heaped in orderly mounds beneath the cracked, discoloured glass of the counter; I could hear the buzzing of the flies, and I could see Kana-babu sitting hunched behind his cash-box, scratching his stomach, the same Kana-babu who had once caught their cousin stealing a rosogolla and poured a whole potful of sticky syrup down the front of his shorts: I could see all that, because people like my grandmother, who have no home but in memory, learn to be very skilled in the art of recollection. For me, Kana-babu's sweet-shop at the end of the lane was as real as the one down our own road, and yet I could not tell whether the lane itself was paved or unpaved, straight or curved, or even whether it had drains running along it.

Mayadebi's new house was at the other end of the city. It was in Dhanmundi.

Because of everything Robi told me about it, that name, Dhanmundi, became one of the secret sounds of my childhood, like the drumming of the monkey-man's dug-dugi, and the tinkling of the bells of the Magnolia ice-cream cart in the stillness of hot afternoons; it became a part of my own secret map of the world, a map of which only I knew the keys and the co-ordinates, but which was not for that reason any more imaginary than the code of a safe is to a banker.

I could not have escaped the name Dhanmundi even if I had wanted to; in the early seventies it was everywhere, in books, in newspapers. Sometimes it seemed to me that everything that happened in the capital of new-born Bangladesh happened in Dhanmundi: that was where ministers issued their statements, and unnamed but reliable Western diplomats confided in reporters; that was where Sheikh Mujibur Rahman lived and it was there that he died, one morning, when he stepped out on to a balcony to confront his uniformed assassins, unable to believe that they, clad in the uniforms *he* had given them, would turn their guns upon *him*, their Liberator. Reading those reports in the newspapers, I used to wonder whether, if Robi had still been there, thirteen years old, he would have heard those first bursts of gunfire which brought down the Sheikh's bodyguard, and have run to the roof and seen the old man's body crashing to the driveway, leaking blood, before Nityananda or his mother came running up the stairs behind him, and clapped their hands over his eyes and whispered breathlessly in his ears: Don't look, don't look – it's just a game.

But in 1964 Dhanmundi was barely a blueprint for the fashionable suburb it was later to become. It was a near-empty wasteland of flooded foundation trenches, boundary walls that enclosed nothing but dust and grass, and a few huge walled-in houses that rose like catafalques above streets which existed only by common consent since they had no surfaces to mark them out from the fields that surrounded them. And so my grandmother, looking, perhaps, for sweet-shops and lanes, could not help exclaiming when she saw the Shaheb's house in Dhanmundi: But this is for foreigners; where's Dhaka? And Tridib could not resist the malicious pleasure of pointing out: But you *are* a foreigner now, you're as foreign here as May – much more than May, for look at her, she doesn't even need a visa to come here. At that, my grandmother gave May a long wondering look and said: Yes, I really am a foreigner here – as foreign as May in India or Tagore in Argentina. Then she caught another glimpse of the house and shook her head and said: But whatever you may say, this isn't Dhaka.

Still, it was a good house to be thirteen in: a wonderful place for Robi. It had a large roof, wide open and breezy, as good a place for flying kites as any one could wish for; you had only to hold up a kite on that roof and the wind would snatch it out of your hands, its glass-coated string singing, and in an instant it would be so far away you would hardly be able to see it and wouldn't have the time to try, because it was all you could do to hold on to the string.

Like all the other houses in Dhanmundi, theirs had a high wall, running all the way around it. At the back, just outside the wall, there was a pond where fishermen would come in the afternoons to try their luck. Usually it was a quiet, tame little pond, but in the monsoons, when the great cyclones of the Bay of Bengal struck Dhaka, that pond would turn purple, mirroring the sky, and it would rise with the wind and hurl itself on the house and go shooting through the driveway, out into the streets beyond. And when that happened, Nityananda, their cook, would run out into the flooded driveway, armed with an old sari, and drive the fish into the puddles in the garage and scoop them up. Sometimes he would keep the fish there for days, in an earthenware pot, and run into the garage and pick out a fresh one whenever he wanted.

At the back was an enclosed courtyard, ringed with coconut palms and papaya plants. Nityananda kept a few ducks and chickens there, and once a week he would act out a play for Robi in that courtyard. This one's been a bad boy this week, he would say, grabbing a chicken by the neck. Then he would raise his sickle and shout an invocation – *Joi Ma Jagad-janani* – and the blade would flash and the chicken's head would jump off its neck and lie at Robi's feet, its beak open in surprise. Robi would run upstairs then, but, unable to resist, he would stick his head through the railings of the veranda at the back, and watch spellbound as the headless chicken flapped around the courtyard. Nityananda would know that Robi was watching, and he would rock back on his heels, squatting on his haunches, and stroke his moustache and puff at his biri, and after a while he would look up at Robi, his bright, black eyes twinkling, and point at the spinning carcass, and say: Do you see – that's what comes of being a bad boy.

It was Nityananda too who introduced Robi to the garden in front: showed him how to suck the watery nectar from the stems of canna lilies, and taught him the trick of catching dragonflies, by pinching their wings together between finger and thumb. But best of all, he taught Robi to climb the mango tree in the middle of the garden. It was a big tree, very difficult to climb, with a trunk that grew straight and smooth out of the earth for a good eight feet or so before it divided into branches. It took a lot of work, but he mastered the trick just in time. And the first thing he did, when he and his parents got back from the airport with their visitors, was scramble up the tree. When he had climbed into the highest branches he shouted down to my grandmother: Look, mashi; look where I am!

She looked up, and when she saw him she said wistfully: I wish I could do that too – maybe I'd be able to see Dhaka from up there.

That evening, sitting out in the garden before dinner, my grandmother asked Mayadebi when they were going to the old house to fetch their uncle.

Whenever you like, said Mayadebi, and my grandmother,

eagerly, cried: Tomorrow – we'll go tomorrow! The sooner the better.

But then, to her surprise, the Shaheb interrupted: No, he said. This isn't a good time to go there. The house is in the heart of the old city and in the Chancery we've heard there's going to be trouble there. I don't think you should go there now.

My grandmother would have despised herself if she had given in to the Shaheb. She leant forward, shook his knee and said: If there's going to be trouble, that's all the more reason to get him out while there's still time. I've come all the way to Dhaka for his sake and I'm not going to put up with any delays now. I'm not going to be scared off by a little trouble. We have to get it done as soon as possible.

But really, the Shaheb protested, spilling his whisky in his agitation. Really – it's not safe to go there now. I can't permit it. You must wait a few days.

He appealed mutely to Mayadebi to reason with her.

Of course we'll go soon, said Mayadebi calmly. We'll go a few days later. A week won't make any difference to anyone.

My grandmother thought this over. We'll wait till next week, she said. Until Thursday. Thursday is a good day. But that's all – not one day later.

I do not remember how long they had been gone when I discovered, one morning, that there was trouble in Calcutta.

I remember my mother had a busy morning that day; perhaps it was one of those days when my father had to leave early for work. Whatever it was, she did not have time to listen to the morning news on the radio and she sent me down to the corner, with my satchel and water bottle, to wait, as usual, for the school bus.

Years later, I used to wonder at my mother's odd relationship with her little transistor radio. It was given a place of singular honour in her room: it stood on the same shelf on which she kept her framed pictures of her dead parents. She never missed the morning news if she could help it: those bulletins were the liturgy of the ritual of our breakfast. In college I used to say proudly to my friends: my mother's really interested in politics – she hasn't missed the morning news in years. Of course, I was merely trying to impress them; I knew perfectly well, even then, that she had no interest at all in the kind of politics that is spoken of over radios. Only I did not recognise that quality as a virtue then, and I could not have brought myself to admit, fattened as I was on promises of bureaucratic progress, like everybody else of my age, that for her, listening to he news was a simple rule of survival. But she missed the news that morning, so I went out to wait for my bus, as usual.

I had to wait a long time. I remember I was jealous when the other two boys who usually caught the bus with me did not turn up. I wasn't surprised, however, because that was the day the first cricket test match of the 1964 series against England was to begin at Madras. I assumed that they had been able to persuade their parents to let them stay back to listen to the radio commentary. Knowing my mother, I hadn't even bothered to ask.

I paced up and down the pavement as I waited: I was worried about the match. The morning newspaper had said that Farouk Engineer was injured and would not be playing; in his place they had included someone called Budhi Kunderan. This was worrying news: Engineer was our hero, the swashbuckler of our side. I'd never heard of Kunderan: without Engineer I couldn't see that we had a ghost of a chance. It was infuriating to wait when I was so eager to talk about the match with my friends on the bus.

Then there it was, our large blue schoolbus, making its stately way towards me, down the avenue. In my impatience, I ran towards it, waving my water bottle. But then, as it drew nearer, something about it began to puzzle me and I stopped. I knew it was the right bus – I could see the name of my school painted boldly on its side – but I could tell there was something wrong. Then it struck me: usually, by the time it reached me, the bus was full, and there were heads and arms sticking out of every window. But today the bus seemed curiously empty: there were no heads outlined against the windows.

The bus stopped and I climbed in. There were only a dozen other boys in it, and they were sitting on a bench at the back, huddled together against the emptiness of the bus. They seemed relieved to see me, although they were none of them my friends. Normally we wouldn't have so much as acknowledged one another, but today they moved up as soon as they saw me and made room for me beside them.

No sooner had I sat down than I noticed that their eyes, all dozen pairs, had strayed towards my shoulder. What's the matter? I said uneasily. What are you staring at? I looked back quickly and saw that it was my water bottle that had attracted their attention.

On my right was a plump boy called Tublu who sometimes played cricket with us in the park. What's the matter? I said to him. Haven't you seen a water bottle before?

His mouth fell stupidly open and he said: So you've brought one too? Before I could answer he pointed at one of the younger boys and whispered in my ear: He hasn't brought any water today; his mother's given him a bottle of soda.

He glared at the cowering boy, and ordered him to tell me why he hadn't brought any water.

I still remember the tearful, sing-song sound of the boy's voice as he told us that his mother hadn't let him drink any water that morning, because she'd heard that they had poured poison into Tala tank, that the whole of Calcutta's

244

water supply was poisoned. I remember how we listened to him and made him repeat what he had said. And somewhere in the rubble exhumed along with that memory there lies another, much smaller detail: I remember we did not ask him any questions – not who 'they' were, nor why 'they' had poisoned their own water. We did not need to ask any questions; we knew the answers the moment he had said it: it was a reality that existed only in the saying, so when you heard it said, it did not matter whether you believed it or not – it only mattered that it had been said at all. Everything fell into place now – the emptiness of the streets, the absence of the other boys – it all fitted. There were no more questions.

Then Tublu said loudly: We'll know at Gole Park.

Why? someone asked.

Because that's where Montu gets on the bus, he said. He'll know; he's a Muslim.

He turned to me and smiled. Of course, he said, Montu's a friend of yours, isn't he?

I remember how my throat went dry as I tried to think of an answer.

Not since we moved away, I lied. I haven't met Montu for months.

I was looking out of the window when we got to Gole Park, watching the spot, right beside the tubewell, where Montu usually waited for the bus. He wasn't there. Stealing a quick glance down his lane I saw a gap in his curtain and I knew he was watching us. I was very glad he hadn't come.

Soon after, one by one, we unscrewed the caps of our bottles and poured the water out.

Our first lesson that morning was in mathematics. Our teacher was an elderly Anglo-Indian lady called Mrs Anderson, a tall thin woman who wore skirts and had short, grizzled hair. There was only a handful of boys in the classroom and Mrs Anderson did not bother with the ritual of calling out our names. This caused a stir amongst us because it was yet another departure from normalcy, and by then we were all silently concentrating our will on keeping everything as normal as possible. But Mrs Anderson rapped on her desk with a pencil, frowning over the top of her glasses. Chastened, we opened our books and settled down. Soon, her soothing, familiar voice was telling us how we could use the letter 'X' to represent any number we liked. In a short while the day seemed almost normal, the lesson no different from any other.

My desk was next to a window. Half-way through the lesson, I thought I heard a noise, somewhere in the distance: It was faint and scattered, like the crackling of a short-wave radio-station. I wasn't quite sure I had heard anything at all, when I saw Tublu, who was sitting next to me, looking up too. I mouthed the words: What is it? But he didn't know either: he made a face and shrugged. Surreptitiously, keeping an eye on Mrs Anderson, I raised my head and looked out of the window. The noise was louder now. It sounded like voices, many voices, but it wasn't the orderly roar of a demonstration. We were used to demonstrations going past our school; it happened every other day and we never gave them a thought. But this was different – a shout followed by another and another, in a jaggedly random succession, and then, suddenly, silence, and just when they seemed to have died away, there they were, one voice, followed by a dozen, and then again a moment of silence.

There is a uniquely frightening note in the sound of those voices – not elemental, not powerful, like the roar of an angry crowd – rather, a torn, ragged quality; a crescendo of discords which you know, because of the slippery formlessness of the fear it creates within you, to be the authentic sound of chaos the moment you hear it.

The others could hear it too now; every head in the class had turned to look out of the windows.

By an effort of will, Mrs Anderson tried to shut the noise out. She began to read louder, rapping on her desk for our attention, filling the room with her voice. But those other voices had grown louder too now; we could hear them surging past the high walls of our school.

Mrs Anderson could no longer ignore them. She laid down her book and marched around the room shutting the windows. The glass panes of our windows had been painted green to keep out the summer sun. Now we sat trapped in a verdant darkness while Mrs Anderson's voice boomed and echoed through our classroom, explaining the principles of algebra.

Mrs Anderson was visibly relieved when the bell rang. She told us sternly to look through our history books, and not to make any noise at all, and then she hurried out of the class.

We threw the windows open as soon as she had left. We couldn't see far because our school had very high walls. The mob had gone away; everything seemed quiet. Then we heard the bells of a fire engine, and a minute later it sped past us. Somebody pointed into the distance and, looking up, we saw a column of grey smoke rising into the sky. We couldn't tell where the fire was.

Wonder who's batting? someone said. Nobody answered: we had forgotten about the match.

Then Mrs Anderson's voice bellowed at us and we dashed back to our desks. She glared at us, with her hands on her hips, but we could tell she wasn't really angry, as she ought to have been. Rapping on her desk, she told us that our classes were being cancelled for the rest of the day; we were going to be sent home in buses.

Why? someone asked. She frowned at him and said: Don't you want a holiday?

We left the room in silence and filed into the playground. The whole school had lined up outside. The massive steel gates swung open. At once, there was a ripple of excitement at the head of the line; the boys in front were craning their heads, looking around in surprise. When we reached the gates we saw that a contingent of armed policemen had surrounded the school.

What are they doing here? I muttered to Tublu.

You idiot, he said. Can't you see. They're guarding us.

We climbed into the buses in awestruck silence. This time, automatically, each of us picked a seat beside a window. As soon as the bus pulled away from the school we could tell that something on those streets had changed in the couple of hours since we had last driven through them: we saw that street twice every day, but now it seemed somehow unfamiliar. The pavements, usually thronged with vendors and passers-by, were eerily empty now – except for squads of patrolling policemen. All the shops were shut, even the paan-stalls at the corners: none of us had ever seen *those* shut before. Then the bus turned off into another, narrower street which we didn't know. The pavements were not quite as empty now; we could see knots of men hanging around at corners. They would look at our bus speculatively as we passed by. They were quiet, watchful; they seemed to be waiting for something.

Thank God, I said to myself, that Th'amma and May aren't here.

Tublu shook my elbow and pointed at a rickshaw that had been pulled across the mouth of a narrow lane. The others saw it too and turned to stare. We couldn't take our eyes off it, even after we had left it far behind. There was no reason for us to stare: we saw rickshaws standing at untidy angles in the streets every time we went out. And yet we could not help staring at it: there was something about the angle at which it had been placed that was

248

eloquent of an intent we could not fathom: had it been put there to keep Muslims in or Hindus out? At that moment we could read the disarrangement of our universe in the perfectly ordinary angle of an abandoned rickshaw.

Then our bus turned towards Park Circus, and suddenly those voices were all around us, those same ragged bursts of noise, but much louder now. Looking ahead through the windscreen, I saw a scattered mob milling around the Circus. As I watched, one limb of the mob broke away from the main body and snaked out towards us. And then I was thrown off my feet as our bus, brakes screeching, came to an abrupt halt.

Wrestling with the wheel, the driver spun the clumsy old bus around. The bus lurched as two of its wheels climbed the pavement, and then it was back on the road again. The gears meshed with a loud metallic screech, and slowly the bus began to move ahead.

The men who were racing after us were no more than a few feet from the back of the bus now. We ducked under our seats as stones began to rattle against our windows. Then the bus picked up speed and we left them behind. When we got up and looked back, some of them were laughing, with their arms around each other's shoulders.

At the next corner the driver swung the bus into a street that none of us recognised. Tublu, who was the nearest to the driver, got to his feet and told the driver that that wasn't the way to his house, he wouldn't be able to find his way back.

Without checking his speed, the driver shot out an arm and shoved Tublu back into his seat.

None of us looked at each other. We could not recognise the streets we were careering through. We did not know whether we were going home or not. The streets had turned themselves inside out: our city had turned against us.

Tublu began to cry. One by one the rest of us gathered around him. At any other time we would have laughed, but now we listened to him in silence, appalled. He was really crying; we could tell – not for attention, nor because he was hurt. There was an ocean of desolation in his sobs. He cried like that all the way home, for all of us.

It would not be enough to say we were afraid: we were stupefied with fear.

That particular fear has a texture you can neither forget nor describe. It is like the fear of the victims of an earthquake, of people who have lost faith in the stillness of the earth. And yet it is not the same. It is without analogy, for it is not comparable to the fear of nature, which is the most universal of human fears, nor to the fear of the violence of the state, which is the commonest of modern fears. It is a fear that comes of the knowledge that normalcy is utterly contingent, that the spaces that surround one, the streets that one inhabits, can become, suddenly and without warning, as hostile as a desert in a flash flood. It is this that sets apart the thousand million people who inhabit the subcontinent from the rest of the world – not language, not food, not music – it is the special quality of loneliness that grows out of the fear of the war between oneself and one's image in the mirror.

When Robi woke up on Thursday morning, he lay in bed for a long time listening carefully to the twittering of the sparrows in the mango tree, the buzz of the traffic on the road that led to the airport, the clanking of milkcans on a bicycle going slowly down their lane. He could not hear so much as an echo of a discordant note in that familiar medley of morning sounds. He got up and went to the window: if there was going to be trouble, he wanted to be the first to see it. He wasn't very sure what 'trouble' was: there hadn't been much of it in Canada or Romania, which were the only two places he had lived in that he could remember, apart from his boarding school in north India – and there wasn't much trouble there either, at least not on their side of the walls.

The expedition to the old house depended on whether there were signs of trouble this morning or not. Of course, he didn't care much whether they went or stayed at home to watch the 'trouble' – it would be exciting either way. But he had a feeling they would be going – despite the rumours, there hadn't been any trouble in the last few days, and in the meanwhile Mashi had grown very impatient. At dinner last night his father had had to give in when she insisted; he had said, all right, they could go, but they would have to take one of the High Commission's security guards with them.

Robi leant out of the window and looked down. The garden was bathed in the tranquil winter sunlight: he could see dragonflies' wings glinting between the petals of the cannas and hollyhocks. Shading his eyes he looked down the road: Mr Haque their neighbour was out in his garden with a cup of tea, sniffing his roses as usual. No sign of anything that could be called trouble. Satisfied, he went down and announced to May and Tridib that everything was all right; they would be able to go after all.

Later, one of the details Robi remembered about that day was that my grandmother changed her sari twice before they left the house. She came down to breakfast wearing a plain but crisp white sari, and announced that she would like to leave as soon as possible. But when their Mercedes came back from the Chancery, with a security guard and a driver, she took a long look at herself, went upstairs, and came back a quarter of an hour later, dressed in a white sari with a green border. So now, ready to go at last, they got into the car. Then my grandmother exclaimed that she had forgotten the present she had brought for the mechanic's wife and rushed into the house. But when she came back again, she was, dressed in a white sari with a red border. He remembered how his mother had laughed at her as she got into the car and said something about her being as anxious as a bride going home for the first time. He remembered too how she smiled back and retorted: You've got it wrong – I'm going home as a widow for the first time.

Robi scanned the streets as they drove through them, watching alertly for signs of 'trouble'. But he was soon disappointed: at the New Market, for instance, all the shops were open and the streets were crowded, as usual, with people and cycle-rickshaws and cars. No one bothered to give their CD number-plated car so much as a second glance.

The driver pointed out the sights to my grandmother as they went by: the Plaza picture palace with a fifteen-foot hoarding of Ben Hur hanging outside, the Gulshan Palace Hotel, Ramna Race Course, and so on.

It's all wonderful, she said. But where's Dhaka?

Then, gradually, soon after they had crossed a bridge, the sights changed; the streets grew narrower and more crowded, the houses older, more dilapidated. My grand-mother was alert now, sitting on the edge of her seat, looking out, sniffing the air. The car turned into a large, bustling square, and all of a sudden she gripped Mayadebi's arm and cried out: Look, Shador-bajar, there's the Royal Stationery, do you remember? Mayadebi threw an arm around her, and then, holding on to each other, laughing, brushing away tears, they explained to May that they had always shopped for textbooks there when they were school-girls. It had looked exactly the same then, Mayadebi said as they drove past the shop, except that the signboard had changed. But my grandmother wouldn't allow even that.

She had said fiercely: No, it's the same signboard. I remember.

A few minutes later they turned into a narrow lane that was lined with shops on both sides. Now my grandmother didn't know where to look, for suddenly the sights were falling into place like a stack of old photographs. She twisted and turned in her seat, pointing at everything: that's where the boys used to play football, that's where Shyam Lahiri used to live, that's Rina's house, I met her the other day in the park, that's where Naresh-babu used to sit – behind the bars in that jewellery shop, sweeping up the gold dust with the hem of his dhoti . . .

The driver brought the car to a halt at the mouth of a narrow lane. Turning to Mayadebi, he pointed down the lane and said: That's your house – that's where Saifuddin has his workshop.

My grandmother, thrown into a sudden panic, began to protest. This couldn't be it, she cried. It can't be *our* lane, for where's Kanababu's sweet-shop? That shop over there is selling hammers and hardware: where's the sweet-shop gone?

The driver rolled his hands sadly in the air and said: There's no sweet-shop here; it's all gone. Now there's only this one.

Then, noticing a sudden movement, he flung his door open and darted off to chase away a boy who had tried to touch the star on the bonnet of the Mercedes. The boy melted back into a knot of young men and children who had gathered around the car. Eyeing them uneasily, the driver beckoned at the security guard and told him to watch the back of the car, while he watched the bonnet.

There! cried my grandmother, pointing down the lane. Look! Our house!

Its edges were blurred with moss, and banyan shoots were clinging to its crumbling silhouette, but the shape of the outline was exactly as she remembered it, large, welcoming and ungainly. My grandmother shut her eyes and would not move until Robi tugged at her hand and said: Let's go and see it, come on.

But before they could go on, the driver came panting up to Mayadebi, whispered a few words to her, and ran back to the car. What did he say? Tridib asked her, but she was gazing at the house, smiling dreamily, and he had to ask her again before she answered: Oh, nothing – he wants us to come back quickly, in case there's trouble.

They went into the lane with a crowd of curious children swarming after them. Most of them attached themselves to May. Robi could hear them whispering to each other about her, and one of them, a little girl, slipped her hand through hers.

They could see the house quite clearly now: wet saris fell from the terrace in wide gashes of colour, like spilt paint, and through the shutterless windows they could see soot-streaked walls, and the tops of mosquito-netted beds, and clothes hanging from nails. A small board hanging under one of the windows on the top floor said: Lutfullah Ismail, BA, MA (Patna), and offered his services for typing and shorthand.

Robi went on ahead, looked through the gateway and came running back. Motorcycles, he said in awe. Motorcycles everywhere.

It costs me no effort at all to imagine the look of amazed disbelief with which Mayadebi and my grandmother received this bit of news. They had known about the workshop, of course, but they hadn't thought that it would be right there; not there, in that little stretch of garden where the two of them had so often sat wondering about the doings in their uncle's upside-down house.

It can't be true, said my grandmother. It must be a lie.

But then, at the gate, throwing up her arms to shield

254

her eyes from a sunburst of blinding silver light, she saw that Robi had told her no more than the truth: the old portico had sprouted a tin shed that was shining in the blaze of a blowtorch as a man worked on a motorcycle mudguard. The patch of grass they had once called a garden was now pitted with pools of black oil and strewn with tyre-tubes and exhaust pipes.

It was all changed, but now my grandmother didn't care any longer. It wasn't the house she remembered, the house she had built for me in Calcutta, but it was near enough.

I can see her, wandering into that yard, heedless of the pools of grease and the discarded tyres, gazing up at the balconies with their spindly wrought-iron railings, tripping over a bent wheel as she looks for the lime trees her mother had once planted, knocking her knees against a set of twisted handlebars, until Saifuddin, the mechanic, leads her gently to a bench and persuades her to sit down. She looks at his grease-blackened face then, and wonders from which part of the house this new relative whose face she can't remember has appeared. And Mayadebi, trying to rescue her from her bewilderment, explains softly that this is Saifuddin, the mechanic who is going to help them take their uncle back to India. My grandmother starts, because she has forgotten all about her uncle, but slowly, with an effort of that prodigious will of hers, she brings herself back to the present, reminds herself that she has a serious duty to perform, that she hasn't come all this way merely to indulge her nostalgia – she hates nostalgia, my grandmother, she has spent years telling me that nostalgia is a weakness, a waste of time, that it is everyone's duty to forget the past and look ahead and get on with building the future – so now, slowly, she reminds herself of the duty that has brought her here, her duty to take her uncle away from his past and thrust him into the future.

Oh yes, Jethamoshai, she said to Saifuddin. And how is he now?

Saifuddin, who was a stocky, powerfully built man, in his mid-forties, explained to her, in rapid Hindustani-accented Bengali, that he wasn't well, that they ought to do something for him as soon as possible.

My grandmother, nodding gravely, looked down at her hands, and saw to her surprise that she was carrying a brown-paper packet. Then she remembered why she had brought it, and thrust it into Saifuddin's hands. Here, she said. It's a sari for your wife.

A smile of pleased surprise appeared on Saifuddin's grease-blackened face. He protested that she shouldn't have bothered, and then thanked her profusely and shouted up to his wife to bring tea for their guests from India.

But shouldn't we go and talk to him now? Mayadebi said. We haven't got much time.

You have to have a cup of tea here before you go, the mechanic said firmly. After all, you've come all the way from India. Besides, it's no use going to see Ukil-babu on your way; you have to wait for Khalil.

And who is Khalil? said my grandmother.

Khalil and his family look after Ukil-babu, Saifuddin explained to her. He's a nice fellow. He came over from India too; from Murshidabad, in Bengal. He's a bit stupid, but he's got a good heart. That's what I always say to people – I say, he may be foolish, but he's got a good heart, otherwise why would he bother to look after that old man, a Hindu too, when he could easily have thrown him out and kept both rooms for his family?

He turned to Tridib, and said: Have you been to Motihari, sahb, in Bihar? That's where I was born.

Tridib shook his head.

Saifuddin pursed his lips in disappointment. That's sad,

he said. You must go and visit Motihari when you get back. It's a nice place, though of course there's a lot of trouble there now.

How does Khalil earn a living? my grandmother asked.

He runs a cycle-rickshaw, Saifuddin said. And does little odd jobs here and there. Just about makes enough to keep his wife and children going. It was all right for them when the Ukil-babu was earning a little. But now that he's bedridden, I don't know how they manage.

He fingered his chin thoughtfully. There must be hotels in Motihari now, he said to Tridib. I believe the town has dozens of cinema halls.

Does Khalil's wife cook for him too? my grandmother asked in a hushed voice.

Of course, said Saifuddin. If she didn't the old man wouldn't get anything to eat.

She exchanged a look of amazement with Mayadebi. Do you know, she whispered to Robi, there was a time when that old man was so orthodox that he wouldn't let a Muslim's shadow pass within ten feet of his food? And look at him now, paying the price of his sins.

Ten feet! Robi explained to May in a hushed whisper, marvelling at the precision of the measurement. How did he measure? he whispered back at my grandmother. Did he keep a tape in his pocket when he ate?

No, no, my grandmother said impatiently. In those days many people followed rules like that: they had an instinct.

Trigonometry! Robi cried in a triumphant aside to May. They must have known trigonometry. They probably worked it out like a sum: if the Muslim is standing under a twenty-two foot building, how far is his shadow? You see, we're much cleverer than you: bet your grandfather couldn't tell when a German's shadow was passing within ten feet of his food.

But how, Tridib was asking Saifuddin, did Khalil come

to move into this house? Was the house requisitioned by the government and divided or something like that?

No, Saifuddin said in mild surprise. He came like the rest of us, only later. Don't you know? After Partition Ukil-babu went around looking for people to move into the house because he was afraid his brother's family would come back to claim their share. He used to stand at the gates, welcoming people in. His own children had gone away long ago, no one knows where. One of his sons came once, but Ukil-babu sent him back. Khalil came much later than the rest of us. He just turned up with his family, and the Ukil-babu let him stay. And Khalil has looked after him ever since.

He glanced at them quickly, out of the corners of his eyes. Of course, he added, it's getting very difficult for him now. He can't afford it any longer.

Poor old man, my grandmother said, shaking her head. Do you think he'll agree to go back with us now?

Who knows? Saifuddin gestured towards the heavens with his open palms: He's very old and not quite right in the mind. He doesn't recognise people any more – that's why you have to wait for Khalil before you go to meet him. You may not find it easy to get him to leave. He's grown old here. I couldn't get my father to leave Motihari to come to Pakistan with us. He'd grown old there too . . . But you will have to try; there's no alternative now.

The reedy blast of a rubber horn sounded in the lane outside. A moment later a rickshaw banked steeply through the gate and came shooting into the yard. The driver was standing poised on one pedal, preparing to jump off.

That's Khalil, said Saifuddin. He usually falls off. *Dhishum!* Right on his head. But he has a hard head.

Khalil leapt off the rickshaw while it was still in motion, fell on all fours and abashedly picked himself up. He was a small, stocky man with powerful legs, broad shoulders, and an indeterminately young face. Respectfully lowering his folded lungi, he shuffled up to Saifuddin and said: Yes, sir? It was evident from the deferential angle of his head that he held the mechanic in considerable awe.

These are Ukil-babu's relatives, Khalil, Saifuddin said. I told you about them. They've come all the way from India to take him back. You must do what you can to help them persuade the Ukilbabu to leave.

Khalil turned to them and grinned: there was a wide gap where his front teeth should have been. May remembered later that her heart was instantly won by that broad smile: it was a shy, simple kind of smile, but looking at his face she knew instinctively that behind it lay, not simple-mindedness, but its exact contrary, a quality of mind.

In a deep, low voice, shaking his head, Khalil said: He won't go. It's no use talking to him. He won't go.

Khalil! the mechanic said sharply. You remember what I told you? You have to do something to persuade him to go. It's for his own sake. It's not safe for him here any more.

Khalil shrugged. All right, he said. You can try. But I tell you, it's no use: he won't go.

He gestured to them to follow him and led the way across the yard. My grandmother had difficulty rising to her feet now; Tridib had to help her up. Mayadebi linked arms with her as they slowly walked across the yard. They both had tears running down their cheeks when they stopped at the door. We're going to find out at last about the upside-down house, said my grandmother.

Khalil pushed open the door and ushered them in.

The room was large and very grimy, not from neglect, but from being too densely inhabited. The plaster drooped in blackened scrolls on the walls, and honeycombs of cobwebs hung down from the ceiling. The floor was littered

259

with old tyre tubes and rusty handlebars while the walls were lined with shelves of peeling books and beribboned files.

Mayadebi and my grandmother began to laugh, hugging each other. Nothing's upside-down, said my grandmother.

A woman, hooded in a sari, with two children clutching her knees, was watching them from the shelter of a curtained door at the far end of the room. *Ei*! Khalil said to her: make some tea for them, quick, they're Ukil-babu's relatives, come from Calcutta.

The curtain dropped and she disappeared, but the children stayed, watching them with bright round eyes.

It was not until Khalil crossed the room that they noticed the old man. He was sitting on a high, four-poster bed at the far end of the room, looking out of the window, unaware of their presence. Robi shrank back. He had never seen anyone as old as that: he was so old he seemed childlike – shrunken, tiny, with spit hanging in threads from the corners of his mouth.

My grandmother's eyes misted over as she looked at the old man. Jethamoshai, she cried. We've come home at last . . .

He saw her then and turned his head slowly to look at her.

She covered her head and hurried towards him. We've come back, Jethamoshai, she said, her voice dissolving into a sob. We've come to take you with us.

Stop! he screamed shrilly, cowering back into the grimy bolsters and pillows that lay scattered around him. Stop, stop, stop! What are you doing woman? Stop!

My grandmother froze, in confusion. What do you mean stop? she said, her tear-choked voice taking on an edge of indignation. Don't you recognise me? I'm your . . .

I know who you are, woman, he said irascibly, his thin

voice quavering. But I never let clients touch me. My father never allowed it. It's a dirty habit, he used to say. Now go and sit on that stool over there and tell me about your case.

My grandmother, taken by surprise, obeyed him and sat down.

The old man shook a twig-like finger at Khalil, and gestured at the others.

Tell them to wait in a queue outside, he said. I'll see them one by one. I can't see more than one client at a time.

Now listen to me, Ukil-babu, Khalil bellowed, at the top of his voice. They're not clients, Ukil-babu. They're your relatives.

But the old man was not listening. His eyes were fixed on May. His sagging mouth had fallen open and his tongue had spilled out from the gaps between his teeth.

Playfully, he waggled his head at her. She smiled back.

She's a foreigner, Ukil-babu, Khalil shouted, so loudly that Robi heard him with his feet. She's come from Calcutta with your relatives.

I know, the old man said, blinking at her. I know. I know everything. Clara Bow, Mary Pickford, I know.

Ukil-babu has so much knowledge in his head! Khalil said proudly to my grandmother.

How do you do? the old man said to May in English, whistling through the gaps in his teeth. How do you do?

A thought seemed to come into his mind and he raised his head and surveyed the walls. The pupils of his eyes had leaked into the whites liked punctured egg yolks. He found what he was looking for and slowly raised a matchstick-thin arm.

There, he said, pointing at a picture. Our King-Emperor. God save our gracious king.

There was so much dust encrusted on the picture that

Robi could see nothing except a pointed beard near the bottom of the frame and a crown floating on a cloud of cobwebs at the top.

The old man began to sing – God save our gracious . . . But then he forgot the tune and managed somehow to convert the words into a cheerful hum.

May laughed and began to sing too: God save our . . .

That's right, the old man said, slapping his pillows in applause. Then suddenly, his mouth fell open and his face darkened with worry.

Khalil! he whispered in a whistle that shrilled through the room. Khalil, run, run, go quickly and buy some toilet paper.

What's that? said Khalil. Why?

What if she wants to shit? the old man said. My father always said: the first thing to remember if a foreigner comes to your house is to buy toilet paper. He knew: he read books.

Don't worry Ukil-babu, Khalil shouted, trying to soothe him. She's already been this morning.

How do *you* know? he snapped. Has she told you? You can't even speak English.

My grandmother was distraught now; she couldn't bear to sit still any longer. She leapt to her feet and shouted: Jethamoshai, don't you know who I am?

His face twisted into a peevish scowl as he turned slowly to look at her. Didn't I tell you to sit down, woman? he snapped.

Obediently, my grandmother sat down again. Can't you see? she moaned, wringing her hands. I'm your own brother's daughter.

All right, then, woman, he said. Explain your case to me. What's it all about?

Then Tridib stepped in. Now listen, he said very loudly. We're your relatives; we've come to take you back. Do you remember your brother who lived in the other part of the house?

The old man's face lit up. They died! he said, his voice quivering in triumph. They had two daughters: one with a face like a vulture, and another one who was as poisonous as a cobra but all pretty and goody-goody to look at.

Tridib began to laugh. Well, they've come back to rescue you now, he said.

They both went junketing off somewhere, the old man went on. And as soon as I could I went out into the streets and got hold of whoever I could and moved them in. Now I'm just waiting for them to come back.

He grinned, and Tridib flinched from the festering malevolence in his bare, black gums.

I'm just waiting for them to come back, he said, so that I can drag them through every court in the land up to the Viceroy's Council. 'Possession is nine-tenths of the law' my cousin Brajen used to say, and he knew because he had taken his uncle's family through every court in the kingdom because they had taken away a handful of soil from the land on his side of the canal and added it to theirs.

It's true, Mayadebi said to Tridib. I remember him: he had to sell his land to pay his lawyers.

For one handful of soil! the old man marvelled, staring up at the ceiling. That's the kind of flesh I'm made of. They'll find out: just let them come back.

They *have* come back, my grandmother said gently. But not to fight you in court. We don't want the house. We've come to take you home with us. It's not safe for you here. There might be trouble any day now. You must move while you can.

Move? the old man said incredulously. Move to what?

It's not safe for you here, my grandmother said urgently. I know these people look after you well, but it's not the same thing. You don't understand.

263

I understand very well, the old man muttered. I know everything, I understand everything. Once you start moving you never stop. That's what I told my sons when they took the trains. I said: I don't believe in this India-Shindia. It's all very well, you're going away now, but suppose when you get there they decide to draw another line somewhere? What will you do then? Where will you move to? No one will have you anywhere. As for me, I was born here, and I'll die here.

At that my grandmother gave up. She sighed and got up to go. There's no use talking to him any more, she said. We've done what we can. We'd better go now.

Then Saifuddin the mechanic, who had been listening carefully, went quickly across the room and said: It's no use talking to *him*. He's not responsible for what he says; it's the same as being mad. You'll have to think of some other way of taking him back.

Suddenly Khalil turned to my grandmother, appealing with open arms.

Don't listen to him, he cried. He's only saying this because he wants to put in a claim for the whole house and he can't do it while the old man is still living here. You can't take him away; he won't go. Besides, he's like a grandfather to my children now – what will they do without him?

The mechanic wrenched him around and pushed him back against the wall.

He's lying, he said. It's got nothing to do with claiming the house. You can see Khalil is simple-minded; he doesn't understand anything. I'm telling you to take him away for *his* sake. He's made a lot of enemies over the years. The last time there was trouble we had a hard time protecting him. Who knows what'll happen the next time?

You can't take him away, cried Khalil. He'll die.

Then a female voice broke in; it was Khalil's wife, half hidden by the curtain.

Take him with you, she said. Khalil doesn't know what he's saying. He doesn't have to cook for him and feed him. We have two other children too. How long can we go on like this? Where will the money come from?

And while they were sitting there, frozen into a tableau of indecision, the driver of their car came running up to the door.

Please come quickly, madam, he shouted. We have to leave – there's going to be trouble outside.

He turned on his heel and disappeared.

My grandmother made up her mind.

Listen, Khalil, she said. What we'll do is this: we'll take him back now and keep him with us for a few days, until the trouble's over. Then if he wants to return, we'll bring him back. What about that?

Khalil's head was hanging down in defeat now. All right, he said sullenly. But he won't go in your car. I'll have to bring him in my rickshaw. I'll tell him he's got to go to court – otherwise he won't leave the house. I'll follow your car.

The mechanic laughed scornfully. How can you follow their car? he said. Have you seen it? It's a Mercedes.

Don't worry, Khalil said, glaring at him. I'll manage: if they go a little slowly.

Then he went up to the old man and said something into his ear. The old man turned his head away and shook his hands wildly in the air. But Khalil argued with him for a while and at last he nodded and stretched out his arms. Khalil took a black cotton coat off a peg and helped him into it. Then, reaching under the bed, he pulled out a pair of shoes, put them on his feet and tied the laces.

All right, said the old man. I'm ready to go now.

Khalil handed him his walking-stick, put an arm around his shoulders, and helped him climb off the bed.

Go on ahead, he said to my grandmother. Get into your car.

They left the room with Khalil and the old man following behind. When they reached the yard Tridib helped Khalil lift the old man into the rickshaw.

The mechanic walked with them as far as the gate.

You're doing the right thing, he said to Mayadebi and my grandmother. It's the only thing you could have done.

Ignoring him, they turned to take a last look at the house: at the balconies and terraces, rising in steps out of the ground; at the garden where they had once spent their evenings making up stories about their uncle's part of the house.

Then they stepped through the gate and set off down the lane.

The children were waiting for them and followed them down the lane, laughing and chattering amongst themselves. The little girl who had befriended May appeared again and took hold of her hand. Some of them ran along with the rickshaw, talking to Khalil, and trying to jump up on the handlebars.

The driver was waving to them frantically from the car. He and the security guard threw the doors open and hurried them in.

Quickly now, madam, the driver said, biting his lip. Quickly now.

Robi had expected to see a crowd waiting for them, but the road was empty, deserted, and all the shops were shut.

There's no trouble here, he said to the driver. What were you so worried about?

Just wait a little, the driver said, wiping his forehead with the back of his hand. Just a few minutes, Robi-master.

He started the car and they set off slowly down the empty road with the rickshaw following close behind.

It was Robi who saw them first, immediately after they turned the first corner, the corner my grandmother remembered so well, where the boys used to play football on a patch of grass.

There were dozens of them, stretched all the way across the road. They had lit a fire in the middle of the road, with a few broken chairs and bits of wood. Some of them were squatting around the fire, others were leaning against the lamp-posts and the shop-fronts. Robi could tell from the way they were watching the road that they had been waiting for their car.

He knew then, because of the chill that was spreading outwards from the pit of his stomach, that trouble had come to him at last.

Every word I write about those events of 1964 is the product of a struggle with silence. It is a struggle I am destined to lose – have already lost – for even after all these years I do not know where within me, in which corner of my world, this silence lies. All I know of it is what it is not. It is not, for example, the silence of an imperfect memory. Nor is it a silence enforced by a ruthless state – nothing like that: no barbed wire, no check-points to tell me where its boundaries lie. I know nothing of this silence except that it lies outside the reach of my intelligence, beyond words – that is why this silence must win, must inevitably defeat me, because it is not a presence at all; it is simply a gap, a hole, an emptiness in which there are no words.

The enemy of silence is speech, but there can be no speech without words, and there can be no words without meanings – so it follows, inexorably, in the manner of syllogisms, that when we try to speak of events of which we do not know the meaning, we must lose ourselves in the silence that lies in the gap between words and the world. This is a silence that is proof against any conceivable act of scorn or courage; it lies beyond defiance – for what means have we to defy the mere absence of meaning? Where there is no meaning, there is banality, and that is what this silence consists in, that is why it cannot be defeated – because it is the silence of an absolute, impenetrable banality.

So complete is this silence that it actually took me *fifteen years* to discover that there was a connection between my nightmare bus ride back from school and the events that befell Tridib and the others in Dhaka. And then, too, my discovery was the result of the merest accident, a chance remark. For a long time after I made that discovery it was difficult for me to forgive my own stupidity. But of course, in a sense, there was nothing to forgive. I was a child, and like all the children around me, I grew up believing in the truth of the precepts that were available to me: I believed in the reality of space; I believed that distance separates, that it is a corporeal substance; I believed in the reality of nations and borders; I believed that across the border there existed another reality. The only relationship my vocabulary permitted between those separate realities was war or friendship. There was no room in it for this other thing. And things which did not fit my vocabulary were merely pushed over the edge into the chasm of that silence.

I could not have perceived that there was something more than an incidental connection between those events of which I had a brief glimpse from the windows of that bus, in Calcutta, and those other events in Dhaka, simply because Dhaka was in another country.

One afternoon in 1979, soon after I began work on my PhD, I went to attend a lecture in the Teen Murti House Library in New Delhi. The speaker was an Australian specialist on Asian affairs, and he spoke on India's war with

China in 1962. He was not a particularly good speaker, and he had nothing new to say, but still, he jogged our memories, and when my friends and I went down to the canteen after the lecture, we found ourselves talking about our recollections of that time.

We were all surprised by how much we could remember of that month – October 1962. I, for one, remembered that we had only recently moved to our new house on Southern Avenue when the war began. It was soon after the Pujas. My mother and I had dressed up in our new Puja clothes one evening, and we were waiting for my father to come home so that we could go out visiting relatives. But he was very late, and when at last we heard the squeak of the front gate, my mother led me out into the garden at once so that we could glare at him. But when he stepped out he was not at all abashed by our frowns. His eyes were bleary and there was a huge smile on his face. He swung me up over his head, grinning (I could smell the whisky on his breath), and he said: Do you know what's happened? Nehru's told the army to drive those Chinkies back from our border. There's going to be a war.

I leapt out of his arms and went running up to my grandmother's room, cheering all the way. Tha'mma, I shouted. There's a war, a war with China.

She laughed, I remember – it was a long time since she had laughed – and gave me a hug, and said: Let's hope we teach them a lesson.

Over our half-pots of tea in the canteen, we recalled how quickly we had taught ourselves to distinguish the shapes of their aircraft from ours, how our mothers had donated bangles and earrings for the cause, how we'd stood at street-corners, taking collections and selling little paper flags. We could all remember how the euphoria had faded into confusion as we slowly realised that the Chinese had driven the Indian army back; how we had

269

wondered whether they were going to occupy Assam and
Calcutta.

One of us, a tall, bearded Marxist called Malik, told us
how his father, who had been a Member of Parliament at
that time, had opened the paper one morning, and shot
straight out of the house, dressed in a lungi, and gone
running down to the Foreign Secretary's bungalow down
the road.

Isn't it odd, someone said, that we can remember it so
well?

Why, no, said Malik. It's not odd at all. It was the most
important thing that happened in the country when we
were children.

The others nodded in agreement, but I had my reputation for contrariness to preserve, so I shook my head
and said: Oh, come on, it was just a stupid little skir-
mish somewhere in the hills. It wasn't important at all.
We wouldn't even remember if it the Indian army hadn't
taken such a beating. It didn't mean a thing to most
people.

All right, said Malik, smiling. You tell us, then – what
was more important than the '62 war?

I was at a loss now that he had called my bluff. They
watched me as I scratched my head, thinking hard.

Suddenly, for no reason that I can remember, I said:
What about the riots . . . ?

Which riots? said Malik. There are so many.

Those riots, I said. I had to count the years out on my
fingers.

The riots of 1964, I said.

Their faces went slowly blank, and they turned to look
at each other.

What were the riots of 1964? Malik said with a puzzled
frown. I could tell that he really had no idea what I was
talking about.

I turned to the others and cried: Don't you remember?

They looked away in embarrassment, shaking their heads. It struck me then that they were all Delhi people; that I was the only person there who had grown up in Calcutta.

Surely you remember, I said. There were terrible riots in Calcutta in 1964.

I see, said Malik. What happened?

I opened my mouth to answer and found I had nothing to say. All I could have told them about was of the sound of voices running past the walls of my school, and of a glimpse of a mob in Park Circus. The silent terror that surrounded my memory of those events, and my belief in their importance, seemed laughably out of proportion to those trivial recollections.

There was a riot, I said helplessly.

There are riots all the time, Malik said.

This was a terrible riot, I said.

All riots are terrible, Malik said. But it must have been a local thing. Terrible or not, it's hardly comparable to a war.

But don't you *remember*? I said. Didn't you read about it or hear about it? After all, the war with China didn't happen on your doorstep, but you remember *that*. Surely you remember – you *must* remember?

Regretfully, they shook their heads and blew out clouds of cigarette smoke.

I stood up and tapped Malik on the shoulder. I was determined now that I would not let my past vanish without trace; I was determined to persuade them of its importance.

Come with me, I said. Let's go into the library and look up the newspaper files for 1964. I'll show you.

He grinned at the others and gulped down the rest of his tea. All right, he said. Let's go.

We went into the quiet, air-conditioned gloom of the library and made our way to the shelves at the back where the bound volumes of old newspapers were kept. The volumes of the newspaper I wanted – a well-known Calcutta daily – were stacked along the third row of shelves. There were four massive volumes for 1964.

Do you remember the date? Malik said. Or even the month?

I shook my head. No, I said. I don't remember.

Well, we can't look through all of these at random, he said, nodding at the four volumes. It would take us days.

Then what shall we do? I said.

Maybe there'll be a reference to it in a book or something, he suggested.

And what if we can't find the right book? I said.

Then, Malik said patiently, we'll have to assume that you imagined the whole thing.

He turned and walked off towards a row of shelves.

Malik knew that library fairly well; he'd been researching one thing or another there for several years. He stopped at a shelf and pointed. It was the section on the war of 1962. There were whole shelves of books on the war – histories, political analyses, memoirs, tracts – weighty testimony to the eloquence of war. He pointed out another set of shelves, smiling broadly: it was the section on the 1965 war with Pakistan.

At least we won that one, he said.

But after half an hour we still hadn't found anything on my remembered riots.

Malik was bored now. He stole a look at his watch and gave me a friendly pat on my shoulder. I've got to get back home now, he said. Maybe some other day . . .

I nodded silently, unnerved by the possibility that I had lived for all those years with a memory of an imagined event. And then, as Malik turned to go, an odd little detail stirred in my mind, a faint recollection of the excitement I had felt while I was standing on the pavement that morning, waiting for my school bus to appear.

No, don't go, I said, clutching Malik's arm. I remember something now. It happened during a Test match – with England, I think. Do you remember that series? When that wicketkeeper who was dropped later scored a maiden century?

Yes, of course, he said laughing. Yes I remember that. It was Budhi Kunderan, wasn't it?

Yes! I cried. Yes, that's it – Budhi Kunderan. So it must have happened during the cricket season – perhaps January or February.

All right, said Malik. But this is your last chance – let's go and look.

We went back to the newspaper section and took down the volume for January and February, 1964. Opening it, we began to go through the papers backwards, turning first to the sports pages. Soon Malik found a reference to the visiting English cricket team. A few pages later we stumbled upon a headline which said: MADRAS TEST BEGINS TODAY.

That's it, I cried triumphantly. That was the day, I remember now. I listened to the commentary on the radio after I got home from school.

It was the edition of Friday, 10 January 1964.

Quickly we turned the limp, yellowing pages back until we came to the front page.

So where's your riot? said Malik.

The lead story had nothing to do with riots of any kind, nor with Calcutta: it was about the 68th session of the Congress Party in Bhubaneshwar. Dazed and disbelieving, I read through a report which quoted a speech in which Mr Kamaraj, the party president, had extended an invitation to everyone who had faith in the ideology of socialism

273

and democracy to come together in the common task of building a new society.

It looks, said Malik, as if your riots didn't manage to make it to the front page.

But a moment later, I found what I had been looking for: a short report at the bottom of the page, with a head-line which said: TWENTY-NINE KILLED IN RIOTS.

There, I said, pounding on the paper with my fist. There: Read it for yourself.

I stood back panting, light-headed with relief, and watched his face as he read the report. He read it once, slowly. A frown appeared on his forehead, and he went back to the beginning and read it through again.

Then he looked up at me and said: Didn't you say the riots happened in Calcutta?

Yes, of course, I answered.

That's strange, he said, tapping the open newspaper. Because these riots here happened in Khulna, in East Pakistan, across the border from Calcutta.

The floor of that quiet, familiar library seemed to drop away under my feet leaving me suspended in space. I would have fallen if Malik had not put out a hand to hold me steady. Holding myself upright with both hands, I leant over the desk and read the report.

It said the army had been called out the day before in Khulna, when a demonstration had turned violent and ended in a riot.

It's strange, said Malik, looking at me curiously. It's really very strange that you should remember a riot that happened in Pakistan.

Then he nodded and went away.

Long after he had gone, it occurred to me that news-papers carry the news a day late. I turned the pages to the edition of Saturday, 11 January 1964, and sure enough, there it was: a huge banner headline which said: CURFEW IN CALCUTTA, POLICE OPEN FIRE, 10 DEAD, 15 WOUNDED.

Indistinctly, through the white haze that was swirling before my eyes, I noticed another headline, at the bottom of the page. It said: KUNDERAN'S DAY AT MADRAS, UNBEATEN 170 IN FIRST TEST. And right above it was a tiny little box item in bold print, with the headline: SACRED RELIC REINSTALLED, which said 'the sacred hair of the Prophet Mohammad was reinstalled in the Hazratbal shrine in Srinagar today amongst a tremendous upsurge of popular joy and festivity throughout Kashmir'.

It was thus, sitting in the air-conditioned calm of an exclusive library, that I began my strangest journey: a voyage into a land outside space, an expanse without distances; a land of looking-glass events.

It is said that the sacred relic known as the Mu-i-Mubarak – believed to be a hair of the Prophet Mohammad himself – was purchased by a Kashmiri merchant called Khwaja Nur-ud-din in Bijapur (near Hyderabad) in the year 1699. The following year the sacred relic was transported to the valley of Kashmir. This is only one version of the provenance of the relic; there are several others. It is agreed, however, that the arrival of the relic was greeted by a great tumult of joy in the valley. People are said to have marched in their thousands from every part of Kashmir – even from such distant and remote eyries as the Banihal Pass – in order to get a glimpse of the relic. Later, the relic was installed at the picturesque Hazratbal mosque near Srinagar. This mosque became a great centre of pilgrimage, and every year multitudes of people, Kashmiris of every kind, Muslims, Hindus, Sikhs and Buddhists, would flock to Hazratbal on those occasions when the relic was displayed to the public. This is well attested, even by those European observers whose Christian sense of the necessity of a quarantine between doctrines was outraged by the sight of these ecumenical pilgrims. Thus, over the centuries, the shrine became a symbol of the unique and distinctive culture of Kashmir.

On 27 December 1963, two hundred and sixty-three years after it had been brought to Kashmir, the Mu-i-Mubarak disappeared from its place in the Hazratbal mosque.

As the news spread, life came to a standstill in the valley of Kashmir. Despite the bitter cold (the weather columns of the Delhi papers note that the water mains were frozen in Srinagar that day), thousands of people, including hundreds of wailing women, took out black-flag demonstrations from Srinagar to the Hazratbal mosque. Schools, colleges and shops pulled down their shutters all over the valley and buses and cars vanished from the streets.

The next day, Sunday, 29 December, there were huge demonstrations in Srinagar, in which Muslims, Sikhs and Hindus alike took part. There were a number of public meetings too, which were attended and addressed by members of all the major religious communities. There were some incidents of rioting and a curfew was quickly declared by the authorities. But the targets of the rioters (and with what disbelief we read of this today) were not people – neither Hindus, nor Muslims, nor Sikhs – but property identified with the government and the police.

The government blamed these attacks on 'anti-national elements'.

Over the next few days life in the valley seemed to close in upon itself in a spontaneous show of collective grief. There were innumerable black-flag demonstrations, every shop and building flew a black flag, and every person on the streets wore a black armband. But in the whole of the valley there was not one single recorded incident of animosity between Kashmiri Muslims, Hindus and Sikhs. There is a note of surprise – so thin is our belief in the power of syncretic civilisations – in the newspaper reports which tell us that the theft of the relic had brought together the people of Kashmir as never before. They ascribe this in part to the leadership of Maulana Masoodi – an authentic hero, forgotten and unsung today, as any purveyor of sanity inevitably is in the hysteria of our subcontinent. He it was, they tell us, who persuaded the first demonstrators to march with black flags instead of green, and thereby drew the various communities of Kashmir together in a collective display of mourning.

In Delhi there was consternation. Prime Minister Nehru appealed for patience and dispatched the highest officials of the Central Bureau of Intelligence and the Home Ministry to find the missing relic. The Premier of Kashmir declared that the theft was a 'mad act of some miscreants'.

In Pakistan there were meetings and demonstrations in towns and cities in both wings of the country. The religious authorities, usually so quick to condemn idolatry, declared that the theft of the relic was an attack upon the identity of Muslims. Karachi observed 31 December as a 'Black Day', and soon other cities followed suit. The Pakistani newspapers declared that the theft was part of a deep-laid conspiracy for uprooting the spiritual and national hopes of Kashmiris, and rumbled darkly about 'genocide'.

On 4 January 1964, the Mu-i-Mubarak was 'recovered' by the officials of the Central Bureau of Intelligence. There were no explanations; indeed, to this day nobody really knows what happened to the Hazratbal relic.

But the city of Srinagar erupted with joy. People danced on the streets, there were innumerable thanksgiving meetings, and Muslims, Hindus and Sikhs marched together in demonstrations demanding that the conspirators be revealed. For the first, and almost certainly the last, time the celebratory slogan 'Central Intelligence zindabad!' rang out on the street of an Indian city.

Within this great festival of joy, there was only one small rumble of warning. In Khulna, a small town in the distant east wing of Pakistan, a demonstration that was marching in protest against the theft of the relic turned violent. Some shops were burnt down and a few people were killed.

When I was reading through that short report for the fifth time, it struck me suddenly, like a slap in the face, that May, Tridib and my grandmother must have left for Dhaka the day before. And then I saw Tridib once again, turning to give me our secret Inca salute for the last time, before he turned to go into the departure lounge at Dum Dum airport.

For a long time after that I could not bring myself to go back to that library. I lay on my bed in my dank hostel room in the university, staring at the furry green patches that had sprouted on the ceiling during the monsoons, wondering how, and why, my father had allowed them to go. It seemed so wanton and senseless – and so uncharacteristic, for he was a realistic, practical, and above all *cautious* man. He must have known that something was going to happen – I distinctly remembered how he had cut himself short when he saw that I had heard him mention 'trouble'. I could make no sense of it, and slowly, watching those green shapes crawling across my ceiling, it began to seem to me that he had sent them there on purpose; that he had conspired in Tridib's death.

But later, when I went back to the library, took down a volume of the newspaper we had subscribed to at that time, and opened it at that date – now branded in my memory – 4 January 1964, I made another discovery. I found that there was not the slightest reference in it to any trouble in East Pakistan, and the barest mention of the events in Kashmir. It was, after all, a Calcutta paper, run by people who believed in the power of distance no less than I did.

There is nothing quite as evocative as an old newspaper. There is something in its urgent contemporaneity – the weather reports, the lists of that day's engagements in the city, the advertisements 'for half-remembered films, still crying out in bold print as though it were all happening *now*, today – and the feeling besides that one may once have handled, if not that very paper, then its exact likeness, its twin, which transports one in time as nothing else can. So, looking at the paper that my father had read that morning, I knew he could not be blamed for ignoring the stirrings of the silence around him: in that paper there was not the slightest hint or augury of the coming carnage; it was replete with the fullness of normalcy. And when I looked back at the editions of 1, 2 and 3 January, they were the same: how could I blame him? He was merely another victim of that seamless silence.

And yet he *knew*, and *they* must have known too, all the canny journalists; everybody must have known in some voiceless part of themselves – for events on that scale cannot happen without portents. If they knew, why couldn't they speak of it? They were speaking of so much else, of the Congress conference, of the impending split in the Communist Party, of wars and revolutions: what is it that makes all those things called 'politics' so eloquent and these other unnameable things so silent? Those journalists and historians were, after all, men of intelligence and good intention on the whole, no less than anyone else, and once the riots had started they produced thousands of words of accurate description. But once they were over and there was nothing left to describe they never spoke of it again – while those other events, party splits and party congresses and elections, poured out their eloquence in newspapers and histories for years and years after they were over, as though words could never exhaust their significance. But for these other things we can only use words of description when they happen and then fall silent, for to look for words of any other kind would be to give them meaning, and that is a risk we cannot take any more than we can afford to listen to madness.

So that is why I can only describe at second hand the manner of Tridib's death: I do not have the words to give it meaning. *I do not have the words*, and I do not have the strength to listen.

Once the riots started in Khulna the government of East Pakistan lost no time in sending the army there to put down the 'disturbances'. But it was already too late. One of the headlines of 7 January reads: FOURTEEN DIE IN FRENZY OFF KHULNA.

Over the next few days the riots spread outwards from Khulna into the neighbouring towns and districts and towards Dhaka. Soon Hindu refugees began to pour over the border into India, in trains and on foot. The Pakistani government provided these trains with armed guards and appears to have done what it could to protect them. At some places on the border the trains were stopped by mobs, some of which were heard to chant the slogan 'Kashmir Day zindabad!' (perhaps at that very moment, the crowds in Kashmir were shouting 'Central Intelligence zindabad!') But there do not appear to have been any serious attacks on the trains. The towns and cities of East Pakistan were now in the grip of a 'frenzy' of looting, killing and burning.

In Calcutta, rumours were in the air – especially that familiar old rumour, the harbinger of every serious riot, that the trains from Pakistan were arriving packed with corpses. A few Calcutta dailies printed pictures of weeping, stranded Hindu refugees, along with a few lurid accounts of the events in the east. On 8 and 9 January, with refugees still pouring in, rumours began to flow like floodwaters through the city and angry crowds began to gather at the station.

And so the events followed their own grotesque logic, and on 10 January, the day the cricket Test began in Madras, Calcutta erupted. Mobs went rampaging through the city, killing Muslims and burning and looting their shops and houses.

The police opened fire on mobs in several places and a dusk-to-dawn curfew was imposed on parts of the city. But the scale of the events had already swamped the police. On 11 January the army was called out of Fort William and several battalions were deployed throughout the city. In the next day's papers, underneath the banner headlines, there are pictures of Sikh soldiers patrolling deserted streets. But in the Moulin Rouge on Park Street, it was business as usual, with a tea dance from 5 to 7 p.m. and a Dinner Dance with Delilah accompanied by the 'popular Moulin Rouge quintette'.

The next day, with patrol trucks roaring through the streets, the Moulin Rouge advertised a twist competition and jam session to 'Bongo rhythms'. Perhaps because of the curfew they couldn't get to the newspaper offices in time to withdraw the advertisement.

'Stray incidents' of arson and looting continued, in Dhaka as well as Calcutta, despite the presence of the two armies, for a few days. It took about a week before the papers could declare that 'normalcy' had been 'restored'.

There are no reliable estimates of how many people were killed in the riots of 1964. The number could stretch from several hundred to several thousand; at any rate, not very many less than were killed in the war of 1962.

It is evident from the newspapers that, once the riots started, 'responsible opinion' in both India and East Pakistan reacted with an identical sense of horror and outrage. The university communities of both Dhaka and Calcutta took the initiative in doing relief work and organising peace marches; and newspapers on both sides of the border did some fine, humane pieces of reporting. As always, there were innumerable cases of Muslims in East Pakistan giving shelter to Hindus, often at the cost of their own lives, and equally, in India, of Hindus sheltering Muslims. But they were ordinary people, soon forgotten – not for them any Martyr's Memorials or Eternal Flames.

As for the two governments, they traded a series of curiously symmetrical accusations. On 7 January, a spokesman of the External Affairs Ministry in New Delhi declared that the situation of 'lawlessness' in East Pakistan was an 'inevitable consequence of the incitement and provocative statements' made by Pakistani leaders and the Pakistani press. A few days later the Indian High Commissioner in Pakistan was summoned to the External Affairs Ministry and informed of the Pakistani government's view that the communal incidents in East Pakistan were being played up by the Indian press in order to 'divert the people's attention from the serious happenings in Kashmir'. But even more curiously, within a few days an almost congratulatory note entered into the exchanges between the ministries as they reviewed their respective success in 'quelling' the disturbances. For a while the presidents of the two countries even seriously considered issuing a joint appeal for communal harmony. But soon enough, that plan went the way of all good intentions in the subcontinent, and the memory of the riots vanished into the usual cloud of rhetorical exchanges.

In fact, from the evidence of the newspapers, it is clear that once the riots had started, both governments did everything they could to put a stop to them as quickly as possible. In this they were subject to a logic larger than themselves, for the madness of a riot is a pathological inversion, but also therefore a reminder, of that indivisible sanity that binds people to each other independently of their governments. And that prior, independent relationship is the natural enemy of government, for it is in the logic of states that to exist at all they must claim the monopoly of all relationships between peoples.

The theatre of war, where generals meet, is the stage on which states disport themselves: they have no use for memories of riots.

By the end of January 1964 the riots had faded away from the pages of the newspapers, disappeared from the collective imagination of 'responsible opinion', vanished without leaving a trace in the histories and bookshelves. They had dropped out of memory into the crater of a volcano of silence.

A few months after I had made my discovery in the Teen Murti Library, I found, at the bottom of my bookshelf, the tattered old Bartholomew's Atlas in which Tridib used to point out places to me when he told me stories in his room. Mayadebi had given it to me many years before.

One day, when it was lying open on my desk in my hostel room, quite by chance I happened to find a rusty old compass at the back of my drawer. It had probably been forgotten there by the person who had lived in the room before me.

I picked it up and, toying with it, I placed its point on Khulna and the tip of the pencil on Srinagar.

Khulna is not quite one hundred miles from Calcutta as the crow flies: the two cities face each other at a watchful equidistance across the border. The distance between Khulna and Srinagar, or so I discovered when I measured the space between the points of my compass, was 1200 miles, nearly 2000 kilometres. It didn't seem like much. But when I took my compass through the pages of that atlas, on which I could still see the smudges left by Tridib's fingers, I discovered that Khulna is about as far from Srinagar as Tokyo is from Beijing, or Moscow from Venice, or Washington from Havana, or Cairo from Naples.

Then I tried to draw a circle with Khulna at the centre and Srinagar on the circumference. I discovered immediately that the map of South Asia would not be big enough. I had to turn back to a map of Asia before I found one large enough for my circle.

It was an amazing circle.

Beginning in Srinagar and travelling anti-clockwise, it cut through the Pakistani half of Punjab, through the tip of Rajasthan and the edge of Sind, through the Rann of Kutch, and across the Arabian Sea, through the southernmost toe of the Indian Peninsula, through Kandy, in Sri Lanka, and out into the Indian Ocean until it emerged to touch upon the northernmost finger of Sumatra, then straight through the tail of Thailand into the Gulf, to come out again in Thailand, running a little north of Phnom Penh, into the hills of Laos, past Hué in Vietnam, dipping into the Gulf of Tonking, then swinging up again through the Chinese province of Yunnan, past Chungking, across the Yangtze Kiang, passing within sight of the Great Wall of China, through Inner Mongolia and Sinkiang, until with a final leap over the Karakoram Mountains it dropped again into the valley of Kashmir.

It was a remarkable circle: more than half of mankind must have fallen within it.

And so, fifteen years after his death, Tridib watched over me as I tried to learn the meaning of distance. His atlas showed me, for example, that within the tidy ordering of Euclidean space, Chiang Mai in Thailand was much nearer Calcutta than Delhi is; that Chengdu in China is nearer than Srinagar is. Yet I had never heard of those places until I drew my circle, and I cannot remember a time when I was so young that I had not heard of Delhi or Srinagar. It showed me that Hanoi and Chungking are nearer Khulna than Srinagar, and yet did the people of Khulna care at all about the fate of the mosques in Vietnam and South China (a mere stone's throw away)? I doubted it. But in this other direction, it took no more than a week . . . .

In perplexity I turned back through the pages of the atlas at random, shut my eyes, and let the point of my compass fall on the page. It fell on Milan, in northern Italy. Adjusting my compass to the right scale I drew a circle which had Milan as its centre and 1200 miles as its radius.

This was another amazing circle. It passed through Helsinki in Finland, Sundsvall in Sweden, Mold in Norway, above the Shetland Islands, and then through a great empty stretch of the Atlantic Ocean until it came to Casablanca. Then it travelled into the Algerian Sahara, through Libya, into Egypt, up through the Mediterranean, where it touched on Crete and Rhodes before going into Turkey, then on through the Black Sea, into the USSR, through Crimea, the Ukraine, Byelorussia and Estonia, back to Helsinki.

Puzzling over this circle, I tried a little experiment. With my limited knowledge, I tried to imagine an event, any event, that might occur in a city near the periphery of that circle (or, indeed, much nearer) – Stockholm, Dublin, Casablanca, Alexandria, Istanbul, Kiev, any city in any direction at all – I tried to imagine an event that might happen in any of those places which would bring the people of Milan pouring out into the streets. I tried hard but I could think of none.

None, that is, other than war.

It seemed to me, then, that within this circle there were only states and citizens; there were no people at all.

When I turned back to my first circle I was struck with

wonder that there had really been a time, not so long ago, when people, sensible people, of good intention, had thought that all maps were the same, that there was a special enchantment in lines; I had to remind myself that they were not to be blamed for believing that there was something admirable in moving violence to the borders and dealing with it through science and factories, for that was the pattern of the world. They had drawn their borders, believing in that pattern, in the enchantment of lines, hoping perhaps that once they had etched their borders upon the map, the two bits of land would sail away from each other like the shifting tectonic plates of the prehistoric Gondwanaland. What had they felt, I wondered, when they discovered that they had created not a separation, but a yet-undiscovered irony – the irony that killed Tridib: the simple fact that there had never been a moment in the 4000-year-old history of that map when the places we know as Dhaka and Calcutta were more closely bound to each other than after they had drawn their lines – so closely that I, in Calcutta, had only to look into the mirror to be in Dhaka; a moment when each city was the inverted image of the other, locked into an irreversible symmetry by the line that was to set us free – our looking-glass border.

There was only one small chink in the armour of austerity that had sat so heavily on my grandmother ever since I could remember: she had a secret fondness for jewellery. There'd been nothing secret about this weakness of hers when she was a girl: it had been a passion.

I know this because I sometimes heard relatives – people who had known her in Dhaka – teasing her about her love of jewellery; asking her what had become of all those necklaces and bangles she had made my grandfather buy her.

Their teasing didn't bother my grandmother at all.

It was a good thing I had something to fall back on,

she would say quietly. How do you think I managed, all those years when I was living in that slum, when all of you'd forgotten about me? How do you think I would have survived if I hadn't had my jewellery to fall back on?

The offending relative would be stung into silence. But later, when we were out of her hearing, they would explain to me, chuckling, that her love of jewellery had been a family joke when she was a girl. She would often be seen at the little gold-merchant's shop at the corner of Jindabahar Lane, peering in through the bars, staring at the gold-smiths working inside. She took so much delight in exclaiming over her married cousins' jewellery cases that they had kept the keys ready on the ends of their saris whenever she went visiting. At weddings, knowing old housewives would ask her for her opinion on the jewellery the bride had been given, as though she were a gold-merchant's grandmother, rather than a chit of a girl.

She had stopped wearing jewellery publicly, of course, after she was widowed, and later, when my father married my mother, she had given her all the jewellery she hadn't yet sold. She loved to see my mother wearing the bangles and necklaces she had given her. But my mother didn't particularly care for jewellery and rarely wore any – even to weddings.

This never failed to infuriate my grandmother. So you're going to a wedding with your neck bare? she would snap at my mother. I suppose you want to give everybody the impression that you're starving here.

But it's horrible to be weighed down with gold in this heat, my mother would protest.

So then what did I save all this stuff for? my grand-mother would say, glaring at her. I could have sold it off, along with all the rest – God knows I needed the money – but I saved it so that my daughter-in-law wouldn't have anything to complain about. And now you tell me you're too fashionable to wear gold at a wedding. The problem is that your generation of girls has grown too used to luxury – you've forgotten the value of things. I'd just like to see you bringing up that spoilt son of yours in a one-room tenement in a slum; I'd just like to see it.

So, to mollify her, my mother would open the steel box in her cupboard, take out one of the necklaces she had been given and put it on.

My grandmother would pretend not to notice for a while, but in fact, of course, she was always delighted. After a decent interval she would summon my mother and run her fingers over the necklace, smiling to herself and reminiscing about the place where she had bought it, trying to remember the name of the shop.

My mother would take it off and slip it into her handbag as soon as she was out of the house (horrible heavy thing!), but my grandmother was not to know, and the mere sight of the necklace would leave her contented.

But there was one piece of jewellery that she had never parted with. It was a long, thin gold chain with a tiny ruby pendant. It was so much a part of her that I hardly noticed it: she had never taken it off, at least not in my recollection.

But all the same, she was very ashamed of wearing it, and went to great lengths to hide it under her blouse, spreading it out over her shoulders, with the pendant tucked deep inside so that nobody would see it. She believed that our relatives would gossip if they saw her wearing it.

I know what they'd say, she would mutter. They'd say: Look at her – she's been a widow for years and she's still wearing jewellery as though she were a girl. Why, I'm sure even your father thinks that, deep down in his heart.

Of course she did not neglect to inform my father of her views. He, for his part, would try to persuade her that he didn't mind about her necklace at all, that, indeed, he would have been happy if she'd worn more jewellery. And perhaps in a way he would have been; perhaps it really would have pleased him to see her, all dressed up, like his fashionable colleagues' mothers, who went to clubs with their sons wearing just the right touches of gold around their necks and wrists, laying claim to chicdom through their defiance of the ancient, but sadly *démodé*, proscriptions.

But my grandmother didn't believe my father when he said he didn't mind, and perhaps she was right: maybe my father, despite his protestations, did mind her wearing even that thin gold chain; maybe somewhere deep in his heart he did really think of it as a sign of disrespect to his dead father.

But my grandmother didn't intend any disrespect to his memory; far from it.

I wear it because He gave it to me, she explained to me once. You know – your grandfather. It was the first thing He ever gave me – in Rangoon, soon after we were married. They have wonderful rubies there. I couldn't bear to give it away now – He wouldn't like it. I haven't taken it off once in these thirty-two years – not even when I had my gall-bladder operation. They wanted me to take it off, but I made them sterilise it instead. I wasn't going to have my operation without it. It's become a part of me now.

Sometimes, while massaging her neck, or when she had fallen asleep in her chair, I would pull the chain out of her blouse and run it through my fingers. It was so scratched and discoloured it didn't look like gold any more. It smelt exactly like her, of soap and starch and powder, but in a sharpened, metallic kind of way. It really was a part of her.

And then, one day in the year 1965, more than one and a half years after her trip to Dhaka, she gave it away.

One afternoon I came home from school to find the

radio blaring at top volume in my grandmother's room, upstairs. It was so loud I could hear it on the pavement, where the schoolbus had left me. I ran in and found my mother lying prostrate on her bed, with her fingers jabbed against her temples and a wet cloth draped over her eyes.

What's going on? I asked her.

Who's to know but God? she said. Your Tha'mma went out of the house at ten this morning and came back a couple of hours later. She wouldn't have anything to eat – I asked her myself, I said, you'll fall ill if you don't eat, but who's listening to whom? – and instead she went upstairs and turned on her radio and it's been going like that ever since. She turns it even higher when the news comes on; it's happened three times already.

Where did she go? I said. I was very surprised, because at that time my grandmother hardly ever left her room: we could count the number of times she had been out of the house in the last year on the fingers of one hand.

My mother shrugged again and pulled a face. Who knows where she went? she said. Who cares?

Didn't you go up and ask? I said, knowing that the answer would be no, because at that time I was the only person in the house whom she would allow into her room.

Why don't *you* go and tell her to turn it down now? my mother said. She might listen to you. It's no use my asking her.

I ran upstairs and pushed my grandmother's door open. I could only see her back. She was crouching over the radio, with both her arms around it, as though she were waiting for the noise to blow a hole through her.

I knew at once, the moment I saw her.

Tha'mma! I shouted. What's happened to your chain? What have you done with it?

She turned to look at me then. Her hair was hanging in wet ropes over her face; her eyes were glazed and her spectacles had fallen off. I was frightened by the sight of her: I wished I hadn't shut the door behind my back.

I gave it away, she said, her glazed, unfocussed eyes alighting, not on me, but on a point on the wall above my head.

Why Tha'mma? I said. Why did you do that?

I gave it *away*, she screamed. I gave it to the fund for the war. I had to, don't you see? For *your* sake; for your freedom. We have to kill them before they kill us; we have to wipe them out.

She began to pound on the radio with both hands. I took a step backwards, fumbling with the doorknob, behind my back.

This is the only chance, she cried, her voice rising to a screech. The only one. We're fighting them properly at last, with tanks and guns and bombs.

Then the glass front of the radio shattered as her fist drove into it. Bits of glass tinkled on to the floor and the radio sputtered and fell silent. She wrenched her hand back, gouging out flesh and skin on the jagged edges of the glass. She gave her bloody hand a shake, put it on her lap and stared at it, bemusedly, as the blood dripped down the sides of her sari, dyeing it a gentle, batik-like crimson.

I must get to the hospital, she said to herself, perfectly calm now. I mustn't waste all this blood. I can donate it to the war fund.

It was then that I screamed. I screamed from the pit of my stomach, holding my head and shutting my eyes. I screamed until my mother and the servants came and carried me to my room, and even then I screamed and would not open my eyes.

I was still whimpering when my mother came into my room with the doctor. She patted my head and said: The doctor's going to give you an injection so that you'll be able to rest for a while.

I struck her hand away and said: What's happened to Tha'mma?

Don't worry about her, said my mother. She's all right. Your father came with another doctor and they took her away to a nice hospital where she can rest for a few days. Doctors and nurses will look after her, and she'll be very calm and happy. Don't worry about her.

Why did she do that? I said. What did she want?

My mother felt my forehead worriedly while the doctor tested his syringe.

Don't worry about Tha'mma, she said. It's this war with Pakistan. She's been listening to the news on the radio all the time and it hasn't been good for her. She's never been the same, you know, since they killed Tridib over there.

'Killed' Tridib? I said, as the needle slipped into my arm. Who killed Tridib? You told me it was an accident.

Yes, yes, my mother said quickly. That's what I meant. Now go to sleep, don't worry.

Why did you say 'killed'? I said. What did you mean?

But the soporific glow of the tranquilliser had already begun to warm my body, and in a moment I shut my eyes and forgot.

That was the first time I had any inkling that Tridib's death was the result of something other than an accident.

I was sent to stay with my mother's brother in Durgapur when his body was brought back from Dhaka. He was cremated while I was away. May left for London the same day, and immediately afterwards Mayadebi and her family went back to Dhaka.

I knew nothing of what had happened, nothing – not even that Tridib was dead.

My parents came to Durgapur a week later, to fetch me, and on the way to Calcutta my father stopped the car at the great temple of Ma Kali at Dakshineshwar. I was taken aback, because I knew my father hated fighting his way through the crowds at the temple. Why have we stopped here? I asked.

Never mind, he said, and I knew at once that it was a special occasion.

We locked the car and went in, followed by a swarm of importuning *pandas*. My father spotted our family priest, and he came running across the great paved courtyard and led us through the crowd up to the inner temple. While we were circumambulating the inner temple, with our offerings cupped in our hands, my father put a hand on my shoulder and said: Listen, there's something I have to tell you. A very sad thing happened while you were away in Durgapur. Tridib died in an accident in Dhaka.

He stopped and bent down to look into my face; I think he'd expected me to burst into tears. But for me 'dead' was just a word, associated vaguely with films and comic books. That was all; I had no means of attaching that word to a real presence, like Tridib's. I felt nothing – no shock, no grief. I did not understand that I would never see him again; my mind was not large enough to accommodate so complete an absence.

What sort of accident? I said.

Their car was stopped by some hooligans, my father told me. Just ordinary ruffians like you have everywhere. But the car swerved and crashed into a wall or something . . . That was all. No one else was hurt.

I nodded and went ahead, my offerings still safe in my hands.

No, wait, my father said, pulling me to a halt. Listen: you have to promise me something. Remember you're holding Ma Kali's flowers in your hands, so you can't ever go back on your word. Promise me that you'll never talk about this anywhere – never, not in school, not to Montu, not to your friends at the park. You know that Meshomoshai – Tridib's father – is a very important man in the government? He

293

doesn't want people to hear about this – it has to be kept secret, so you mustn't talk about it. Most of all, you mustn't ask your Tha'mma any questions about what happened. She's already very upset, and it would only get worse if you made her talk about it. You're growing up now, you're a big boy, and you have to understand that there are things grown-ups don't talk about.

I nodded, but I didn't really give him my word – not because I did not think I could keep it, but merely because I could not understand why he was making such a fuss. My friends wouldn't have been interested in an accident in some far-off place anyway. There was nothing to talk about: an accident was such a petty way to die.

The first time Robi ever talked about Tridib's death was in London: at the end of that beautiful September day when Ila took us to Lymington Road to meet Mrs Price.

Ila had promised to give Robi and me dinner at her favourite 'Indian' restaurant – a small Bangladeshi place called the Maharaja, in Clapham – after we'd been to see Mrs Price. She did her best to persuade Nick to come with us too, when he walked us back to the West Hampstead tube station. But Nick declined politely: he had something to do that evening, he said; he would have to put it off till some other time. He waved us goodbye at West Hampstead station.

Ila was so disappointed she did not say a single word all the way to Clapham Common.

The restaurant was only a few minutes' walk from the underground station. Ila pointed it out to us as soon as we climbed out – a dimly lit plate-glass window, with heavy velvet curtains, wedged in between a dozen other eating places, ranging from Guyanese to Turkish. When Robi pushed the door open, we found ourselves in a narrow, rectangular room, divided into little cubicles, each with its own table and chairs. The tables were lit by brass lamps with tasselled shades and the chairs were upholstered in worn purple cloth. The room smelt powerfully of spices, as though the central heating had grafted the odours of the kitchen deep into the wallpaper and upholstery.

The restaurant was almost empty when we went in. The man behind the counter, at the far end of the room, waved when he saw Ila, and came hurrying towards us.

How are you, Rehman-shaheb? Ila said as she handed him her coat.

I'm very well, he said, smiling broadly. He was a short, middle-aged man, with round cheeks and greying hair, dressed in a black jacket and a white bow tie. He spoke Bengali with a nasal Sylhet accent, and we had to listen to him carefully to follow, even though he was obviously making an effort to match his speech to ours.

Where have you been all these days? he was saying to Ila. We haven't seen you in here for so long we thought you'd moved away from Stockwell.

Ila laughed. Oh no, Rehman-shaheb, she said. I wouldn't move away without telling you first.

Rehman-shaheb ushered us to a table, pulled back the chairs and handed us each a menu. Robi opened his, looked at it for a moment, and gave me a sidelong glance.

Chicken Singapore? he said under his breath.

Prawn Bombay? I responded.

Robi sighed and snapped his menu shut. Why don't you order, Ila? he said. You obviously know the place.

Ila ordered quickly, without bothering to look at the menu. When Rehman-shaheb had taken our orders and gone into the kitchen, she leant towards us and whispered: Treat it like something exotic – like Eskimo food – and you'll enjoy it. You're not going to get your mothers' chochchori and bhat; you mustn't expect anything familiar.

She was proved right when the food came: everything

fell just beyond the border of familiarity – the usual taste of spices transformed by stock and cream and Worcestershire Sauce. But the food was delicious in its own way, and we ate heartily while Robi told us stories about his colleagues in the Indian Administrative Service – funny stories about lonely young men who lived in huge colonial mansions in remote districts and spent their time writing symbolist poetry and masturbating.

After the plates had been cleared away and Ila had paid for the dinner with her credit card, Rehman-shaheb came back with three cups of coffee on a tray.

This is from us, he said. I mean, 'Compliments of the House', *ar ki*; you know? It's a custom over here.

Oh, Rehman-shaheb! exclaimed Ila. Why did you do all this? You shouldn't have. But now you have to sit with us for a while.

Yes, do sit with us for a bit, I added. For me the experience of hearing Bengali dialects which I had never heard in Calcutta being spoken in the streets of London was still replete with unexplored ironies.

All right, Rehman-shaheb said, and pulled a chair up to our table. There was an awkward moment of silence, and then Ila said: Rehman-shaheb, do you know, my uncle Robi over there lived in your part of the world when he was a boy, in Dhaka.

Oh, is that so? said Rehman-shaheb. I lived there too for a bit. When were you there?

It was a long time ago, said Robi. From 1962 to 1964.

I see, said Rehman-shaheb, I left before that – joined a ship, you know. Have you been back after that? After Bangladesh became independent?

Robi shook his head.

You must go, said Rehman-shaheb. It's completely changed now – so modern. You won't believe it. But tell me, which part of the city did you live in?

In Dhanmundi, said Robi.

Ah there, said Rehman-shaheb. That was for rich folks and foreigners. Did you ever go into the old city? Now that's where you should have gone: the sweets you'll get there! Like nowhere else in the world, not even Calcutta. And the people! They're so hospitable, they'll take you straight into their houses.

Robi smiled thinly.

Ila gave me a worried glance and pushed her chair back.

But I don't suppose you've ever been into that part of the town, have you? said Rehman-shaheb, smiling at Robi.

Yes, said Robi. As a matter of fact, I have. You see my mother was born there.

Really? cried Rehman-shaheb. Where? Do you remember where?

Robi's smile was like a grimace now. Yes, he said. I do remember. You had to go past Shador-bajar, and then turn off the road and go down a long road crowded with shops, and then you had to turn off at a corner where there was a kind of field where the boys used to play football, and then there's a hardware shop, and that's the corner of the lane where my mother was born – Jindabahar Lane, Dhaka.

Allah! said Rehman-shaheb. You remember it very well I can see. But you must have been very young then. How is it that you remember?

I pushed my chair back and stood up. We ought to go now, I said.

But Robi didn't hear me. He was leaning towards Rehman-shaheb, gripping the table, his knuckles white.

I remember it because my brother was killed there, he said. In a riot – not far from where my mother was born. Now do you see why I remember?

Rehman-shaheb leapt to his feet, his face red with embarrassment.

Robi stood up, pushed his way past us and went out.

Oh, I'm so . . . Rehman-shaheb said to Ila. I didn't mean . . . I really didn't.

Don't worry, Ila said quickly. It's not your fault. I know you didn't mean it. It's mine – I shouldn't have brought up the subject. Ila snatched up her coat, gave Rehman-shaheb's arm one last pat and whispered: It's all right, don't worry. Then she followed me out of the restaurant.

He was gone by the time we were out. It was a while before we saw him, in the distance, as he passed a lamp-post. He was striding fast down the Clapham Road, towards Stockwell. We began to run.

When we caught up with him we tried to fall in step, but his strides were so long we virtually had to run to keep up. We walked past the fast-food shops on the Clapham Road, beneath the railway bridge and the underground station at Clapham North. At length Robi came to a halt. He shook his arms free and said: I need to sit somewhere. Just for a minute.

There was an overgrown garden to our left, and within it a derelict white church, with a short flight of steps in front. Robi led us through the gate and up to the steps. Clearing a space for himself among the leaves on the stairs, he sat down and lit a cigarette.

It's a dream, you know, he said, blowing a plume of smoke at his feet. I only get it about twice a year now, but it used to be once a week, when I was younger – in college, for instance. But I learnt to control it – I often know when it's coming, and on nights like that I try not to sleep. It always begins with our car going around a corner. There's a muddy kind of field on one side, a very small one, but it's got a crooked goalpost stuck in the mud. We turn the corner and there they are, ahead of us, strung out across the road. Sometimes it's a crowd, sometimes just a couple of men. I know their faces well now, better than I know my friends'. There's one with a very thin face and a wispy moustache and a crooked mouth. He's always in it. The odd thing is, that no matter how many men there are – a couple, or dozens – the street always seems empty. It was full of people when we went through it – a bazaar, all the shops open, people going in and out, rickshaws, thela-garis, vendors, donkeys. And there were people in the houses above the shops too, looking down at us, from the windows and balconies. But all the shops are shut now, barricaded, and so are the windows in the houses. There's no one on the balconies. The street's deserted, but for those men. I can see little details sometimes: a green coconut, for instance, lying in the middle of the road, wobbling when the breeze catches it; a slipper on the pavement – not a pair, just a single rubber slipper, lying there abandoned.

There's a grinding kind of noise somewhere inside the car, and it lurches, throwing everyone forward, so that I almost bang my head against the dashboard. Someone in the back seat, I think it's my mother, but I've never been sure, cries: Don't stop, go on.

And the car does go on, in fact the driver had merely changed gears without declutching properly. It's moving forward again now – not steadily, but in short jerks, because the driver's so scared he's lost control of his right foot. His cap's fallen off, and he's sitting hunched over the wheel, with sweat dripping down his face. The security guard, sitting beside me, in the front seat, is looking ahead, fingering his shirt.

Then the men begin to move towards us – they're not running, they're gliding, like skaters in a race. They fan out and begin to close in on us. It's all silent, I can't hear a single thing, no sound at all.

The security guard pushes me down and reaches back to make sure our doors are locked. I can only see his blue uniform now, from where I am. I can't see his face and I can't look outside. I see him reaching under his shirt, and when he pulls out his hand there's a revolver in it, a very small one. It's got an odd colour, sort of slate-grey. I can see it in detail because it's right next to my face.

Then the car veers away, and suddenly there's a huge thump on the bonnet, and somebody screams at the back. I look up then, lifting my head just a little, until it's level with the bottom of the windscreen, and there's a face there, on the other side of the glass, the nose flattened, the eyes looking in. It's the man with the crooked mouth; he's lying flat on the bonnet, and he's seen me. He raises his arm and swings it back; there's something in it, but I don't know what it is, I can never see it. His arm comes swinging down, over his head in an arc, and suddenly the windscreen clouds over and crashes in. When I look up at the driver there's a cut across his face, and he's clutching a flap of skin trying to hold it in place, on his cheek. He doesn't have either hand on the steering wheel. The car lurches, rolls forward, and stalls, with its front wheel in a gutter.

The security guard pushes me down again, and then he throws the door open and jumps out, with the revolver ready in his hand. He shouts something, I don't know what, and then he shouts again, and there's a crash, and I know he's fired a shot. I look out then, out of the window, and I see the men, circling around us, drawing back, and the sound of the shot is still echoing off those closed windows and empty balconies.

There's a moment of absolute quiet as they watch us and we watch them. It's so still I can hear the sound of the driver's blood dripping on the steering wheel. And then the silence is broken: there's a creak somewhere behind us – it's a small sound, but in the quiet it sounds like a thunderclap. We all turn: we in the car, they outside. And do you know what it is? It's the rickshaw – Khalil's rickshaw – with the old man, our grand-uncle, whom we'd gone to

300

rescue, sitting at the back, all dressed up in his lawyer's coat.

And as I watch, the rickshaw begins to grow. It becomes huge, that rickshaw, it grows till it's bigger than the shops and the houses; so big that I can't see the old man sitting on top. But those men are running towards it, as fast as it grows, they're scrambling up its wheels, up its poles, along the sides. They've forgotten us now; there's no one around us – they're all busy climbing up the rickshaw. The security guard jumps in, grinning, and shouts something to the driver: he's telling him to start the car and get going while he can – to think about his face later. And they're shouting at the back too, telling the driver to be quick, to get going. The driver reaches for the key, he's stretched his arm all the way out, as far as it'll go, but it doesn't reach, no matter how hard he tries. And while he's straining to reach the key, somebody gets out at the back; I hear the door slamming shut. When I look around I see May: she's tiny, shrunken, and behind her is that rickshaw, reaching heavenwards, like a gigantic anthill, and its sides are seething with hundreds of little men.

May is screaming at us; I can't hear a word, but I know what she's saying. She's saying: Those two are going to be killed because of you – you're cowards, murderers, to abandon them here like this.

The door opens again, and I know in my heart that Tridib is going to get out too. I stretch out a hand to pull him back into the car, but my hand won't reach him; I try to shout, but I have no voice left, I cannot make a single sound.

And that is when I wake up, gagging, trying to scream.

Robi shook another cigarette out of his pack and tried to strike a match. The first match broke, and he threw it away and struck another, held it steady and lit his cigarette.

I've never been able to rid myself of that dream, he said. Ever since it first happened. When I was a child I used to pray that it would go away: if it had, there would have been nothing else really, to remind me of that day. But it wouldn't go; it stayed. I used to think: if only that dream would go away, I would be like other people; I would be free. I would have given anything to be free of that memory.

He laughed, looking at the glowing tip of his cigarette.

Free, he said laughing. You know, if you look at the pictures on the front pages of the newspapers at home now, all those pictures of dead people – in Assam, the north-east, Punjab, Sri Lanka, Tripura – people shot by terrorists and separatists and the army and the police, you'll find somewhere behind it all that single word; everyone's doing it to be free. When I was running a district I used to look at those pictures and wonder sometimes what I would do if it were happening in my area. I know what I'd have to do; I'd have to go out and make speeches to my policemen, saying: You have to be firm, you have to do your duty. You have to kill whole villages if necessary – we have nothing against the people, it's the terrorists we want to get, but we have to be willing to pay a price for our unity and freedom. And when I went back home, I would find an anonymous note waiting for me, saying: We're going to get you, nothing personal, we have to kill you for our freedom. It would be like reading my own speech transcribed on a mirror. And then I think to myself, why don't they draw thousands of little lines through the whole subcontinent and give every little place a new name? What would it change? It's a mirage; the whole thing is a mirage. How can anyone divide a memory? If freedom were possible, surely Tridib's death would have set me free. And yet, all it takes to set my hand shaking like a leaf, fifteen years later, thousands of miles away, at the other end of another continent, is a chance remark by a waiter in a restaurant.

He shrugged, threw away his cigarette, and stood up. I suppose we should be going, he said.

Then Ila, who had been sitting beside him, stood up too and put an arm around his shoulders and another around mine, and held us together. We stood a long time like that, on the steps of that derelict church in Clapham, three children of a free state together, clinging.

I had hoped to spend my last day in London visiting my old haunts – West End Lane, Lymington Road, Stockwell and the Embankment – one last time before leaving for India. In the evening I was to go to Islington because May had invited me to dinner.

But, as it turned out, the day went past in a breathless rush, and I almost forgot about dinner.

I had to make the journey from Fulham to the West End twice, with my suitcase still unpacked: once when I discovered that I had merely overlooked two of the names I thought I had already ticked on my list of presents. I ran all the way from the house to the tube station at Putney Bridge, sweat pouring down my face, my shirt clammy on my back. Then I pushed my way out into the crowds on Oxford Street, into teeming, confused shops, and then out again, clutching morose little parcels – brushed-denim jeans of just the right length and colour for a friend in Delhi, and a digital watch for a family friend in Calcutta – and back into the bowels of the tube station and into the first train, drumming on the armrest of my seat, trying to avoid the glare of the Walkman-ed skinhead opposite me. Back to my room, to pull everything out of my suitcase and start all over again, only to find a note I had left for myself in my ticket folder, which told me that my ticket had not yet been confirmed. So back again then, all the way to Regent Street, the chilly wind grafting my shirt to my back, running all the way to the airline office, and of course, when I get there, the girl in the uniform, behind the counter, tells me, smiling kindly, seeing me mopping the sweat off my forehead: You could have done it over the phone, luv. Back again to Fulham, my feet aching, nothing done yet, so much left to do, and no time to do it in.

I have to be at Heathrow, tomorrow at midday.

At lunch-time I telephoned Ila at her office.

Oh, it's you, she said abruptly, when she recognised my voice.

There was a short silence, and then I said: Ila, don't you remember? I'm leaving for India tomorrow.

I know, she said, with an unfamiliar note of awkwardness in her voice. Puzzled, I asked her whether there were other people in the room.

No, no, she said quickly, it's not that. There's no one here.

Then what's the matter? I said. Why do you sound so odd?

Look, she said. I meant to come to the airport with you, to see you off. I really meant to, you know. But . . .

Don't worry about that, I said. What's happened?

Well, it's like this, she said. Nick and I are driving down to Cornwall for the weekend. We're taking a little holiday.

That's nice, I said, in my most neutral voice.

You mustn't pay any attention to what I said the other day, she said in a rush. I wanted to tell you that. I was just overwrought, and it made me suspicious. Nick wouldn't dream of doing anything that might upset me, really, believe me. You mustn't believe a word I said. I made it all up. That's what I did, I made it all up. That's the truth of it. I talked to him later, and he showed me how silly I was being. It's all fine now. We need a little holiday, that's all.

She was speaking very fast, in an unnaturally high voice.

Of course I believe you, I said. Why shouldn't I? I hope you have a nice time.

I know you don't believe me, she said.

There was a catch in her voice, she sounded almost as though she was choking.

Ila, I said. Shall I come over? Are you all right?

Of course I'm all right, she shouted into the phone. I'm fine. Have a nice flight.

There was a click as she slammed the receiver down, and the line went dead.

I went back to my suitcase, upstairs.

At about seven in the evening, when my packing was nearly done, I found myself trying to make room for a small porcelain vase in a corner of my suitcase. It was soon evident that it would break if I put it in. Scratching my head, I wondered what had possessed me to buy it in the first place.

And then I remembered. I had bought it a week ago, when May had telephoned to ask me to dinner. I was so touched I'd gone out and bought her a present that very morning. That was what that vase was, her present, and I was meant to give it to her that evening.

I raced out of my room, hurled myself down the stairs, burst into the kitchen, and more or less snatched the telephone out of the hands of the Scandinavian flagellationist. He glared at me, banged a fist on the tin-topped kitchen table and stormed out of the kitchen.

An age seemed to pass before I heard May's voice.

Hullo May, I cried in relief. I'm coming; I'm on my way. I hope you hadn't given me up yet.

Of course not, she said, I wasn't expecting you till half-past.

I'll be with you in half an hour, I said. I'll take a taxi.

That's all right, she said. There's no hurry. Come when you like.

Within a short while I was standing at her door, with the vase stuffed into my pocket.

Later, when I was back in Delhi, I often used to wonder whether I would ever have had the courage to ask May the one question I had so long been longing to ask. I don't know, and I never found out, for she spared me the task. It was she who ended the desultory conversation about my thesis that had sustained us through dinner, and raised her head to look at me, her blue eyes clear and forthright, and said: Why haven't you ever asked me how Tridib died? I thought it would be the first thing you'd ask.

I told her the truth: that I hadn't known how to ask, that I simply hadn't possessed the words; that I had not had the courage to breach her silence without a solid bridge-head of words.

You should have asked, she said. It was your right and it is my duty to try to find an answer.

She was sitting bolt upright, her hands on the table, one upon the other.

I suppose you know most of it already, she began.

I could tell that she had been preparing herself for that moment.

We were on our way back from your grandmother's ancestral house, she went on. The car was stopped. By a mob. I'm sure you know that. Some of them attacked us. They broke the windscreen and injured the driver. We had an armed security man with us. He fired a shot at them. They drew back. They might even have gone away. But your grandmother's uncle was following behind us. In a rickshaw. The man who had looked after him all those years was driving the rickshaw. The mob went after them instead. Your grandmother wanted the driver of our car to drive away. She shouted at him to get away, fast. I shouted back at her and got out of the car. Your grandmother

306

screamed at me. She said I didn't know what I was doing, and I'd get everyone killed. I didn't listen; I was a heroine. I wasn't going to listen to a stupid, cowardly old woman. But she knew what was going to happen. Everyone there did, except me. I was the only one who didn't. I began to run towards the rickshaw. I heard Tridib shouting my name. But I kept running. I heard him running after me. He caught up with me and pushed me, from behind. I stumbled and fell. I thought he'd stop to take me back to the car. But he ran on towards the rickshaw. The mob had surrounded the rickshaw. They had pulled the old man off it. I could hear him screaming. Tridib ran into the mob, and fell upon their backs. He was trying to push his way through to the old man, I think. Then the mob dragged him in. He vanished. I could only see their backs. It took less than a moment. Then the men began to scatter. I picked myself up and began to run towards them. The men had melted away, into the gullies. When I got there, I saw three bodies. They were all dead. They'd cut Khalil's stomach open. The old man's head had been hacked off. And they'd cut Tridib's throat, from ear to ear.

That was that; that's all there is to tell.

We cleared away the dinner-plates then, I remember. I wiped up some ice-cream I had spilt on her table while May washed the plates and the knives and forks. She had cooked a nice dinner – a rich tomato soup and a spinach and asparagus flan. There was ice-cream, too, and a bottle of white wine. I had made a mess around my plate as I often did and it took me a while to clean it up. When I finished, May was still in her small kitchen, wiping her plates dry.

I looked at my watch and saw that it was almost eleven o'clock. May, I said, I must go now, tomorrow I have a plane to catch.

I suppose you must, she said briskly.

She was in the kitchen, so I couldn't see her face. But there was a note in her voice that made me wonder. I stepped into the kitchen and touched her arm, and when she turned to face me, I saw that her face was wet with tears.

Don't go, she said. Please; I don't want to be alone – I'm afraid.

I grasped her shoulder then, and she leant her head against my chest so that I could feel her face wet against my shirt. I stroked her hair, once, twice, and then, afraid of frightening her as I'd done once before, I tried to step back. She held me for an instant and then she let go and straightened up.

Do you think I killed him? she said.

I stayed silent; I did not want to answer her.

I used to think so too, she said. I thought I'd killed him. I used to think: perhaps he wouldn't have got out of that car if I hadn't made him, if I'd understood what I was doing. I was safe, you see – I could have gone right into that mob, and they wouldn't have touched me, an English memsahib, but he, he must have known he was going to die. For years I was arrogant enough to think I owed him his life. But I know now I didn't kill him; I couldn't have, if I'd wanted. He gave himself up; it was a sacrifice. I know I can't understand it, I know I mustn't try, for any real sacrifice is a mystery.

She touched my face gently, with her fingertips, and said: Why don't you stay here tonight? I'll come to the airport with you tomorrow morning.

I stayed, and when we lay in each other's arms quietly, in the night, I could tell that she was glad, and I was glad too, and grateful, for the glimpse she had given me of a final redemptive mystery.

Read more . . .

Amitav Ghosh

SEA OF POPPIES

An epic seafaring adventure set against the backdrop of the Opium Wars

Deeti is a widow to opium, saved from her husband's funeral pyre by the low-caste Kalua, who has been waiting for her. Paulette is the orphaned daughter of a French botanist and Jodu, the son of her wet nurse, is the only link to her past. A bankrupt raja is chased from his estates which fall into the hands of an avaricious opium dealer. Fate throws these characters, and a host of others, together as a motley crew on an old slaving ship, the *Ibis*.

Set against the backdrop of the Opium Wars, this unlikely dynasty is what makes *Sea of Poppies* so breathtakingly alive – an absorbing masterpiece from one of the world's finest storytellers.

'Profoundly moving' *The Times*

'A remarkably rich saga' *Guardian*

'It is the sheer energy and verve of Amitav Ghosh's storytelling that binds this ambitious medley' *Daily Mail*

Order your copy now by calling Bookpoint on 01235 827716 or visit your local bookshop quoting ISBN 978-0-7195-6897-8 www.johnmurray.co.uk

Read more . . .

Amitav Ghosh

THE CALCUTTA CHROMOSOME

Winner of the Arthur C. Clarke Award

A computer programmer trapped in a mind-numbing job hits upon a curious item that will change his life for ever. When Antar discovers the battered ID card of a long-lost acquaintance, he is suddenly drawn into the strange life of L. Murugan, a man obsessed with the medical history of malaria. Before he knows it, he is caught up in an adventure spanning centuries and taking him across the globe in search of the elusive Calcutta Chromosome.

'With its dazzling and haunting mix of science fiction, thriller, ghost story and postcolonial allegory, Amitav Ghosh's new novel is – like his previous work – wonderfully clever as well as a good read' *New Statesman*

'Mesmerizing . . . a mind-boggling conspiracy saga' *New York Times Book Review*

Order your copy now by calling Bookpoint on 01235 827716 or visit your local bookshop quoting ISBN 978-1-84854-415-4
www.johnmurray.co.uk

Read more ...

Amitav Ghosh

THE CIRCLE OF REASON

Orphaned at the age of eight and sent to live with his aunt and uncle in a small Bengali village, Alu's start in life is not an easy one. He devotes himself to his uncle, a fanatical phrenologist, involved in an ongoing local feud. When both his aunt and uncle are killed, Alu is wrongly suspected and takes flight. He travels from Bengal to Bombay and on through the Persian Gulf to North Africa pursued by a birdwatching police inspector and helped by a series of unlikely candidates along the way.

'A remarkable achievement' Anthony Burgess
'Gave me more pleasure than I've had in the longest time'
Toni Morrison

Order your copy now by calling Bookpoint on 01235 827716 or visit your local bookshop quoting ISBN 978-1-84854-416-1
www.johnmurray.co.uk

From Byron, Austen and Darwin

to some of the most acclaimed and original contemporary writing, John Murray takes pride in bringing you powerful, prizewinning, absorbing and provocative books that will entertain you today and become the classics of tomorrow.

We put a lot of time and passion into what we publish and how we publish it, and we'd like to hear what you think.

Be part of John Murray – share your views with us at:

www.johnmurray.co.uk

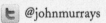 johnmurraybooks

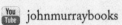 @johnmurrays

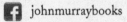 johnmurraybooks